OBERLIN'S ANOMALY

L CHANCE SHIVER

L Chance Shiver
Asheville, North Carolina
www.chanceshiver.com

Cover Art by Susette Shiver
Art Photography by Ian Loring Shiver
Book Cover Design by Tanja Propek
          of Book DesignTemplates.com
Production by IngramSpark

Oberlin's Anomaly - Paperback 1st ed.

ISBN 978-0-578-44813-8
eBook 1st edition
ISBN 978-0-578-44814-5

FOR SUSETTE

Acknowledgements: First, thanks to my bride, Susette Carter Shiver, without whom these pages would be blank. Thanks to Tommy Hays, Vicki Lane, and the good folks in The Great Smokies Writing Program at the University of North Carolina Asheville for mentoring, critical insight, and review. And thanks to Betsy Thorpe for invaluable editing.

Special thanks to Patricia Poteat whose dedicated reading and critiques were instrumental in the completion of this book. And to David Moltke-Hansen, for his historical contributions and valuable edits.

I couldn't have done it without you all.

L Chance Shiver, November 25, 2018

Contents

CHAPTER ONE

THE CANOEING SOCIETY

GEORGETOWN, DC   SATURDAY

MAY 20TH

Jack Starkey opened his eyes and looked at the passenger beside him. Ethan still sat there on the worn, grey seat of the Subaru staring straight ahead. His son's long red hair escaped from his baseball cap and hung down, mostly covering his face. He looked like his mother in subtle ways, with his high cheek-bones and small ears. He'd been tall for his age and thin. Of course, Ethan wasn't really there. Ethan was dead.

The therapists told him to stop speaking to the boy. Then the hallucination would go away. *If only.* He'd driven his son to school every morning. Now it had been five years since his death. Ethan turned towards Starkey and looked at him, slowly fading.

He started the car and backed out of the parking lot of his condo building. His mind got a little clearer driving down Wisconsin Avenue towards the beltway. The therapists also said he needed to lay his wife Jane's memory to rest. But how to do that? Her long, slow, cancerous death a year after Ethan's suicide carved out crevices in Starkey. Seek closure even of small things, they told him in his six months at Sheppard Pratt. Don't forget, they said when they released him. And take your medication. He didn't forget.

Since his release he'd often seen canoes on top of cars on his commute along the Potomac River into DC and they always reminded him of Jane. The Potomac Canoeing Society was visible during his daily run along the Chesapeake & Ohio canal that took him past the society's island. Five years had passed since he and Jane applied for membership. She'd wanted so much to join. She'd loved to canoe that stretch of the Potomac River beside the little island where the society lay. They thought of how convenient it would be if they could have a canoe there instead of hauling one down to the canal every time. They didn't know how the odds were stacked against them until they visited the island. The waiting list ran in the hundreds, they were told. After that Starkey never expected he would ever set foot on the funny little island again, but Jane kept up hope. People died waiting to be members. It wouldn't hurt, he supposed, to go down to the river to talk to them. Focus on something healthy to do the therapists said. And Starkey felt it meant something to try again. He just didn't know what.

He now no longer even owned a canoe. He held on to Jane's for a long time after she died, but eventually he couldn't stand to look at it sitting there in the garage and sold it. But he knew he needed exercise more now than ever. Exercise helped with the depression, physically and mentally. It would be worth his time just to ride the little ferry and walk on the island. So he went.

He parked along the Clara Barton Parkway in the turnout above Chain Bridge. He took the dirt trail leaving the parking lot. It led down the steep face of the palisades beside the canal to the footbridge that crossed over to the towpath. The bridge's heavy iron frame wore some rust on the railings, and the wooden planks squeaked a bit underfoot as he crossed above the murky water of the canal. He stepped down from the bridge stairs and approached the little society dock. He could see the hand-pulled ferry. It floated some thirty yards across the water at the end of the steel cable that stretched away from the bank beside him. He reached up and pulled the chain to ring the tarnished brass bell.

After the third ring, a figure in a red leather hat, a tan field jacket, and faded blue jeans appeared beside the small dock across the branch of the river that separated the island from the bank where Starkey stood.

"Hello," Starkey called out.

The figure in the red hat said nothing, but peered at him across the water. His wide eyes and puzzled brow gave him an owlish look.

"Can you come across to get me, please?"

The ferryman glanced over his shoulder, staring up to the building behind him. Then, as if in answer, shrugged his shoulders and stepped onto the small ferryboat. He pulled brown leather work gloves from the pocket of his jacket and slowly put them on. He continued to glance over his shoulder towards the low, rambling clapboard building on the island behind him, as if indecisive.

This man either didn't want to come and get him, or he was the most incredibly slow moving person Starkey ever saw. At last, the ferryman reached over his head to take hold of the rusted steel cable, and began to pull the wooden ferry across the slow current of the river water. He kept his head down during the crossing, and Starkey couldn't get a good look at his face. The little ferry reached the dock.

"Thank you," Starkey said as he stepped aboard. The ferryman nodded, still head down, but he did not speak. Starkey noticed an odd smell about the man. It must be something on his clothes, Starkey supposed, a sort of damp, musty odor. The man's clothing badly needed laundering. Turning his back to Starkey, the ferryman hauled them across to the island. The skin on the man's neck was sallow above his frayed and dirty collar.

When they landed at the dock the ferryman raised his hand to point to the clubhouse building, but continued to avoid eye contact. Then, without a word, he turned away quickly and disappeared behind a low outbuilding that sheltered canoes.

"Thank you, again," Starkey called after the man. Starkey walked up the steps and onto the wooden porch of the clubhouse. The door stood ajar, so he stepped inside. The stale air carried dust motes floating in the dim light that came in through dirty windows.

The man at the desk didn't look up at first, intent on some papers he held. But when he did, his large, pale, and protruding eyes startled Starkey. The irises of the man's eyes—nearly the color of the whites—looked like a frog's that lived too long in a darkened cave. Otherwise, the man's appearance was unremarkable. He had thinning gray hair, metal-frame glasses, a pale complexion, and dark work clothing. That strange smell hung about him also, like mildew, musty and dank.

"Excuse me," Starkey said. "My name is Jack Starkey."

After a long pause the man spoke. "My name is Simmons. Can I help you?"

"Well, I'd like to join the canoeing society."

The man looked over his shoulder to the doorway behind him, and then answered. "I'm sorry but the membership is full." His speech sounded slow and deliberate.

"I see. Is there still a waiting list? I used to be on it years ago," Starkey asked, glancing around. The place looked nearly abandoned, generally disorganized, and swallowed up by thick layers of dust. It didn't look that popular or well used.

A raspy cough interrupted. Another man stood in the doorway behind Simmons. He stepped forward.

"Mr. Starkey, I'm Henry Grimes, the president of the society."

The tall thin man wore clothing identical to Simmons, and he had the same pale, protruding eyes, though they were less pronounced. Like the other man's his speech sounded labored. Starkey found himself taking a step back. These were not the

friendly people Jane and he had met before. But it
had been years.

"Well, Mr. Starkey, you are in luck," said
Grimes. "Mr. Simmons here has not heard. We just
lost one of our members. We have an opening for
one. Step this way."

Grimes led him to a dusty, unused desk and
chair and handed him a membership form. "Just fill
this application out."

What about the waiting list? Better not to ask.
The men and the office and the whole scene put
Starkey off. But he went on with it. Closure, the ther-
apists said. He must follow through.

He wiped aside some of the dust on the desk
with his hand and wiped it on his jean. He filled out
the short form, signed it, and gave Simmons a check
for three months' of dues. "I don't have a canoe today, but I'm going to buy one. When can I drop it
off?" Starkey said. He hadn't expected this to be so
easy.

"Our hours are on this card, Mr. Starkey,"
Grimes said, handing it over. "Just call to let us know
when you're coming."

Starkey backed out of the office glancing
down at the smudged card. *As easy as that.* The ferryman met Starkey by the water and took him back
to the other bank. They crossed in silence. Starkey
felt some resolution, and also a sense of relief. *But*

relief from what? As he climbed the hill back to his car his mind shifted and he wondered if Ethan sat waiting for him in the front seat. But he wasn't there, and Starkey drove thinking about the uneasiness that came over him around Grimes and Simmons. He re-played it all again and again until he reached the parking lot of his condo. Probably just his own weird reactions—his mind hadn't been right since the death of his family.

Nothing to do but go on. And buy a canoe.

CHAPTER TWO

THE BLACK ARROW

C&O CANAL PAW-PAW ISLAND MD
MONDAY MAY 22ND

After work Starkey ran through the shade of the sycamore and maple trees that lined the towpath along the C&O Canal. Off to his right the Potomac River shot brilliant flashes of reflected sunlight through the trees. Calling what he did "running" exaggerated his speed. Jogging would have been more accurate, but he held a tight grip on that verb. Slowing, he straightened up to almost all of his five foot ten, breathing hard. He carried a hundred and eighty-five pounds down the towpath despite his almost daily runs there just outside of Georgetown, DC. Starkey looked his age at forty-three and a little extra. Worry lines had invaded his face, and the graying reddish-brown hair didn't help. The lids becoming heavy on his blue eyes didn't either.

Starkey slowed to a walk and invoked a familiar daydream he often played and replayed, a kind of tonic for sadness. In the daydream the melody of Maria Elena played on the Spanish Guitar, and provided the background music for the sweet touch of his lover's lips. Today his fantasy lover wore the face of Jane, his wife. Since her death the face of his girlfriend, Sheila Cartwright, appeared in his fantasy more often, but today Jane was on his mind. For once he felt almost at peace, but he didn't say it out loud. Peace seldom stopped by or stayed long. Something disturbed the murky surface of the canal near him on the left, a turtle perhaps.

His walk took him below the semi-restored buildings of Glen Echo, now a preserve run by the National Park Service, on the high bank's crest above the canal. The old amusement park peeked through the trees above—a place out of time. He could see the back of the Crystal Ballroom and its Spanish Revival beige stucco and red tiled roofs. Broken tiles had fallen on the bank above, sliding down the palisades hill.

Now he walked parallel to the island of the canoeing society. Jane and he had made walking and biking this stretch of the towpath into a courting ritual for them before and after marriage. They often stopped at the Sangamore Store nearby for picnic sandwiches and cold drinks. There they first heard of the exclusive canoeing society and the private island that housed it. He walked past the ferry as it drifted back and forth with the current. He was pulled out of his daydream. Remembering his strange visit there a few days before had brought back waves of suspicion.

Starkey leaned against the giant sycamore beside him, his hand on the smooth, whitish bark. He didn't see the round circle of a red targeting light on the side of his head. He did see a large freshwater clam shell on the path at his feet. He stooped to pick it up. He heard a hiss and sharp thud as something hit the tree inches above his head.

Starkey twisted and looked up in the direction of the sound. A short, black arrow quivered in the trunk of the tree. He stiffened with shock, and looked back across the canal. A widening circle of waves rocked the canal's surface. Something large moved off, back up the canal, a shadow beneath the water. He heard voices. Two bikers approached on the towpath.

Rising, he took a forward defensive pose, and looked for his enemy. But he saw no one. *Time to run away.* He jerked the arrow from the tree and raced up the steps of the footbridge that crossed above the canal, taking them two at a time, to reach the parking lot and his car. He felt fear ignite something inside him, something that flamed and spread. He raced over the wooden planks and across the bridge, the pounding of his running echoing back from the far bank. He reached the hilly path at the other end and pushed long strides upward. Half way up he slipped and fell onto his hands and one knee in the gravel and dirt, but he pushed up and forced himself on, his hands stinging. *I can't run any faster, it never seemed this far before.* Yet he reached down deep inside himself and there he found a new strength. He ran harder, faster, maybe faster than ever before. The trees and bushes around him became obscured. The motion of his arms and legs blurred in revolution and his sense of time distorted.

At last he reached the top of the hill and crossed into the parking lot. He sprinted past the parked cars to his own, fumbling with his keys. Once inside, the old Subaru station wagon engine sputtered, but caught easily for once. He backed out and sped off down the parkway, veering onto the beltway entrance south towards Silver Spring.

He remained disoriented as he drove amidst the converging traffic. The scene at the canal replayed continuously in his mind. The same questions arose again and again. Where should he go? Who should he talk to? He should call the police. What he really wanted was a drink. Calming slowly, he became less numb. His hands stung with the gravel embedded in his palms. His feet hurt. His running shoes felt tight, too small suddenly. He shivered in his jersey, still soaked with sweat. Loose before, now it stretched tight across the chest, binding and chilling him.

Who could have shot at him? It made no sense. And with a bow and arrow? But who else could have been the target? He was alone. Someone tried to kill him right there by the towpath, which had been his place of solace after his release from the hospital. Running there had eased the pain.

Rush hour traffic slowed on I-495, hundreds of cars packed in rows of six lanes like cattle in pens. It seemed to take forever, but eventually Starkey got to the Georgia Avenue exit. The arrow lay on the passenger seat next to him, black feathers and all. It didn't seem quite real. A widening wave in the canal water and the dark shape that moved off beneath the water were all he saw. Then the realization hit. If he hadn't seen that clam shell and stooped to pick it up, he'd be dead. The chill returned and shook his body in a single, violent convulsion. The pain in his feet grew sharp. He slipped off his shoes at a stoplight. *Call the police. But he really wanted a drink first, just one to calm his nerves.*

The old Subaru rattled on, following a well-worn track. Starkey's car carried him into the parking lot outside St. Andrew's Pub. Only mildly surprised to find himself there, he took off the wet jersey and pulled on a running jacket and sweatpants. He crossed the street lifting his bare feet high after each step on the hot pavement. He pushed his way through the mahogany-stained door and into the pub. The air conditioning gripped him in its chill and sent waves of shivers through him.

Clasping his arms around himself, Starkey walked the length of the bar, greeting the regulars. He caught sight of himself in the big mirror across the dining room. His reflection looked hunched over, but also bigger, somehow. He slid onto the next to the last stool. The dark green walls and mahogany bar's familiar surroundings calmed him. Large hands pushed a pint of beer at him. This reality made some sense.

The bartender, a tall, squarely built man, had a head slightly too large for his body. His green logo t-shirt stretched tight across his heavy shoulders. Paul struck Sharkey as a friendly man, quick with a joke and a story. Starkey got on well with him. Today Starkey saw him smile at first, but then the corners of the man's mouth turned down and Paul began to stare at him. Then he turned away.

The slightly bitter taste of Bass Ale began to relax him, but his hands shook as he lifted the pint. His running shorts felt tight across his hips. Someone had tried to kill him *and* he was getting fat. Great. He got up and went to the men's room and changed out of the running shorts. The sweat pants fit looser.

Back at the bar, Starkey drained the last bit of the pint and set the mug a bit forward on the bar where it would be noticed. Another pint appeared. He caught the beginning of a conversation down the bar. Turning on the stool he saw Paul leaning in, one foot up the cooler, tapping his forefinger on a newspaper, and speaking to a man wearing a red baseball hat and grey plaid shirt. The man sat two stools down from Starkey. The heels of his work boots hooked on the rungs of the stool.

Paul thrust the Metro section of the Washington Post towards the man and stabbed with his forefinger at an article on the front page.

"There you see, three pregnant women," Paul said. "Three pregnant women missing or drowned in the last seven years down there along the canal near lock 7, it says."

"My God, that's strange." The man frowned as he read.

"Strange isn't the word for it," Paul said.

"No, I don't mean just about the three women," the man said. "My grandmother used to say more people drowned or got lost between locks 5 and 7 than any other stretch along the canal..."

Starkey interrupted. "Excuse me," he said.

The man in the red baseball hat turned to-wards Starkey. He had a small, but sturdy stature. The dark, closely cropped hair around his cap added to the impression of deliberateness that he gave. He looked to be about Starkey's age.

"I'm sorry to interrupt, but I'm interested in that section of the canal," Starkey said. "Do you mind if I ask why your grandmother thought that?"

"Have you ever been to Fletcher's Boat House?" the man asked.

That question dropped Starkey in a pile of memories. "Sure, I've gone to Fletcher's off and on forever," he said. "I park there sometimes to run along the towpath."

The man took off his red cap, placed it on the bar, and ran his fingers through his hair. "Well, the whitewashed stone house there on Canal Road above the boat house? That belonged to Granny," he said. "She lived there all her life. Her father worked as the lock keeper. He tended lock number seven. When the canal shut down he bought the house from the canal company. My grandmother inherited it. Later on the Park Service bought it from her when they turned the canal into a national park, with the provision that she could live there until she died."

Starkey passed that house frequently. Tall and thin, it stood two stories tall, unlike most of the lock houses along the C&O.

Paul interrupted, smiling. "This fellow who butts into other people's conversations is Jack Starkey," he said. "Starkey, meet Bob Warfield."

Starkey stuck out his hand and the other man shook it firmly. "I'm sorry your grandmother isn't still with us. There are some questions I'd like to ask her," Starkey said.

"Well, you can try me," Warfield said, sipping his beer. "She pretty near raised me. I stayed with her every summer while my folks worked. I played in and around that house and along the river afternoons during the school year, too. My folks lived up on MacArthur Boulevard, close by."

"Did your grandmother ever mention anything else odd about that section of the canal, besides the drownings?" Starkey asked.

"Well, yes," Warfield said. "She also used to say that bad luck followed a pregnant woman if she walked along that part of the canal."

"Did she tell you anymore?"

"No, at least not that I remember," Warfield said. "I once asked her how she knew, but she just said 'Never you mind, just remember it'." I always wondered about her answer. But then I recall getting that 'Never you mind' answer about a lot of things when I was a kid."

"I'm writing a book about life on the canal," Starkey said. He didn't know exactly why he lied.

But he knew he needed to think before he talked about what happened to him there today. "Is there some way I could get in touch with you in case I have more questions about your grandmother's stories?"

"Sure, why not?" Warfield said. He stood and drained the last of his pint. "Let me give you my card."

As Warfield left the pub Paul replaced Starkey's empty beer mug with a full one. "Since when are you writing a book, Starkey?" he said.

"Since today." Paul didn't seem to notice the fear Starkey knew was on his face.

"Are you putting on weight, squire? You look bigger."

"Thanks a lot, Paul. Well, yes, these clothes do seem tight all of a sudden."

"And when did you start dyeing your hair?" Paul stared at him for a moment, but then went off down the bar to serve someone else.

Starkey looked in the mirror behind the bar. His hair did look darker. Why? *Wait, I haven't called the police*. Christ what would he tell them? They wouldn't believe the crazy story. Someone he didn't see fired a strange black arrow at him? And then disappeared under the surface of the canal? He could picture the disbelief on the face of the cop already. But he must report it. If the arrow truly targeted him, as unlikely a target as he thought himself to be, next time the archer might not miss. He had to make the call. Starkey pulled his cell phone. He dialed 911, and it directed his call to the Glenmont Police Station.

"No, it's not an emergency," Starkey said. *I wish I knew.*

"Hold on."

Starkey told the story to the cop who came on the line. The man listened patiently enough, but sounded dubious. The cop told him to come by the station and fill out a report. "Be sure to bring the arrow," he'd said.

Back at the bar, Starkey pictured the arrow lying on the passenger seat of his car outside. He knew something of archery, but next to nothing about unusual arrows. He would need Sheila's help, if she could get over being pissed off at him. Starkey had accidentally called her Jane when they were making love the other night. Big mistake. But he needed her knowledge and clarity of mind, especially when his wasn't working so well. Plus she studied archery with Hiro Yamashima, their martial arts master. Master Yamashima introduced Starkey to Sheila when they shared private classes with him. Over the ten years they continued as his students they became his disciples, and scholars of the master's form of martial art. After Jane's death they'd slowly gotten closer. Some time passed before it grew into a relationship.

Starkey raised his pint to his lips and looked into the mirror behind the bar. At first he saw only his own reflection. Then his breath caught in his chest and the mug dropped from his hand, crashing onto the bar and spilling beer across the polished surface. He saw Ethan's reflection in the mirror, sitting on the stool beside him.

Paul's hands appeared to retrieve the glass and mop up the beer from the bar. "Jesus, Starkey, look at this god-awful mess you've made here. What are you staring at? You look like you've seen a ghost."

Starkey dragged his eyes away from Ethan's image and looked at the bartender.

"I have," Starkey said.

When he turned back to the mirror Ethan had disappeared, and he saw only himself. Starkey put twenty dollars on the bar and hurried out of the bar.

Ethan didn't reappear in the car. Starkey drove to the Glenmont police station. He swallowed six breath mints to disguise the smell of beer, and drank some water. He thought about what he would tell them. He knew they would keep the arrow if he took it in, but Starkey wanted to show the arrow to Sheila and Master Yamashima. He knew he needed their help to deal with the attack. With everything. So he put the arrow under the front seat and went inside.

"You didn't mention this happened in DC, Mr. Starkey. Why didn't you report this at the McArthur Boulevard station?" The uniformed policeman didn't introduce himself, but his name plate said Rasmussen. Late fifties and on the heavy side, his expressionless face told the story. His made it clear he viewed the attack as one of too many things already on his plate. And not his plate at all, really.

"I called from Wheaton and 911 connected me to you," Starkey said.

"Okay, well, I can take your statement, but you'll still have to talk to the DC police. The incident took place there, not here in Maryland. We don't have jurisdiction."

"Ok, just tell me what I have to do."

"You say somebody shot an arrow at you? Do you have it?"

Starkey lied. "No, I just ran, so I guess it's still in the tree."

"A critical piece of evidence, that."

"Well, I panicked. I didn't think about evidence."

Rasmussen frowned at him. "All right, Mr. Starkey." He gave Starkey a form. "Write out your statement and don't leave anything out."

Rasmussen took his finished statement. "Ok. Mr. Starkey. You'll be hearing from the DC police."

With what little he knew about crime rate in Washington, DC, Starkey had his doubts.

CHAPTER THREE

MIRROR IMAGE

BETHESDA, MD TUESDAY MAY 23RD

The coffee smelled better than usual as it brewed the next morning. It tasted better too. Same beans, same half and half creamer. Sunshine streamed into the kitchen of his condo and Starkey opened the window and let fresh air in. He'd felt refreshed, like he'd had a good long night's sleep. But he phoned the secretary at work anyway to say he'd be off on personal leave. He just needed a little time to process what had happened to him. Plus he felt too damn good to go to work. He didn't tell her that.

Drinking his second cup of coffee he realized he hadn't taken his medications yet. What passed for his reality didn't feel frayed at the edges, and no shadows slipped at the sides of his vision as in days past. Maybe he'd wait a little longer to take them. He shaved half his face before he realized Ethan didn't appear in the mirror beside him, either. Ah, but the mirror. A few small items called that reality thing into question. First the hair. The Starkey in the mirror this morning had reddish brown hair. Hair like he'd had ten years ago. No grey. Longer now than yesterday, it hung over his ears and reached down his neck. Oh, and the small item of his size. There was no question he stood taller in the mirror and over the sink. Two days ago he stood five feet ten, maybe slightly less. He guessed his height at six feet today. Last time on the scale Jack Starkey weighed one eighty-five. Today the scale said one ninety-five. And if the mirror told the truth, then twenty pounds of it didn't laze around his middle like before. He had abs. Abs you could actually see. And well-defined muscles. Not bulging like a weight lifter's, but damn big. His shoulders were broader and his hips slimmer. Maybe he'd take his meds.

His psychiatrist told him the antipsychotic she prescribed would help keep him in touch with reality. Rein in illogical thoughts and perceptions. Right. Better take it. Then he'd see if he looked like yesterday's Jack Starkey or the new, improved model. He didn't feel even slightly depressed, but he took that medication, too. She said they worked together. He'd wait an hour and see what happened. These new hallucinations, if that's what they were, scared him. His dead son's apparition showed up too often to surprise him now and he'd gotten used to it. But his sudden growth spurt astonished him. It felt different than a hallucination. He couldn't touch Ethan's ghost, but he could run his fingers through his own gray-less hair. He felt the muscles in his arms and legs. They seemed awfully damn real. The black arrow sitting on the table beside him looked damn real, too. The medication would kick in in forty minutes. He waited. He had more coffee, and breakfast. A big one.

An hour later he stood in front of the tall mirror on his closet door. His Bermuda shorts and underwear still fit, better really without the belly overhang. He'd dug a huge old sweatshirt out of his closet that did the job. So there he stood. Six feet tall and one ninety-five. And he felt great. Fantastic, really. Wait until Sheila saw him. How would he explain it? He couldn't. And he didn't have that fuzzy feeling the medication usually gave him. He didn't feel held down, or held up. Just good. He liked this. *What the hell constituted real anyway?* The first stop out the door would be the mall, much as he hated going there. He needed clothes. Saturday he'd try to get Sheila to go to REI with him to buy a canoe and then hit the river. The hell with whoever shot at him on the canal

CHAPTER FOUR

THOMAS JEFFERSON

COLLEGE OF WILLIAM AND MARY VIRGINIA 1761
And
CASSIDY'S TAVERN GEORGETOWN DC 1801

In the spring of 1761 Tom Jefferson sat shivering in the College Building at William and Mary. Snow still covered the grass of the quad outside his window, for a cold spring had followed an unusually bitter winter. Jefferson turned the pages of his notes with finger tips extended from fingerless gloves, sitting with a woolen blanket around his thin shoulders. A wool cap covered his head and ears, but a few flaming red wisps of hair had escaped. The meager wood fire in the red brick fireplace behind him did little to alleviate the cold, and Jefferson cupped his hands and blew on his fingers. Intent on the mathematics that sat on the desk before him, he ignored the first knock at his dormitory door. At the sound of a second, heavy knock he reluctantly raised his head and answered.

"Come in." He expected a classmate waiting to draw him away from his studies.

The door opened and a very large man ducked his head and side-stepped through the low doorway. "Am I disturbing you?"

Jefferson leapt to his feet. "Professor Aldwin. No, of course not, please come in."

Now inside, the man dwarfed Jefferson's small room, his head nearly brushing the ceiling, and his shoulders almost seeming to touch the walls. Jefferson's visitor looked at the sparsely furnished room around him with its cot, washstand, and desk and chair where Jefferson stood, and the one, frost-covered window in the wall beside him. "I fear I have interrupted your studies," Aldwin said.

Jefferson threw off the blanket and hurried around the desk and extended his hand. Aldwin took it, his larger hand enclosing Jefferson's. Jefferson looked up at the man's face. He himself was over six feet at seventeen years old, but Aldwin stood more than a head taller. Much more. So broad of shoulder and narrow through the hips, Aldwin was an imposing figure. He wore no hat or scarf and his black hair hung loose in a queue. The man's large dark blue eyes were set below a high forehead and above a long, sharp nose, giving him an odd, hawkish look, but he wore a warm, open smile.

Aldwin withdrew a book from an inside pocket of his frock coat and offered Jefferson the well-worn, leather-bound volume. "I have brought you a copy of John Locke's Second Treatise of Government. After our discussion in class today I thought you might like to have a copy of your own."

Jefferson took the book from the man's hand and opened it. Turning pages he observed the clear, concise hand-written notes in the margins.

"Your own copy, sir?"

"As it happens I have another copy given to me by an acquaintance of mine." Now the man's smile had become a wry grin and hinted at something like mischief, but Jefferson couldn't guess what it might be.

"Professor Aldwin, I am most grateful for the gift. But how did you know? I had indeed thought I'd like to examine Mr. Locke's philosophy on my own. This is very kind of you."

"Just a guess," Aldwin said, his smile broadening again. "In my own study I have marked some chapters and sections in that copy that I found most compelling. I recommend them to you for your contemplation. I particularly direct you to Chapter II, sections 4 and 5, wherein Locke writes that the natural state of man is equality and all power and jurisdiction is reciprocal, no one having more than another, as we discussed in class this morning. It's essentially a declaration of independence for all men." Aldwin said.

"I don't know what to say, sir, this is extremely generous." Jefferson said.

"Not at all, Tom, the pleasure is mine. It is most encouraging to see a young man so diligent in his studies. Your classmates tell me you can barely tear yourself away from your books. I predict great things for your future." The look on Aldwin's face had grown serious, and he stared directly into Jefferson's eyes.

Jefferson thought the man looked through him, and beyond. Aldwin's words stirred something in him. The man's tone seemed to convey a message and conviction. Jefferson found he could not answer. An uncomfortable silence began.

"Well," Aldwin said, "unfortunately I have also come to say goodbye. Your Professor Small returns tomorrow and my time here at William and Mary as his replacement is done."

"Will we see you here again, sir?" Jefferson said.

"Perhaps, Tom. But whether I return or not, you and I could continue our discussion of philosophy if you would like. Inside the back cover of the book there is an address where you may write to me. I promise to answer your letters."

"I will, sir."

With a nod, Aldwin turned on his heel, and ducking low beneath the door jam, went out, closing the door behind him. Tom watched the man go and then opened to the last page of the book Aldwin had given him. There he read,

John Aldwin
2 Fishing Lane
Georgetown, Province of Maryland

>>>

Early the next morning, Aldwin sat on his large, black Percheron horse atop a low hill overlooking William and Mary. His hooded and robed companion hovered at his side as they gazed down at the first rays of the rising sun illuminating the school.

"The seed is planted, Proteus, but will it take root?" Aldwin said.

"So the history books will write, John. It all started here."

>>>

35 years later.

Grabbing a straw broom from the wall as she passed, Mary Catherine began to mutter aloud, mimicking *his* haughty voice. "Surely you know women should not worry their heads over politics, so a book discoursing on the subject would be of no use to you. I fear your reading and self-education will be of little use to you." She continued sweeping as she moved down the hall of Cassidy's Tavern, passing the tools and tack that hung on the plastered walls. The girl attacked the ever-encroaching dirt clods that were tramped in to the hardwood floors from the courtyard that opened on to Fishing Lane by the Potomac River. She swept her way to the wooden outdoor kitchen attached to the tavern's back wall. There she left her cleaning chores and turned to serving breakfast. She struggled to control the anger that came in waves still, carefully retrieving the plates that the cook set out for her. Finally taking hold of herself she gathered the breakfasts and backed through the taproom door. She stopped halfway through and looked in.

Colors of sunlight blazed across the ivory walls from the floor to ceiling windows. The bright light revealed scars and dents in the chair railing that girded the room and lit the pastoral paintings of the English countryside hung about. There *he* was. She moved through, carrying a large tray on each arm that held pots of coffee and tea and milk and honey. She slid them carefully onto the walnut sideboard. The taproom was nearly full, for Cassidy's Tavern was where travelers to the new Washington city lodged and conducted their business, there in the most famous of the area's hostelries. Tom Jefferson sat with his friend, John Taylor, by the river-stone fireplace at the far end of the room. Mary Catherine took up a cup and saucer from a tray and walked down behind Jefferson. He jumped when she virtually dropped the cup and saucer on the table in front of him.

She let her anger come out in her tone of voice. "Would you care for coffee or tea, *Mr. Jefferson?*"

Jefferson looked up at her, a stiff frown on his face, but it eased and he spoke quietly. "Tea, please, Mary Catherine."

"And you, Mr. Taylor?" She placed a cup and saucer in front of him as well, but much more delicately.

"Coffee for me Mary, thank you. How are you this fine morning?"

"Fine," she said, filling the cups, her voice clipped, and she turned on her heel to move on to the next table.

"I'll have you gentlemen's breakfast shortly," she said over her shoulder. She accented the last syllable in 'gentlemen' in a distasteful way, but subtly. Nothing they could complain about.

She overheard their conversation as she served the other customers. The two men made no effort to lower their voices. Taylor spoke as he began to butter his toast. "What has put our girl Mary off this morning, I wonder? I've never seen her anything but bright and cheerful before."

"I'm afraid I have," Jefferson said.

Taylor smiled at his friend. "What have you done? You haven't trifled with that young girl's affections, I hope?"

Jefferson leaned forward, speaking quietly. "In a way that is just what I have done. I have encouraged her to read and think and learn for some time, but last night I told her education would avail her little, and not to bother her head with politics and philosophy."

Mary Catherine continued about the room, listening and growing more and more angry, finally retreating into the kitchen. The sounds of plates crashing to the floor reached the taproom.

"Why on earth did you dash her hopes that way, Tom? Was that necessary? Everyone knows how she looks to you for encouragement. Why man, the girl very fairly worships you."

"It was time she faced reality. I was wrong to have encouraged her. I simply told her the truth. This girl is unusual, true, and I have done with her as Adams has with his daughters, encouraging them to read Locke, Newton, and Descartes, but to what end? It will profit them nothing."

Mary Catherine swept out of the kitchen and dropped an empty tray on the sideboard near the two men with a loud clatter. She heard Taylor change the subject. "Tom, I am thinking of alternating a white clover crop with tobacco, there's some that say the clover will restore the vitality of the soil and improve the tobacco yield."

"Well, Mr. Jefferson, what have you been saying to my Mary Catherine?"

Taylor and Jefferson turned to the sound of the voice. The tavern owner, Hannah Cassidy, stood behind them. She stood out, physically, from most of her customers. Standing less than five feet tall and almost as wide, she stood face-to-face with Jefferson although he was seated. Her skin, dark and tobacco-colored, and high cheekbones clearly showed she was Native American. Her face, always wrinkled and serious, looked like a thunder storm approached now, dark and foreboding. Despite her diminutive size she possessed boundless energy, a surging vitality, and a temper to match. People went a long way out of their way to stay on the good side of Hannah Cassidy.

Mary Catherine came forward to stand behind her mother, looking over her shoulder and frowning.

From the sound of her voice, Hannah Cassidy was just getting started. "Well, sir, what do you have to say for yourself? Our Mary Catherine has her nose completely out of joint this morning. She's been out there slamming the crockery around in the kitchen. She's mad as a box of snakes and giving no sign of calming down. And when I ask her what's wrong all she will say is 'ask him.' You're mostly all she talks about, you know, so likely it's you as has put her knickers in a twist. The girl thinks you walk on water." She paused to take a breath, obviously ready to go on in this way for some time.

Jefferson broke in. "Yes, yes, Mrs. Cassidy, I am at fault." Jefferson stood up, dwarfing the small woman. "But I simply told her the truth."

"And what is the truth, Mr. Jefferson?" The small woman peered up at him, not the least daunted by the sudden height of the man. Jefferson measured six feet two, and his slenderness and erect bearing made him seem even taller.

"I simply told her education in other than the fine arts would avail her nothing, and politics was not the proper subject for a young woman's contemplation." He seemed to be attempting to rewrap his dignity around him as he stared down at her mother.

"So that is the truth in your opinion. Now I understand." Mrs. Cassidy pulled over a tavern chair and clambered on to it—once again eye to eye with

Jefferson. "Well, the truth, *in my opinion, Mr. Jefferson,* is that Mary Catherine has an excellent mind, and is more capable than most men, as you yourself have often commented to me. A prodigy is what you have called her. Since she was a small child you have encouraged her and instructed her each time that you have stayed in my tavern. And now that she is nearly a woman grown and can dispute with you, you have suddenly changed your mind."

Jefferson strove to interrupt. "Yes, I did encourage her, but..."

"So it always is," she said, beginning to bounce her finger at Jefferson's chest, just short of striking him. "You men are eager enough for women to learn and think as long as they do not step outside the narrow boundaries you place around them."

When she stopped Jefferson tried to respond. "I am sorry if I have offended the child..."

"Enough—I must attend to my other guests now, but mark me Mr. Jefferson, future president or not, you have done yourself no credit today. There will come a day when those fine words of yours— "All men are created equal"—will mean men *and women*, yes, and black as well as white." And with that, Hannah Cassidy climbed down from the chair and turned to go.

Jefferson caught at her sleeve, and when she turned toward him, spoke with some agitation. "Nobody wishes more ardently to see abolition, not only of the trade, but of the condition of slavery. But I do not believe Negroes can live under the same government. Nor do I believe women should leave their place in the home to traffic in the outside world as do men."

Hannah Cassidy pulled her sleeve free. "Then sir, I say to you that you have lied to us with your *declaration of independence.* You truly meant to say that all *white men* are endowed by their creator with these inalienable rights. My God, sir, can you stand there and tell me you believe the creator created you with more rights than a woman, or a black man?"

Jefferson did not answer. After a time of looking into his eyes, Hannah Cassidy seemed to shake herself and then walked away, gathering up dirty dishes and glasses from tables as she passed. The other customers found something else of interest to focus on as the innkeeper strode by.

Mary Catherine stood frozen. She watched as Jefferson stared at the back of her mother.

Taylor spoke first. "Mrs. Cassidy is a remarkable woman, but I do not believe women can or should be equal to men, or blacks to whites."

"Indeed, John, she is remarkable." Jefferson continued to stare after the small woman.

>>>

Mary Catherine knocked on her mother's door in the dark hours after midnight. Dim light projected out from under the wood paneled door.

"Mary?" her mother called.

"Yes, can I come in, please? She opened the door.

Her mother sat upright in bed, the room lit by a single candle. Mary Catherine went in and sat next to her mother on the bed, leaning over to bury her face in Hannah's shoulder.

Then her mother spoke. "Mary, it is time for you to meet someone, a friend. Do not be afraid."

Mary Catherine heard a small sound. She turned to see a hooded and robed figure glide out of the shadows in the corner of the room. A voice spoke from out of the hood, strange to her ear, and yet somehow not unkind. "Hello, Mary Catherine, I am Proteus. Have no fear. Just sit quietly and listen while I speak to your mother. Can you do that for me?"

"Yes."

Proteus' voice turned stern. "Your outburst today was unfortunate, Hannah."

"I know. I became angry. I cannot understand how that man can hold two clearly opposing views in one mind, and I cannot understand why it has taken him so long to fully grasp the fundamental concepts."

"Your frustration is warranted, but you must remember you have the benefit of training and many years of experience that Jefferson has not. Your emotional outburst today might have destroyed years of slow development with this man. You must control your temper as you have been taught. Do you believe you have the right to jeopardize the future of this species because you are impatient?"

Hannah's voice sounded contrite. "No, of course not, I am sorry. In the future I will hold my temper in check."

Proteus spoke more kindly. "You must. Jefferson is a unique individual poised at a critical juncture in human history. You have been instrumental in reaffirming Brother Locke's concepts to Mason and Jefferson, and the future ramifications are inestimable. But if the die is hastily cast it may yet fail. Centuries of effort will be lost. I sense in him strong reluctance in the wake of your hastily flung epithets, and all may be lost. But truly Hannah, I have feared from the first that this species is not ready to receive full enlightenment, and our efforts are premature. Alas, Thomas Jefferson may be our greatest failure."

"Mother, I don't understand."

"There, now, child, everything is going to be all right. I have a long story to tell you, and in the end you will understand what has happened and who you are. You will be the mother of a special child, and you yourself were a special child. You see, it began long ago in a distant land, so long ago that it had no name except 'this place', and the people there simply called themselves 'the people'."

CHAPTER FIVE

CASSAVETES

WASHINGTON DC WEDNESDAY MAY 24TH

The black arrow sat there on Starkey's desk at work, impossible to ignore. Otherwise Starkey would have done his usual procrastination routine. But for the first time in many months of being unable to think clearly, Starkey knew just what to do. If someone did a survey and asked who knew an odd-ball genius, Starkey would have raised his hand. If a thing was old or strange, Randall Meyers knew something about it, or knew someone who did. Myers ventured down into DC every day to work at the Smithsonian Institution where he built models and exhibits. Starkey felt certain Myers could connect him with someone to help identity the arrow.

Starkey called him.

"Hey, this is Starkey. How the hell are you, Randall?"

"Oh, about a six," Myers said.

"Leaves room for improvement. I have a question. Are you still working on models down at the Smithsonian?"

"Steam engines, miniature of course, why?" Myers said.

"Good. I need a favor."

"What?"

"I need to talk to someone who could identify an object for me."

"What kind of object?" Myers said.

"It's an arrow."

"I really don't know anyone," Myers said. He sounded reluctant.

"Randall, you owe me for that water ram I found for you." Starkey stumbled across the antique hydraulic pump in a junk shop and called Myers to tell him about it. Starkey waited through a silence at the other end of the phone.

"Okay, Jack, where's the arrow?" Myers asked.

"Just have the person call me, please."

"What's so damned special about this arrow?"

"Just do me this favor and we're even, Randall."

That afternoon, Starkey sat at his desk at the Harmon Group, a Pharmaceuticals corporation on K St in downtown Washington. He slowly processed the mounting pile of marketing proposals that seemed to comprise ninety percent of his job of late. Most days Starkey regretted winding up in this job. He didn't know what to do with himself in college. He'd drifted into marketing and finally into pharmaceuticals with a vague notion of contributing to the public good. It didn't work out that way, of course. It was all about money. He made a living, went home at night, and lived his real life on the weekend like most of the commuting workers in Washington, DC. Today he couldn't muster even the smallest concern for the pile of stuff on his desk. He no longer cared if Congressman Whoever voted in favor of or against the Pharmaceuticals agenda, if he ever did care. These days the best thing the job had going for it was the short ride on the metro to the stadium to watch the Nats play baseball on a summer afternoon. Baseball proved to be a tonic for his depression, like exercise. He used the game as a metaphor for life. You won some and you lost some. He'd been on a losing streak for a while.

But Harmon's personnel people didn't give him a bad time about his hospitalization. When he

ran out of sick leave they carried him. His boss welcomed him back, and made things easy for him. But
he couldn't muster any enthusiasm for his job after
returning. It all seemed so pointless.

He shoved the pile aside, turned to his computer, and began to scan his email. No more en-
thralled with what he found there, Starkey did enjoy
each little execution.

"Pointless," he said aloud. He hit the delete
key.

"Waste of time." Delete.

"Go away." Delete.

"Jackass." Delete.

"This is going to be the week when I have a
bale of straw delivered to his office. Jackass." Delete.

Of course, his appearance made new problems. The security guard at the front desk asked for
ID when he signed into work that morning. The man
looked him up and down, dubious, even when he
showed his company badge. Jack knew he'd grown
another inch. That made him three inches taller than
when he came to work Monday. The guard didn't
ask, and Jack didn't offer an explanation. The secre-
taries on his floor stared at him, but he just smiled at
them and hurried to his office. He didn't know what
to say. Sooner or later he'd have to tell them and his
boss something. A glandular condition? The doctors
weren't sure?

He turned to glance at the arrow on his desk. It didn't look quite real, somehow, with its strange feathers, black as night but with the faintest traces of a color he couldn't give a name to. The shaft looked eons old and pock marked, or pitted with craters like the surface of the moon. He picked the arrow up and then held the point up to the light. At first the arrowhead looked completely black, but there were small areas through which he thought he could see light. Was it quartz? No, it didn't look crystal-like. Glass? What was the name of that black glass that formed at the site of volcanic eruptions? Obsidian. Was the arrowhead made out of volcanic glass? Obsidian or not, it felt incredibly sharp. The arrowhead appeared polished, honed to be razor-like, but with a broken tip, and he wondered if he did that himself when he yanked it out of the sycamore. The edges of the arrowhead were serrated, as if designed to tear as well as pierce. It scared him just to touch it. He jumped when the telephone rang. After two rings he answered it. "Starkey here," he said. He smiled at his disregard for the company telephone policy that obligated him to say, "Hello, Harmon Group, Jack Starkey speaking."

"Hello? Jack Starkey? This is Peter Cassavetes," a voice said.

"I'm sorry, I don't place the name," Starkey said.

"Randall Myers gave me your number," the man said. "It's about the arrow? I owe him a favor, and it appears he owes you one as well."

"Oh yes, thanks for calling. I'm wondering if you can help me identify a strange arrow I found."

"Perhaps I can. I'm an anthropologist down here at the Natural History Museum, and the weapons of primitive cultures are a special interest of mine. What does the arrow look like?" Cassavetes asked.

"Well, it's short, too short to fit anything but a pigmy's bow. It's about fifteen inches long and black as night. It has a dark, wooden shaft of what looks like ebony, black feathers, and a black, polished arrowhead. The arrowhead looks to me like obsidian," Starkey said.

"Fifteen inches long. Interesting. Feel free to bring it by the museum for me," Cassavetes said. "Just call first so I can be sure I'll be here when you come. I teach a few classes at Catholic University during the week. Wait, Starkey, did you say the point was obsidian?"

"I'm guessing."

"Well, I can't tell you much without seeing it, but you've reminded me of something. I can't be sure how it relates until I do some checking. But now I'm intrigued. Can you come tomorrow?" Cassavetes' voice pitched higher now.

"Yes, that would be great. After lunch? That would be good for me," Starkey said.

"Excellent," Cassavetes said. He gave Starkey his number.

Later that day, Starkey ducked out of his office on K St early and caught the Metro at Farragut North. The subway car sat waiting, nearly empty, but it held a few early bird civil servants and a group of boys. Two of the boys carried gym bags with the logo of Sidwell Friends, the Quaker School. The boys wore the skinny jeans, long sleeve shirts with the shirttail hanging out, baseball caps, and skateboarding sneakers that passed for young men's fashion. Seeing nothing of particular interest, Starkey returned to his book, a Poirot story he'd read before.

Startled by the laughter of one of the boys, Starkey looked up. The boy's voice sounded so much like his son Ethan's that Starkey felt a chill go up his spine. He turned to the window at his side. He met his own reflection in the glass, though he could see through to the concrete sides of the tunnel racing by in shadow. Ethan's reflection sat beside him on the seat. Then memory overtook him and the lines of the concrete wall morphed into the razor blade slices his son Ethan cut into his upper arm. Perfectly parallel, like the hash marks on the sleeve of a soldier's uniform, each carved the same, deliberate length. Some cuts were broader than others, where it seemed the blade delved more deeply and the flesh separated more. Blood seeped from each gash down over the ones below like dripping paint. Together they composed a kind of abstract in Ethan's flesh. Ethan lay in an emergency room under shockingly bright lights. Starkey's child balanced on the brink of death. The child whose warm newborn face Starkey had pressed to his cheek lay there, seventeen years later, with tubes running in and out of his body.

The subway car stopped with a lurch. He watched the boys exit the train and followed them out onto the platform and up the stairs. The late afternoon sun shining down on the Grosvenor Station was warm.

>>>

Starkey left his office at 12:30 the next day and set off to meet Cassavetes at the museum. He'd always longed to go behind the exhibits of the Natural History Museum, to venture behind those closed doors marked "Staff Only" that admitted only those lucky folks who worked there.

Cassavetes met him in the rotunda by the giant African Elephant. Cassavetes was short and somewhat rotund. Starkey might have recognized him from the man's tweed jacket and checkered bow tie alone because even his voice had sounded tweedy on the phone. He looked up at Starkey.

"You're younger than I expected from your voice on the phone," Cassavetes said.

"Thanks, I think," Starkey said.

After a brief introduction and a handshake, he took Starkey up a steep marble flight of stairs. And yes, damned if the man didn't lead him right through one of those Staff Only doors. They went down a long hall and through one of the many glass-paned doors. Cassavetes' office was long and rectangular with high ceilings and tall double hung windows at the rear. A window unit air conditioner ran, dripping water onto the hard tile beneath. Floor to ceiling shelves covered the walls and were filled by books, as he expected, but there were weapons of every description also. Spears and shields and daggers and swords and clubs hung from the walls like icons, and crowded every shelf and table and windowsill, spilling out onto the floor.

Cassavetes closed the office door and came back to perch on the corner of his desk. He looked to be in his fifties and graying, with a small, neatly trimmed goatee that exaggerated an already pointed chin.

"Come in and sit down." Cassavetes said. He gestured to a chair. "Is that one big enough?"

"It'll do." Starkey sat down, removed the arrow from his briefcase, and handed it over. The anthropologist took it and examined it. His right forefinger traced the length of the shaft. Then he held the dark arrowhead up to the light of the windows. Starkey thought he saw a shiver run through the man.

"Where did you get this, Mr. Starkey?" Cassavetes asked.

Starkey told him about the attack at the canal. "Well, is the arrow head obsidian? Do you recognize it?" Starkey asked.

"Yes, it is and yes, I do."

Cassavetes placed the arrow carefully on the desk beside him. He took a long look at Starkey, as if appraising him.

"Have you ever heard of Oberlin's Anomaly?" Cassavetes asked. He rose and walked around behind his desk and sat down in the worn leather swivel chair.

"No," Starkey said.

Cassavetes leaned back and steepled his fingers.

"Well, this is the story. In 1948, a photographer named Cardiff was taking pictures of a trench dug for a cable to be laid by the Potomac Electric Power Company. The trench cut across the C&O Canal at 34th St. in Georgetown."

"What does this have to do with the arrow?" Starkey asked.

"Patience, Mr. Starkey, you will see. When the excavation crew touched off a blast and the dust cleared, the photographer saw something. Through the camera lens he saw what looked like bones protruding from one wall of the trench. When the local coroner arrived he determined that some of the bones were human. Those were excavated and sent to the morgue. The other bones were not human. They and some other objects they found with them were shipped here to the museum."

Cassavetes must have seen Starkey grow impatient. "You can't understand unless you hear the whole story," Cassavetes said.

"Okay, okay, I'm with you, go on," Starkey said.

"The bones and the other objects were placed in the hands of a paleontologist named Robert Oberlin. This is a picture of the bones," Cassavetes said.

He pulled the photo from his top desk drawer and handed the black and white photograph over to Starkey.

"My story reminded you of this?" The photo showed the large bones of some kind of creature jutting out from a wall of dirt. "What is it?" Starkey said, handing it back.

Cassavetes slipped the photograph back into his desk. "Nobody knows. Oberlin might have classified it as a pterosaur, a flying dinosaur that became extinct sixty-five million years ago, except for one thing."

"And what's that?"

"His colleagues would have laughed him out of the institute," Cassavetes said. "The skeleton wasn't a fossil. It wasn't more than a few hundred years old. It takes at least ten thousand years to make a fossil. But here is the really strange bit. The skull held sockets for three eyes."

"Three eyes? Dammit, I should have known. That Myers has set me up," Starkey said, standing up and turning to go.

Cassavetes started to laugh and held up his hands.

"No, no, wait, please sit down. I know how it sounds, but I assure you, every word is true."

Starkey sat back down and Cassavetes went on.

"Of course Oberlin's colleagues then and everyone since have dismissed it as being impossible, and called it a hoax," he said, "and somehow faked. Three eyes makes it unknown and likely not of this planet. As soon as you say 'extra-terrestrial' legitimate scientists run and hide for fear of being called frauds."

"Except you," Starkey said.

"Yes. Well, almost everyone here at the museum has seen it or heard of it. Every few years, someone pulls it out of storage to examine it." Cassavetes said. "One of those times, twenty-five years ago, a brash young anthropologist thought the ridicule of those around him would mean nothing to him."

Starkey watched the man's eyes stare off in the distance, and something like regret crept into his face.

"That was you, right?" Starkey asked.

Cassavetes looked at him again. He shrugged. "I was wrong."

"Why are you telling me this story? What does this have to do with the arrow, Doc?"

Cassavetes leaned forward and spoke more quietly. "Well, here's the point. Pterosaur wings are forelimbs adapted for flight," he said. "The wrist bones, the hand bones, and the fingers and claws are attached to the top of the wings. In this skeleton, however, those structures are attached directly to the chest."

"What does that mean in plain English?" Starkey asked.

Cassavetes, paused, looked over Starkey's shoulder at the closed door, and leaned in still closer.

"There is no way this creature could evolve from a terrestrial species."

"You mean on Earth?"

"Yes."

"Are you trying to say it is extraterrestrial? Alien?"

Cassavetes pulled back. "I didn't say that. No one knows. It remains an anomaly, and largely avoided like the plague by scientists. As I said before, the vertebrate paleontologists either dismiss it out of hand as a hoax, a composite, or they pretend as hard as they can it does not exist."

"This sounds more like a cover of a tabloid magazine than science," Starkey said, "but you still haven't told me what this has to do with the arrow."

Cassavetes took a key from his pocket and unlocked a drawer in the credenza behind him. He pulled it open and took out another arrow and placed it on the desk between them. Starkey stared.

"Where did that arrow come from?" Starkey said.

"This arrow was found with the skeleton of the anomaly in Georgetown in 1948. As you can see they are identical. After you and I talked on the phone, I retrieved it from the subbasement where the anomaly is stored."

Cassavetes leaned further back in his chair and watched Starkey's face.

Starkey pulled it all together in his mind.

"Did the arrow kill the thing?"

"No," Cassavetes said, laughing. "In a way, I wish that were true. Somehow it would be easier to categorize the whole thing. No, the arrow rested amongst the bones of the anomaly's hand, as if being clutched."

He took a larger object out of the same drawer and placed it on the table. "This was found with the bones of the anomaly also."

Starkey leaned forward to touch the object carefully. "Is that what it looks like, Doc?"

"It depends on who you talk to," he said. "Privately I would classify it as a 3rd century Chinese crossbow, at least the mechanism is. The stock appears to be made of the same stuff as the shaft of the arrow. I have no idea what that is."

Starkey looked at Cassavetes and waited, wondering if there was still more to come. There was.

"I told you before. Some of the bones found in 1948 were human. Remember those were the bones the coroner examined and took possession of at the scene. They were the remains of a young woman. She was nine months pregnant when she died."

"So this thing, whatever it was, attacked a pregnant woman by the canal?

"Looks that way, doesn't it? But there's no proof," Cassavetes said.

"Ok," Starkey said. "Now that's really bizarre. Did you see the article in The Post just today about pregnant women disappearing by the canal? It said three had gone missing in the last seven years." Starkey told him about the man he met at the pub, Warfield, and lock number seven of the canal.

"That puts an entirely different face on it, doesn't it? Now it seems these bones are speaking to us from out of the past," Cassavetes said.

"But what do we do about it?'

"First I'm going to do what I should have done years ago. I'm going to send the anomaly bones to Ann Wilson's lab at NIH. They will test the DNA. Then we'll see."

CHAPTER SIX

DAVE VAUGHN

SILVER SPRING MD THURSDAY MAY 24TH

Just out of habit Starkey stopped by St. Andrew's Pub. It's what he'd done for months. He knew he needed a change. *But what?*

"Are you ready for another?" Paul said.

"Absolutely," Starkey said, pushing his pint glass forward.

"I'm not complaining, Starkey my lad, but you've been in more these last few weeks. Did you strike out with Sheila?" Paul asked. A stronger hint of Dublin sounded in the bartender's voice this evening.

"You know we don't live together, Paul. You sound like you've been back home today."

"I talked to my brother, Brennen, on the phone this morning. Starkey I'd swear you're an inch taller than you were the last time you were in here. When was that?"

"Monday. Yeah, I know, I know. Give me a break, Paul. I don't know what the hell is causing it. And since you asked so politely, no, I'm still in the ballgame with Sheila, maybe. But I haven't made it to first base for quite a while, either."

Why had he been spending more of his free time at this bar than with Sheila? Now his mind had cleared enough to see that it was a little game he'd played with himself. He'd been trying to pretend Ethan didn't commit suicide and his wife didn't die and there wasn't a great gaping hole in him he couldn't drink enough to fill. But the time for that was over.

Starkey watched as the bartender wiped the mahogany bar and took his glass. Starkey saw a man who looked Native American coming into the bar. *Shit.* Dave Vaughn. The man walked the length of the bar and sat down on the empty seat next to Starkey. *Great, just what I need.*

Meeting Dave Vaughn the first time was disillusioning to say the least, shattering Starkey's naïve illusions of Native American social graces. It happened late one Thursday night back in the fall when Starkey should have been home in bed hours before, but he still sat at the bar. Sometimes a few pints of Bass could put a brighter face on his past. That night he reached equilibrium after three pints. Dave Vaughn had walked into the pub and taken the stool next to him. Starkey thought he saw a look of chagrin pass across Paul's face. Shortly Starkey began to understand his first impression was correct.

Vaughn stood a little short of medium height with a stocky build. Starkey guessed his age as being around forty. He wore his hair in long braids, and his face reminded Starkey of the color of oiled leather. Acne scars marred his beardless cheeks and a large hooked nose completed an otherwise handsome face. He wore a dark, well cut suit and a conservative tie.

Dave proceeded to tell the most gross and disgusting stories Starkey could imagine. He told one dirty joke after another, and the personal anecdotes were even worse. To hear him tell it you would think the man spent his every waking moment philandering. Even worse, he spoke of the women in these scenarios in the most demeaning way possible. Trapped, Starkey saw little choice. It was listen or leave.

"Hey Paul didja you hear the one about the two squaws standing in the train station in Baltimore?" Vaughn asked.

"Yes, twice," Paul said.

Instead the man told another joke, something about 'hoss-style' and 'dog style'. Starkey left early, an unusual occurrence.

So tonight when Starkey saw Dave Vaughn come through the door, he wished he'd left a half hour before. It didn't help any that Dave seemed to have decided he liked Starkey. He made it a point to sit next to Starkey whenever he found him at the bar. And over the months Starkey came to know the man and found reason to tolerate him. Starkey recognized another tortured soul and felt some sympathy for Vaughn, as he called himself. It couldn't have been easy for a Native American living in this culture. Starkey believed he sensed more to the man underneath all the crude, womanizing bullshit.

Then Starkey thought about being attacked by the canal, the arrow, and the revelations of Cassavetes. When they first met, Vaughn told Starkey he belonged to the Piscataway tribe, native to the area along the Potomac in Maryland. He supposed it couldn't hurt to ask him if his people ever mentioned a creature with three eyes. Maybe Vaughn would shut up about his "young Indian girls" for a few minutes.

"Hello, Dave," Starkey said. "How are you?"

"Excuse me, but who the hell are you?"

"I'm Jack Starkey, Dave."

"Sure." He laughed that short laugh that ended most of his sentences. Starkey didn't know if it
was derisive or just a nervous habit. "Hey, Paul can I
get a fucking beer down here?" Vaughn said.

Starkey sighed. "Look, Dave, I grew, ok? The
doctor says it may be glandular. He doesn't know."

"Ok, Starkey, or whoever. Why should I
care? Did I ever tell you the one about the Arapaho?"

"Yes, twice," said Starkey. Then he spoke
quickly, not allowing the other man to respond.
"You're Piscataway, right?"

"Yeah, so what? Did I tell you the one about
'hoss-style'?"

"Yes, three times," said Starkey. "Do you
speak the language?"

"Fuck no," Vaugh said, laughing again. "But
then nobody else does either. Most of our language
and customs were lost during what the white man
called our *assimilation*. A few words survived among
the old women. Why the hell do you care? Hey, Paul,
what about that goddamn beer?"

"Well, I'd like to know if the phrase 'three
eyes' or 'three-eyed' means anything in the language
of your people," said Starkey.

"*Three eyes?*" Well, it don't mean shit to me,
but I'll ask around if you like. Say can I get some of
that stuff you're taking to get pumped up like that?"

"Sure I'll bring you a bottle. Paul, put his beer on my tab will you?" Starkey gave Vaughn his card with his address and phone number on it, drained his pint, and stood up. He left a twenty beside the bill Paul put on the bar, and hurried out.

>>>

Later that evening, Dave Vaughn adjusted the ball cock just slightly and pushed down the handle to flush the toilet. This time the water rose and shut off the flow, just like it should. He placed the toilet lid back on the tank and left the small, tidy bathroom. He walked down the narrow, short hall to the kitchen of his father's trailer.

"The toilet's fixed, Pop."

"Good," the old man said. He didn't look up from the small, portable television on the kitchen table in front of him. He reached over to adjust the rabbit ears. Dave's father was smaller than Dave, more like his Piscataway people. Though his skin looked lighter than his son's, he had the same high cheekbones and long, black hair. Dave got his skin color and size from his mother who belonged to the Lenape tribe. Painfully thin, and his back permanently bent from long years of day labor, his father looked frail.

"There's beer in the icebox," Pop said, waving a can of Milwaukee's Best at him. The kitchen, like the bathroom, was small but immaculate. The single, plastic window over the sink stood open to the warm weather, and a bird's song came in through the checkered curtains.

"No thanks, I got to get going," Dave said.

"You'd rather drink with those white folks down at that place where you go than here with your old man, I guess?"

"Don't start that shit again, Pop." But he remembered Starkey's request. Taking a can of beer from the mostly empty refrigerator, he sat down across from his father at the small, scarred, Formica-topped table. Dave pulled the pop top and took a sip. "Do you know how to say 'three-eyes' or 'three-eyed' in the language of our people?"

"I don't know how to say 'shit' in the language of our people," his father said, rolling his eyes.

"Ok, Pop, but do the words mean anything to you?"

"Nope."

"Well if you remember, ask some of the old women down at Bingo if it means anything to them."

"It might be a while, son. I spent all my bingo money 'til I get my next check."

"Damn, Pop, you hittin' the wine heavy again?"

His father didn't answer and Dave took ten dollars out of his wallet and, putting the money down on the kitchen table, pushed it across to his father. His father grunted and pushed the money to the side by a white, plastic toaster.

"You could ask that man from the university, he seems to know more about us than we know about ourselves," his father said. "He showed me a little stone thing with three big eyes, now you mention it."

"He visited here again?"

"He came yesterday, I think. This time he's been digging around in something called a mizzen, or midden, or something like that out on Heater's Island near Frederick, which he says is one of our garbage dumps from three hundred years ago."

"What did he find?"

"He brought some stuff for me to look at. A leg bone and some teeth from one of our ancestors, he said. He said he was having them tested for something, I forget what. He said he'd be back another day. His card is on the table by the door."

Dave reached for the card and examined it. He read it out loud. "Joseph P. Wilson, Ph.D., Physical Anthropology, University of Maryland."

"Garbage dumps." His father gave a dry laugh. "I told him our garbage was sacred and he'd better stop digging it up. His face got all pinched and he looked mighty put out, until I couldn't hold it anymore." Pop's shoulders shook with silent laughter. "I nearly bust a gut laughing at him."

"Real nice, Pop. The man respects you."

"Just a little joke."

"Ok, Pop. Can I have this card with his phone number?"

"Take it. The goddam phone company cut off the phone again anyway."

"What the hell didja do with the money I gave you to pay the bill, Pop?" The old man didn't answer. Dave opened both hands and held them up. "Never mind, where's the bill? I'll take it with me and pay it."

"It's there on the table in the hall somewhere, boy. Quiet now, Wheel of Fortune is on," his father said, turning to the television.

Dave rose to leave. "O.K, Pop, I'll see you later."

"Dave?" the old man turned down the television and looked at his son for the first time.

"The professor guy wants me to give him a sample of my blood."

"Why does he want that?"

"He wants to run some tests. Something about comparing my DOA to some from the bones he found out there."

"It's DNA, Pop. Where out there?"

"That garbage dump."

"So?" Dave said.

"Well, I've never given blood. I didn't go for the draft. I don't like needles, so I always refused down at the clinic. They didn't give a damn, anyway. Is it okay, do you think?"

"Pop, it doesn't even fucking hurt. The man respects you. He just wants your help. Yes, it's okay."

"All right. He said I was near about the only full blood Piscataway he was sure of. He said he'd pay me. I told him I'd let him know. He's coming back tomorrow at 2:00 o'clock if you want to talk to him."

"Maybe I'll stop by if I can leave work early. See you later, Pop," Dave said, but his father had turned back to the television.

CHAPTER SEVEN

SHEILA CARTWRIGHT

SILVER SPRING MD WEDNESDAY MAY 24TH

Starkey left St. Andrew's glancing over his shoulder. Starkey thought Dave Vaughn might follow him out of the pub and into the parking lot, anxious to tell another dirty joke. He warned himself to avoid coming to the pub on future Thursdays. The engine of the Subaru ground for a few minutes, but coughed to life. He backed slowly out of the space and pulled out of the parking lot onto Georgia Avenue, darkness falling. Starkey checked his watch. Six. Sheila would be home. He turned right onto University, making for Sheila's place. He pulled downward on the legs of the new slacks he'd bought yesterday. They seemed tight in the crotch though they'd fit well enough in the store. How could his inseam have gone from thirty-one to thirty-three in three days? The extra-large polo shirt he bought for casual Friday at work seemed tight already. What was happening to him? Maybe he should see a doctor about his sudden growth. He lifted his right hand from the steering wheel. He almost didn't recognize it. No doubt about it. He'd grown bigger again. It seemed to be accelerating.

Wait, wait, of course. Starkey hit the steering wheel with his hand. It started right after the attack at the canal when he'd felt that sudden surge of strength running across the bridge and up the hill. He'd run so fast his legs began to blur. He could tell Sheila that.

Before the black arrow hit the tree and his universe shifted he'd been fantasizing about Jane. Now it came back to him in disjointed pieces. Of course it wasn't only about her. The woman in his fantasy formed a composite. Sheila played the main role, but a great deal of his wife, Jane, appeared as well, and both were romanticized. He tried only once, as in the fantasy, to listen to Ry Cooder's recording of "Maria Elena" while making love with Sheila. That went wonderfully well until he whispered Jane's name in Sheila's ear. Almost a week had passed and she still didn't return his calls.

He didn't blame her. Starkey mourned Jane and he mourned Ethan. The same old blues song played over and over. It was five years ago this month Ethan committed suicide. Starkey's thirteen year old son overdosed after a long bout of depression and took much of the light out of his life. *No wonder I'm seeing him again.* That happened for a long time after his son's death. In a way, he'd grown used to the ghost. Sometimes he'd even talked to it. After Sheppard Pratt released him he stopped, and eventually it went away, at least for a while. Starkey missed talking to him sometimes. But now Ethan had reappeared.

Maybe if he opened up about how poorly he coped with the anniversary of Ethan's death Sheila would listen, and he could get past it. Talking about his depression since the death of his family got harder for him, even with her, who he knew stood firmly on his side. But what would she say about his size?

The memories of both members of his lost family left little of Starkey for anyone or anything else. Sooner or later, the women who came after Jane all figured it out. Sheila knew now, too, that down in the marrow Starkey still loved Jane. But why not? It would be strange if he didn't–and didn't he love Sheila, too?

Maybe he should just give up on relationships. But then what would he do? Sit with the regulars at the pub and drink until the pain went away every night? No, it was way too early in his career to start drinking full-time. Although, that might be the way this story ends. Plenty of time remained to become an alcoholic after he retired. Screw that. He wanted things to work out with Sheila. When they stood shoulder to shoulder in training with the Master or in moments when the ghosts of Ethan and Jane retreated to the background while he and Sheila were together, he felt centered and complete. Starkey believed Sheila represented his last best chance for happiness. Starkey decided a 'relationship discussion', as Jane used to call it, could no longer be avoided. It was time. He didn't feel afraid to let go and really love her anymore. A clear vision of her face appeared in his mind. But should talk of their relationship happen first? Nope. His size alone would force the story of the attack.

Starkey turned into Sheila's neighborhood. The houses that lined her street were those typical, brick Silver Spring split-levels, each much like the other. The sidewalks at this time of evening were alive with the families of conservative Jews, all walking to their temple under the streetlights. The fathers wore dark fedora hats and dark pants and coats and white shirts. The mothers wore long skirts or dresses and often wore hats. The boys wore yarmulkes and white shirts a well, with dark trousers like their fathers, and the girls dressed much like their mothers. The whole scene made him feel even lonelier.

Sheila never once let him down. He tried to remember this as he pulled into her driveway. It was almost a week since he'd seen her and he had no idea how he'd be received, showing up unannounced like this. And lots bigger. The woman was gutsy, for sure, or she wouldn't be hanging around with him at all. She was, in fact, the most fearless person he'd ever known. Five feet nine in her bare feet, with broad shoulders and narrow hips, Sheila possessed strength, mentally and physically. She seldom missed a rally for a cause she believed in. She'd get right up in the face of her opponents, and the cops. Her green eyes stared directly into theirs, unflinching. Her strong personality dominated their relationship. Starkey wasn't always so pliable, perhaps, but there it was.

He really needed a friend tonight. He needed a friend who could disregard the fantastic nature of the story he told her, and just listen. It would be nice if there was Bass ale in her refrigerator as well. The fact she had a great body and strong hands couldn't hurt, either. Not for the first time, he marveled at her presence in his life.

It started out as a damn good friendship. Master Yamashima introduced them since they both studied martial arts with him. After Jane's death they slowly got closer. Some time passed before they developed a relationship. Sheila thought of herself as a recovering romantic and hadn't encouraged intimacy in the beginning. Her previous relationships soured her on love affairs, and she'd never married. They both joined a mystery book club in a small bookstore in Takoma Park, Maryland, and the shared books and martial arts gave Starkey things to talk about with her beside his troubles. Singing the blues achieved limited attractiveness in dating, he'd discovered. Somehow the friendship and relationship that followed deepened, all due to Sheila's patience with him, he thought, for he did tell her his troubles. Yet, for reasons known only to her, she seemed to love him. But she never said it out loud.

He pulled into her driveway and parked. He put the arrow into his backpack, zipped it up, and got out of the car carrying it. He locked the car and glanced around him, cautious after the attack at the canal. The houses were lit brightly around him, and everything seemed just as it always had. Only he had changed. He shrugged his shoulders, crossed the yard, went up the steps, and rang the bell.

After a moment, Shelia opened the door.

"Hello, Sheila," Sharkey said.

Sheila turned on the front porch light and stared at him. "Yes?"

"Ok, I know I look different, Sheila."

"Do I know you?" She said.

"Damn, Sheila, it's me, Jack. Who do you think?"

Sheila looked him up and down. She took a step closer and looked up in his face. She took his sleeve and pulled him more into the light. "Jack? Wait, you're huge. How…what happened? This can't be real."

"My thought exactly. Except it is. Can we go inside? I'll tell you what happened. Ok?"

Sheila looked wary, but she seemed to recognize him, and she motioned for him to follow her in. "This ought to be good." She flung the words over her shoulder as she turned her back to him and walked toward the kitchen. He watched her shoulder blades move under her sports bra as she strode down the hall, her backside lean and muscular in her exercise tights. She turned back once to stop and stare at him again with those striking green eyes. He loved those eyes, even when they bored into him, like now. Her long, shining black hair hung down to her shoulders. He'd seen these things about her, but he hadn't opened to them.

But he didn't say those things. He fell back on the old familiar smartass routine. "Won't you come in, Jack? How nice to see you."

"Well, what did you expect?"

"I'm sorry, I didn't know what to expect." He put his backpack on a table in the foyer and trailed her down the short hall and into the kitchen.

"If you are Jack you'd most likely like a beer." She turned, holding an open bottle of Bass Ale. There in the bright lights of the kitchen she looked him up and down. Eyes wide, she stood with her mouth open. She took a step back, shifting her weight to the rear leg.

"Who the hell are you?" She sounded serious. You're three inches taller, your pot-belly is gone, and your hair is red."

He should have known. Sheila set the beer on the table between them and moved into a defensive pose.

"Can we sit down and talk about this, Sheila? It's a long story and that beer would be very welcome," he said. She didn't answer, but she pointed at a chair. She sat down across from him. Where to begin?

Her eyes still looked at him in disbelief. "I don't even recognize the clothes. You never buy new stuff."

"Everything got a little tight."

"A little tight? You're one helluva lot bigger and an entirely different shape than the Jack Starkey I know. It's too weird. It's not possible. How could you grow like this?"

"I don't know. But I know when it started. I'll tell you the story if you'll give me a chance."

"Ok. Maybe. The voice is right. If I close my eyes you're Jack. I like the hair. Good dye job. It makes you look younger. The red in it kind of suits you."

He expected the hair color comment. "I didn't dye it. It used to be all reddish brown before I went grey."

"I don't know what to say. I'd call you a liar except there you sit. Big as life. If you'll pardon the expression." She pushed the beer across to him and watched as he sucked down a third of it straight away.

"Thanks." He felt a smile start to form on his face. But Sheila wasn't smiling.

"Well, Jack, Big Boy, or whoever you are, that's the last of those." The shock and surprise left Sheila's face, and disappointment and sadness replaced them.

Starkey watched the change, and set the beer bottle down on the table. "Do you mean you're out of beer or the ball game's over?"

"It depends, Jack."

"Depends on what?"

She looked down at her hands on the table. Her beautiful, long fingers showed calluses along the sides from continuous martial arts practice. Strong hands. He loved those, too.

"Look Jack, let's leave aside your ridiculous growth spurt for the moment. I'm sorry for you, but the big blue eyes and mournful looks aren't going to cut it this time. Jane's dead, and your son is dead, I know, and it's awful. But you bring them with you every time we're together. Even when you aren't singing the blues, they stand like ghosts in the corner behind me. I see them reflected in your eyes."

"I know. I don't see Jane. But I saw Ethan in the mirror at the pub after the attack, and again on the subway, but not since then. Look at me, Sheila. Do you see them now?" Starkey asked.

She took a long look. "Ok, maybe not so much today. You think I'm hurt and angry because you called me by her name the other night, right?"

"Aren't you?"

"No. Okay, yes, a little. But the point is you can't continue to mourn them full time and be here with me. I've seen enough of your emotionally unavailable act. My parents already taught me all I needed to know about emotional unavailability, thank you very much. Not to mention my previous boyfriends. I need more than pity in a relationship."

Starkey looked at the table for a long time. As usual Sheila said exactly what she thought, point blank, no bullshit.

"Is it so obvious?" he asked. "Look, Sheila, I want things to work out with you. I don't want to lose you."

Sheila rose and went to the refrigerator and got a bottle of white wine, grabbed a wine glass off the rack and sat back down at the table. "That's nice to hear, but it doesn't change anything," she said, pouring the wine.

"I know. Look, I need someone to talk to tonight."

"If it's more blues, just take it back down the road to St. Andrews." Sheila said, shaking her head. She sat quiet for a moment and sighed, "Okay, what? I have no clue how to talk about your size."

He stood up and walked to the kitchen window. "May I close these blinds?"

"Yes, of course, but what's wrong? What are you looking outside for?"

Not answering, he retrieved his backpack from the hall, opened it, and pulled out the black arrow. He placed it on the table in front of Sheila.

"Three days ago I was attacked along the canal. Someone shot that arrow at me. If I hadn't bent over to pick up a clam shell, I'd be dead. Totally dead. Since then I've been growing like this. Big and getting bigger."

"Someone who? Where were you on the canal? How do you know you were the target?" Sheila's questions spilled out.

"I don't know who. I saw circles over in the canal near me and a shadow moving away, like something sunk below the surface. I didn't see anyone else except some bikers farther down the towpath."

Starkey paused to take a breath and Sheila broke in. "You still don't know they were shooting at you."

"Nobody else was there, Sheila. The arrow struck the tree beside me right where my head would have been. What would you think? And it happened by the island of the canoeing society."

"So?"

Starkey told her about his visit to the canoeing society a few days before the attack and the creepy guys and the weird reception they gave him.

"Ok, that is weird. But why would they want to kill you, Jack?"

Starkey's voice went up higher. "Damn, Sheila, I don't know. But don't you think it's a little odd they acquired a very convenient opening just when I showed up?"

"Coincidences do happen, Jack. Calm down, I'm just going over the facts," Sheila said. "Did you go to the police?"

"Yes, but I went to the pub first."

Sheila laughed a very short laugh. "Surprise, surprise."

Starkey told her about Warfield and the deaths along the canal near lock Number Seven.

"I went to the police station in Glenmont. I gave a statement, but the cop said the incident took place in DC so they'd be calling me. He wanted the arrow, but I didn't give it to him."

"So what now?" Sheila asked.

"There's more. I went to see an anthropologist at the Smithsonian to show him the arrow. This is where it really gets strange." He told Sheila about Oberlin's Anomaly.

"Come on Jack, space aliens? You can't be serious."

"I didn't believe him at first, but he showed me an arrow identical to this one. And he's not a crank. He's an anthropologist at the Natural History Museum, for Pete's sake. I believed him."

Sheila picked up the arrow and took a closer look. "What is this point made of? It looks like stone but it's so light. And if the shaft is wood it's a kind I don't recognize."

"Cassavetes said the arrowhead was obsidian. But I'd like to show it to the Master. I'd like to see what he thinks about this whole thing."

"Ok, let's put the whole thing together."

They laid out the sequence of events. First the strange reception Starkey received at the canoe club. Then the attack on him by the canal. The black arrow that almost struck him. Then Starkey's sudden growth. Finally the meeting with Cassavetes and Oberlin's Anomaly. In the midst of all this Starkey noticed his mind held focus, connecting the events and circumstances logically. The mental fog he had lived in for so long had disappeared.

"Jack," Sheila said. "Somewhere in all of this is the reason for your sudden growth. I know it."

"That's when it started. But how, and why? I know I was afraid, really afraid for the first time in my life. Maybe the Master will have an idea. "

The Master formed a magnetic center in Starkey's life. Inexorably drawn to Master Yama-shima, the needle on Starkey's compass stopped spinning when he interacted with him. Starkey drew strength from their relationship, calibration, and a sense of direction he had sorely needed in the last few years. The dojo felt like home, particularly now when Starkey's own home harbored painful ghosts. Sheila and he trained side by side there with the Master, eventually being accepted as his disciples. Starkey brought everything to Master Yamashima, even Ethan's suicide and his wife's subsequent death. The Master became more than teacher to Starkey, almost like the real father Starkey never knew, though they didn't speak of it. Starkey's adopted father had been benign and well meaning, but somehow distant. Both his adopted parents died relatively young. And so Starkey would bring the arrow and the attack on him to the Master as well. Although he told himself the Master held special knowledge of archery and weapons, Starkey knew fear drove him.

CHAPTER EIGHT

VIOLA

C&O CANAL GREAT FALLS MD
JUNE 1901

Vernon Hilliard raised the boat horn to his lips and blew a long, groaning call. He squared himself on the rear deck of the canal boat, Shenandoah, and set aside the horn. He took the tiller with both hands, planted his bare feet wide, and steered down the center of the canal. Blackish water passed beneath the boat, sliced by the rudder, and the green bottom of the boat left a wide wake behind. Away down the canal he saw Violet's Lock, still distant, through the white oak trees that lined the shore. Spring had come early, and the redbuds along the bank of the Potomac River began to bloom as the days started to heat up.

Vernon rubbed the back of his neck, stiff
from an overnight at the tiller. He pulled off his bat-
tered grey fedora and wiped his balding head with his
shirt sleeve. Yes, he was tired. The run down from
Cumberland always took its toll, but Vernon made no
complaints. He'd come out of the mountains, like
many men before him, seeking a living wage, and
he'd found he enjoyed life on the canal. He had been
'a-boatin' some five years now, hauling coal down to
Georgetown, and empty barrels or general merchan-
dise back up to the towns along the canal. He was
judged to be one of the best of the boat captains that
plied the C&O Canal from Cumberland, Maryland to
Georgetown, DC. That meant he stayed unusually
sober for a canal boat man. Most of the captains and
the crew who worked for them drank heavily, and the
taverns along River Street in Georgetown and all the
towns up and down the Potomac River knew them
well. Vernon avoided their company. He drank little
and only between runs.

His older sister Ophelia climbed out of the little cabin of the boat onto the narrow deck and stood
with her back turned to him. Her long gray hair
pushed up, she pinned it there to keep it off her neck
in the heat. Tall like her brother but broader built,
people called her horse-faced behind her back, but
never to her face. She was fearless and proud and
stronger than most men, with large muscles knotting

her arms and legs. A life of physical labor spent on a hardscrabble farm in the mountains had made her formidable. She wore bib overalls like her brother, frayed and patched many times, but clean.

Ophelia's daughter, Viola, poked her head out of the cabin and clambered onto the whitewashed deck beside her mother. Vernon reached out to smooth her blond hair with one brown, callused hand. "Well, looky here, if it ain't my new little boater," Vernon said. "Did the horn blowin' wake you up, honey?"

"Yes, Uncle Vernon," Viola said. She pulled down on the hem of her yellow sundress to straighten it. "What's the horn for?"

"That's how we tell the locktender we're a'comin' and to ready the lock," he said. "You re-member I told you how the locks lower you when you're going down to Georgetown and raise you up when you're a'comin back?"

"Yes, sir," said Viola.

Ophelia climbed up on the canal boat roof, stepped down a bit, and sat down cross-legged. She took her banjo out of its tow sack and launched into an old ballad, "Little Omie Wise," her voice spare and lonesome.

"Here, now we got to get a line on you, Viola honey," Vernon said. "You know you can't be out here on deck without your line until you get used to walking around the deck."

"'Deed I know, or I might fall in the canal and drown like Omie Wise," Viola said.

"We don't talk about drownin' much out here on the canal, honey, it's bad luck," he said, raising his voice so Ophelia could hear. He threw a half-hitch around and above the girl's waist, and snugged it up under her arms. When her eyes were elsewhere he looked down at the growing bulge of her stomach and shook his head slowly.

"Viola," Ophelia called. She stopped singing and set her banjo down, waving a hat. "Come get your straw hat, that sun's got the power today."

"Ophelia, can you bring it down here?" Vernon said, "I've put the line on her."

Ophelia shuffled along the narrow white deck and brought the hat down to Viola. She stood watching her daughter as she put the hat on, and the love in his sister's eyes for her daughter seemed nearly overflowing to Vernon. Gentle and caring with the children, she loved her Viola, and Vernon's own boy, James, with the fierce love Appalachian women can have for family. 'Come not between a mother and her child', the mountain saying went, and if it was ever true of any woman, it was surely true of Ophelia Hilliard.

Vernon looked to James up ahead on the shaded towpath. The boy had sprouted this past winter and his long arms stuck out of his shirt sleeves and his pants legs rode up past his ankles. The old snap brim cap James wore to keep the sun out of his eyes barely covered his clump of red hair. The boy steered the big mules along the gravel towpath, stooping once in a while to pick up a rock and skip it across where the river cut in close. Ophelia acted as a second mother to his boy. His sister came down from their home place in the Blue Ridge Mountains to 'do' for James and Vernon after Vernon's wife died. Vernon knew the real reason she'd come, though. Ophelia also left to escape the prying eyes and wagging tongues of the backward villagers of their home back 'up the country' when Viola's 'condition' began to show. But now folk began to talk around Cumberland, too. She could expect more of the same. So, given the way things were, Vernon reckoned the girl and his sister might as well come 'a-boatin'.

Ophelia went back to her seat on top of the cabin and took up her banjo. Vernon heard her start playing again. Damned if she didn't start to sing that one about Johnny Howard who got hanged for killing his boat captain.

"Christ Almighty, Ophelia, can't you sing no songs 'cept about murder and drownin'?" Vernon said.

"Vernon Hilliard, do not take the Lord's name in vain," Ophelia said. She didn't seem offended, however, and paid him no mind. She finished that song and struck up "Banks of the Ohio," another murder ballad.

Vernon shook his head. *She's mighty contrary sometimes.* He heard the relief mules scuffling about in the forward cabin, their big hooves scrapping against the bottom of the boat. Ophelia's songs or something else made them uneasy. He reckoned they didn't like banjo music too much. He put his mind on steering the canal boat down towards the lock, watching James out ahead passing under the big sycamore trees that lined the canal along here.

The Shenandoah moved on down, arriving at lock #7. The warm afternoon sun filtered through the trees along the towpath. Vernon's sweaty overalls and shirt stuck to his back. Green shadows and light flickered on the red roof of the boat, and Vernon watched Viola, her back against the cabin wall, dangle her pale legs over the rail, the heels of her black shoes clicking against the gunnels. He heard Ophelia frailing away on the banjo, no words this time, just an old fiddle tune she called "Sally Ann".

"Whoa, Jack, whoa Tom." Vernon heard James yell out ahead on the towpath. "Oh, ouch goddamit, he's stepped on my foot!"

Up ahead, Vernon could see James hopping on one foot and struggling to hold down Jack, the big lead mule and Tom, the second, as they reared and pulled at the leads. Jack, lurching about the towpath, stamped his huge hooves.

"Are you all right, James?" His father called from the stern.

"No, Daddy, something spooked the mules, and this god dam' jackass has stomped my foot." James said. He hopped to the side of the towpath and tied the mules' leads to a big white oak.

"There's no excuse for cussing," Viola said. She said it again, 'sing-songing' it this time.

"Let the boy be, girl," said her uncle. "I reckon you ain't been stepped on by one of them big hooves of Jack's, it's enough to make anyone cuss."

Vernon put the tiller hard over and brought the canal boat to the towpath side. He slid the fallboard off the roof and made a bridge to the towpath. *God help us if he's hurt bad.* The next doctor lived some two hours away in Georgetown. They'd barely passed lock number seven.

"Ophelia, come take the tiller," Vernon said. "I'll take Viola and see how bad the boy's foot is."

Ophelia hurried to put her banjo back in the tow sack and climbed off the cabin roof. As she stepped down to the deck from the roof, Vernon heard the relief mules inside the small stable area lurching about. She teetered along the narrow deck beside the cabins and took the tiller from Vernon.

Vernon removed the line from around Viola's waist and, holding her hand, stepped on the fallboard to cross over to the towpath.

The two had side-stepped halfway across the wooden fallboard when the canal boat lurched away from the bank. The end of the fallboard slipped off the deck, and, turning slowly downward, dumped Viola and her uncle into the dark, murky water.

Vernon surfaced, coughing. He saw Viola rise further out in the canal.

Viola screamed. "Mama!" She disappeared beneath the water.

"Vernon, oh my blessed Jesus, what is that?" Ophelia said.

Vernon looked where she pointed and saw a shape in the water at the back of the canal boat becoming partly visible now, its broad and scaly back breaching the surface. He glimpsed Viola's blond hair and blue dress beneath the surface of the water, starting to move away with the thing.

Vernon stared, stricken.

"Viola!" Ophelia flung herself off the stern of the canal boat and onto the monster that clutched her child. She clambered astride, gripped the thing's back with her left hand and striking it with her right fist, rained blow after blow upon it, hammering at the thing.

"No, no, no, God damn you. Let her go." Ophelia bit and scratched and clawed at the creature until at last it reared, heaving the woman up and off its massive back. Long yellow talons at the end of the wing-like arm slashed backward at the woman's face as she hurtled through the air. She landed like a broken thing half on the gravel towpath and half in the water.

Vernon, standing up to his waist in the canal, stared in horror at Ophelia lying beside him. Three razor-clean cuts had sliced away the left side of her face, cuts so deep that the cheek and jaw bones lay bared. Her left eye completely gone, Ophelia lay quaking. The blood from the deep gouges in her face ran in rivulets across and down the grass and green leaves of the weeds on the canal bank into the water, and the red stain spread away on the current that flowed south down to Georgetown.

CHAPTER NINE

HIRO YAMASHIMA

ROCKVILLE, MD FRIDAY MAY 26TH

Master Yamashima's dojo, a converted warehouse, stood on Stone Street in Rockville, Maryland. To the casual observer little distinguished it from the many other buildings that populated the small industrial zone at the northwestern edge of the DC area, but if you looked closely there were subtle differences. Recently painted, the building was spotless, and the windows were clean. That alone would have set it apart. In addition, instead of an industrial chain link fence, a pristine cedar fence stretched along the sides and back, enclosing a private garden. Bamboo peeked over the fence and tall green fronds extended into the alley. A small, inconspicuous Shinto gateway framed the entrance's double doors and the wooden sign on the wall simply said 'Yamashima'.

Starkey had called ahead to see if the Master could see Sheila and him. He'd given the Master a short summary of what had happened. Now they waited outside the open doors of the zendo with Michael August, the Master's assistant, while the Master completed his meditation. Starkey starred at the back of August. Something about the man bothered him, but he wasn't sure what. Yamashima sat forward on a small round pillow, legs folded in a lotus position, both knees pressed firmly against the floor. His feet aligned under the necessary pressure points, he bent slightly forward from the lower back. His left hand lay palm upwards in his right hand, the little fingers of each hand pressing against his stomach. Half-closed, his eyes focused about three feet out before him on the polished wooden floor.

The tatami mat where he sat ran forward to an altar that held an emerald green vase holding a single sprig of pink lotus and a burning stick of incense, two brass candlesticks with white candles, and a photograph of a monk seated in meditation. The other walls were each hung with a single scroll or woodblock print.

Just as the joss stick burned out, a soft bell sounded. Master opened his eyes, raised his arms to shoulder height, hands together, palms touching before him, and bowed slightly. He rose in one fluid movement to stand, red Chuck Taylor sneakers just showing beneath his black robe, and turned to face the open doors. Starkey did not know Yamashima's age, but the Master retained the agility of youth. He stood no more than five feet five, and his shaved head and too large robes made him look even smaller.

Michael August stepped forward bowing, his head shaved, also. But August stood well over six feet, a little taller than Starkey. He also wore the Buddha's robe, though it fit tightly across his wide shoulders. His dark blue eyes were fixed on the floor, and he spoke quietly.

"Two of your students, are here, Master, Jack Starkey and Sheila Cartwright, but they do not have lessons today."

"It's cool. I have been expecting them, Michael." The Master pronounced his words carefully, while his native Japanese accent remained apparent.

August stood aside for Starkey and Sheila to enter. The Master reseated himself on the tatami, this time facing the doors, and waited for them to approach. Sheila and Starkey had progressed beyond the basic martial arts training Yamashima's dojo usually provided. They had advanced to the Zen Buddhist practice given those who demonstrated the aptitude and interest, and higher martial arts training.

Both were now his disciples. Sheila entered first. She bowed, giving the required salute, right fist covered with open left palm, representing the warrior-scholar. Her hands extended forward, her form perfect. Starkey followed closely and saluted as well, if less adroitly. Yamashima returned their salutes and motioned for them to sit on the floor before him. Michael August remained standing just outside the zendo doors.

Starkey did not know August well. Sheila and he tried to befriend him, but the man seemed distant somehow, and little came of their efforts. His tone of voice always seemed on the edge of dismissal. But they did not question the Master's choice of assistants. The Master seemed to trust him, but they didn't. Starkey wondered why he stood there listening now and thought the man stared at him.

The Master looked at Starkey for a long time and Starkey and Sheila waited for permission to begin. When the Master nodded at last, Sheila spoke first.

"Thank you for seeing us today, Master."

"Yeah, yeah, it's cool. Lay it on me." The Master said, smiling. He loved American slang, but used it with varying degrees of success. Sometimes Starkey and Sheila felt on the verge of laughing, but never would.

Starkey produced the arrow from inside his jacket and placed it on the tatami in front of the Master. "Three days ago someone may have tried to kill me. Someone shot this arrow at me on the canal towpath by the Potomac. It struck a tree behind me just as I bent over to pick up a shell. I didn't see who shot it. We were hoping you might be able to tell us something about the arrow. We think the arrow head is obsidian."

Yamashima picked up the arrow and examined it closely. Then, putting it back down, he pulled a pair of reading glasses out of his surplice and placed them carefully on his face. He examined the arrow again, his face remained impassive.

He reached up and rubbed his bald head with one hand. He looked at them for a long moment. His eyes rested on Starkey last. He nodded slightly. When he spoke again the slang had vanished. "Yes, it is obsidian and I recognize the stone. Wait here."

The Master rose and left the zendo through a bead-curtained door at the side. When he returned, he held a dark object in his hand. He reseated himself and placed the object on the floor next to the arrow. There sat a dagger cut from obsidian, and it closely resembled the arrowhead in appearance. It could have been cut from the same piece of volcanic glass.

"This piece came from my home in the Oki-Shotto Islands in Japan. It's from an archeological excavation site of the Jomon culture. It's thousands of years old." Yamashima looked at the two objects for a long moment, and then again at Starkey and Sheila.

Starkey shook his head. "This gets crazier all the time," Starkey said.

Sheila recovered first. "They appear to be identical. But can we be sure without having them tested? It looks like the obsidian arrowhead could have come from there also."

Yamashima shook his head no. "Maybe the same, maybe not,"

Starkey went for it. "Why do you say that? They look the same to me."

The Master smiled the same smile that so often infuriated Starkey when he argued with him on the 'battlefield of truth'. The seemingly irrational Zen sayings, the Koans, typically frustrated the linear, pragmatic mind of Starkey, and The Master often smiled at his student's dogged pursuit of their literal meaning. Yamashima told them obsidian artifacts just like that were found in other sites, Russia for example, and very old sites like those near his home. It looked identical, but it could have gotten there another way. The Master's people originally came down from central Asia, out of Siberia, down into Japan, and on to the Oki islands. So it may have traveled along a trade route. The obsidian may have come from Oki, or not, and the arrowhead could have been cut elsewhere.

Starkey shrugged. "So we're no better off than we were before."

Yamashima pointed to the arrow. "Don't forget the shaft of the arrow, the feathers, and the fletching itself, but today I can't tell you anything more. As we talked about during your phone call, it is no small thing to be the victim of an attack. We will act. I will contact my brother, a Zen priest, and historian."

"Wait, Master, there's more," Starkey said. He told the Master the story from Warfield about the history of missing pregnant women by the canal, and the article in the paper of recent incidents. The Master said nothing. Starkey went on with the story of Oberlin's Anomaly and Cassavetes. The Master still sat silent.

"Will you please advise us, Master? We are at a loss. What should we do now?" Starkey said.

The Master sat quietly for a few more moments, and then spoke. "First, since violence seems to occur by the canal, stay away from there for the time being. My brother Masato is in Japan on Oki at the monastery there, but I will email him today about all this," Yamashima said. "I think we need his assistance."

"Master," Sheila said. "You are more somber that I have ever seen you. Is there something you haven't said? What aren't you telling us?"

Yamashima did not answer at first. "Jack barely escaped dying. Isn't that enough?" He paused, looking away and then back at her. "But I will tell you this. I fear there is evil here."

"What is it, Master Yamashima?" Starkey asked. "What does this mean to you? And Master, about my size…"

"Sometimes people grow. I can tell you no more yet, I am sorry–but, yes, these events taken together disturb me. Now remember. You are students of martial arts, yes, but you are ordinary people. You are not the police. I want you to do nothing beyond what we have discussed."

"It is very hard to do nothing, Master," Sheila said.

The Master looked pointedly at Sheila. He held up the arrow. "We must go carefully. Allow me to state the obvious. If you get shot with one of these, Sheila, then we will drink no more Pina Coladas. The greatest of the warrior monks of the past died just like that. Do not overestimate your abilities. I will help you if I can, but I can do little if you're dead or in jail." He looked Jack in the eyes as he said this.

Starkey must have looked horrified.

"Chill out, Jack, don't get all bent out of shape," the Master said. "When there is work, work. When tired, rest. When hungry, eat. After eating wash your bowl." He waved them away, laughing.

As they rose and bowed out, the Master called after them, "And stay away from the canal."

Starkey and Sheila walked out of the building and into the noonday sun. The humidity hit Starkey hard after the cool of the dojo. "Did you get the feeling the Master knew a lot more than he told us?"

"Oh, yeah. Lots more. And whatever it was, it was serious like a heart attack. Did you notice he didn't want to talk about your size? What the hell have you gotten us into, Jack?"

CHAPTER TEN

RENDEZVOUS

SILVER SPRING MD FRIDAY MAY 26TH

The sun beat down on the afternoon and the smell of hot macadam rose up in the small parking lot. Starkey and Sheila stood by her car looking back at the building, their meeting with the Master still swirling around in Starkey's head. Some of the anxiety surrounding the attack on him had abated.

"I feel like I've woken up in an alternate reality," Starkey said, opening the car door. "Either that, or I've been blind to what really went on around me." He looked down at the road dust on his hand. "The Porsche could use some soap and water, Sheila. It's looking kind of grey instead of black." He held up a dirty palm.

Sheila drove a 1978 Porsche 911. It was ten years old when her dad, an amateur mechanic, gave it to her as a present when she graduated from college. Sheila maintained it like the true classic it was, so the dirt was unusual. She even changed her own oil.

"The hose and the bucket are waiting patiently back in the garage at my house, Jack. Feel free to wash her when we get back. I know I may live to regret this, but I suppose you may as well stay for dinner."

"Do I detect a certain thawing in your mood?"

Sheila opened the car door and sat down, putting the key in the ignition. "Don't count your chickens before they're roasted, sport."

"Baby let me wash your car," he said, grinning, as Sheila started the engine. "If you'll stop at the Safeway, I'll buy the beer."

They always drove to the dojo together for their lessons. Starkey left his car at her house, even when Sheila made it clear a few weeks ago their love life was stalled, that didn't change. Sheila liked to drive, and she hated his old station wagon. Today, for once, traffic was light on the beltway, the sunlight warmed the inside of the car through the windows, and Sheila's deep leather seats were comfortable. Starkey started to drift.

"When you saw Ethan in the mirror at St. Andrew's Pub," Sheila said. "How many pints of beer did you drink before that?"

It took a moment for his mind to clear. He'd nearly fallen asleep. He knew what she meant, though. "Two. I spilled most of the third one. And no, I wasn't drunk." Starkey watched as Sheila took the University Blvd exit. Red brick Cape Cod houses and little mom and pop stores and restaurants populated the four lane street. Big cumulous clouds drifted across the sun, hanging low in the sky over Wheaton's hill, layered colors promising a grand sunset. People strolled by on the Saturday sidewalks in shorts and flip-flops, dressed for the heat.

"Why then? Why that day?" she asked.

"I think because it was the anniversary."

"You mean of Ethan's suicide."

Starkey didn't respond. Sheila turned in and parked in the Safeway lot. She switched off the engine and turned to look at him. But Starkey opened the door and jumped out. "Just beer?" he said over his shoulder.

"Pick up some Tylenol. I have a feeling I'm going to need it," she said.

Starkey hurried through the grocery store. Sheila finally seemed to have forgiven him. Somehow this arrow thing had brought them closer again. An ill wind did some good, it seemed. Whatever the reason he'd take it. A good mood started to rear its pretty little head, and Starkey whistled 'Maria Elena' as he crossed the parking lot back to the car. He put the groceries in the boot behind his seat. "I got some Brie and crackers, also."

Sheila slipped out into the traffic on University and they drove in silence for a few minutes. When she turned the car onto her street Starkey saw a few men dressed in white, short sleeve shirts and dark trousers standing outside the synagogue. Stern faces turned to watch the Porsche go by. Their black wool fedoras looked like they would be hot. *Would God care if they wore straw hats?*

Sheila turned in her driveway and parked in front of the white frame garage. A bent basketball hoop hung over the door. Magnolia leaves and fading blossoms lay along the walk in front of her brick rambler. Rain had been scarce, and the daisies and dahlias in the flower boxes by the door looked wilted.

"I could water your flowers when I wash the car."

"One criticism—implied or otherwise—is all you get today, Mr. Observation."

Once inside the house, she took the Safeway bag from his hands and walked down the hall to the kitchen.

"You know where the car stuff is."

Starkey opened the garage door. He liked the smell of garages, a little gasoline, a little oil, and rubber. He found the bucket and car wash soap on the workbench beside Sheila's jeep. Washing a car satisfied something in Starkey. A job well done. One thing made clean. Even someone else's car. Starkey went all out. He vacuumed the carpets, Armoralled the vinyl, and buffed the leather seats until they shone and his hands tingled. He opened the hood, drizzled water over the engine, sprayed it with cleanser, and came back with a light water shower. It removed all the road dust. He hosed the car down, cleaned the windows, and scrubbed the hood and side panels and back. Starkey rinsed the car thoroughly, dried it, and buffed it with a chamois cloth. Then, he got down on his knees and washed and polished the chrome wheels. He even blacked the tires. As the sun went down, he began to feel tired. Good thing Sheila didn't have any car wax. As the last of the summer twilight faded he stood up, stretching his back. The garage light came on, reflecting in the deep black of the hood. The Porsche looked good. *Friday evening, washing my girlfriend's car.*

The front porch light turned on then and Sheila opened the screen door. She walked out to the driveway with a bottle of beer in her hand. She eased around the car whistling and trailing her fingers along the finish. She opened the hood to look at the engine.

"Credit where credit is due, Jack Starkey, you know how to detail a car. I'll give you that." She handed him the beer and slipped her arm around his waist and looked up in his face, green eyes smiling. "I've got dinner ready." The last of the pinks and whites and blue of the sky dimmed.

They stood side by side, washing and drying the dishes after dinner. Sheila talked during the meal about her problems of finding funding for taekwondo in the county schools. If it wasn't related to football it received short shrift in the budget. Starkey listened, but his mind drifted. She must have known.

Sheila folded the dishtowel, led him over to a seat at the kitchen table, and sat him down. She sat down across from him and looked him in the eye. "Ok, Jack, this is the place in the script where we talk about the rhinoceros in the room. Your job is to explain to me how you caused Ethan's suicide."

"Sheila," Starkey said, holding up both hands for her to stop.

"Can you even say the word suicide, Jack? Are we ever going to be able to talk about this? Don't you see it's trying to eat its way out from the inside of you?" Sheila was a master of the curve ball.

Here it comes again…but she's right. "I don't know if I can talk about it, Sheila."

"Jack, they diagnosed your son as bipolar."

Starkey leaned his elbows on the table and put his face down in his hands.

"No, Jack, no more hiding." Sheila reached over and pulled his hands away. "Look at me. You and your wife tried every intervention available, all of them, all, again and again. It was an awful, tragic death, yes, but you were not at fault."

"Yes, Sheila, I know, I was there," Starkey said, looking up. "I know it wasn't anything we did or didn't do."

"So?"

"So Jane kept on asking, over and over, why this happened to him, but they couldn't give us any reason. Finally, they told us there was a strong hereditary factor in depression."

"Ok, go on."

"No history of depression or mental illness existed in Jane's family," Starkey said.

"What about your family?"

"That's just it. I don't know. My family adopted me. I don't know anything much about my real family. All I know for sure is my mother's name, Beryl Starkey. She died giving birth to me. The orphanage ran ads in the paper for relatives, but there were no answers. It was at the end of the war, 1945. I have my mother's wedding ring and nothing else. That's all my adopted parents knew."

"You never told me you were adopted, Jack."

"No, I don't think about it much."

"Okay, so it wasn't Jane's family, and maybe it was yours, but that's a big maybe. It could have been something else entirely. And even if it was, Starkey, for God's sake, you are not responsible for your own DNA."

"I know that Sheila, I am not an idiot. You don't understand."

"Then help me understand."

Starkey put his face down in his hands again. Sheila sat quietly, waiting. Starkey finally raised his head. "Jane always wanted two or three kids, but Ethan's birth was difficult. He was born prematurely, and I was out of town, traveling for my job when she delivered. She was alone. They both almost died. The doctors saved them, but they told her she couldn't have any more children."

Sheila rose and went to the refrigerator and got two more beers, twisting off the caps. She set one in front of Starkey. "Did you feel guilty for not being there? You couldn't have known."

"It started that way, but things got worse."

Starkey told her it took months for Jane and Ethan to recover. Jane constantly expressed her fear she'd lose him. Even after he seemed to recover she never let him out of her sight. When he got older, she could hardly stand to let him go to school. He was her only child, the only one she'd ever have. She'd placed all the love she owned in that one cradle, and when he turned thirteen and became seriously depressed she was distraught. When he committed suicide, she couldn't blame Ethan. So the blame fell to me. Where else?

"Jack, holding you responsible was irrational."

Starkey held out his two hands palm up and shrugged his shoulders.

"She never stopped blaming you?"

"Oh, she said she did, when I asked. But mostly she just stopped talking to me. I watched her flounder in silent despair and anger and grief until finally she just disappeared. Her body still existed, but her heart and soul withered away. She went through the last days of her life AWOL, until finally cancer put an end to her misery."

"Jesus, Jack," Sheila said, taking both his hands in hers. "No word, no sign, nothing left for you at all?

"In her last moments, lying there in the hospice she opened her eyes and looked at me for one moment. I thought I saw the ghost of a smile, but I might have imagined it. But then she turned her face to the wall and died."

Sheila watched as tears began to roll down Starkey's face and fall into small, round puddles on the kitchen table. She got up to get a box of Kleenex.

"Here, blow your nose."

He did.

Gradually the lumps in the silence that followed smoothed out in the gentle atmosphere of the summer night outside. The sound of a whippoorwill came in through the open kitchen window with a breeze wrapped in the smell of flowers.

"Sheila, what's that smell?"

"It's the Chocolate Cosmos flowering behind the house."

Starkey pushed himself up from the table. "I think maybe I'd like to take a walk. Would you walk with me?"

Out on the sidewalk, she took his arm and he placed his hand over hers. Their walk took them down the street and around the corner to the elementary school and the playground. They paused to watch a few parents pushing children on the swings, listening to the laughter, families starting out the weekend. Lightning bugs glimmered under the trees out beyond the reach of the playground lights. Old oaks and maples canopied the sidewalk. A stray cool breeze slipped out from under the trees. Starkey and Sheila walked on companionably.

They passed a bench and Sheila pulled him down to sit beside her. The wood of the slats felt cool to the touch. Starkey sat listening to the sounds of the night. After a few minutes Sheila shifted over to look up at him.

"I wish I knew what Master Yamashima held back from us," She said, "and why he wouldn't talk about your size."

"That scares me," Starkey said. "When we gave him the arrow, you could tell he recognized something about it that really worried him. I think the research he said he'd do was a smokescreen. I think he recognized it and didn't want to tell us. "

Sheila stood up to go. "I suppose all we can do for now is wait."

"Tomorrow is Saturday. I want to go buy a canoe. We could take it out for a bit on the river and then drop it off at the society island," Starkey said.

"What? That's not a good idea Jack. The Master told us to stay away from the canal. I agree with him."

"But you said yourself, those society guys may be weird, but why would they want to kill me. It's just coincidence it happened there. The master didn't tell us not to go canoeing on the river."

"I don't know. You're splitting hairs."

"All right, we'll just paddle on the river and bring it back home. No canoeing society. I'll take you out to breakfast anywhere you say."

"Anywhere? Wait, what makes you think you're staying here tonight?"

"Well, can I?"

"I don't know. I'm still not sure you're who you say you are." She punched him on the arm. Hard.

He slipped his arm around her shoulder, leaned over, and kissed her cheek.

"Perhaps I could be convinced," she said.

Starkey pulled her closer. "Would I be sleeping on the couch?"

"We'll let the Whippoorwill decide, if he calls again, you bunk with me."

CHAPTER ELEVEN

BENEATH

PAW-PAW ISLAND MD
SATURDAY MAY 27TH

Saturday dawned sunny and warm, a perfect canoeing day. After breakfast at the Tastee Diner they hit REI, the outdoor store in Rockville. Starkey bought a sixteen foot Old Town canoe friendly to sometime canoers and roomy enough for his size. Sheila picked out life vests and gel seat pads. Starkey brought his old paddles. They lashed the canoe to the rack on top of the Subaru and headed down to Hank Dietle's tavern on Rockville Pike and picked up sandwiches and beers to go on the way to the river.

Starkey parked the Subaru at Fletcher's Boat house off Canal Road and put in at the Potomac River there, carrying the canoe and gear across the wooden bridge over the canal, but avoiding any travel along it. Starkey and Sheila hoisted the canoe and threaded their way through the crowds of bikers and picnickers taking advantage of the weather. They launched the canoe into the river and loaded up. Starkey sat in the rear e to steer and guided it out of the cove. He watched Sheila paddling ahead, back and shoulder muscles working. In front of him the small cooler of beer and food waited. The world looked pretty damn good.

Once out of Fletcher's Cove they paddled the canoe up river passing beneath Chain Bridge. Tiny, rocky islands dotted the river here. They surprised one heron and lots of turtles that scooted off logs along the shore. Paddling against the current going up river, they knew they would enjoy an easier ride coming back. Sunlight reflected off the water and a gentle breeze came across from the Virginia side. They left behind the noise of traffic on the bridge and heard only the sound of the paddles and water splashing against the bottom of the canoe. After some forty minutes of paddling they drew up in sight of Paw Paw Island.

Sheila pulled in her paddle and turned around to face him. "Jack, I think it's time to head back down river. Remember what the Master said. We don't want to approach the island."

"Ok," Starkey said, digging in with his paddle to swing the canoe around. As it turned the canoe seemed to drag over something. It lurched sideways as the bow swung down river and ground to a halt. They leaned into their paddles, struggling to get the canoe moving again. But they couldn't budge the canoe.

"We're dragging over something," Sheila said.

Jack pushed again and grunted with the effort. "Maybe a river shoal caught us. There are shallow spots all through here and rocks aplenty." Jack bent over the gunnel. "I see something dark in the water under us, but I can't tell what it is. Dig your paddle in and push. Maybe we can shove off it."

Starkey moved his paddle around searching for an advantage and pushed, giving it all he had, but made no progress. "I guess I could get out and try to free it," he said, but he didn't do it. "I don't know what's down there." He stared into the water beside the canoe.

"Jack?" Sheila's voice grew louder. "We aren't just stuck. Look at the shoreline. We're moving backward upriver."

Starkey looked up when he heard the fear in her voice. "No way. It's got to be an illusion caused by seeing the current moving past us down river."

The canoe lurched backward and began to pick up speed, leaving no doubt in Starkey's mind. They turned in their seats and watched for a long moment. They started paddling, struggling against the canoe's motion, but failed to slow it.

"Ok, you were right, Sheila. Something is dragging us backward."

"I don't want to be right. I want it to stop. What the hell is going on? And Jack? Look where we're headed."

Starkey looked ahead. The canoe was headed directly for the canoeing society island, and, what's more, it was accelerating. The canoe gained speed quickly, moving faster and faster. The distance to the island grew less and less. The canoe bore through the water, beginning to lurch from side to side. They dropped their paddles and grabbed on to the sides of the canoe. A wake formed at the bow and water splashed over it as they flew towards the island.

Sheila yelled over the sound of the gushing water. "There are people standing on the bank."

Starkey yelled back. "I see them. Not good. I think one of them is Grimes, the president of the society." The fast moving canoe halved the distance. A hundred yards, fifty yards.

"Jack. He's holding some kind of weapon."

"I see it. I can't be sure at this distance, but it looks like a crossbow," Jack said. "I think the other man is the boatman I told you about."

Moving still faster, the canoe drew ever closer. The water grew shallower and they caught sight of a dark shape moving under and ahead of them with something like wings of a sting ray that swept back and forth.

"Oh my God, Jack. What is that thing under the water?"

Jack didn't answer. He just stared at the thing as the island got closer. Twenty-five yards, ten, five. Still accelerating, the canoe surged across the remaining distance. It ran aground, striking the shore at tremendous speed. Starkey was thrown through the air. He landed, striking the ground head first, and blacked out.

>>>

Starkey opened his eyes and tried to sit up. Nausea and a blinding headache forced him to close them again and fall back down. His head spun. He felt a hand clutch his arm.

"Jack, are you all right?"

He heard Sheila's voice through the dizziness and pain. He struggled to answer. "Yeah, apart from a major headache and some dizziness." He managed to sit up with Sheila's help and looked around. Empty shelves, dust covered tables, and chairs surrounded them. "Where are we?"

"In the clubhouse on the island. Grimes and the other guy brought us here and locked us in this storeroom. They had to carry you. You were knocked out."

"Tell me about it. Are you hurt?" Starkey asked.

"A few bruises, mostly just wet. When the canoe hit the bank I landed in the water. Grimes pulled me out. You know your face is bleeding, right?"

Starkey put his hand up to the side of his face and winced, pulling away fingers smeared with blood. "I think I lost some skin." Starkey looked around. They sat on a dusty floor of the storeroom. A little light filtered through one dirty window.

"And you've got a helluva lump on the side of your head."

They heard the sound of a key in a lock and the door opened. Grimes stepped in pointing a handheld crossbow. A red laser light moved across them. "I see you're back with us Mr. Starkey. Well, well, so kind of you to drop in. This saves us a lot of trouble," he said. "Get up. Raise your hands and move out through the door."

Starkey and Sheila obeyed, passing into the next room. Starkey limped, moving slowly. Grimes shoved him forward as they approached some stairs leading downward. Sheila, ahead of Starkey, stopped and turned.

"Where are you taking us?" Sheila asked.

Grimes moved the crossbow laser sight to focus on Sheila's face. "Just go down the stairs."

Starkey saw the red dot appear on Sheila's forehead. "Do as he says, Sheila."

Sheila just stood there, defiant, but Starkey put his arm around her and walked her across the room where stairs at the end led down to a lower floor. The room below held some scattered furniture, a table, and stacked wooden chairs. A strong smell of mildew and mold pervaded.

"Keep moving," Grimes said.

They reached the end of that room where more stairs descended into relative darkness, lit by wall sconces. The air rose from below, damp and chill, toward them. Starkey stood beside Sheila, looking down, and saw rough stone walls and a landing below. Another set of stairs led down from it. A hand rail ran down the right side of the steps. Sheila held onto the rail and started slowly down, step by step, with Starkey following. He could feel her reluctance, but Grimes kept the red laser light aimed at the back of her head. When she paused Starkey urged her on, his hand on her shoulder. The lights in the sconces continued down the second flight of steps, but the next flight descended far into the darkness and the lights grew dim. Starkey stayed close behind her, listening to the heavy, uneven steps of Grimes. Now rivulets of water ran down the dark rock walls and smelled like river water. Down and down they went, and Starkey counted four landings and four sets of stairs. Once Starkey turned to speak, but Grimes pointed the crossbow at his head, the red light of the laser shining in his eyes. Starkey turned and continued down.

At the bottom of the last set of stairs, Sheila stopped. Starkey stepped down on the smooth stone floor and looked ahead over Sheila's shoulder. An arched tunnel turned sharply left and led on, now cutting through bedrock, lit by a strip of light that ran overhead. *We have to be under the river now.*

Grimes spoke from the stair above them. "Go on. You're going to see something no one of your kind has ever seen."

Sheila spoke in Starkey's ear, under her breath. "He's only got one arrow."

"Don't you think one's enough?" Starkey asked.

"Don't talk, move," said Grimes.

They entered the tunnel and walked on for what seemed to Starkey forever, passing branching tunnels that disappeared off into darkness. Turning a corner, they saw a widening of the tunnel in the distance and large, indistinct figures moving in the dim light. Here the vibration they felt above grew heavier and the rumbling louder. It shook the walls and floor of the tunnel.

A dull thud sounded behind them. They turned to see Grimes slump to the floor. A robed, cowled figure hovered over him, holding a baseball bat. The figure appeared short and wide and somehow indistinct in the dimly lit tunnel. Starkey could see no face under the cowl, but two eyes seemed to shine out of the darkness. The figure pushed the bat inside its robe, turned and signaled for them to follow him back the way they came.

Starkey looked at Sheila and she shrugged. *What choice did they have?* Starkey followed, staying close behind the figure, with Sheila in tow. She pulled back once.

"Who the hell is that, and where is he taking us?"

"I don't *know*, Sheila. But he knocked out Grimes, so he must be on our side. Hopefully he's getting us out of here. Personally I am completely lost. I could never navigate back down all those branching tunnels we came through."

They came to an unlit side tunnel and headed down it. Whoever was helping them moved soundlessly, and seemed to float over the floor of the rough passage. Directing a beam of light ahead, their guide plunged on, gesturing at them to hurry. He moved with surprising speed down this smaller tunnel. After many turns and forks Starkey felt completely lost and disoriented, but stayed close behind their guide. Sheila had pulled a small flashlight from her pocket and shined it on the figure ahead, staying close to Sharkey. He examined the back of the heavy wool robe and cowl their rescuer wore as they walked. The robe reached the floor of the tunnel, and the feet of the figure could not be seen.

After some minutes, their guide stopped and shined his light on a tall, round, rusted steel door in the rock wall. Starkey could just read the words, Washington Aqueduct, in raised letters on the door. Just below it said The Army Corp of Engineers. The cowled figure took hold of the wheel in the center of the door with two heavy leather gloves and turned it to the left. The metal screeched in protest, rust spraying from the mechanism, but the wheel turned and the hatch-like door swung inward. Following their guide, Starkey stepped through and found himself in another dark tunnel that arched overhead. A huge pipe lit only by the rays of the figure's light surrounded them. The pipe, nine or ten feet in diameter, led off in either direction in total darkness. Sheila came through to stand beside him. Her flashlight lit a few inches of water at their feet and it seemed to be running to their right.

Starkey watched as their guide swung the steel door closed and spun the wheel clockwise, and then set a locking clamp on the wheel. He then moved off down the tunnel in the direction the water flowed, motioning to them to follow.

This time they walked much longer, but they came at last to a shaft of light that shown down into the tunnel from above. It illuminated a steel ladder that rose up to the light. As Starkey approached, their guide turned toward them and held up a leather glove signaling them to halt. A distant sound of running water dampened the silence around them until their guide spoke.

The voice, oddly resonant and crystal clear, struck Starkey as familiar. "Jack Starkey, this is where I leave you. This ladder leads up to an exit at the Dalecarlia Reservoir on Fox Hall Road. The access hatch will open easily." Starkey's thoughts were awash with memories of the voice he couldn't quite grasp on to. He felt disoriented.

Sheila could contain herself no longer. "Now wait just a goddamn minute. Who the hell are you and what the hell is going on here?"

Here it comes. She was scared and that made her angry. Sheila angry was not a pretty sight.

"First we're abducted at arrow point, threatened, and kidnapped. Then you come along and slug Grimes with a baseball bat. We've followed you under the ground, into and down this water pipe for a couple of miles..."

Starkey finally found his voice and interrupted. "Sheila, stop."

Sheila seemed to shake herself. "Okay, I'm grateful you took Grimes out and rescued us, but I still want to know what's happening."

The cowled figure answered in a patient, kind voice, almost as if to a child. "So brave, you are, Sheila Cartwright. Yes, I know your name. I have learned much about you in the past year."

Starkey knew that tone of voice would antagonize Sheila, but she said nothing.

Their guide went on. "You, Starkey, I have known since the night of your birth. It is time for all to be revealed to you. I didn't plan on Sheila's presence, but I see now she must be involved. However, it is a long story, an ancient story, and it cannot be told here." Their guide reached a thick leather glove into its robe and thrust a card at Starkey. Sheila stepped closer and shined her flashlight on it. The card read, The Protean Society, 3525 K Street St. NW, Washington, DC.

"Come tomorrow at 6:00 pm. You will have all your questions answered, my children. Do not call the authorities. It is not yet time."

"I am not your child, whoever you are," Sheila said.

"Ah, but in a very real sense you are." Turning, the robed figure moved off with surprising speed back down the tunnel.

"Wait," Starkey said, "who are you?"

Stopping and turning the figure said, "Call me Proteus." Then he disappeared down the tunnel into the darkness.

Starkey watched the figure go, then started up the ladder, reached overhead, spun the wheel on the hatch, pushed it open, and climbed out. He stood on an access tower at the rear of the reservoir, above the river. He could see the familiar 'castle' of the pumping station in the distance. Sheila climbed out onto the platform beside him. He closed the hatch and climbed down the steel ladder to the ground. He led the way through the holding ponds to a locked chain link gate. They climbed up and over and stood together beside Foxhall Road.

Starkey hailed a passing cab that took them back down the parkway to their car. They sat silent in the cab. It dropped them off by Starkey's Subaru. Once inside it, they sat staring straight ahead without speaking for some time.

Finally Sheila broke the silence. "What next, Vulcans and Klingons?"

"I wouldn't be surprised. Whatever it is, I'm hungry, Sheila. What do you say we hit the Tastee Diner?"

CHAPTER TWELVE

REDWING

LOWER POTOMAC RIVER
circa 1650 CE

One-Woman reached the bottom of the rocky trail that led across the face of the palisades above the Potomac River. He strode forward, holding himself erect, a big white-tailed doe slung across his shoulders. The brown skin of his cheeks was tattooed with antler symbols in vivid blue. Tall for his Piscataway people and broad in the shoulder, One-Woman looked strongly built but lean as the grey wolves that sometimes shadowed the fish camp. That morning his woman, Redwing, shaved the hair from half of his head and reapplied the copper-green and yellow paint to his body and face.

He approached the branch of the river that separated the island from the shore and sprang lightly from rock to rock. When he crossed the clearing in the center of the island the village children ran to flock around him, pulling at the doe on his shoulders, and competing amongst themselves for his notice. He laughed, pleased by their adulation, and held the doe down for the children to touch.

He reached the small lodge of bent branches and skins, their temporary home here by the fishing grounds, and found Redwing there. She sat upon her knees with her legs folded underneath her doeskin. He saw a string of fresh water clam shells newly woven into her long, straight black hair. The wing feathers of a Red-winged Black Bird, tied up in her hair, shimmered in the sunlight. He paused to watch her. The muscles in her bare, reddish brown back and shoulders and arms worked rhythmically as she ground corn in a soapstone mortar. Hungry from the hunt, he relished the thought of the taste of the corn-pone she would bake, slathered with the fat of the doe he carried.

She looked up from her work to smile at him. "It's a fine doe," she said.

He squatted down without speaking and slid the deer from his shoulder on to the ground near her work. Redwing rose and stepped to him. She extended her hand. He took it and allowed her to pull him to his feet.

"I want to tell you about my dream," Red-wing said. She led him to sit on a log near their lodge. "First I saw only darkness, and then I felt wet and cold. Then I thought I lay in the water and I was drowning, and I felt a great pain in my stomach. Then a tall man came and spoke to me. A great owl sat on his left shoulder and a huge grey wolf sat by his right side. I did not know the tall man. He did not tell me his name. He did not look to me like anyone in our families. He called me daughter."

"Did he say anything else?"

"He said Okee comes."

"Okee? It means nothing to me."

"We will go to see the Old One. He is supposed to be able to tell the meaning of dreams." Red Wing laughed. "We will let him earn his venison for a change."

Later that day One-Woman cut a large steak from the hindquarter of the doe. Redwing took the meat from him and wrapped it in cornhusks. They crossed the village and made their way north along the river's eastern shore. The water of the Potomac had risen in the spring rains. They left the river side and climbed up to the rim of the palisades. There a footpath wound its way up the face of the stark, lonely rock formation that towered above. Blooming redbuds lined the path and the air smelled fresh and sweet. Higher up, only a few cedars clung to the bare, gray rock of the pinnacle.

They found the Old One waiting for them at the mouth of his cave on top of the promontory. The threshold overlooked a rocky gorge where the river burst loudly over the rapids below. His body bent and twisted, the Old One wore his ceremonial deerskin cloak ornamented with circular rows of freshwater clamshell beads and bird feathers. One-Woman thought great age must lie on the old man's shoulders. A thousand wrinkles scarred a face that might have been cut from the gray bedrock of the cave floor on which he stood. The Old One's pale eyes bulged slightly from out of his face above high cheek bones. One-Woman's people said no one living remembered the Old One's true name.

The shaman began to speak as if they were in mid conversation. "Dreams can be an omen of the future, or nothing but the result of eating rancid deer fat." He took the deer steak from Redwing and laid it aside.

"How did you know we came about a dream, old one?" Redwing said.

"Why else? No one comes here just to visit. Births or deaths or sickness bring visitors, but none of these has happened. So it is a dream."

The old one turned and led them deeper into the cave. One-Woman caught the strange smell of him, musty and damp. *But he lives in a cave, how else would he smell?*

"What is Okee?" Redwing said when they were seated around the old man's meager fire.

The old one stared at her quietly for some moments. Then he grunted heavily and began to speak.

"So you are the one, Red Wing. Tell me your dream, and do not leave anything out."

After listening in silence to Redwing's telling of her dream, the Old Man spoke in a small, quiet voice. Redwing and One-Woman leaned forward to understand his words. His story began in the middle.

"I traveled north in my youth to the distant land of the Leni Lenape, your mother's tribe, One-Woman," the old man said.

He told them the Leni Lenape were a people who shared ancestors with the Piscataway, but the tribes separated after the great migration. At a gathering of shamans there, he saw The Walam Olum, the greatest totem of their ancestors. The Walam Olum was the chronicle of their people in the old times. It was recorded in pictures painted on birch bark scrolls. The Great Shaman of the Leni Lenape sang the verses that accompanied each picture. The verses told the story of how their people came down from the great white land in the northwest, and how they crossed the bridge of ice and snow through the hunting grounds of the seal killers.

One-Woman stopped him. "What is a seal?"

Redwing clapped her hands together. "What about my dream?"

"Patience, both of you, I'm coming to that."

The Old One told them one set of verses told the story of Manitou and the creation of the earth and the heavens, and it was Manitou who came to her in the dream with the wolf and the owl. Another verse told of the coming of the other god of their ancestors, the one that came from the outside, who is called Okee. Okee was not of this world, they said, but came from the sky, from a place beyond the stars that take the shape of the great bear. The story told that Okee would sometimes take to wife a pregnant woman. 'Brides of Okee' they were called. Later the child would be found in the wilderness, a holy child who possessed great wisdom or power over others, even while still young. These children often became shamans or chiefs. 'Children of Okee', they were called. Sometimes they grew to great size and were powerful warriors.

"I have heard enough," One-Woman said. He stood and thrust his jaw in the old man's direction. "Okee can go mate with himself. Redwing will be no one's bride but mine." He turned to leave, walking back towards the mouth of the cave, motioning with his head for Redwing to follow.

"But what shall I do, old one, what does this dream mean?" said Redwing.

"Go with your husband, Redwing, there is nothing more I can tell you." The old man rose up stiffly and hobbled after them out to the promontory. "Just do your work, pass your days as you always have."

One-Woman led Redwing down the steep path to the river. He stopped when the path reached the river side. The cold, rushing waters leapt over the rocks beside them. "He gave us no help."

"No." Redwing took his hand. "I am more afraid now than before."

"Dreams are not real." One-Woman pulled her close to him. "Tonight the striped fish will come. That is real. Soon our child will come. That is real. Let the old man rattle his bones and grunt." He took her chin in his hand. "What will you name our child?"

"I will name her Sooleawa if it is a girl."

At dusk, One-Woman and Redwing sat in their dugout on the river. All around them the men and women of their village waited for the first big surge of fish. Some stood in the shallows to spear the shimmering Rockfish as they tried to force their way upstream. Others like One-Woman and Redwing readied bow and arrow and spear to harvest the fish in deeper water. Other tribespeople grasped nets, preparing to haul the snared fish aboard their dugouts.

The big surge came. Frenzied fish hurled themselves against the current, up and over the foaming falls below. They came leaping, hurtling upward, cresting, and falling away, the falls becoming a fountain of fish, with many throwing themselves upward and over the fall line, but nearly as many falling back. One-Woman watched as the first full wave of fish moved up river past Little Falls. He saw a great female, her belly swollen with eggs, come abreast of their dugout and plunged his spear down. The obsidian point pierced her side, just behind the gills. He drove it through her and out the other side, spitting her upon its length. Her pale red blood oozed from the wound and ran down along the length of the spear as she was levered from the water and held high overhead. He cast her down into the bottom of the dugout, jerking the spear out the fish's side as he did so. The eggs the fish carried for so many miles leaked through the great rent in her side and onto the wooden bottom of the canoe.

One-Woman turned to speak to Redwing but froze, for behind her he saw a large, dark shape moving in the water towards the dugout. Coming closer the shape hovered just below the surface. Three

large, yellow eyes broke the surface, watching him.
Then, the dark shape sank beneath the blackish water.

The dugout heaved upward and to the left,
clearing the surface of the river by some five feet,
then turning slowly downward, dumped Redwing
and One-Woman into the water. One-Woman came
to the surface, coughing, but Redwing did not. He
dove beneath the surface, searching for her in the
dark roiling water. He rose and cried out her name.
Then One-Woman saw the shape again moving
away from him, partly visible now, its broad, scaly
back breaching the surface. At first he froze, stunned.
Then he roared in fear and anger and Redwing's
name came out at the end of the roar that became a
scream. He saw Redwing's feet trailing behind in the
water as the beast crested the surface of the river.
Frozen no more, he thrust forward fiercely through
the water, and, drawing his knife from out of its
sheath, he screamed the war cry of his people.
Scrambling onto a river outcropping, he leapt high
into the air, hurling himself onto the massive back of
the creature. He seized the head of the creature under
the jaw in the crook of his left arm. Gritting his teeth,
One-Woman heaved backwards with all his strength,
lifting backward the head of the creature and baring
its throat. Then One-Woman brought his father's
fathers flint knife down from high above his head in

a powerful arching blow. Again and again he stabbed at the thing that clutched his Redwing. The men and women in the water and the other canoes looked on in horror, transfixed by the nightmare tableau, and no one moved to aid him.

But the knife glanced off the neck of the creature, doing little damage. The creature reared, heaving One-Woman up and off. Long yellow claws at the end of one wing-like arm slashed out, arching backward. But One-Woman twisted in the air, avoiding the talons by inches. Pivoting in the air and diving as he hit the water, One-Woman thrust forward under the water and came up under the creature, stabbing savagely at the leathery abdomen. As before, the knife glanced off, inflicting little damage. Now the creature plunged its head below the water and seized One-Woman by the neck and shoulder, lifting him above the surface of the water in its yellow, beak-like jaws. One-Woman's screams of agony filled the night, yet he ever twisted and writhed seeking to stab at the creature. The creature, jerking its head upward, violently snapped One-Woman's body like a dried branch and hurled it back over its head many yards and into the river behind.

CHAPTER THIRTEEN

BETRAYAL

BETHESDA, MD MONDAY
MAY 28TH

The extensive campus of the National Institutes of Health sat on Rockville Pike in Bethesda, Maryland like a scientific colossus. If you were a scientist in the fields of health and medicine anywhere around the world, you knew the cutting edge of science sharpened itself right there. Nobel Prize winners, hungry, private company collaborators, and state of the art technology wielded the scythe and separated the wheat from the chaff. Graduate students around the world sat in labs and daydreamed about working there or receiving a grant to do research funded by them. Brilliant discoveries waited for them in a kind of scientific Disneyland, and for

the chosen few working there would be a dream
come true. But for others it would be only a dream.

Building Thirty-One sat at the north end of
the campus, surrounded by trees and carefully maintained gardens. The National Human Genome Research Institute lived in eleven stories of pale, grey
concrete. Architecturally bland, it brought nothing to
mind unless you thought of an elongated beehive
with rectangular cells for windows. Today, like so
many other days, Phillip Lipscomb worked in his
windowless office to extract and analyze DNA in the
clean room of the Ancient DNA lab on the seventh
floor. Fluorescent overhead lights sharply illuminated the laminar flow hood, a specialized work area,
where he sat extracting Neanderthal samples. Sterile
white walls surrounded him, and the low hum of the
air filtration system droned in his ears. Phillip suffered. He'd been a postdoc too long, and whatever
scientific promise he had demonstrated in his youth
never bore fruit. He suffered because of the pain
from fractures in his too long legs and arms. Phillip
had Marfan syndrome, a genetic disorder that affected the body's connective tissue in the presence of
abnormal bone growth, and osteoporosis. And he suffered because his life felt like an automobile tire that
was slowly losing its pressure.

He was clothed from head to foot in a long,
hooded, white cleanroom suit, affectionately called a

bunny suit by those who, unlike Phillip, still showed
a sense of humor. His humor had disappeared as his
dreams of success faded. He did not feel even slightly pleasant today. His safety glasses fogged, his allergies brought tears to his eyes, and his nose dripped
mucus into his face mask. His right shoulder ached
from hours of holding his arm forward under the
hood. Against all the rules, he pulled the tray forward
to the edge of the hood to make it easier to reach the
tube tray and ease the pain. Grasping the Pipetman,
he loaded a new pipette tip, immersed the tip into the
DNA sample, and began to dispense the sample into
the receiving tubes.

Phillip sneezed violently, and his head
snapped forward, hitting the glass hood. His face-
mask slipped down below his nose. *Oh, God, I've
contaminated the whole tray.* He looked around to
see whether anyone saw him. No one else worked
nearby. He pushed his mask back up over his face
and stood up. He put the contaminated tray back in
the rack. He had no more trayed samples prepared,
and he was just too upset to go on today. Rubbing his
shoulder and neck, he walked, shoulders rounded
forward and stooping, to enter the cleanroom Pass-
Thru. He was too tall to stand up straight in the unit.
His gangly form limped down the aisle, passing
black-surfaced work tables loaded down with beak-
ers, boxes, tubes, and white-labeled brown bottles.

He squeezed behind his desk in the dimly lit corner of the lab. He scraped his knees on the sharp underside as he sat down. The space was just too small for his six-foot seven frame. He stripped off his blue rubber gloves, massaged his long, pale fingers, and placed them on his keyboard, but then stopped. He'd caught sight of his reflection in the blank screen of the computer. There he sat, protracted jaw, sparse beard, and long, lank hair, looking back at himself, his eyes swollen with allergies. He looked guilty, knowing he'd have to tell Dr. Wilson about the contaminated tray. The protocol would have to be redone. She would be furious. The Neanderthal samples were beyond precious and he'd screwed up hours of careful preparation.

It was her fault, he rationalized. If she'd just let him continue working on the Piscataway research, it wouldn't have happened. She'd pulled him off that project as soon as the alien DNA sequence revealed itself last week. It was the discovery of a lifetime—a career-making find—and she wanted to pretend it never happened. There could have been a major scientific paper written with his name on it and published in a top journal, Nature or Science. *But, noooo.* Instead, today he was back sequencing Neanderthal DNA, whose entire genome was already mapped and they were replicating studies just to verify results. With no new discovery possible, no innovation, there was no chance he'd receive any attention for his contribution. All because she was frightened of what the scientific community might say. "Flying saucers and space aliens with green skin and antennae, they'd laugh us out of NIH," she'd said. "What would happen to my reputation?" *Her reputation?* What about his reputation? She didn't care about that. Why would she never let him do anything important?

His boss, Ann Wilson was success personified. She had her own lab at NIH, many scholarly publications, a noted anthropologist for a husband, children at Harvard and Princeton, and a beautiful home in Potomac, MD. What did he have? A PhD in molecular biology from a minor university in West Virginia, a loving, but relatively dim sister in Charleston, West Virginia, and early onset osteoporosis. He lived in a one room efficiency apartment on Wisconsin Avenue. Some life. No wife, no children, and no career to speak of. How many years did he have left to make his mark before the disease overcame him? It just wasn't fair. He'd tell Wilson about the contaminated tray later. Maybe he could redo it without her finding out.

He'd been the one who saw the alien sequence first in the Ancient Piscataway DNA from Dr. Wilson's husband. She laughed at his results and made him run the tests again. And again. Until after the seventh run she logged on to the server system and did the DNA extraction and analysis herself. Phillip never saw her shaken before. If you looked up "self-assured" in the dictionary there would be a picture of Ann Wilson, but this time she looked shocked, staring at the results. She didn't say a single word to Phillip, nothing like "you were right", or "sorry I doubted you", for example, *oh no*. She just shut down the system and stood up and walked back to her office.

Then Phillip made the mistake that really put it all over the top. Before she caught him and pulled him off the project, he turned the computer server system back on and began transferring DNA sequence data into the analysis software and using the workflows to identify variants. But he'd transferred the wrong ones. When he ran the filters to compare samples with the Ancient Piscataway, he compared one that was extracted from the bones the Smithsonian anthropologist, Cassavetes, sent over to be tested. Not only that, but he also loaded one from the blood sample taken from the modern Piscataway man Dr. Wilson's husband took. That's when things got really crazy. Bells and whistles started sounding and flashing red words blazed across the computer screen. There was a three way match. The same alien DNA sequence appeared in the modern Piscataway man, the Ancient Piscataway DNA from the Heater's Island dig, and Cassavetes' bones. There was no doubt. The software identified a three way match of Extraterrestrial DNA.

His chair was yanked back violently. "What are you doing, Phillip?" Ann Wilson stood behind him. "Get out of that chair." Her face contorted in anger, she jerked one thumb upward, and one greying strand of hair fell down into her eyes. He lurched up and stepped aside.

Dr. Wilson sat down and worked backward and forward through screens of the software as Phillip watched over her shoulder, verifying every setting, entry, and the results. The rest of the lab workers had heard the alarm bells when the sequences matched as well, and pressed close to Philip's sides, gathering around the computer station. After a very long five minutes Ann Wilson turned in the chair and looked up at him, and Phillip read anger now tinged with fear in her face.

"Export the results and print two copies on my office printer," she said, emphasizing each word. "Then, Phillip, shut down the computer and go back to your desk. Do not touch those samples again, ever. Do you, understand?" She stood up and looked around at her staff. "The rest of you get back to work, the show's over." Phillip watched her turn and walk away, heels echoing on the linoleum floor, her starched, brilliantly white lab coat stiff on her back.

Nice. No congratulations, no recognition. It was like he just discovered a cure for cancer and she told him to hand it over and go sit down and shut up. Ok, it was an accident, but didn't great discoveries sometimes begin with accidents? Fleming got a Nobel Prize for discovering penicillin when he accidentally let mold grown on his flu cultures. A Nobel Prize. *But no*, Ann Wilson shoved him back into his corner, and hushed it all up.

Dr. Wilson went back to her office and called her husband out on the dig. She must have been really upset because she forgot to close the door. Phillip overheard her tell him what they'd found. He could tell Joe Wilson was excited, and they'd argued about releasing the results. But in the end her husband seemed to acquiesce, agreeing their reputations might be ruined if they did release the DNA results. Phillip heard Ann Wilson use the word "crackpot" several times. The outcome came as no surprise. In all the years he'd worked for her, she won every argument he ever witnessed. She got the last word every time.

It still made his stomach hurt to think of it. Phil moaned just a little and began to read his NIH email. Vendor's ads mostly filled the screen, and there was the daily one from his sister. She wrote the usual fare about her children and her day at the elementary school where she taught. She always asked about the pain in his legs and reminded him to use his cane as the doctor advised. Today she told him it was a shame his big discovery wouldn't be acknowledged. Now he regretted writing to her about it yesterday, but he just couldn't keep from telling someone. He knew from the boring and continuous NIH training sessions its email systems were not for private use. So now he could fret over that as well.

CHAPTER FOURTEEN

AFOSI

WASHINGTON, DC WEDNESDAY MAY 30TH

After a nearly sleepless night with a dark dream of bones and Jack Starkey's face, Peter Cassavetes leaned on the moving black handrail of the steep escalator as it rose towards the oval of light and escaped the darkness of the metro station. Warm humid air streamed down from outside as he launched himself off into the crowds of multicolored tourists that poured out of the Smithsonian exit. Cassavetes soldiered his way across the thinning grass of the Mall to the museum. Pausing under a giant elm tree, he looked up at the somber Romanesque building and the dome of the rotunda. He crossed the street and plodded up the grey granite steps between the soaring columns, through the heavy bronze doors, and into the central rotunda. It echoed there with the voices of early visitors. He signed in at the guard station and nodded to the familiar faces of the uniformed guards. The huge African elephant on display in the center of the Rotunda stopped him briefly. Cassavetes tried to remember when he first dreamed of working here in the Natural History building, or becoming an anthropologist, but he knew it began when, as a little boy, he had stared up at that elephant for the first time. Today that seemed a very long time ago.

Cassavetes' morning coffee wasn't doing the trick. Still feeling a pint low, he got more coffee in the atrium, climbed the worn marble stairs to the third floor, and eased down the long hall of plate glass and mahogany doors. That's when it really hit him. History was about to be rewritten and big scary change neared. Usually history curled up under his desk and went to sleep. Change, when it happened at all, moved at glacier speed here in the museum. Now change waited for him behind his office door and an unknown future would begin here today. He squared his shoulders, opened the door, and went in. He eased himself into his chair, leaned back, and almost recovered that once familiar feeling of knowing his reality and where he belonged in it. After Starkey's visit nothing in the world would fit back in place.

Nope, that wasn't going to happen. Massaging his forehead, he reached over and pulled the plain brown folder holding the results from Ann Wilson's DNA analysis off the top of a stack of papers. He knew he should have analyzed the pterodactyl-like bones as soon as reliable DNA tests became available. But the fear of being called a fraud again still lingered in his mind. A yellow note attached to the front read "Show this to no one, Peter. I'm serious. Ann." The manila envelope containing the test results from her lab at NIH arrived by special courier late yesterday afternoon. He'd almost gotten over the initial shock.

He leafed through the charts and graphs to get to the final page. He read the conclusion at the bottom for the umpteenth time, **Unknown DNA sequence - Extraterrestrial**. A slight chill shook him, just like when he'd first read it. Of course, he'd known it all along, or he'd suspected it, and yet a part of him had still hoped it wasn't true. He dropped the report on the pile again, and leaned back in his chair. He ran his hands through his thinning grey hair and reached for his coffee. His fifth cup today and it was doing damn little to replace the sleep he'd lost. He pulled a bottle of Tylenol out of his desk drawer and gulped two down. Not for the last time he asked himself why he'd agreed to get involved with Starkey. Cassavetes didn't know whether he felt thrilled the DNA analysis proved the alien origin of Oberlin's

Anomaly, and that it was no hoax, or scared to death the story would get out and still be disbelieved. He didn't want to live through the scorn of his peers again, and this time the media would spread it around the world, guaranteed. Ann's note on the folder made it clear she would suppress the results, but what about the rest of her lab, or her husband? But shouldn't the truth be told? Could he let his fear of the loss of reputation keep him from doing the right thing?

The temperature rose in his office. The museum's ancient air conditioning units always lost the daily battle with DC's heat. He took off his jacket and hung it on the back of his chair. Loosening his tie, he swiveled around to look out his window at the front of the museum. Below on the Mall, walkers and joggers passed by and people sat on benches basking in the sun. A few kites hovered in the air above with long strings leading down to the hands of running children and were framed by the pale blue sky with great white cumulous clouds voyaging slowly across. It looked like just another day on the National Mall in Washington, DC, with nothing to distinguish it from the thousands of days when he'd looked out his window. Now, however, he recognized the fluid nature of reality. Cassavetes picked up the phone to call Starkey, wondering how the man would take the news.

The knock on the door startled him. He did have the presence of mind to hang up the phone and shove the DNA analysis into the top drawer of his desk.

"Come in," he said.

The door opened slowly and two men stepped in. They stood just inside the doorway and looked around the room, their eyes carefully noting the weapons hanging from the wall and crowding the shelves. Then their eyes came to rest on Cassavetes, but they still did not speak.

"Can I help you?" Cassavetes asked, rising from his chair.

"Dr. Peter Cassavetes?" said the taller of the two men.

"Yes, what can I do for you?"

"I'm John Petrucelli." The man reached inside his jacket pocket and produced a leather ID wallet. He held it out for Cassavetes to read. "This is Frank Novovaski." The other man stood quietly, looking at Cassavetes, his head cocked slightly to one side.

The taller man's identification said AFOSI. Cassavetes did not recognize the acronym. "What is AFOSI?" he asked.

Petrucelli closed the leather wallet with a snap and slipped it back in his pocket. "We are from the Air Force Office of Special Investigations."

"The Air Force," Cassavetes said. *What in the world?* "What brings you to me?"

"Mind if I sit down?" Petrucelli asked.

"Oh, sorry, of course, just let me move these things." Cassavetes came around and gathered various daggers and clubs from the two wooden chairs in front of the desk and piled them on the tile floor behind him.

Petrucelli sat down, but Novovaski remained standing. He walked over to the cluttered bookshelf near him, picked up an object, and examined it closely.

"That's an atlatl, a Toltec spear thrower," Cassavetes said. "It is nine hundred years old and priceless, so please be careful."

The agent nodded slightly and stepped into a shaft of sunlight from the tall windows. Starkey saw heavy wrinkles in the agent's dark blue suit. It fit his heavyset frame poorly, straining at the shoulders and too long in the sleeves. The sunshine highlighted his short brown hair and revealed a scar across his scalp above his ear. More, smaller scars lay along his heavy, beard-darkened jaw line and dotted his jutting brow.

Petrucelli cleared his throat and Cassavetes looked back at him. This agent's hair, cut longer than Novovaski's, lay tight, slick, and black on his skull, combed back straight from his forehead. A severe part divided the man's pomaded hair. Cool blue eyes stared out of an otherwise non-descript face with an olive complexion. His suit, also dark blue, was immaculately pressed, and his crisp white shirt sported a bright blue paisley tie. A matching handkerchief pushed out of his breast pocket.

"We have a few questions, Dr. Cassavetes. First, do you know Ann Wilson in the Ancient DNA lab over at NIH?"

"Yes, but what's this about?" Cassavetes said.

"Let's focus on our questions first, alright, Doc?" Petrucelli asked. "Did you recently send Dr. Wilson a bone sample for DNA testing?" Cassavetes watched Novovaski set the atlatl back on the shelf carefully. The agent moved closer to the desk and focused on Cassavetes' face, putting his hands on the back of the empty chair. The knuckles of both hands were scared. The man smiled slightly, but Cassavetes still felt threatened. He wondered if it showed.

"Yes, I did. Why?" Cassavetes said.

"Where'd that bone sample come from, doctor?" Petrucelli asked

"It came from Oberlin's Anomaly, a set of bones…"

Petrucelli held up both hands to cut him off. "We know about the Anomaly, Doc. It's an unidentified skeleton unearthed in Georgetown in 1948. We also know some bones of the skeleton are missing from its storage unit here in the museum. You don't happen to know their present whereabouts?"

"Why in the world would the Air Force be interested in the Anomaly?" Cassavetes said.

"That information's classified, doctor. Just answer the question, please," Petrucelli said.

Cassavetes' looked at the two agents. *Why do I feel threatened? I've done nothing wrong.* Government agents in your office did that, he supposed. He swiveled in his chair and opened the bottom drawer of the credenza behind him. He removed the white plastic container that held two finger bones of the creature, leaving the crossbow and arrow in the drawer. Turning back, he pushed aside a stack of papers and placed the container on his desk. "They are here. I removed them from storage for testing."

Petrucelli picked them up and handed them to Novovaski who opened the box and then nodded to him. Petrucelli removed a black fountain pen from his coat pocket and a black notebook. Cassavetes watched him write out a receipt.

"We'll be taking those with us," Petrucelli said, handing it to him.

At first Cassavetes didn't know what to say. He sat looking at the receipt in his hands. Then Petrucelli stood up and began to walk toward the door carrying the container.

"We'd appreciate it if you stayed in the area, doctor. We may want to talk to you again," Petrucelli said.

"Wait just a minute, those bones belong to the museum. You can't just take them," Cassavetes said.

"Oh, yeah we can, Doc," Petrucelli said, heading for the door.

Cassavetes picked up his phone. "Security, this is Dr. Cassavetes. I need immediate assistance. I have two Air Force Agents here who are attempting to remove…" Cassavetes paused, listening. "I see. Thank you." He hung up the phone and looked at the agents. "Well, it seems you can."

Novovaski nodded. "One more question, Dr. Cassavetes. The museum held those bones for eighty years." The agent's accent sounded mid-western, and his tone seemed almost friendly. "Why send the bones for DNA testing now?"

Cassavetes thought about Starkey and hesitated before answering, but he saw no reason to bring up Starkey's name. So he gave a partly truthful answer. "DNA sequencing is a relatively new technology. We just never got around to testing the bones of Oberlin's Anomaly. There's a lot of stuff like that that ought to be tested. And it's expensive."

Novovaski tilted his head again and looked thoughtful. He lifted his hand in a dismissive wave, turned and walked out. He left the door open.

CHAPTER FIFTEEN

BERYL STARKEY

WASHINGTON, DC JULY 15TH 1945

On a brilliant Saturday afternoon in mid-July of 1945, a light breeze, sweet with the smell of honeysuckle, drifted through the half-open window of the streetcar. The breeze washed over Beryl Starkey and the other riders of the pale green car as it clattered and climbed up the 14th Street hill past Meridian Park's fountains and gardens. Beryl paid no attention to the sounds of laughter and cheerful chatter from the streetcar's riders. Almost all women, the riders seemed excited that the workweek was finally over. Last night's *Evening Star* reported good news from the war. The allied forces were advancing and the end of the war in Europe seemed to be in sight.

Beryl and her friend, Flora Doval, sat together on the last seat at the back of the streetcar, apart from the general gaiety. Beryl spoke little to her friend, her arms folded over her stomach. Her dark auburn hair curled beneath a navy blue hat with a small veil, and she wore a navy blue suit hemmed just below the knee, with a neatly pressed white blouse pinned with a small silver-colored broach. She wore her best outfit, complete with the matching blue purse and pumps and precious silk stockings. Flora, the older and larger of the two, wore a brown tweed suit and a brown hat. Her hair defied curlers, thin and stringy and blond, it would hang straight regardless of Flora's nightly ministrations.

The older woman tried more than once to strike up a conversation with Beryl since they boarded at H St., but the younger woman barely answered Flora's questions and volunteered nothing. Beryl sat, bent slightly forward, one hand on her stomach, staring out the window at the row houses and storefronts that lined 14th St., the *Washington Post* folded neatly in her lap. She hardly moved except to bite her nails while she glanced at the ads in the paper for "National Baby Week."

Beryl usually chattered away incessantly on these rides, regaling Flora with tales of her day. Flora hung on every word of the stories her friend told every evening on the streetcar. The customers who came to Beryl's candy counter at Liggett's Drug Store provided daily tales to be shared with her friend.

"Beryl Starkey, you ain't said five words to me since we got on this streetcar. 'Deed you ain't. What in the world is wrong with you today, honey? And you still haven't told me why you put on your best blue suit to go to work." Flora said.

Beryl sat perfectly still without answering, with only the clanging and clanking of the moving streetcar and the hubbub from the other passengers filling the silence between them.

Getting no answer, Flora went on. "Well? I ain't talking just to hear myself."

Finally, after a pause, Beryl opened her purse and removed a manila envelope. Without looking up, she handed it to Flora. Flora stared at the envelope for a moment before she noticed the return address. "The War Department? Why would they be writing to you?" Then, at last, Flora understood. "Oh, God, honey." She put her arm around her friend's shoulder, and then she too fell into silence. There was little to say. Beryl continued to stare out the window as the streetcar crested the hill, but she leaned into her friend's arm.

>>>

The months after Jim's death passed quickly, racing toward the birth of her child, and Beryl didn't feel ready. She just felt just scared. This day, Beryl rode the streetcar alone. She went with Flora for their usual Sunday breakfast, chipped beef on toast at the Blue Mirror down the street from their boarding house. But instead of riding the streetcars with Beryl the way they always did on Sunday, Flora got off to visit some friends from the Navy Yard where she worked. Flora offered ride on, but Beryl insisted she'd be fine and would take the Sunday ride alone, maybe go out to Glen Echo Amusement Park.

Beryl changed cars at Pennsylvania Avenue and took the Glen Echo Line. She could have spent the afternoon at the movies. The uptown theater was near her boarding house. But these days she still liked to go to Glen Echo. Flora said she ought to take it easy when she was nearly due, but she loved the trees and the stream and the sounds of the children laughing on the rides. She felt good, and still strong. She had purchased her weekly pass, and now she sat staring at it. The picture of the Crystal Pool reminded her that she forgot to put her towel and swimsuit in her bag. She stared out the window of the streetcar as it turned on to M St., and a memory of Jim's face came into her mind, smiling as he did that first day they met. The passing houses and storefronts blurred with the memory.

Eight months ago she went with Flora to
Walter Reed, the army hospital, up on 16th Street.
They visited Flora's brother, Buford, some week-
ends. Buford and Jim served in the same regiment
and were wounded in the same campaign in Sicily.
Having wound up in adjacent beds there at Walter
Reed, the two men quickly become friends. Jim said
he lay there waiting for Beryl, although it took a
world war and a leg filled with shrapnel to bring
them together.

Beryl noticed him right away. She passed
right in front of him and sat down across from him
on Buford's bed that Sunday morning. She pretended
she didn't notice, of course. Feeling his eyes on her,
she carefully crossed her legs and tugged at her skirt
to pull it down below her knees. But soon she could
bear it no more. She just had to turn and look at him.
She thought he looked awful skinny in the striped
hospital pajamas, but she liked his wavy brown hair.
Jim stared at her, his head cocked to one side, his
blue eyes wide and smiling. Beryl blushed deeply,
and looked away. She tried to pay attention to Flora's
animated conversation with Buford giving him all the
latest news from 'up the country,' as they called their
Shenandoah Valley home town. Beryl had been painfully shy of all strangers and most men all of her
twenty years, but when Jim Starkey smiled at her the

first time she opened like a rosebud. She started to shine just as she did in her story-telling with family and friends.

Beryl stirred on the streetcar seat as she remembered Jim's smile and the way it reached right down inside of her and grabbed something, something she hadn't known lived in there. She had never had such a feeling, as if recognition and surprise and desire all came wrapped up in a single moment. For the first time in her life she wanted someone, wanted him badly, and that feeling never went away. She still wanted him, perhaps even more.

In case the smile alone didn't do the job, luck had stepped in. A nurse arrived to raise Jim's bed for lunch. She bent over and grabbed the crank at the foot of his bed and wrenched it hard. An ear-splitting rasp of metal grinding on metal screeched out across the whole ward. Everyone on the floor turned to look in the direction of the awful sound, Beryl included. She saw that Jim still stared at her, but the nurse kept on turning the crank and the screeching noise kept going on and on until it finally distracted him and Jim began to laugh. Jim's loud and altogether infectious laughter soon got the nurse laughing. The laughter spread until Buford and Flora joined in and then the rest of the nurses and patients on the ward. Finally Beryl couldn't help but laugh as well. That was all it took. Her shyness just fell away. After that Beryl found it easy to talk to him.

After she met Jim that day, she began to go with Flora on her visits to the hospital every Sunday afternoon. At first she would spend a good bit of the time visiting with Buford. But as the weeks went on, she spent more and more time with Jim, sitting on his bed while they talked. Then Buford, released from the hospital, went back home to Stanley, Virginia for good. The war had ended for him. Beryl just kept coming, however, and she could no longer pretend she came to see Buford.

As Jim's wounds healed she began to take him for walks around the grounds of the hospital. At first he rode in a wheel chair while she pushed him, but later when his leg was almost healed and the doctors ordered exercise, they would walk together. They talked as they walked and came to know each other, drawing closer. In that setting they were always surrounded by others, nurses and doctors and patients, however. Beryl resisted his efforts to hold her hand or embrace her. They would talk for hours, often sitting by the fountain on the hospital lawn, but they did not touch. She was too self-conscious to physically express her affection for him in front of others, or to allow him to do so. One day, though, she plucked up her courage and asked where else they could go. The hospital staff told them about the park nearby. Finally, when his leg grew stronger, they crossed 16th Street to walk and picnic in Rock Creek Park where at last they could be alone.

The streetcar came to a stop at Wisconsin Avenue, and Beryl watched as a woman boarded carrying a small child. The woman turned and came to the back of the streetcar and took a seat across from Beryl. She watched as the woman arranged the child on her lap. The woman began to talk, as if to the child, but actually to Beryl.

"We're off to Glen Echo to ride the carousel today. We'll ride the ostrich, won't we, Billy? And the rabbit, too?" she said. The boy, who looked to be two or three years old, laughed and clapped his hands, and then he turned to stare at Beryl. He continued to stare, in an odd, direct way for a child. Beryl saw that the mother watched her out of the corner of her eye. The mother, very short-statured and unusually wide in the body, had a dark complexion like an Indian, Beryl thought. *A Red Indian*.

When she found her fingers drumming on her knees she clasped her hands together and turned back to the window. She wondered if a boy grew inside her. Would he have Jim's smile? Where would the baby sleep? Who would watch the baby while she worked? What if she died in childbirth? Sometimes women did. *Why, oh why did she ever fall in love with a soldier?* Her hands made fists on her knees. *Jim Starkey, if you weren't already dead, I could choke you for leaving me to go back to the stupid war, and making me a widow and a pregnant widow, to boot.* "Oh, what must I do?" The last few words she spoke aloud.

"What did you say?" The woman with the boy asked.

"Nothing," Beryl said. Mother and child looked at her. Beryl felt like they looked right inside of her, and knew her in some strange way. She felt embarrassed and knew she must be turning red. She spread her hand on her knee showing her wedding ring. *Beryl Starkey get hold of yourself.* She couldn't afford to go to pieces now. She must set things in order. A baby was coming, a baby that would never know its father, and it was up to her to make a way for it. Who else would care for it? At least it would have a mother, a mother who loved it. She'd never known her real mother. A foundling they called her, left on the doorstep of the orphanage in Luray, VA. Beryl was adopted by the Cubbages. They gave her a home with them in Stanley, VA. And she was loved.

The streetcar lurched to a stop, staunching the memory. Beryl looked up to see a soldier and a young woman at the stop by the theater on MacArthur Boulevard, and they climbed on board. They sat near the front behind the driver. Beryl watched as they sat close together, his arm around her shoulders. The young woman leaned her forehead against the soldier's. They spoke quietly, almost nose to nose.

Beryl turned back to the window and her memories. She sat like that with Jim on a blanket on the grass in the park.

In silent agreement, they walked until they found a secluded spot in a grove of trees on a little hill above Rock Creek. They spread the blanket and opened the picnic basket she had borrowed from Mrs. Patterson, her landlady. Sitting beneath an ancient sycamore tree, they opened the pop bottles and ate cold chicken sandwiches she had made the night before. Beryl told him stories of the characters that lived around her home in Virginia. The village folks, Keysers and Caves and Cubbages and Campbells, came alive in her stories. Heroes and fools, shiftless and lazy, plain and hardworking, her stories found humor and humanity in all of them.

Then Jim put down his sandwich and took her hand.

"I love you, Beryl," he said out of nowhere.

"Oh shoot, you do not. How could you? You've only known me three months."

Jim laughed. "How long does it usually take?"

"I don't know, but..."

"Beryl," he said, "Don't you love me?"

She looked down at her hands, and then slowly she nodded.

Jim slid closer to her on the blanket and took
her in his arms. He kissed her gently on the lips once
and then a second time. It was just like she'd always
thought it ought to be. She agreed soon to marry him,
and so the service was performed by the Army Chap-
lin at Walter Reed in a simple ceremony, with only
Flora there.

Jim hadn't been released from the hospital
yet, and housing wasn't provided for couples at Walter Reed. Beryl could have no privacy at her rooming
house. Mrs. Patterson allowed no gentleman callers
in the women's rooms, of course, not even husbands.
She could have him visit in the sitting room of the
old brownstone on Belmont Street or on the front
porch swing on Sundays between two and five with
no exceptions. Mrs. Patterson stood for no hanky-
panky, as she called it. And so it was that her child
would be conceived outside, in a glade among the
trees, on a borrowed blanket in Indian summer when
the first maple leaves were beginning to turn red.

She didn't plan to get pregnant so soon, of
course. If their relationship had a fault it was that
talking about some things like sex and children and
the future just never happened. It might have been
easier to talk about them if Jim hadn't been a soldier,

and a soldier the army wasn't quite through with. He would be found fit for duty soon. What would happen then? But the desire within her and Jim did not wait for talk or planning. Once they began to be intimate the current buoyed them up and carried them along without a single spoken word being necessary.

"Glen Echo, end of the line," the streetcar driver called out. Beryl returned slowly to the present, and looked through the window to see the stone facade and the high arched sign of the amusement park. She stood when the car stopped.

"Goodbye." The mother of the boy smiled when she spoke. They didn't seem to be getting off. Beryl nodded and walked down the aisle to the streetcar's steps and pushed open the folding doors to get off. She walked under the stone arch at the entrance and joined the small stream of people that flowed down the hill into the park. Lining up to purchase tickets at the red and white booth, she turned to look over her left shoulder in the direction of the carousel. Parents and children were waiting outside the carousel house for their turn to ride. They looked anxious to climb aboard, select the animal of their choice, and wait for the sound of the bell. The carousel let war-weary adults ride as children once more. The circular carousel house, built of painted red and green wood and columns of local stone, had large open windows. Through these Beryl could see and hear the carousel as it whirled round and round. The band organ that made the music for the carousel broadcast "American Patrol" across the park. She heard it echo off the beige stucco buildings around her.

She watched the carousel as it turned, ringed with elaborately carved animals that circled on a wooden platform suspended several inches above the floor. Decorated in carnival colors and gold leaf, the animals formed a menagerie of horses, rabbits, ostriches, and more. Beryl, stepping one step forward with the ticket booth line, glimpsed her favorite animal, the King Horse, leading the animals round and round to the music. The little money she could afford bought tickets for three rides. Her favorite was the carousel of course, but she liked the bumper cars and the swings, too, but she knew she shouldn't ride them now, with the baby so close. She passed the walk that led down to the Tunnel of Love. *I'll save the carousel for last.* She went off in the direction of the picnic ground.

She slowed as she neared the Dodgem' car pavilion, and stopped to watch and sit for a while on a bench. It wouldn't do to rush through the park. These small pleasures acted as a refuge from the worries that circled around her. She sat up straight, right leg crossed over the left. Posture was so important, all the ladies magazines said. She withdrew her compact from her purse, and opening it, examined her appearance. Her hat sat straight on her head, and her hair laid just right on her collar and behind her ears. Her nose looked too shiny, however, and she quickly applied a layer of powder. She had smudged her lipstick as well. As she reapplied it she thought, biting my lip again. A tiny drop of the precious Evening in Paris perfume Jim had given her and a pat of powder on each cheek helped to refresh her. Now, satisfied with her appearance, she began to take notice of her surroundings.

One didn't come to Glen Echo for the quiet. The screams of the people on the Coaster Dip could be heard throughout the park. Beryl loved the sense of peace that came with watching the couples strolling arm and arm as they passed the Dodgem' and entered the Spanish Ballroom. The exhaustion from the war brought men and women here for sanctuary, for recovery. The ballroom seemed so foreign and exotic to her, with its stucco walls and Spanish-mission style. But as she watched the couples today, she suddenly felt terribly alone. She allowed herself to daydream a bit, replaying nights she danced there in the ballroom to the Paul Kain orchestra. That was before she met Jim. She found the park soon after she arrived in Washington, but in her daydream she managed to put Jim's face on the young men she danced with.

Then the pain in her stomach jabbed her and bent her double. A couple stopped to ask if she needed help, but she waved them away. These pains came almost daily now, but she'd put them from her mind along with the strange dreams that came with them. This time, after a few moments, the pain slowly began to ebb. She started at the music of the carousel. The band organ struck up "The Volunteer March", and the stirring music pulled her out of her seat and drew her towards the sound. The pain receded into her subconscious like a crab scuttling back into darker waters.

Beryl decided to walk back to the carousel. A sharp pain in her left ankle caused her to limp slightly. One ankle was tender, and both were swollen this week. She gained little weight during the first five months of pregnancy. Being a bit pudgy and given to softness around the middle no one noticed her condition until she was nearly six months. But now, at nearly eight months, her condition could not be more noticeable. Beryl knew she shouldn't have come to the park in her final months of pregnancy, but she was afraid that soon she wouldn't be able to come, and she loved it so.

Beryl saw the carousel attendant watching her from the open window as she approached. She'd noticed him in weeks before. He made her nervous. He seemed to work and lurk at the same time. His movement looked furtive, his shape oddly bent. She saw him mount the turning platform with practiced timing and begin to move amongst the animals and their riders, calling for tickets. He glanced over at her. After finishing taking tickets, he worked his way to the interior of the platform and stepped off it into the drum at the center of the carousel. Beryl watched as he grasped the lever, slowing the carousel and bringing it to a stop.

Beryl entered the round house, crossed the polished hardwood floor, and stepped carefully aboard the platform, holding on to a carriage. She passed among the menagerie, looking for the King Horse. She walked past the lesser animals but a little girl and her mother beat her to it. Disappointed, she moved on and climbed carefully aboard the ostrich, another favorite. The carousel started up again.

As the speed increased, Beryl saw the carousel attendant step on the platform again, threading his way among the moving animals and across the revolving platform to step down on the hardwood floor. He moved quickly out of the exit to the back of the carousel. *Good, he's gone.* "La Gitana," the song then playing, came to an abrupt halt, the castanets suddenly silent. A new song began. "My Blue Heaven" rang out, one of Beryl's favorites. As she hummed the familiar tune her spirits began to lift. By the time the band organ reached the second verse, Beryl began to sing the words happily. She sang along until the chorus reached the line "just Molly and me, and baby makes three, we're happy in my…" Then the full meaning of the words came home to her, her voice trailed off, and she began to cry. Looking up she caught sight of herself in the mirrors above bordered by plaster carvings of jesters and cupids. *What a little fool I look, riding a carousel, and crying my eyes out.* The plaster faces seemed to be laughing at her.

"Ticket, please."

Beryl turned to see the carousel attendant standing beside her, and much too close it seemed to her, with his hand outstretched.

"Ticket, please," he said woodenly, as if he did not fully understand his own words.

Beryl handed him her ticket. As she did so, she noticed a peculiar, musty, dank smell about the man, and she could not help but stare at his queer, protruding eyes. He quickly turned away, as if to avoid her gaze. After taking the remainder of the tickets from the other passengers, he disappeared into the opening in the drum. Beryl could see him just inside each time she circled past.

Beryl forgot him. Catching the thrill of spinning round, she leaned over quite a bit backwards, holding on tightly to the brass tube. She watched the thousand lights that circled round on the inner drum and their reflection on the rounding board above. She heard laughter behind her and turned to see the mother and daughter on the King Horse behind her. The little girl, perhaps three years old, laughed and laughed with the up and down motion of the horse. She squealed each time the horse reached bottom and began to climb, bouncing in her mother's arms. But watching the girl brought back echoes of the pain in her stomach. Beryl saw the country scenes painted on the inner drum of the carousel stream by, but the colors seemed garish to her now. The fun had gone out of the ride for her.

The carousel slowly came to a stop. The music played on as the riders dismounted. Beryl's first ride ended. But crying or not, creepy attendant or not, she would take all of her three rides here. She could not bring herself to waste them, and she continued to hope the free, joyful feeling she usually had there in the park would return. It did not. There were too many things that made her think of Jim and the baby. She supposed it would be the same wherever she went now. There were children and soldiers everywhere.

She left the park rather late, after most of the other visitors. The Coaster Dip stood still in shadow, screams silenced, as she passed. She looked at her watch and thought the last street car must be getting ready to leave. She hurried up the little hill towards the gate and the platform.

Just as Beryl came through the gate, crossing beneath the bright neon sign above, an empty street-car rolled up. No one else stood waiting to board, and she did so alone. She was glad for that. The worst thing about riding the streetcar was sitting next to people you didn't know at all. You felt the heat of their bodies, the press of their weight against you. The car moved off immediately. Beryl held onto the stainless steel pole next to her. Its cold surface reminded her of the dining hall at Walter Reed. The tables and chairs there were all of stainless steel. *Jim, how could you leave me like this?* Beryl gazed out of the car window into the darkening forest outside.

Startled when the streetcar stopped, Beryl looked up to see the driver get up from his seat, turn and look in her direction as he made to get off. The driver stepped down from the car into the light of a street lamp. She saw his large, pale eyes reflect that light. He stepped out of the circle of light and disappeared into the woods.

This wasn't a stop. The first real stop was the Sycamore Store, and this wasn't it. She stood up slowly walked through the car, grasping the poles as she passed. She stepped down to the open doors and onto the first step and looked out into the darkness.

"Driver?" she called out, though she did not see him.

She looked at the half circle of light that lay outside the folded doors. Beyond the circle the spreading sycamores stood silent, wrapped in gloom. Then the pain in her stomach returned, doubling her over, horrible, excruciating pain, more pain than she could bear. She stumbled blindly down and fell heavily to the ground in the pool of light.

When she opened her eyes she saw a dark figure come out of the shadows into the light. The figure, cowled and heavily robed, looked short and wide, too wide for a man. She could not see a face. She struggled little when it lifted her up in its arms, then started to carry her. She lost consciousness as they traveled down the streetcar tracks into the night.

She heard voices, voices in the dark.

"I can't save her Proteus. I can save the child, and normalize his appearance."

"Can we keep her alive until she reaches the hospital and he is born, Panacea?"

Beryl came awake at the sound of a bell. She lay on the concrete step by a door. A single lamp lit the sign above, Glen Echo Fire Station. A man opened the door and looked down in her face.

"Harry, come here and bring the stretcher, there's a woman lying outside our door." Another man joined him and they stooped down to examine her, taking her pulse.

"She's alive, but we need to get her to Georgetown Hospital now."

"Harry, she's pregnant, and her water's broken."

CHAPTER SIXTEEN

DNA

BETHESDA, MD THURSDAY
JUNE 1

Daylight blasted the Murphy bed, seared through Starkey's eyelids, and excavated him from an exhausted sleep. His apartment sat on the twelfth floor of the Grosvenor, an older high rise at the edge of Bethesda, MD. He forgot to close the balcony drapes last night and his windows faced east. The merciless sun burnt through the June haze outside, throwing even the darkest corners of the small efficiency into sharp relief. The clock on his bedside table read 9:37am. Good thing he'd left a message the night before with his office that he wouldn't be in. Starkey rolled over away from the attacking light and willed himself to sleep. Instead his mind kept tracking back to replay the scenes of the morning before like a needle skipping on an old 78 record. Grime's crossbow, the baseball bat in Proteus' hands, and their flight through the tunnels came round again and again. Then his cell phone rang.

He fought his way out of the twisted covers and grabbed his phone off the bedside table. "Hello?"

"Starkey? This is Cassavetes."

Starkey rubbed his face with his hand. "Hey, Doc. What's up?"

"Can you meet with me today? I need to see you."

"Well, yeah, maybe later, but what's going on?" Just getting out of bed seemed too much at the moment.

"I'd rather tell you in person. Can you meet me in the Haupt Garden behind the old Smithsonian building? Eleven o'clock?"

Starkey said he would. Still trying to process what the call could mean, he eased over to the sideboard of the small kitchenette and poured coffee beans into the grinder. He covered the grinder with a dish towel, but it didn't muffle the painfully loud sound well. The ceramic tile cooled his bare feet.

Starkey waited for the coffee maker almost prayerfully. He gathered up scattered Styrofoam trays and plastic forks and cardboard coffee cups and tried to shove them in the overflowing trash compacter, but most spilled out onto the floor again. *Forget it.* He poured his coffee with reverence. Holding the chipped blue cup in both hands and leaning against the kitchen counter he looked around the tiny, one room box that held his life now. *How depressing is this?* He couldn't face the rooms of his little rambler in Silver Spring after Ethan and Jane's deaths. He still didn't let the real estate agent list the house, though, but he knew the slogan for the sign, "Three Bedrooms and Two Ghosts."

Starkey shaved, showered, and ran a comb through his hair. Dressed in a new white shirt and new dark grey slacks, only slightly tight, he hurried downstairs and through the short tunnel under the highway into the Grosvenor Metro station. Starkey crossed the dimly lit platform hunching his head into his neck and shoulders. He changed trains at the Metro Center, shrinking from other riders who brushed past or turned to stare at his size. His eyes searched down side corridors and behind him on the escalator, half expecting to see Grimes following him. *On the other hand, I am awake, totally awake for the first time in a long time, as if the fog of grief has at last cleared away.* He stood up straighter as he left the Smithsonian exit and crossed over Jefferson Drive to enter the Haupt Garden at the rear of the old Smithsonian castle. His watch read 11:10. Cassavetes should be waiting for him. The anthropologist's cryptic phone call contributed one more cause for the tension in Starkey's neck, and the headache that lingered behind his eyes.

>>>

John Petrucelli and Frank Novovaski sat in a spotless black Chevy Suburban parked on Constitution Avenue behind the African Art Museum. The darkened windows of the SUV reflected the traffic and pedestrians that passed. Novovaski reached over to boost the volume on the sound of the laptop mounted on the dash. On the other side of the wall beside them, their camouflage-painted drone hovered in the sweeping canopy of a magnolia tree. Novovaski focused its mike and camera on the wrought iron bench where Peter Cassavetes sat. The agents watched the video's live feed on the computer screen. The sound was so sensitive they could hear Cassavetes' rapid breathing. The bench, partly surrounded with euonymus hedge and tall Hibiscus flowers in beds bursting with color, seemed to have been chosen for seclusion. The agents watched as a grey-suited man approached and sat down on the bench beside Cassavetes.

"Hello, Doc," the man said.

"Hello, Starkey," Cassavetes said. "Wait. Is it my imagination or are you a lot bigger than you were a week ago? I'd swear…"

Starkey cut him off. "Yes, I am. I don't know why and I'm scared shitless about it. Let it go for now. You sounded excited when you called. What's happened that we couldn't talk about it on the phone?"

Cassavetes looked around them in the garden and then spoke in a quiet voice. "Ok. This morning, two agents from the AFOSI came to see me. Before you ask it's the Air Force Office of Special Investigations."

Starkey turned on the bench to look directly at Cassavetes. "The Air Force? Why? What did they want?"

"They wanted the finger bones of the anomaly I had in my office. Somehow they knew I'd removed them from storage."

"But what's it about, why did they want them?" Starkey asked.

"I don't know. They wouldn't answer any questions, but they also knew about the DNA testing. My friend, Ann Wilson over at NIH, sequenced the DNA from the bones of Oberlin's Anomaly. Well, she sent me the results." Cassavetes ran one hand down his goatee and his neck.

"Okay, okay, go on, what'd she find?" Starkey asked.

"The DNA's nucleotide structure tested all wrong. It held five bases instead of four. *Five*. And the fifth defied identification, completely unknown."

Starkey rubbed his forehead and looked up at the trees overhead. "Doc, what does that mean in plain English?"

"It means that the DNA—if we can call it that—is so different it could not have occurred here on Earth. The bones of the creature are not Terran."

"Okay, so the creature came from another planet." Starkey didn't sound very surprised.

Novovaski looked at his partner in the car.

"I believe it. You suspected this all along, right?" Starkey asked.

"Yes, but before there was no proof. Ann Wilson didn't believe it, either. She made her postdoc run the tests seven times and she still didn't believe it. Then she extracted the DNA herself and ran it yet again. Same result."

"No chance of error then?" Starkey said.

"None. And it gets worse. Her postdoc also accidently compared it with DNA Ann's husband extracted on a project of his. And I can't believe this part at all. Her husband, Joe Wilson, is a Cultural Anthropologist who studies Piscataway Indians in the DC and Maryland areas. Joe took a blood sample from the only full blooded Piscataway he knew of to compare his DNA with that of his samples from the Piscataway fossil record."

"And?" Starkey asked.

"They found a match."

"The Piscataway man is an alien?"

Cassavetes slid closer until his shoulder touched Starkey's. "No, of course he isn't. But the man's DNA did hold some sequences that matched the alien DNA from the bones," he said.

"A part alien Indian and alien bones, but how can this be?"

"Who the hell knows? But what's made you so accepting all of a sudden?"

Starkey moved back slightly on the bench. "Wait," he said. "Did you tell the air force agents about me?"

"No, I didn't. They didn't seem to know about you. They just told me not to leave town. They'd be coming back to see me. You need to put me in the picture, Starkey. Tell me what's happened since I last saw you."

Starkey looked down. "I don't know if I should tell you, because it may put you in danger."

Cassavetes put his hand on Starkey's shoulder. "It's too late, my friend, I'm already too far in. Besides, this is exciting stuff. I *want* to be in on it."

Starkey told Cassavetes about the canoeing society, Sheila, and their capture at the society's island. He described their abduction and the strange, cloaked guide that saved them.

The garden where they were talking grew more crowded. One couple walked close by Starkey and Cassavetes and sat on a nearby bench. Starkey leaned forward, speaking even more quietly.

Novovaski turned up the volume on the computer.

"Our guide told Sheila and me to meet him at someplace called the Protean Society this evening down on K St. by the river. He told us not to involve the police any further. I'm scared not to, but they'll think I'm nuts if I do anyway, so it's easier to play along for now."

"It's certainly intriguing. I've never heard of the Protean Society. But I'd go, if it were me," Cassavetes said.

"That's how I feel," Starkey said. "How could I not? Plus our guide seemed to know me, and I don't know, I just trusted him somehow. Don't ask me why he felt familiar, I don't have a clue. But if something happens to us, Doc, it will be up to you. You will be the only one who knows the score."

"Now I see why you could accept the alien DNA findings so easily." Cassavetes put his hand over his mouth, and then went on. "What's really scary and yet fascinating, Starkey, is all this seems to fit together. The Anomaly, the attack on you, and the canoeing society men, and now the DNA, all point in the same direction. Give me the address where you're going,"

Petrucelli and Novovaski watched the screen as Starkey pulled out a small note pad and wrote the address down and passed it over. Novovaski zoomed in for a close up of the note. He pressed a button to do a screen capture.

"What will Dr. Wilson do with the results of the DNA test?" Starkey asked.

Cassavetes gave a short laugh. "She won't do anything for now, and never if she can help it. No, she'll sit on it, and Joe Wilson will do the same, until we can publish without fear of becoming laughing stocks."

"But what about those two Air Force agents, what if they come back?"

"What if they do? I don't really know what their interest is in the DNA or the anomaly, but space aliens and the air force? It's like a grade B movie. If they do come back, I'll have to tell them the truth, but I guess we can hope they won't ask me about you."

"If they ask, tell them everything, Doc, don't try to cover for me. We haven't done anything wrong. I don't want you in trouble because of me, but I really appreciate your help. It means a lot to have someone to talk to about this who doesn't immediately dismiss me as a loony."

Cassavetes held his hand out to Starkey, who shook it. "I think, Jack Starkey, those DNA results prove you're on the trail of something real." Cassavetes rose to leave. "I have a departmental meeting across the Mall. You've got my phone number, call me tonight. I want to know what happens."

The two AFOSI agents in the suburban looked at each other. "The Protean Society," Novovaski said, starting a search on his laptop.

"I would say I told you Cassavetes was hiding something, but I know how you hate it when I do that," Novovaski said.

"Gee, thanks."

Petrucelli retargeted the drone.

>>>

The next morning Frank Novovaski hit the enter key on the laptop sitting on his knees. "I give up. There's nothing." He sat back and loosened his tie, a few more coffee stains showing down the front. He rubbed the ache in his neck and resumed staring at the Protean Society building. All night surveillance had gotten harder in the last few years.

John Petrucelli shifted in the car seat to stare at his partner. "What do you mean nothing? How can there be nothing? The damn building is sitting right there in front of us, Frank, big as life, on K St. in Washington, DC, the nation's capital, with a brass plaque on the door that says The Protean Society. How can there be no records?"

"Oh, there are records. The 'FOSI network searched every DC database out there. I found tax records going back to the Civil War, and several building permits here and there over the last fifty years. When I say nothing, I mean I found nothing that really tells me who they are or what they do there. There is a reference to a tavern that stood on the site before. The tavern functioned as a meeting place for politicians and landowners. Thomas Jefferson slept there, you know, the usual stuff. There's also a statement from an interview done by the old *Evening Star* in 1952."

"Well, what does that say, Frank?" Petrucelli said, annoyed with his partner's bit by bit responses.

"There's just a mission statement. I'll read it to you. The Protean Society is one of the nation's oldest patriotic organizations, founded in 1799. A hereditary society, its mission is to promote knowledge and to foster fellowship among its members. Now a nonprofit educational organization devoted to the principles and ideals of its founders, the modern Society maintains its headquarters, library, and museum in Washington, D.C."

Petrucelli ran both hands along the sides of his head smoothing his pomaded hair and turned back to stare at the brick building across the street. "What the hell does that mean? That's suspicious all by itself."

"Let me tell you something else suspicious, John. The drone's camera spotted a Black Hawk model helicopter on the rooftop when we arrived yesterday. I just checked the live feed and it's not there anymore. And no, before you ask, it didn't take off. One second it was there and the next it wasn't."

"I would say helicopters don't just disappear, but I know how that annoys you when I do that," Petrucelli said. His lopsided grin annoyed Frank even more than the words.

"Disappearing helicopter or not, I think it's time we brought in the whole team. Ancient bones, three-eyed monsters, secret societies, it's all just too damn much. Add alien DNA to that?" Frank said.

Petrucelli shrugged. "If you say so. It could be all bullshit."

"Oh, it smells alright, John, but the odor just ain't right."

CHAPTER SEVENTEEN

PROTEUS

GEORGETOWN DC THURSDAY
JUNE 1 6:00PM

Starkey wiped the drops of moisture from St. Andrew's dark mahogany bar with his hand and placed the card on it. It struck him as incredibly ironic. The card sat there, plain white, printed in the simplest typeface, and as mundane as concrete. Yet, it sent waves of chills through him and tumbled him in and out of vague memories that shook him, bizarre but somehow intriguing. It held an address, nothing more. He found 3051 K St. NW on a DC street map. The label read The Protean Society. A short search online turned up nothing about the society except an obscure historical reference to a former tavern that stood on the site, and a brief mission statement from a newspaper article. *Well, it's a real address, any-way.* He'd half expected the address to be a fake.

Sheila came through the door and walked down past the bar. She greeted a few regulars and waved at Paul the bartender. She was dressed in all black, from her fitted leather jacket to her high-heeled boots. The boot heels clicked on the tile floor all the way down the aisle. "Are you ready?" she asked.

"You look like a secret agent." He smiled at her, and gave her a kiss. "I'm waiting to hear a spy movie soundtrack come on." He looked down at his new blue jeans and running shoes. "I feel under-dressed."

"You saw the Georgetown address, decidedly up town. It seemed appropriate."

Paul appeared across the bar. "Do you want a drink, Sheila?"

"No thanks, Paul. We're just leaving."

"I haven't finished my pint, Sheila, and I could stand one more," Starkey said.

"You can always stand one more, Jack, and whatever is up tonight, we need you rational, given what we have to work with. Let's hit the road." She turned and high-heeled her way toward the door.

What could he do but follow?

Starkey got into Sheila's Porsche and buckled up. "I told Cassavetes the whole story. I just thought someone else should know where we're going."

"Will he be discrete?" She asked this as she started the car.

Starkey nodded. "I trust him, and he won't jeopardize his career again. But there's more. I'll tell you while we drive." He told Sheila about the DNA results from the NIH testing of the skeleton, the Piscataway man, and Cassavetes' artifacts from the Anomaly.

Sheila braked hard and pulled into a parking lot. She jerked the emergency brake up and turned to stare at him. "Starkey, are you kidding me? This is too goddam much. This woman at NIH thinks the DNA is from space aliens? Some Native American guy is part space alien? This gets worse all the time. We've been kidnapped at arrow point and rescued by someone who is four feet tall, four feet wide and floats in midair. Now you tell me they're all aliens?"

"Well, when you put it like that." Starkey sat silent for a long minute. "Okay, you're right. But we still have to go, don't we?"

"Hell, I guess so." Sheila pulled back onto Connecticut Ave and drove on. She stopped at a red light at 22nd St. and turned to look at Starkey.

Starkey's mind cleared. "Sheila, I don't know about you, but I'm starting to get really tired of being jerked around. Aliens or not, I'm tired of being threatened and I'm tired of being afraid and feeling helpless. I'm going to get myself ready to respond instead of just react. Will you help me?"

Sheila looked at him, eyebrows up, and her head to one side. "Well, well. Yes, I will."

A horn blew behind them. She let out the clutch and moved out with the traffic. Sheila took Connecticut Avenue and Wisconsin all the way down to Georgetown. Traffic moved slowly, but still Starkey's watch said ten before 6:00 when Sheila parked on K St.

Starkey looked at 3051, and turned to Sheila as they crossed the street. "Well, I'm impressed." It was a colonial-era, three story, red brick building that took up most of the block. Multiple dark, grey slate roofs topped several wings, with twin chimneys on each wing. The door and eight tall windows on the front first floor were painted white and had Italian marble thresholds and sills. Above the ornately carved entrance a large oculus centered the front of the building. In contrast, a small, unobtrusive brass plaque below the heavy brass knocker on the door simply said The Protean Society, 1799.

"Tell me again who these people are," Sheila said.

"All I know, Sheila, is from that one article. It said it's a hereditary society of patriots."

Sheila shrugged, stepped up, and started to grasp the door knocker, but the door swung open. A short and wide woman stood holding the door. She nodded at them. Clearly Native American, her face was an artwork of wrinkles. An ancient face. But her smile welcomed them. Her ornate dress had an embroidered white lace collar. It buttoned down to her waist, and the skirt reached the floor. She wore white gloves on her small hands.

When she spoke her voice rustled like silk. "Please come in, you are expected." "Please" sounded like "pless" when she said it.

The woman closed the door behind them and led them down a walnut-paneled hall carpeted with deep oriental rugs and lit by fluted wall sconces. At the foot of a large, curving marble staircase she turned and opened the double doors of a room on the right. Starkey stepped in first and saw a huge granite fireplace along one wall and several huge red leather wingback chairs arranged before it. The surrounding walls were hung with large portraits of men and women. The faces were familiar.

A giant of a man whose face looked Japanese rose from one of the chairs. "Jack Starkey and Sheila Cartwright, I am honored to meet you. I am Masato Yamashima, your Master's brother." He bowed deeply, stepped forward, and extended his hand.

Starkey shook the offered hand, feeling almost normal for once. His hand and Yamashima's were nearly the same size. He knew for certain Masato Yamashima was the biggest Japanese man he had ever seen, at least seven feet tall and with broad shoulders. Masato's face, like the rest of him, looked lean and hard. The dark oval pupils of his eyes nearly filled the irises. He wore an exquisitely tailored black suit and a black silk shirt, open at the collar. His voice, deep and resonant, had only a hint of an accent. Starkey appraised him slowly. Masato resembled Master Yamashima in the face, yes, but his size belied their family relationship. Masato seemed somehow larger than life. Starkey felt an immediate rapport. The man's face looked open, receptive.

"How do you know our names?" Starkey asked.

"Hiro emailed me about your experience along the canal. He summoned me. I arrived from Osaka this morning. And, Proteus told me you were coming..." Masato said.

A voice interrupted from the far end of the room. "Welcome, Jack and Sheila."

Turning, Starkey saw a large, six-paneled Japanese screen, but no speaker. The panels held paintings on silk of cherry blossoms and cranes. Four high-backed chairs were drawn up to face the screen. A low, marble-topped table sat before the chairs.

The voice spoke again from behind the screen. "Come my children, sit and we will talk, I am Proteus."

Starkey saw Sheila stiffen, but she moved to the chair on the left and sat. Starkey and Masato took adjacent chairs.

"You have met Masato. He has come from Japan to help us meet the threat we face."

Starkey saw Sheila struggle with herself and lose. "What threat? Who are you?" Sheila's voice sounded angry. "Why have you brought us here? And why are you hiding behind that screen?" Sheila's questions streamed out like angry bees in a swarm.

They heard a soft, bell-like laugh and then the voice of Proteus grew patient, parent like. "Damn the torpedoes, full steam ahead!"

"That's full 'speed' ahead," Sheila said.

"I ask for your patience, Sheila," the voice said. "All will be revealed. It is a long story, but if you will please indulge me a little longer, I promise all your questions will be answered. But first, we will take refreshment."

Almost immediately the woman who answered the door entered the room carrying a large silver tray with coffee, a plate of cheese and breads, ice water and glasses. The tray looked heavy, but she carried it effortlessly.

Proteus spoke while the woman placed the tray on the table before them. "This is Hannah. She is not a servant, she is an associate. Hannah, please join us and let me introduce you to our guests."

Hannah sat down in the remaining chair. She looked first at Masato, then at Starkey, and finally at Sheila. Her large, oval, pale blue eyes remained fixed on Sheila's. "My name is now Hannah Cassidy, but my birth name was Sooleawa. I was born in the Piscataway village on what is now called Heater's Island near Frederick, Maryland in 1699."

Starkey slipped forward to the edge of his seat. *1699? Piscataway.* A silence fell that went on for a long moment. As impossible as Hannah's statement seemed, Starkey believed her. At least he could not doubt the sincerity in those eyes.

Sheila spoke first. She spoke to Masato. "You say you are my Master's brother, and if so I must respect your presence here—but how can what this woman says be true?"

"Sheila, this is only the beginning. I met Hannah for the first time when I arrived today, but I knew of her before I came. I assure you she speaks the truth. My brother Hiro knows all you will hear today, and that is why he summoned me."

Proteus interrupted. "Sheila, please hold your questions for now. I will begin the story, and perhaps

Hannah and Masato will add their own stories as we go along."

Starkey refilled Sheila's coffee cup and then his own. He again experienced the feeling of mental clarity that he had had the last few days. Sheila and Masato looked completely focused also. Starkey sipped his coffee and listened.

Proteus began his story. "Your astronomers and astrophysicists today will tell you Earth's galaxy, quaintly called the Milky Way, is one of billions of galaxies in the universe. Moreover, they estimate that over eight billion earth-sized planets exist in the Milky Way alone, and many of these orbit around stars that resemble Earth's sun. These estimates are actually too conservative, but they will do for now. Therefore it should not surprise you that life exists, indeed, has existed for countless billions of years, beyond your small planet. But beyond even these easy concepts, galaxies were formed and life began shortly after what your scientists so familiarly call the Big Bang. Life began on planets warmed by cosmic radiation." The six-paneled screen shimmered and then became white and then black. The white light of an explosion burst outward in the center of the blackness and thousands of points of light scattered from the center.

Proteus continued. "And these galaxies are still pumping out stars at a prodigious rate. As Professor Stein at Harvard has recently said, 'the entire universe has been an incubator for life'. Yours is far from the only intelligent life in the universe, and you are not alone on the earth, Jack and Sheila, nor has your species evolved from its earliest days in isolation."

Starkey felt recognition, not surprise, during the silence that followed. *I have known this, but how?* He tried to get his mind around the immense implications of Proteus' statements, and his own realization.

Proteus told them mankind remained largely ignorant of the millions of inhabited planets in the galaxy beyond the solar system. That was by design. Earth, like thousands of others in the galaxy, has been in development, and likewise the human species has been in development, for more than two million years. For most of those long years the motives of the developers were progressive and constructive. The genetic changes that developed Homo sapiens out of early Hominids in Africa half a million years ago were not accomplished by blind evolution. Directed effort and resources accomplished it. Further genetic changes brought forth modern man some 100,000 years ago, also by design. All of this design and development here on Earth began and continues to be the work of representatives of what humans would call "The United Planets", the central governing body of the galaxy.

"My creators—the Museons—are a species whose altruistic efforts have fostered the cultures of many species across the galaxy. They support my efforts here on earth."

Starkey realized he'd been holding his coffee cup up for some time. He set it down and listened as Proteus continued. In some strange way all this also sounded familiar.

Proteus explained that Earth, previously little known to the rest of the galaxy, had rested in the benign influence of the galaxy's social scientists. Galactic expansionism and commerce had largely overlooked it. Unfortunately that was no longer the case. The Archarans, a species from the distant edge of the galaxy, had discovered this planet and its rare earth elements. One of these, scandium, could be mined on earth despite its scarcity elsewhere, and therefore was highly sought after and beyond value across the known universe. Alloys produced from this element could withstand the tremendous ionizing radiation in deep space. These alloys were used in most systems found aboard inter-galactic star cruisers. The United Planets' Covenants forbid the conquest of worlds, the subjugation of species, and the theft of minerals and commodities from primitive societies. The incredible value and demand for these rare earth elements, however, have tempted the Archarans to break the covenants. At this distance from the galactic center, enforcement remained weak, and the Archarans wielded significant power in the governing body, blocking close examination of their exploitation. Reports of the plundering of the scandium had reached the assembly of the United Planets, but were negated by political influence.

Proteus's voice softened, as if remembering. "Long ago I arrived on the earth to begin my work of contributing to the cultural, philosophical, sociological, and scientific development of man. Some 13,000 years ago I visited the island of Kyushu, the southernmost island of Japan. There I made my first direct contribution to Masato's ancestors—pottery. This is a fundamental building block of civilization.

"My specialty was not genetics, or warfare, but rather sociological development. But with the Archarans arrival, some 40,000 years ago, my role changed. Now I am like a double agent in your spy novels. I endeavor to thwart the Archarans while continuing my benevolent work with mankind."

Proteus explained that the Archarans began to genetically modify humans and train them as agents to accomplish their illegal mining in secret. The DNA of captured human females was modified when the women were pregnant in order to produce offspring that could be caused to undergo a metamorphosis. This metamorphosis made them more useful as warriors or slaves. The unsuspecting descendants of these offspring carried this DNA and were later enslaved when the Archarans needed them. Indigenous populations in remote areas around the earth were manipulated by these agents, covering up the extraction and off world transport of the scandium. Proteus and others dedicated to the protection of human rights and the defense of earth's resources intervened to free and sometimes retrain these agents to protect the planet.

"You, Jack Starkey, are also a product of that genetic modification," Proteus said.

Shock, doubt, and recognition rolled over Starkey in waves. With that one sentence, Proteus tore aside the veil that obscured the true architecture of Starkey's life.

Sheila, of course, spoke first. "Ridiculous. Surely, Starkey, you don't believe all this space alien bullshit."

"Sheila, just listen, please. There is something here. I know it. I don't know how, but I do. Somehow I've always known I was different, an odd man out. Like I was pinch hitting in my own life."

Sheila gave a short laugh. "Every adolescent thinks that."

Proteus interrupted. "Jack, the Archarans attempted to abduct your mother, Beryl, hours before you were born. She was one in a long line of people we suspected of being observed by the Archarans. When she met your father and became pregnant we began to watch over her closely. You, her child, were destined to become an agent of the Archarans, but I interceded. Unfortunately I did not manage to save your mother's life, but I did save yours. I hid you from the enemy's sight with your adopted parents. Now, the time has come for you to face your destiny."

But Sheila wasn't done. "Ok, Proteus, how is it that those mutants at the canoeing society had yellow eyes and Jack doesn't. Tell me that."

"When I rescued his mother, our healer, Panacea, altered Jack's DNA slightly to normalize his eyes before he was born. The same is true of Darake and the other Warriors you may meet. I interceded before they were born and brought them to Panacea here, or in our other, older enclaves. We have moved many times over the centuries as you might guess," Proteus said.

"So if you don't intercede the children are born with those yellow, bulging eyes and become slaves of the Archarans." Starkey said.

"Yes, but they are not always evil. Some resist their enslavers." Proteus told them that over the centuries some of those so mutated had joined him, becoming helpers and even Warriors. Proteus had observed that the second and subsequent generations mutated were more likely to become willing agents of the enemy.

Starkey tried to take in all that Proteus said. He'd known his mother's name and nothing else except she'd died in childbirth. He almost believed it all. But the huge expanse of time overwhelmed him.

"Proteus, you can't expect us to understand, or believe you could have been on earth for 400,000 years. I can't believe any living creature can exist for that long."

"Jack, you're right. None can. But I did not say I have been here on earth continuously for that time. Nor did I say I am alive. I am not, not in the sense you mean, though I am sentient. I am a SyLF—a Synthetic Life Form."

A hooded and robed figure came out from behind the screen. It came soundlessly and smoothly to hover facing the four people. One gloved hand rested on the back of an enormous wolf that moved beside it. Starkey felt a deep sense of recognition at the sight of the wolf, and somehow, a profound affection. The wolf looked directly into Starkey's eyes and held its gaze there. It padded over and sat down beside him, looking up at him.

Then Proteus removed the hood and the robe. A dark, metallic silver-green and generally ovoid figure revealed itself. Proteus' head had an over-sized helmet-shape, and a kind of translucence that allowed indistinct shapes to be visible through the surface. Two of these appeared to be large, spherical eyes, and one which Starkey thought had to be a mouth smiling. Proteus' trunk appeared also semi-translucent, having two arms with five-fingered hands and an opposable thumb, but no appreciable shoulders. He had no lower appendages. Overall he measured perhaps four feet in height, but hovered some two feet off the floor. The metallic surfaces of his body, despite their translucence, reflected the light from the tall windows at the end of the room. Starkey could see his own reflection and others in the room in Proteus' exterior. After a long moment, the figure spoke.

"I am Proteus. I have been the friend of Archimedes, Galileo, Isaac Newton, Thomas Jefferson, Louis Pasteur, Marie Curie, Darwin, Faraday, Einstein, and many, many others whose names you do not know. And I am your friend, Jack Starkey."

CHAPTER EIGHTTEEN

METAMORPHOSIS

C&O CANAL FRIDAY JUNE 2 2AM

Sheila drove them away from the Protean Society on K St. He replayed the evening in his mind. Masato and Proteus and the wolf all seemed too fantastic to be real. But there they were—what other explanation could there be? He tried to find a way to discount everything he heard, but belief flooded back in. It all explained much about the history of mankind. From his experience and knowledge of history, he thought it would probably take alien intervention just to save mankind from the war, climate change, and genocide it inflicted on itself. What's more, his mother, Beryl, and he were products of Archaran genetic alteration. His adopted parents told him only that his mother had died at Georgetown Hospital. He doubted if they knew more to tell him, and Starkey never tried to find out more. *Why did I never try?* Most adopted people wondered who their real parents were, but he never gave it much thought.

Sheila headed south and turned onto White-hurst Freeway, exiting onto I-66. She took the George Washington Parkway up the Virginia side of the Potomac River. Starkey stared out the window. In his mind he pictured Proteus floating two feet off the floor right in front of them. He looked for all the world like a four foot high, stainless steel, Japanese Kokeshi Doll with arms and hands. And the wolf. *Why did he feel he had known that wolf all his life? He'd never seen it before, had he?*

GW Parkway rode the crest of the palisades, rising above the Potomac. As Starkey watched the streetlights across the river on the Maryland side illuminating the Clara Barton parkway along the canal, he lurched upright and stared as the streetlights became obscured. A shimmering whiteness crossed the river towards them, flowed into Sheila's headlights, and closed around the Porsche. Sheila flicked on her high beams but switched them off again.

"What the hell is this, Starkey? A fog?"

"I don't know. I can't see the road. Can you?"

"No, I can't see anything."

"Slow down," Starkey said.

Sheila braked and came to a stop as vertigo began that made Starkey feel dizzy and disoriented.

"Jack, I'm getting seasick, what the hell is happening?"

"I don't know, but I feel it, too."

Starkey sat frozen, blind, and captured in the whiteness, as time seemed to slow. Starkey felt a kind of slipping, and then a lift, as if a tow truck had grabbed on to them and raised the car to its bed. He felt a jolt and sharp movement to the side and the vertigo got worse. The car bounced once and came to a stop. The whiteness gradually thinned and Starkey slowly began to make out their surroundings. They sat beneath a streetlight in a parking lot. Sheila's engine had stalled.

"Jack. Where are we?" Sheila said.

"Well, it looks like the parking lot above the canal by the society island."

"Yes, I know. Jack? One more question. Just how the hell did we get here?"

"I don't know, but I don't like it. Back the car out of here. Let's not hang around to see what happens next."

Sheila tried to start the car, the ignition grinding away, but the engine wouldn't catch. "Jesus, Jack, it won't start."

"Wait. There's something out there in the dark under the trees. No, don't wait. Whatever it is it's coming closer. Start the god damn car, Sheila."

"Can't you see I'm *trying* to start the god damn car, Jack?"

Finally the engine roared and Sheila shifted into reverse, gunning the motor, but the car wouldn't move. The rear tires spun, smoking, but they were held in place, the engine straining.

"There's something over there under the trees at the edge of the parking lot. Someone's moving in the darkness."

The Porsche engine died as a shadow darker than the dark slowly moved towards the car. It approached until it entered the circle of light beneath the street lamp.

Starkey heard the sharp intake of Sheila's breath. "It's Grimes," she said. Grimes neared the car holding the crossbow. The red targeting laser reflected off the windshield. A shadow fell across Starkey's face and his car door jerked open and tore away. Two hands pulled Starkey out of the car and pinned his arms behind him. He struggled to free himself, but failed. He watched Sheila being pulled out as well. *Grimes.* The strange guy from the Society gripped her by one arm, holding the crossbow aloft, but the man misjudged Sheila. She jerked her elbow down and around and smashed it into her attacker's gut and then up again into his face, her *Kiai* resounded off the forest wall mixed with the sound of crunching cartilage. Grimes stumbled, and dropped the crossbow, but still held on to her arm.

Then Starkey heard a shrill, harsh, animal-like cry from above and looked up to see a nightmare. A huge black shape descended on wings, long yellow talons at the end of the wings extended. A grotesque head with three eyes sat in the midst of the wings and a red light blinked on a small metallic panel in the middle of the creature's chest. The talons were aimed at Sheila. It landed on two scaly, clawed leather feet and hopped forward like a giant bird of prey. The talons clutched Sheila by the forearms, cutting deep gouges, blood squirted from the wounds and Sheila cried out.

"No, no, no." Starkey's mind began to scream, over and over until he felt his heart begin to race. He struggled and pulled against his attacker again and again, and sweat began to pour off him. And then everything changed. Starkey felt a current surge through him bringing a razor-sharp clarity of mind. His vision became sharper also and his surroundings grew more distinct, but a crippling wave of intense pain began at the base of his skull and radiated downward. Every cell in his body felt on fire. It seemed to him his skin and flesh and bone were melting in fire, dividing in fire, growing in fire. His back arched in agony and his arm pulled free and flew back. He felt his forearm smash into the skull of his attacker and then Starkey jerked free. Turning, Starkey saw Simmons from the canoeing society fall to the pavement, his skull crushed and shoved down into his shoulders, his brains splattered across the pavement.

As the pain subsided, he turned and saw the nightmare creature flap its leather wings, rising in the air, clutching Sheila with the hand-like appendages at its chest. Then, without thinking Starkey vaulted to the top of the Porsche and into the air, coming down on top of the creature, astride one wing. Clutching the wing, Starkey hammered at the creature's eyes with his fist, smashing two of the three eyes, and yellow fluid exploded from them. The creature shrieked and dropped Sheila. She fell to the ground. The creature crashed down onto the Porsche with Starkey astride its back. Starkey griped the black leathery wings in his hands and pulled back with all his strength, hearing the sounds of tearing muscle and fiber and tortured metal. The creature screamed again. Starkey and the creature rolled off the top of the Porsche and they landed on the ground beside the car, with the creature on top. Starkey held his grip and continued to pull back on the wings. But the creature kicked back at Starkey with spurs on its legs, slicing Starkey's ankles with the claws behind

its feet. Starkey's grip weakened and the creature
pulled one wing free, struggling to rise, but Starkey
held on, raining blows on the back of the creature's
head, denting the leather-like skull. Then Starkey
heard the sound of a helicopter, and looked up to see
it lowering to hover a dozen feet above. Starkey saw
Masato in the cockpit at the controls and the wolf
crouched by the open door. The wolf dove through
the air down onto the chest of the creature. Starkey
heard sounds of ripping and tearing, and then the
wolf leapt down to the ground, clutching something
in its teeth. The wolf had pulled a small, red, screeching body from the winged creature's abdomen and
held it to the ground with one paw, growling and
gnawing at it. The wolf raised it in its jaws and shook
the red thing until the screeching stopped. The
nightmare creature's body that Starkey held went
limp, collapsing, and Starkey shoved it off and away
from him and leaped to his feet. He heard Sheila cry
out. He turned to see Grimes lifting her by her arms.
Starkey reached them in one fierce stride and took
Grimes by the back of the neck and held him aloft in
one hand and squeezed his neck until Grime's bulging eyes began to leak, and then closed. The body of
Grimes went limp. Starkey caught Sheila as she fell
and cradled her with his other arm, lowering her to
the ground. He flung the lifeless body of Grimes
aside.

The wolf brought the body of the small, red creature and laid what Starkey thought must be an Archaran at his feet. The wolf looked up into Starkey eyes. And then Starkey truly began to understand.

They boarded the helicopter. Starkey held Sheila unconscious on his lap as the helicopter rose into the dark.

Masato landed the helicopter on a helipad on the roof of the Protean Society building. Starkey stepped down to the concrete carrying Sheila and followed Masato into an elevator at the back of a tower. He marveled at his new strength. She felt as light as a child to him. Six floors down the elevator door opened and Masato led Starkey down a brightly lit hall of glass and stainless steel. He carried the still unconscious Sheila through a wide door and into a large laboratory. Proteus waited by a stretcher.

"Put her here," Proteus said.

Another SyLF appeared in a doorway across the lab and glided over, gently moving Proteus aside. Shaped like Proteus but slightly smaller, this SyLF possessed a gleaming, brilliant white surface. The SyLF carried blankets and sheets in its arms. Realigning Sheila slightly, the SyLF covered her. The SyLF began to examine the deep cuts and abrasions on Sheila's arms. Starkey heard quiet sounds, very like concern, emanating from the SyLF.

Then it lowered and reached down to touch Starkey's trouser legs where the blood had stained them. "This must wait. The woman's injuries take precedence."

"This is Panacea, and as you might guess from her name, she is our healer," Proteus said.

The Panacea's voice sounded gentle, female, and soothing. "This will block the pain, should she wake up. She held a small device against Sheila's neck. Starkey heard a quiet sound of air pressure Panacea waved a hand held device over Sheila and read the display. She turned to look at Starkey.

"Her vital signs are strong," she said. "She will recover fully, Jack."

"Thank you." Starkey said. "How do you know my name?"

"I have known you since you were born, Jack. I will see to the wounds on your legs soon, have no fear, my son," she said.

"I don't feel any pain," He said.

Panacea pointed to a table where instruments lay. "Proteus, please hand me the laser suture beside you."

Proteus retrieved the instrument from a near-by counter and handed it to her.

She set to work. "This procedure will clean and suture her wounds. I will cover them with plasticast sleeves to protect and rebuild the tissue. Healing will be quick, for it stimulates cell repair and growth, but she has lost some blood. Do you know her blood type, Jack?"

"Yes, I found out when I took her to the emergency room last year. She slipped and cut her leg on some rocks during a portage up on the Shenandoah River where we canoed. She lost a good bit of blood before we got to the hospital. It's O positive."

"Good, we have plenty of that," she said. "I will set up for a transfusion just in case."

Proteus took Starkey's arm, urging him towards the door. "Don't worry, Jack, Panacea will look after her now. Perhaps you and Masato would like to wait in the room next door. Sheila will come to find you there. I know you have questions, and Masato is the one to explain what's happened to you."

Starkey followed Masato into an office door. Starkey sat down in a deep leather chair. He felt completely disoriented, as if he wore someone else's body. The wolf came and sat down next to him. Starkey put out his hand automatically and stroked the animal's head. The wolf lay down by his chair.

The room around them silent, Starkey felt the beginnings of a nausea start, but something within him rose and quelled it. An injection of well-being. A strengthening.

"We're going to have to get you some new clothes, Jack." Masato said.

Starkey looked down at himself. His clothes were stained with Sheila's blood and his own, and he saw that, unaccountably, his pants were too short and his shirt too tight. It strained at the shoulders. The sleeves fell three inches too short. *Cripes, I've grown again.*

Panacea came in and cleaned and attended to his ankles where the creature sliced his skin, he saw that the wounds closed rapidly. He felt drowsy, his eyelids growing heavy. She left as quietly as she came. Starkey dozed again. He awoke to Masato speaking.

"When the change comes there is much pain and then you grow larger. I know, as it happened to me. Ten years ago Hiro and I were the same size. We are only half-brothers, you see. The Archarans abducted my mother—my father's first wife—but not Hiro's. Like you, Proteus rescued me, and returned me to my father later, protecting me until the threat passed."

"What change?" Starkey whispered as the room began to fade away. He didn't hear Masato's answer. He fell sound asleep.

Starkey woke with Sheila's hand on his shoulder. She stood over him, smiling, with Masato sitting nearby. Her forearms were covered with smooth white sleeves that looked like plastic, but otherwise she looked great—beaming in fact.

"How do you feel? You've been asleep for an hour. Wow, what's happened to your clothes? They've shrunk." Sheila asked. "No, you've grown. A lot. But that's impossible isn't it? Before I passed out, I thought I saw you fly through the air and attack that monster. What happened? Panacea wouldn't tell me anything. Can you believe her name?"

"Slow down, Sheila, I'm just waking up here. First, I didn't fly. I sort of jumped on your car and then onto the monster," Starkey said. "I think the wolf killed it when he pulled the red thing out of the monster's chest. I just held on for dear life. I think Masato began to explain it to me before I fell asleep."

Masato began again. "Last night, Proteus told you about the enemy, the Archarans, who have broken the galactic covenants and mined scandium and other rare earths here on the planet, exporting them off-world. He also told you the enemy kidnaps pregnant human mothers and modifies the DNA sequences in the unborn fetus to create worker-slaves. Pro-teus stopped short of telling you what would happen when you confronted these Archarans and their crea-tures, the Okees, and their deadly force for the first time." He paused then went on. "Think about it, Jack, have you ever faced violent death before? No, I don't mean the sad death of your wife or even Ethan's sui-cide, but an attack, an immediate threat of violent death to you or someone you love?"

Starkey saw Sheila stir at this—someone you love. "No, I guess I hadn't, until now." *How does he know about Jane and Ethan?*

"Because Proteus saw to it you did not. You have been watched over all your life, in recent years by my brother." Masato paused and leaned forward in the chrome chair. "Proteus used many generations to refine his methods of developing warriors like us, and he believes it is best to keep them unaware of their identity until the fullness of time. But this time he miscalculated. He did not predict your abduction at the canal today."

Masato stood up and moved closer to Stark-ey. "You were followed, and our drone relayed the live feed, but we were too slow to avoid the confron-tation. Yet, we always knew it would come some-time. Your realization of your destiny begins now, Jack."

Starkey and Sheila looked at each other. Questions flooded in to Starkey's mind, but Sheila spoke first. "So Grimes and Simmons were genetically modified humans working for these Archarans? Ok, I get that, but what was that monster?"

Masato told them he didn't know its true name. The Archarans brought them from off-world and modified them to be their surface transportation, their means of interaction, and a weapon. "The small red creature Wolf killed was an Archaran. Earth's gravity is too much for their frail bodies. Hannah's people called the monster the Archarans use an Okee."

"Well, I guess it appears I have to take back what I said last night about space alien bullshit, Jack," Sheila said. She removed her hand from his shoulder and pulled over a metal chair. It scraped on the cool white tile floor, echoing in the silence that hung around her words.

Starkey reached over and touched her face. "It's ok, Sheila. Masato, all this doesn't explain what happened to me when we were attacked. What is the 'change'? All I know is it hurt like hell, and I know I should have been afraid of that monster. But I felt anger, not fear."

Masato looked into Starkey's eyes for a moment, as if gauging his recovery, and seemed to come to a decision. "Jack, I will try to explain. You underwent a global change in your genome, the hereditary information in your DNA."

Masato explained to Starkey that the violent threat to Starkey's life and Sheila's triggered the change because Starkey's DNA held, as Proteus told him, an additional alien sequence. Until the first attack at that canal that sequence remained dormant. Tonight Starkey's fight or flight response during the attack completed a massive epigenetic change, a chemical change that turned on the alien DNA sequence. The pain Starkey felt accompanies the first stage when the surface receptors in every cell in the body enhance skeletal bone density, and size and muscle oxygenation increase. In other words, he got bigger, faster, and mentally and emotionally stronger.

"There's more of course, how much do you want to know?" Masato said.

"I want to know how to make it stop. I don't want to be some kind of comic book freak," Starkey said.

"I am sorry, Jack, there's no going back. And this isn't the comic books, Jack, this is as real as it gets. But we are not alone. You are about to join Proteus' Warriors."

"Proteus' Warriors?" Starkey said. "Who the hell are they? How many are there?"

"They are the warriors that battle our ancient enemy, the Archarans. As to how many there are, that depends on how many answer the call," Masato said. "We shall see. There have been many over the centuries. How many are still living, I am not sure."

Sheila stood up and moved to place both hands on Jack's shoulders. "How do you feel now?"

Starkey took stock. "I feel fantastic, really." Starkey stood up straight and stretched even higher, extending his arms. For the first time, when he looked down into Sheila's eyes, Starkey realized he felt love for her, love uncompromised by the past. But he still didn't say it out loud. Wolf stood up beside him.

Hannah came in with a stack of clothes and shoes and gave them to Masato. "Put these on, Jack, they are mine," Masato said, taking them from her. "A little large, perhaps, but you'll soon grow into them. The growth associated with the metamorphosis has not stopped, you may rest assured." Masato stood up. "I will take you back to Sheila's car. You can assess the damage and see if it can be driven. I believe the threat is over for tonight. The enemy forces will not attack again so soon. Yes, you have destroyed some of them, but they are not alone. We believe they will have to regroup. You may return to your homes for now, but we will need to meet here again tomorrow to talk about the future. This is far from over."

"When will we be able to go back to our old lives, Masato?" Sheila asked.

"I'm sorry, but you won't ever. Your lives have changed beyond all reversal," Masato said. "The truth about who you are, Jack Starkey, has opened doors that cannot be closed. Yes, and introduced you to worlds far beyond what you knew."

CHAPTER NINETEEN

EREBUS

CABIN JOHN, MD FRIDAY JUNE 2 4AM

Dave Vaughn woke, startled from a restless sleep. At first simply uneasy, he soon began to feel a kind of unfocused fear growing and spreading inside him like burning grass. Vaughn sat up and his eyes searched the gloom of the bedroom. The feeling he was not alone crept over him, cut into him, but at first he saw nothing. A voice from a shadow among shadows spoke in a sibilant, harsh whisper. Vaughn knew the voice. *Erebus, shit.*

Forcing down his panic and revulsion at the sound of the voice, Vaughn rose and moved into the living room of the small townhouse. Erebus floated ahead of him, barely visible in the dim light of street

lamps outside the windows. Vaughn stood and waited. Seven years had passed almost to the day since he
first heard that voice. He had tried very hard to forget
about its owner. Mostly he'd succeeded. As the years
passed the terror and despair faded, and the revelations of that night about his origin and mutation grew
less and less real. Until now, that is.

When he could stand the silence no longer,
Vaughn spoke to the figure that hovered in the
blackness of a corner. "What the fuck do you want,
Erebus?"

"Jack Starkey, the man you were assigned to
watch, has become a problem," Erebus said.

"Starkey? What could he do?"

"He and other M-Museon agents have destroyed an Okee, an overlord, and two human slaves.
In the process, they have compromised the mining
operation below the Potomac River, and now I need
an agent to handle several tasks until others arrive
from off-world." Erebus said.

"I don't give a damn. I don't want to know
anything about any of that. Go away and leave me
the hell alone."

Erebus went on as if he didn't hear. "The
common need for secrecy of our enemy and us m-
may yet save our operation, but we must eliminate
those who have gained knowledge of our presence
and destroy the M-museon SyLF and his soldiers."

Vaughn's legs began to tremble and he fought to control it. "No, please don't make me do it. I don't want to be a part of your operation."

Erebus' voice became a hiss. "Oh, yes, you will do it Indian m-man, you are ours—we m-made you. You and your father and his fathers have been bred for this very purpose." Erebus opened his cloak to reveal a small control panel on his chest. He flew forward and clutched Vaughn's shoulder and pressed a stunner against Vaughn's neck. Vaughn felt his consciousness drain away.

When Vaughn came to, he lay on the wet grass in front of his father's little house trailer in Cabin John, Md. His head ached, and he felt dizzy. Lifting his head saw the single, bare light bulb that lit the entrance of the trailer. The trailer sat on the back of the last loop of the rundown trailer park, now surrounded by a dim, murky dawn. His father stood on the top step looking down at him, his thin, bent form haloed in the trailer's light. His father looked frightened, but his voice sounded determined when he spoke to someone behind Vaughn.

"You. I thought we were done with you. What have you done to my son?"

Vaughn heard the now familiar, harsh voice behind him. "I have done little so far, but I can kill him now, Indian m-man, or he can live. The Okee will gut you both like animals. Your son will fulfill his destiny, or you will both die here and now."

A rasping, guttural noise like a giant vulture's screech sounded above and Vaughn looked up. A huge pterodactyl-like shape perched on top of the trailer. He watched as the monster flapped its dark wings once and dropped to the ground. It hopped towards Vaughn's father, long yellow talons extended forward from its chest. The old man shrank backwards, falling into the doorway.

Vaughn, struggling, cried out. "God damn you, Erebus—stop that thing. Don't let it hurt him."

A metallic, clicking, somehow like laughter, came from Erebus. "Too late, Indian m-man, the Okee is going to have to hurt him a little now."

"Stop, I'll do whatever you want," Vaughn begged now. "Just don't hurt him."

"Yes, yes, you will. You will do everything we ask. Watch and r-remember, Indian m-man."

Vaughn struggled to rise, but something held him to the ground as if by a tremendous weight. Sweat began to pour from him and his heart began to pound in his ears as he strained to move. Then a sudden change began. His senses seemed to sharpen. The murk around him grew lighter. He could hear the monster breathing heavily as it approached his father. Its rank, fetid stench attacked his nostrils. Then he heard his own heart beating, quickening. The bitter taste of bile filled his mouth. He felt a sudden surge of strength, but simultaneously the pain began. Intense pain, more and more pain. It burned—it seared, as if his bloodstream carried lava, as if his heart pumped pain that flowed from his head down throughout his body. Fire seemed to rage over the surface of his body, as if the skin would soon stretch, tear, flame up, blacken, and peel away.

Even in the midst of his agony, Vaughn saw the Okee seize his father and lift him into the air. The old man screamed as the talons tore into the flesh of his arms and chest. Flinging the old man to the ground, the monster placed one three-clawed foot on his chest. It leaned over him, thrusting its beak forward as if to bite the old man's face. Desperate, Vaughn thrust his anger and fear deep inside himself and felt a barrier fall as he struggled to rise. His father screamed again and struggled to avoid the maw of the hideous creature.

Vaughn felt himself growing still stronger, until at last he rose under the crushing weight that held him down. He leaped to his feet, flexing his arms and hands as more power flowed into them and at last the pain subsided. He sensed his body growing taller and wider, his arms thickening and growing longer.

With a loud cry Vaughn charged forward to attack the Okee as it bent over his father's writhing body. It turned towards him, lifted its head, and gave a deafening, high-pitched screech.

Then Vaughn heard Erebus's voice command him. "Halt, Indian m-man, or your father dies now."

Vaughn's body stiffened and froze in response to the voice command. Though he struggled to resist, he was forcibly turned around to face Erebus. He saw the SyLF held a crossbow, the laser light targeting his father's head.

The Okee straightened up. A small panel opened in the monster's chest revealing a small, red, vaguely humanoid shape. Erebus addressed the creature whose three eyes shone forth in the gloom. "Lord, I ask that you take the Okee and withdraw."

The monster snarled, but slowly removed its foot from old man's chest and withdrew further into the darkness beyond the trailer's weak circle of yellow light.

A small, whining, metallic voice answered. "Control these monkeys, Erebus. I grow tired of this dalliance." The creature flapped its wings and, rising, disappeared up into the night.

Vaughn sensed his release and began to move toward his father's side.

"Stop there, Indian m-man. Approach and stand near me."

Vaughn stopped, wooden once more, and moved stiffly to comply. Erebus pressed something

in his control panel and Vaughn watched as everything, the trailer and the forest and his father's still
body began to shimmer and fade into whiteness.

Vaughn stood captured in the whiteness, disoriented, as time seemed to slow. The whiteness gradually thinned. He found himself in a dank tunnel with
walls of cut stone. Banks of lights high above lit the
scene. He stood at the entrance to an immense cavern
where giant machines moved, some carrying loads of
rock and dirt. Vaughn saw there were no operators
on the machines.

"Now, Indian m-man, you will listen."

Vaughn turned to the sound of the harsh
voice and saw the hood and robe were gone. A shape
of lustrous black floated beside him, two feet off the
cavern floor. The spherical head appeared featureless, save for the cold blue lights that flickered and
danced across the luminous face. The ovoid body
carried two arm-like appendages that extended as if
from shoulders. Vaughn saw himself reflected in the
brilliant black of Erebus' body. Lit by the bank of
lights overhead, his reflection revealed the now great
size of Vaughn's shoulders and arms and the increased height of his body. If it didn't hurt so damn
bad, he would have thought he hallucinated.

"What have you done to me, Erebus? I'm
stretched or something."

"I gave you a little pain to r-remind you who you are. And the Okee hurt your father a little to give you a dose of re-reality. You are mine to use as I see fit. Your little pain and suffering triggered a change, a change in your DNA. I placed an additional alien sequence in your ancestors that re-remained dormant until I chose to call it forth. It increases skeletal bone density and size and muscle until you are a useful tool for my purposes. That is all you need to know."

One hand-shaped, three-fingered glove held articles of clothing out to Vaughn. The other held a handgun-shaped weapon aimed at his chest. The crossbow from before was replaced with something even more threatening.

"Here, put these on," Erebus said.

Vaughn took the offered clothes. "What are you?" He stripped off his shredded pajamas. "How did we get here?"

"I am a Synthetic Life Form. SyLF, if you like."

"Where are we and how'd we get here?"

"We are deep below the Potomac R-river where we mine the r-rare form of scandium oxide we ship off-world. It is one of only a few such mines on your planet. As for how we got here, it is a Molecular Vector Re-recombinator, but MoVR or just Mover will do for your simple mind. It disintegrates, trans-ports, and re-reintegrates ma-matter."

"Let me go back to my father," Vaughn said. "He needs help."

"Soon. He will survive. You and your kin are tough in fiber, and heal quickly. You will learn this. First you must know your tasks. You will kill Jack Starkey and Sheila Cartwright."

Vaughn jerked his head back in surprise. "You mean the guy from the pub? Kill Jack Starkey? Kill him? What's he got do with this?"

"He has become an agent of that old fool Proteus, our enemy. It is Proteus who stings us like a wasp and moves away to hide, always working a clandestine, minimalist campaign. He strives to keep the pitiful humans ignorant of our operations, but that is in our favor as well. He is soft and m-maternal about these humans, and therefore weak."

Why does it keep stuttering? "But I've never killed anyone. I wouldn't know how, no matter what you've done to me." Vaughn said, staring at the bulging muscles in his arms and thighs as he put on the sweat shirt and pants.

"Then you will learn. You will use your size and strength to do our bidding, the task for which you were bred."

Vaughn raised his head to stare at Erebus. He began to understand, but his fear caused him to lower his eyes in submission. Erebus floated nearer and seized Vaughn's right arm in a fierce grip. "Now you know enough. Go and kill Starkey and his woman, Sheila Cartwright. Ma-make it look like an accident if you can, but kill them or you and your father die. Begin with the woman. Starkey will be with her. I will return you now to your father's home. A higher overlord is coming from the home world. His ship bends space even as we speak. We must be ready when he arrives."

Vaughn watched as Erebus and the cave began to fade to white.

>>>

Erebus moved swiftly through the cavern's bedrock corridors, deeper into the mine. He passed giant prospecting, mining drones that moved silently in rough-hewn, excavated tunnels. Erebus had ordered mining to continue, but he halted off-world shipments, and he knew the overlords would not be pleased. Nevertheless, protocols demanded a halt until the resolution of the security breach.

Erebus entered a chamber off the main tunnel that held a control room. He approached the central console and moved his hands over the orange lights of the surface that gleamed in the dimness of the chamber. He waited, watching the large, oval screen. A small red figure emerged, shimmering, from the darkness. It sat in the hollow of a larger, half seen structure, suspended and surrounded with controls. An umbilical connection emerged from behind the figure's side, connecting to the adjacent, striated wall of its recess. Three bulging yellow eyes stared out of the small, vaguely humanoid, hairless head. The third of the large eyes formed the apex of a triangle in the forehead. The tiny hands and wrists that gripped controls emerged from the chest and were covered with three fingered-gloves. The distorted face twisted in an ugly leer.

"Well, Erebus, have you dealt with Proteus and his pathetic humans? We do not appreciate being called on to resolve these petty matters."

"No Prefect Ukruek, our efforts have failed and the situation worsens. I fear Proteus' Warriors m-may risk exposure. They are angry and overconfident since their re-recent encounter with the Okee and an overlord at the canal," Erebus said.

"What has changed? The monkeys have been more timid in the past."

"Exposure ma-may mean less to them now than defeating us. I suspect that they may r-reason exposure could be in their favor. Or Proteus m-may be losing control."

"Why have you not repaired your vocalization circuits? Your stuttering grows more and more irritating."

"I have told you r-repeatedly that I need off-planet r-resources. You have r-refused to supply them."

The Prefect's sneer grew sharper. "You are far from our first priority, Erebus. We are not pleased with the manner in which you have handled this situation. You have failed to eliminate the pitiful humans involved. They have remained alive long after threatening our operations. Perhaps it is time to replace you with someone more, shall we say, effective?"

Erebus dissembled, attempting to shift the blame for failure to the sub-overlords and their Okee hosts, accusing those assigned to earth oversaw the onsite operations of carelessness, but he knew the overlords seldom accepted responsibility for failure. The blame would be placed on him, no matter the circumstances. The fact that sub-overlords were present on the planet and shared the failure meant little.

The flashing lights within Erebus dimmed. "I assure you I have taken every step possible within the r-restrictions you place on us. Your protocols forbid us to use more than the most primitive of weapons and methods with these humans, and have forced us to engage them as we have for hundreds of years."

"Grake your excuses for failure, they mean nothing to us. Halt all operations. Bring together our remaining agents and wait for our arrival. Is the mole you have planted within Proteus' midst providing you with the enemy's plans?"

"Yes, Prefect."

"Good. We want to know what Proteus' warriors intend in order to determine what actions are necessary upon our arrival in orbit. In the meantime, seal and disguise the entries to the mines. It must be impossible for the earthlings to discover or enter these sites until we determine how to proceed. This would all be much easier if our graking scientists would come up with a way to use the MoVR to transport scandium through space without it destroying itself in the process."

"Our mole has discovered little, but our efforts continue. I promise it will be as you order, Prefect," Erebus said. *Grake yourself, Ukruek. I hope your arrogance opens you to defeat and Proteus and the humans destroy you.*

CHAPTER TWENTY

WOLF

SILVER SPRING, MD FRIDAY JUNE 2 6:30AM

The Porsche had stood up to the heavy weight of the monster pretty well. The roof did cave a bit, but only a few inches. The headliner crowded the heads of Starkey and Sheila now, but the car was drivable. But surveying the damage solidified the reality of what had happened.

The wolf rode back with them in the helicopter, and remained with them after Masato set them down in a quiet clearing near the car. Starkey didn't question this—somehow it just seemed right. The wolf barely fit in the small back bench seat of the 911, hanging over between the bucket seats. Starkey squeezed in with some difficulty. The Porsche just wasn't designed for someone his size—his new size. The wolf sat silent, watching ahead, his head between Starkey's and Sheila's.

Sheila drove them back to her house. Starkey supposed neither of them saw a need to discuss it. It only made sense for them to stay together. Sheila rolled down the windows and welcomed the cool air into the car, thinking of Wolf. She placed her hand on Starkey's in between shifting. She turned frequently to look at him. Starkey tried to understand the changing looks on her face he saw there. Some looks were of warmth. Some might be gratitude. Some might be a new respect. But there seemed to be looks of wonderment, too, and maybe a little fear, he thought. But Sheila holding on to his hand for so long was a new experience. He liked it. He also liked the feeling of his new body. The strength, even in exhaustion, exhilarated him and an extreme sense of well-being uplifted him. He realized he ought to have been afraid and traumatized, but he wasn't. *Well, maybe a little.*

They got out of the car in the dim light of dawn. Starkey looked carefully around them, scanning the sidewalk and street and the tidy brick ramblers mostly surrounded by spruce and pine. The wolf walked across the front yard, circled the house, and came back to Starkey and looked up into his eyes. Starkey thought the look meant reassurance.

Starkey gazed up into the dark sky where the first pale, yellow pink light of sunrise appeared in the east. The old friendly stars, so commonplace and benign before, hung silently above them. Now he saw them as teeming with life, and some of it wasn't so benign. A chill ran down his back.

"Are you hungry?" Sheila asked, once they were inside.

"Ravenous. Do you have eggs? I'd kill for an omelet." He paused. "Sorry, poor choice of words. And do you have something for Wolf?"

Sheila looked in her refrigerator. "I've got eggs. I'd guess wolves eat raw meat. I do have some ground chuck. Perhaps he'd like some water, too? I can make you a cheese omelet." Starkey took the food and water from her and placed in front of the wolf. The animal waited, looking at Starkey.

"Go ahead, boy," Starkey said. The wolf began to eat.

Starkey and Sheila sat at the table and ate in a comfortable silence. Starkey watched Sheila's face, and thought he saw the events of the night play back behind her eyes, but he felt reluctant to speak of it yet. He quite enjoyed the new, silent closeness and the feeling of calm between them. Sheila rose without speaking and cleared the dishes away. The wolf went to the kitchen door and turned to look back at Starkey. Starkey stood and opened the door for him.

Sheila watched the wolf go out. "I hope he doesn't wander too far. He'll scare the living hell out of the neighbors if they see him."

Starkey held the door open and stepped out on the porch. "He will circle the house again and come back, I think."

"How do you know that?"

"I don't know how I know. I just do. Or I think I do."

Sheila sat back down at the kitchen table and waved to him to come closer. She put her arms around his waist and pulled him close. Her arms didn't make it all the way around. "Your new size is going to take some getting used to." She paused and leaned back to look up at him. "The question is what do we do now? I don't mean right now, I know we need to rest and sleep. But what do we do tomorrow? And the next day? Can you go back to work looking like this? How do we go on with our lives?"

"Tomorrow isn't yet here. I'm being here now, Sheila. And right now I feel like Basho's haiku."

"In my new clothing
I feel so different,
 I must
look like someone else"

Sheila stared at him. "Where did that come from?"

"I don't know, really. It just popped into my mind," he said.

There came a quiet sound at the door. Starkey opened it and the wolf walked in on silent paws. Wolf sat down and looked at each of them in turn. Starkey thought he looked satisfied and reassuring.

"There's way too much to think about now." Starkey reached down to rest his hand on Wolf's head. "I don't know if it will be any easier to answer your questions tomorrow. But can we sleep now?"

Sheila took his hand and led him to her bedroom. She sat him down on the bed and helped him undress, pausing to gently touch the muscles that moved in his back and shoulders, and rolled him under the covers. He watched as she undressed, turned off the lights and slipped into the bed beside him. Starkey nearly fell asleep almost instantly, but he felt her body slide closer and she rested her head on his shoulder. She reached out and put her hand on his chest, lightly touching him, and moved her leg over on top of his. This time he didn't feign sleep or make excuses as in the past. This time he turned and opened to her completely. Waves of love and tenderness flowed out from inside him and he felt the waves return from her. Then desire and passion gathered and rose and surged past the emotional dam that had blocked him so painfully in the past. But he hesitated.

"Are you in pain? Should we wait?" Starkey asked.

"I want you now."

When Starkey woke, Sheila's clock read 11:30. Wolf stood up and came round to his side of the bed. "Good morning, boy." Wolf came forward and allowed the hand on his head. *There is no subservience there.*

Sheila rolled over to face him. "Hey, Big Boy. So last night was real. I thought perhaps I dreamed it. After we made love, I lay awake next to you for a while. I saw Wolf sitting in the corner near the foot of the bed and at first it bothered me he'd watched us. He looked alert, and seemed to be listening. But before I drifted off, Wolf came over and looked into my eyes with such affection. Then he lay down beside my side of the bed. I remember feeling safe, and I wished he would watch over me forever."

"I dreamed about him also, and Proteus." Starkey told her about the long series of past scenes played back in the dream. He'd heard Proteus' voice speaking to him. First while he played on the sidewalk as a small child, and then riding his bike in front of the house where he grew up on Woodridge Street in Kensington, Md. Wolf was there in the dream watching him from a distance. When Starkey got older and Ethan was small, Wolf watched when he walked with his wife in Rock Creek Park. Starkey carried Ethan on his shoulders, and then played catch with him. Wolf, or a wolf that looked like him, watched from the trees on the hill above them, standing sentinel.

"It was a dream, yes, but they were things I believe really happened."

Starkey took a shower and returned to dress in Masato's clothes. *I must find some of my own today, though the clothes do seem to fit perfectly this morning.*

He went to the bed side and sat down beside Sheila. He took her hand and held it in his, and spoke quietly to her.

"Before last night, I'd been blind to who I truly was and what was actually going on around me." Starkey pulled her hand from under the patchwork quilt and held it. "Most of the people in the world still know nothing of the Archarans. Perhaps that's for the best. But now it seems like it's my job to take part in this unseen war, confronting the enemy we now know exists. I wasn't happy with my life at all before now. But I wouldn't have chosen this. I am not the hero type."

Sheila squeezed his hand hard. "You weren't the hero type before. I kicked your ass to get you moving half the time. But the Jack Starkey I knew before didn't leap thirty feet in the air and bring that monster down, or rescue me from those men, or zombies, or whatever they were. You did."

"Yes, but what about our old lives?" Starkey lowered his head rubbed his temples. Then he looked up again at Sheila. "What have I become? What about my job? What about your job? Can I go back to work knowing all this? Can you go back to your life as it was without living in constant fear? What the hell do we do now? We've still got to eat and pay the rent, or mortgage, or whatever."

"Now we do the tasks in front of us at this moment." Sheila rose, pushed her chair back, and put both hands on his shoulders. "We need breakfast. You need to buy some clothes and then we go as planned back to the Protean Society to rejoin Proteus and Masato. Just take one step at a time. You said last night you were being here now. Focus, Jack,"

"Yes, ok, you're right. I have little choice in any case. Masato said it. There's no going back. It's just, well, the old Jack Starkey is still in here somewhere, you see, and I think he's scared."

"You are not alone, Jack. Remember what Master Yamashima has taught us—a true warrior is not fearless, but he channels his body's response to fear into heightened awareness and capability. That is exactly what you did yesterday."

"Master Yamashima, of course," Starkey sat down. "We need to talk to him. He knew about Masato and the Archarans long before. He can help me to accept this and adapt to what has happened. Next to you, Sheila, I trust him more than anyone alive." That brought a smile to her face.

>>>

Michael August, Yamashima's assistant, answered the phone on the second ring. "The Master expected your call, Jack. I will see if he will speak to you now." Now Starkey knew what it was that bothered him about August. The man's tone carried a subtle irony, sarcasm, or condescension.

After a short pause, the Master began without preamble. "I am glad you called, Jack. We waited for this. Yes, what you have learned from my brother, Masato, and Proteus is true and as real as it gets in what we call this life. I anticipated Proteus might reveal all this to you sooner. But that is old news. I am sorry I could not answer you completely before, but it was not my story to tell. Now a crisis is upon us. I believe the Archarans and their soldiers will try to kill you and all those connected with you in order to preserve the secrecy of their operation here."

"Master, I don't understand why you didn't tell me yourself. You have been my mentor and friend. I feel somewhat blind-sided by all this," Starkey said.

"I am sorry I could not tell you before. Proteus leads our forces and we all must follow his direction. I strove to prepare you mentally and physically through our martial arts for what lay ahead."

"I see that, and I guess you have." Starkey said. "I still don't see why you couldn't have given me a clue to all this."

"Would you have believed me if I told you that you were abducted by aliens and rescued by a Synthetic Life Form?"

"Well, I…" Starkey started to argue but then realized he wouldn't have believed it. So he said nothing.

The Master went on. "You will be asking yourself what to do next. The answer is not easy, but I believe a confrontation is coming. An Okee has been killed, and not just the creature itself, but the Archaran that controlled and exploited it. We believe they have a SyLF operating here also. There may be time for planning, but we must hurry. I will meet you at the Protean Society this afternoon."

"I understand and I will do as you say, Master. But must I bring Sheila with me? I'd like to avoid putting her in danger again, if I can."

"I am afraid it's too late for that. Don't underestimate her. The forces of the enemy will be gathering, and we must all stand together. We'll be there."

Jack hung up. "Sheila, we must go to Proteus this afternoon, the Master will meet us there. Can you cancel your Taekwondo classes and let them know you'll be unavailable for a while?"

"What about my students? They depend on me. I can't just disappear on them." Sheila said.

"Just tell them you've got a family crisis out of town or something, and you'll let them know when you're back."

"All right, this is going to upset a lot of things. I may lose my job, you know. But I suppose we have no choice. How long should I say?" Sheila asked.

Starkey shrugged. "I don't know how long. It's a brand new ballgame. I'm going to call my office and tell them I need leave for a few weeks. They may fire me, or want a doctor's note or some justification. We'll just have to see what happens. I think we know what we need to know about the obsidian and the arrow. Make the call and then we'll go shopping."

"Shopping? You? Last time you bought new clothes I dragged you there by the collar."

"This is your chance to dress me in the style you'd like me to become accustomed to."

CHAPTER TWENTY-ONE

DAMN THE COVENANTS

GEORGETOWN, DC FRIDAY
JUNE 2 5PM

Hannah Cassidy opened the Protean Society door and welcomed Starkey and Sheila. Hannah's strong-featured face looked more worn and worried than the night before. She turned and led them down the wood-paneled hall to the large, double doors. Their steps rang hollow on the oak floor. Wolf walked beside Starkey. The wolf's shoulder tracked his left side. Sheila stepped behind the two and followed them. Somehow overnight they had become a unit, their relationship clearly defined. No words were necessary.

They found Masato seated in the same deep, red leather chair as before, with his brother, Hiro, beside him. Proteus floated a few inches off the dark blue oriental rugs next to them. The midday sun shone through the clerestory windows above and reflected in the silver surface of Proteus' chassis. Michael August, Master Yamashima's assistant, stood behind the Master.

Proteus waved one glove to indicate the two remaining chairs. "Starkey and Sheila come in and sit down. We have just begun." Wolf sat down between them.

Proteus hovered before a huge painting of John Locke. "I expect the Archarans to respond with violence to the confrontation at the canal soon." He waved his hand and the painting faded away, now replaced by a real-time display of the earth. "These red circles indicate locations of suspected alien installations as well as the one we now know exists under the Potomac River."

"What are the aliens likely to do now that we've discovered them there beneath the island?" Starkey asked.

"If they follow the same protocol as in other confrontations in the past, I believe they will shut down the mining operations temporarily and disguise the site. In the past another overlord-bearing Okee arrived from off world or transferred from another site on earth," Proteus said.

"You mean there are more of these overlords and Okees here on earth?" Sheila asked.

"Yes, Sheila," Proteus said. "We have evidence that one oversaw mining in Northern Russia, and perhaps one more operates in the Japanese Archipelago, north of Hokkaido."

Starkey saw Master Yamashima stir at this, but the Master said nothing.

Proteus told them they could expect no help from off-world until circumstances convinced the Inner Council of the United Planets that intervention was justified. The Archarans shared no such restrictions, and would likely be sending support.

Sheila stood and interrupted. "So you're telling us these aliens, these *Archarans*, can send all these reinforcements down here and your people will stand by and do nothing?"

A long silence followed. Starkey smiled at her, shaking his head. *She gets right at it.*

"She's right," Master Yamashima said. "This is unacceptable."

Proteus raised both hands. "We must tread carefully. Fortunately the Archaran home world lies at the other end of the galaxy, and even allowing for bending space a few days may be necessary for that support to arrive."

"The Archarans are unlikely to act," Masato said, "until a higher overlord arrives. Events have now escalated, and no doubt one would be summoned since they will suspect there exists a serious security threat to their mining operations."

"Yes," Proteus said, "and there is no guarantee we have even a few days—so we must prepare now. We must attempt to predict the Archaran's response, and marshal our resources. But first, Masato, do we face a threat from forces already on earth?"

Masato updated them on the search for an alien mining site in the islands to the north of the Japanese mainland, but no tangible evidence had been found. Fisherman told stories of strange sightings, underwater shapes, lights and distant sounds in the seas, but there were thousands of islands to search. "So far, we have found nothing concrete. If you have information, Proteus, we will act on it."

"Unfortunately, no." Proteus told them that unusual seismic activity detected near Etorofu in the Kuril Islands that the Russians call Iturp concerned him also. It might be an indicator that the deep disposal of waste salt water associated with the Archaran's scandium oxide extraction set off minor earthquakes in that area. However, other possible explanations existed for these events, and the Russians did not publish the whereabouts of fracking operations or methane extraction, for example.

Proteus returned to the display of Locke's portrait. "So there again we have no useful data, only suspicions."

Sheila interrupted again. "Why can't we just call the police or the army and send them down into the tunnels under the river? We wouldn't have to mention aliens. We could just report suspicious activities, and the investigation would lead to their discovery."

"No, Sheila, that option is not open to us. The Archarans will have sealed those caverns and removed any evidence. Even the communicating of knowledge of off-world intelligence and other inhabited worlds is forbidden. Accidents may happen, but direct information may not be given."

Starkey placed his hand on Sheila's shoulder. "Sheila has a point. How we can we face this challenge alone? We are the rookies here, I realize, but it seems to me it doesn't much matter whether these Okees come from Japan or Russia or from outer space. If they show up and attack us, we're screwed. There are only five of us, not counting Wolf. They would go through us like Sherman across Georgia."

"You're not wrong, Jack, but there is hope," Proteus said. He explained that the Archarans didn't particularly care about breaking the covenants of the United Planets, but secrecy made it safer for them to continue to mine and transport the scandium ore as they had done in the past. Discovery by the earth's nations would force the United Planets Council to act. Trade sanctions against the Archarans at the least, and possibly intergalactic police action would result. These possible consequences were bad for business and profits. The Archarans were here for the gigantic profits of mining and marketing rare earths in the galaxy. But they would resort to concealed violence, since they knew Proteus' group was bound by the covenants to keep secret the presence of aliens on Earth. The Archarans sought what human covert agencies call 'plausible deniability'.

"Does that deniability explain," Sheila asked, "why they use the crossbows and the arrows instead of ray guns or something?"

Proteus moved closer to her when he answered. "Yes, but don't be fooled. They have far more deadly and advanced weapons at their disposal, and will have no qualms about using them where secrecy is thought possible—or failure of their enterprise seems imminent."

"Okay, okay. I get it," Starkey said, "but what do we do *now*?"

Masato broke the silence that followed. "Defending ourselves is one issue, Proteus, but there is also the overarching issue of ridding the earth of this enemy who…"

"I take these two issues as one only," Master Yamashima said, interrupting his brother. "I believe we must not wait to be attacked—that time is past. Too long we have sat ignoring the clandestine crimes of our enemy through fear of discovery. We must attack while the Archarans are wounded and vulnerable."

"But, Hiro, we must remember we don't know the full extent of their forces on the surface or in space above," Masato said.

"Also Hiro, what about the Inner Council? What about the covenants?" Proteus said.

"Damn the covenants." Master Yamashima's voice became strident. "Live with cause and leave results to the great law of the universe. Must our species continue to be brutalized in the name of those covenants while the leaders of the galaxy sit in chambers and play at politics and intrigue? No, we do not know the extent of their forces, nor they ours. While we sit cowering, the Archarans grow bolder, gather strength, and continue to abduct our people and commit their atrocities. No, we must go down into this cavern and destroy them there and their machines. And we must marshal our forces here and worldwide in order to do so."

Masato turned to his brother. "I agree, but we few are not enough, Hiro. We must first call our brother and sister Warriors around the world—we must gather the faithful."

"Wait, how many more are there?" Starkey asked.

Proteus moved in front of Master Yamashima. "What you suggest could jeopardize thousands of years of careful secrecy. Our responses to the Archarans have historically been defensive, occurring only when threatened and then carefully restrained. We have rescued individuals that have been genetically altered, yes, but we have always acted in response, where our actions could still be interpreted as defensive. I don't have the authority to go fully on the offensive. My charter is for human development, not violence."

Masato forged on. "Does that mean you are not capable of violence, Proteus?"

"Theoretically, no, and it is true the circumstances have changed. Technically we didn't have the authority to defend ourselves either, but I thought justification could be made." Proteus waved his hand and John Locke's portrait reappeared.

Starkey watched Proteus as the SyLF stared at the group in silence for long minutes. Finally Proteus spoke. "But my children, I fear you are right. We have no choice. I will put out the call to the Warriors. I will also contact the Museons, my creators, and our other supporters who sit on the council. I have provided them with intelligence in the past, but the council has been reluctant to use force. Violence is anathema to the Museons."

But Starkey would have his clarity. "Could someone please answer my question, Proteus? Are there others like me?"

"Yes, Jack, there are. It is a long story, but I will abbreviate it for the sake of time constraint."

Proteus told him that about 100,000 years ago he first modified the mitochondrial DNA of a female human ancestor in East Africa. The results of that modification subsequently made possible what human anthropologists now call The Great Leap Forward, exemplified by the use of fire, finely made weapons and tools, art, cooking, and primitive music. This began the long development of human ancestors. No further modification took place for tens of thousands of years. But prospecting Archarans discovered scandium and the planet's other rare earth resources, and they began to kidnap human females. They further modified their DNA to produce mutated offspring whose behavior could be controlled, providing workers for their mines.

Proteus explained that in response to the enemies' agents, he had made a DNA modification in a band of Denisovans, an early species related to Homo sapiens. That modification resulted in the metamorphosis Starkey experienced.

"I am still troubled by the ethics of that modification," Proteus said, "but there seemed to be no other choice. I created a cadre of Warriors to combat the enemy's activities."

"How many are there still living?"

"As far as we know, there are now five living warriors, Jack, including you and Masato," Proteus said. "One hunts our enemies in Northern Russia, and another hides in plain sight amongst humans, attempting to lead a life free of this intrigue. One lives here in the society enclave. A sixth may yet come to answer the call, we do not know. I shall not count him until I see him."

"What about Hannah," Sheila said, "is she not a Warrior?"

"No, Sheila, Hannah's metamorphosis took a different course, and we're not sure why. Her special skill is in communication across distance," Proteus said.

Hiro stirred at this. "Don't count out the Eldest, our sixth warrior, I believe our old friend is still alive, but Proteus' Warriors do not stand alone in any case. Our brotherhood of warrior priests formed in alliance with Proteus centuries ago, would respond now as in the past. Is it time for me to reach out to them?"

Proteus raised an arm. "No, Hiro, a call to your warrior priests would compromise our secrecy, without doubt. Please give me more time to gather the dedicated Warriors and speak to the Museons on the inner council. I need to give them our updated assessment, and I hope to receive their support in the confrontation that comes."

Starkey saw disagreement in Master Yama-shima's face. But the Master remained silent. And silence was assent.

"In the meantime, Jack and Sheila, I think you can expect a visit from our enemies tonight. They will attack you first Sheila, believing you to be the weaker," Proteus said.

"Shouldn't we move to the Protean Society so we can protect her?" Starkey said.

"Wait one more night. I believe they will send a slave first before attacking in force. But Masato and Wolf will go with you. They are more than enough to protect you," Proteus said.

CHAPTER TWENTY-TWO

TRUST

SILVER SPRING, MD FRIDAY
JAN 2 6PM

Dave Vaughn began his mission to find Starkey by going to St. Andrews Pub. He never saw Starkey anyplace else, and knew nothing about him or Sheila Cartwright, though he'd met her once. He pushed open the big mahogany door and walked the length of the barroom. No one looked up as he entered. The pub held few patrons in the early afternoon, but the regulars leaned into their beers along the carved, ornate bar. The bartender, Paul, finally came down and asked what he wanted to drink. Vaughn ordered a beer and asked Paul if he knew where he could find Starkey. But the bartender wouldn't answer at first, and just stared at him. He acted as if he didn't know Vaughn at all.

"Who are you, mister?

Vaughn, completely frustrated, set his beer mug down on the bar with a thump. "What? You don't recognize me? I'm Dave Vaughn, for Christ's sake."

Paul put both hands on the bar and looked him over. "Well, you resemble Dave Vaughn, but you're a hell of a lot bigger than I remember."

"I'm Dave Vaughn. I'm just grown. The doctor says it's glandular or something. He doesn't know what caused it."

"Well, if you say so, then you are, it doesn't really matter to me." Paul didn't like him before, Vaughn knew, and from his tone the bartender seemed to like him less now. Paul turned back to the bottle-lined shelves and grabbed a fifth of Dewars and a glass for another customer. He didn't look convinced, and when Vaughn asked him again about Starkey and Sheila Cartwright, the man would tell him nothing. After Vaughn left the pub he realized his appearance must have been suspicious. He kept forgetting about his new size. He still didn't feel that big on the inside. Even after buying new, larger clothes and shoes that morning, his new size hadn't sunk in. He didn't recognize the stranger in the mirror at the store.

A phone booth sat on the corner by the pub, but the directory gave no listing for Starkey. Vaughn caught better luck with Sheila Cartwright. There was only one in the book. He walked back to his car and searched for her address on his DC map. It was near-by. Twilight fell, and the street lights came on around him while he drove. Her street lay just off nearby University Boulevard. The house, a red brick split-level, like so many in suburban Maryland, sat in a quiet neighborhood. A few flower beds and shrubs broke up the otherwise plain front yard, and the green lawn looked cared for. Vaughn noticed things like that. He liked flowers. His mother grew flowers around the trailer where he grew up in Cabin John. But when his mother died the flowers went out of his life. He eased past Sheila's house, made a U-turn at the corner, and parked at the end of the block across the street. He began to watch and wait. It got darker.

About 9:00 o'clock, a car turned the corner and came down the street. The black Porsche pulled into the driveway of the house. Vaughn watched as first a woman and then a man got out of the car. Vaughn didn't recognize the man as Starkey at first. This man looked too big. Then what appeared to be a very large dog jumped out of the back of the Porsche. It put its nose up in the air and seemed to catch a scent. It started to walk slowly across the street and down towards Vaughn's car.

Vaughn sucked his breath in hard. *Shit.* He started the car, mashed the accelerator, and rushed off down the street, away past the advancing animal and the man who started to follow it. Vaughn hoped Starkey—he thought it must be him—didn't recognize him. *Why did there have to be a dog?* He really liked dogs. He hoped he didn't have to kill the dog. He turned out onto University Boulevard and drove back towards Wheaton and the pub. He watched the rearview mirror.

The traffic rolled along, and his pulse slowed after several blocks. This was ridiculous—he didn't know how to kill people. He didn't know anything about hunting or stalking, or whatever. Come to that, he didn't know anything about any of that old Indian stuff. He liked to screw with people sure, but he'd never hurt anyone. Starkey looked dangerous. *He's even bigger than I am. Why?* And what about the dog? It was huge, and looked like a wolf. That meant something, but he didn't know what. *Yet Erebus and that monster are going kill my father if I don't kill Starkey.* He rubbed his temples where the headache that started at the trailer kept getting worse.

Starkey was the only white man he even kind of liked. Never mind Erebus forced Vaughn to watch him, get to know him. Over the last three years Starkey sat in the pub lots of nights and listened to his stories. Some of the stories about the women were lies, and the jokes were stupid. But Starkey put up with the phony Red Man vs White Man act. Vaughn played the Wronged Native American so often that he spouted it out of habit. Starkey listened, though, and actually seemed to give a damn. *Why did it have to be him?*

He stopped for the light at Connecticut Avenue. The bright neon lights of the storefronts hurt his eyes. He didn't own a gun or knife. Some Indian he was. He'd never even lived on a reservation. The Piscataway didn't even have one. Screw all that Indian Brave stuff. He'd struggled into some over-sized sweat clothes at home so he could make it to Sears to shop for some things that fit. How the hell could he explain to people why all of a sudden he stood seven feet tall and was built like a brick shithouse? What would he say? It was all so fucked up.

Vaughn found he'd pulled into the parking lot of St. Andrews Pub again, but he realized he couldn't go back in without raising more questions he couldn't answer. He got out of his car and walked up the street and across to the Army Navy Surplus Store with the Cigar Store Indian standing out front. The Indian held a rubber tomahawk. *That's my speed.* He went inside.

The man behind the counter stared at him. Vaughn walked down the aisles past counters stacked with camouflage clothes and paratrooper boots.

Vaughn remembered a TV show where they'd given a pit bull meat with sleeping pills inside. He could do that with the wolf-dog. *I have those sleeping pills.* He picked up a bayonet and put it back down. *The ma*chetes might be better. *I can buy meat, but how many sleeping pills should I put in? Just crack the capsules and dump them all in? I hope it doesn't hurt the dog.* The edge of the machete felt pretty dull. The hunting knives were sharper, but the machete had a longer reach. Maybe he could cut Starkey's throat while he slept? Vaughn cringed. He hated the sight of blood. The woman would be easy, no contest. He was big and strong, now. He didn't know how he'd get into the house without waking Starkey, or where the dog would be. The sales clerk looked scared with his presence in the store. Would people always be afraid of him from now on? Part of him like that idea, but it made him an outsider, and just being Native American did that too often in his life. Shaking off that idea, and thinking of the threat to his father, he bought the machete and a hunting knife and a camouflage hoody.

Two hours later, Vaughn drove back to Sheila's house after picking up the meat and the sleeping pills. He parked at the end of the block again, turned off the ignition and waited in the car. He rolled down the window and watched. The unusually hot DC June night was humid with no relief coming until the wee hours. The sweat ran down his back in rivulets. Vaughn took off the hoody and looked at his watch—11:30. This time all the lights were turned off in the house. He just didn't have the patience to wait any longer. Taking the machete and the drugged meat wrapped in foil, he got out of the car and walked up the block on the opposite side of the street. He could see people in the front rooms of some of the houses. The flicker of TVs shone out. The street lamps were sparse on this block. He crossed, came back down, and stopped behind a neighbor's dark green Euonymus hedge that hid him from view. The leaves smelled acidic. He liked the smell. He waited and watched. There were no lights or sounds in the house. The big dog didn't seem to be outside.

He walked down the side of the yard towards the back. Another dog barked at the fence right be-hind him. It startled Vaughn and he dropped the meat on the grass. The foil fell open. He ran across the front lawn back to his car and got in. Lights came on in the house. His breath caught in his chest. The front door opened and the big dog came out. The lights went back out. The dog circled around the house, past the garage to the back, and came out from be-hind. It found the meat and stopped. The dog's body blocked Vaughn's view. He waited and watched. A few minutes later the dog lay down beside the bait, and rolled over on its side.

Vaughn waited long, long minutes, but finally could wait no more. He got out of the car and walked across the lawn, approaching the dog. It sure looked like a wolf in the dim light. It didn't stir, and Vaughn crept past it. He crossed in front of the house and went around the end through a chain link gate. He walked along the back, his hand trailing along the rough surface of the bricks. He tried each white-framed window, but they were all locked. A small stoop fronted the back door. He stepped up the three concrete steps, one step at a time. The machete felt light, strange in his hand when he pulled it from the scabbard. He gripped the door knob, his palm sweaty. It turned in his hand. *Unlocked.* A warning bell went off in his head. He started to shrink back, but stopped. The image of his father and the Okee and Erebus's threat came back into his mind. He felt his guts twist. He pushed open the door and stepped into a kitchen. He saw a sink and a stove in the dim light. His shoulder twitched and he started to turn. Then he felt a sledgehammer-like blow to the side of his head. He went down to one knee but jumped back up. He heard a short word shouted behind him, and felt a blow on his lower back near the spine. He went down again, this time for good. He felt paralyzed.

Bright lights came on. He tried to move his head, but he couldn't. He couldn't feel his body at all. *What had they done to him?* He looked up into Starkey's face. The neon light on the yellow ceiling shone in his eyes.

Jack Starkey looked down at him. "Dave Vaughn? Sheila, this guy looks like Dave Vaughn from the pub."

Another very large man moved into Vaughn's view. "The paralysis will only last about twenty minutes—we need to secure him."

A woman's face came into view over him. Must be Sheila Cartwright. "There's climbing rope in the garage, Masato. I'll get it."

Vaughn tried to speak, but couldn't. He watched out of the corner of his eye as the dog came in and sat down beside his head. No, it really was a wolf. It looked intelligent. Green eyes stared down at him. It didn't move or make a sound. How was he even awake?

The man Sheila called Masato spoke to him. "You aren't very good at this, are you? We were expecting an attack, but something a bit more competent."

Starkey came to stand over him again. "Dave Vaughn. I almost wouldn't have known him. He's huge."

Sheila brought the rope. "Whoever he is he came into my house with a machete in his hand. We expected trouble, but what's he got to do with it? How do you know this guy? Why would he do that?"

Starkey shrugged. "I know him from St. Andrew's. We've drunk a few beers together. You met him once. He's kind of a pain in the ass. But I have no idea why he would do this."

Masato trussed Vaughn up from shoulder to ankle and left him on the floor. "I am afraid your beer-drinking buddy is an agent, however inept, of our enemy." Masato gave a short laugh. "He's nearly as big as I am. He is not the first Native American to be involved. Remember Hannah Cassidy is Piscataway and Proteus rescued and recruited her from the Archaran's ranks."

"Hannah's not huge," Sheila said.

"Proteus thinks the Archarans used a different DNA sequence with her," Masato said. "She has the same strength as the larger warriors, but also the power to communicate telepathically."

Vaughn struggled to speak. He only managed a groan.

"Wait. Dave Vaughn is Piscataway," Starkey said. "I forgot that until now."

Starkey picked Vaughn up like a sack of snakes and carried him into the next room. Starkey put him on a couch and turned on more lights. Some feeling started to come back into Vaughn's body. His head really hurt now. Sheila sat down in a black, wooden rocking chair across from him, but Masato and Starkey stood. Wolf sat beside the couch, still watching him. There were scrolls hanging from the walls. *They look Japanese.* A ceiling fan turned slowly overhead. They were waiting for him. *No, they expected someone more competent.* No one would mistake him for competent.

He struggled to speak, and the words came out slurred. "He-He said they'd kill my father if I didn't help them." Vaughn laughed his short, nervous laugh.

Sheila leaned in toward him. "Who is 'he'?"

Vaughn's words got clearer. "His name is Erebus. He's some kind of frickin' robot thing. He called the monster that attacked my father an Okee. But something he called an overlord sat in the Okee's chest." He told them the whole story, from Erebus' first visit to him years ago, to the attack at his father's trailer. Erebus told him that he and his father were bred by the Archarans to be servants of these monsters. He said their DNA or something had been changed. Erebus sent him to kill Starkey and Sheila Cartwright tonight.

"Look, I didn't want to come here. I'm not a killer. I've never killed anything. They made me bigger, but they didn't change me inside. But they said they'd hurt my dad again if I didn't do what they said. I didn't know what else to do. I don't want my father to die."

Masato motioned Sheila and Starkey to step outside on the front porch. He closed the storm door before speaking, but Vaughn could hear through the screen. "What do you think of our would-be assailant? Does he speak the truth?"

Starkey answered without hesitation. "I believe him."

Sheila leaned against the porch railing. "I believe him, too. But he seems weak-minded."

"Right now he's confused, paralyzed, and frightened. He's not at his best. We must decide if he can be turned," Masato said. "His father means a lot to him. If we harbor his father, then we might be able to recruit him. He might be unskilled, but it took courage to come here."

When they went back inside, Wolf sat next to Vaughn, staring into the man's eyes. Wolf placed one paw on the man's knee and turned and looked up at Starkey.

Starkey read Wolf's eyes. "I believe Wolf wants us to save them. Let's do it. But before we take him to Proteus, Sheila and I have got to gather our things and move to the society building as well."

"Yes, you must," Masato said. "Do that. I'll wait here with Mr. Vaughn. We're going to get to know each other."

CHAPTER TWENTY-THREE

SPIRIT OF THE WARRIOR

KOLA PENINSULA RUSSIA
SATURDAY JUNE 3

Snow lay deep on the brown bear skins draping the shoulders of the huge Sami warrior. The sun slowly crested the spruce and larches of the vast snowforest that surrounded him. He did not feel the biting, arctic wind, but the blind, killing delirium had finally drained away. Darake found himself on his knees with clarity of mind and vision slowly returning. The long hooked blade of the knife in his right hand plunged deep through the neck and up into the skull of his enemy. His left hand held the head down and the body's bulging eyes leaked yellow fluid. Turning, he saw many more enemy bodies piled around him. Beyond the carnage, men, women, and children sat on the ground encircling him.

He shook his head vigorously to further open his mind. Long braided locks of black hair cast snow and ice crystals through the air. He rose, collecting his juoska bow from the ground beside him. He towered over the bodies and the people who watched—their yellow eyes staring. Darake coughed, clearing the bile from his throat. His dry voice sounded rasping, but still deep and resonant. "How long was I unconscious?"

The man nearest him spoke. "We have watched over you for two days."

Two days. That might be a record. Darake looked around. "No more came?"

The man gave a short laugh. "One, Darake, but the women and children killed him before we came back from the mine."

Memories opened like stuttering film images. He found the underground caverns and the mine. He lured the Archaran soldier mutants out into the open. He shot nine with his crossbow until the enemy came too close. Then the killing delirium took him. In his memory he began to accelerate, blurring as he swept through the mutants in a maelstrom of dismembered bodies. Only isolated freeze panes of the battle remained for him after that. But Darake did remember slaughtering his way through the waves of enemies

until he reached the Okee. He sliced open its carapace with his knife, gutted it, and extracted the
squealing overlord. He tossed the Okee's carcass
aside and held the overlord aloft, writhing in his grip.
Darake walked to a huge larch nearby and beat the
head of the overlord against the tree again and again
until it burst like a yellow paint balloon.

Darake regarded the man before him now. He
knew before he asked. "I don't see the bodies of the
Okee and the overlord."

A bitter smile wrinkled the man's face. "The
women burned them," the man paused, "after they
hacked them into little pieces."

Darake stepped over the bodies around him.
The people approached slowly and gathered about
him. He had freed them. He allowed them to thank
him, and then it was finished. He turned and walked
away through the forest towards his waiting snow-
mobile. Now he could come out of hiding and answer Proteus' call.

>>>

Hannah Cassidy prepared herself. Sunlight
filtered through the blinds and lit the colonial writing
desk where she sat. Her small office in the Protean
Society building held only a few treasures preserved
from that long-ago time when it all started for her. A

necklace of freshwater shells encircled a quill pen and ink bottle. Her green, glass, ship's deck prism, a gift from Jefferson from his travel to France, reflected the sunlight in a green band of color on the sheen of the desk from the oculus above.

Masato had brought Vaughn and his father to the Protean Society, and Proteus told her he believed these newest arrivals might be better approached by her. The SyLF reasoned that their common Native American heritage might ease their transition, and partially quell their fears. Proteus hoped Dave Vaughn could be recruited to join his Warriors in the coming confrontation. Vaughn in particular could be a great asset if he could be realigned and trained. The Warriors numbered too few. And so, she must try.

Hannah took the wide wooden stairs down to the basement of the society building. Her steps echoed down the hall on the marble floor, and the sound reverberated off the white, half-tiled walls that gleamed in the bright overhead lights. She found Vaughn at his father's bedside in a room just off the infirmary. She unlocked the door, stepped just inside and waited. The room's white walls felt clinical to Hannah, but the leather arm chairs and carved oak tables softened the room somewhat.

Vaughn stirred, looked up, and saw her. He stared for a long time before speaking. "You're Indian." His voice sounded small, but curious.

"Yes. Is your father better?" Hannah took a chair beside Vaughn.

"Why do you fucking care? Maybe. The robot closed his wounds with that laser thing. He's asleep. What's an Indian doing here?"

"I live here. Her name is Panacea, and she's not a robot. She's a SyLF—a Synthetic Life Form."

"Like that thing Erebus. Whatever. I don't even know where I am. What kind of place is this? I mean, who are you? And why did those two huge men and that woman bring us here?" Vaughn said.

"They brought you here to protect you from the Archarans. My name now is Hannah Cassidy, but my tribe called me Sooleawa." Hannah leaned forward and spoke to them in a kind, quiet voice. "I am Piscataway like you, though during my Indian life long ago we just called ourselves 'the people'. Bred by the Archarans like you were, I slaved for them for many years—until Proteus saved me."

"Is that what I am, a slave?" Vaughn stared at the floor. "So what happens now? Am I a prisoner? What about my father?"

"That depends. Wolf chose you. Starkey brought you and your father here because of that alone." Hannah tried to sense if the man's mind focused and he was ready to listen. She drew in upon herself, visualizing a pivotal moment. *Can he be realigned? How shall I explain what he has to know?*

The Warriors numbered too few, and so she must try. She sat up straight, her decision made. "Come with me, your father will be all right." She stood and drew closer to Pop Vaughn where he slept, speaking in a softer voice. "Please wait for us here."

Hannah took Vaughn by the arm. She led him out and down the hall through two large double doors. They went down twelve steps into a large, high-ceilinged room. Weight machines, free weights, and large areas with mats lined the walls. A large, rectangular open space occupied the middle of the room.

"What are we doing here?" Vaughn said. His voice sounded hoarse with insecurity.

Hannah tightened her grip on his arm and forced him to turn to face her, standing close. "This is our dojo, our training room. You see, we here at the Society, along with allies around the world, defend mankind from the enemy, the Archarans. For thousands of years, they have kidnapped pregnant women, tortured and mutilated them in order to harvest their fetuses. From these unborn children they create the mutated slaves that work in their mines and do their bidding."

Hannah paused, watching Vaughn's face for a reaction. He listened intently. "We are the soldiers who meet the enemy in battle to protect those who are in danger, the same enemy that attacked your father. We want you to join us." Vaughn made no answer. Hannah pressed on, her outstretched hand indicating the room where they stood. "Here is where you will learn to be the warrior you were destined to be, but for the right side."

"Who will teach me, little woman? You?" Vaughn loomed over Hannah. His voice betrayed a mix of fear and bravado.

Hannah struck him with the flat of her hand just below his rib cage. The force of the blow doubled his body over, lifted him off his feet, and flung him against the mat on the wall ten feet behind. The force of the blow held him there for a few seconds, until he slowly slid to the floor.

Hannah walked over to him, raised his chin with one hand, and looked again in his face, eye to eye. Satisfied, she offered him a hand and pulled Vaughn to his feet. "I could, though I have never gained the size of a warrior. My talents are mental. I can communicate around our world and even across time. Yet the same strength is within me that you possess. But I will not be your teacher. You will have a much tougher teacher, NiTawis, his name is Masato."

Vaughn stood, bent inward, his breath rasped. "What did you call me?"

"NiTawis. I have given you a new name for a new life. It means 'my cousin' in our language."

The double doors opened above and Masato and Starkey stepped down into the dojo and stood watching. Wolf sat on a step beside them.

Hannah's voice grew deeper and more resonant as Masato walked closer. "The Spirit of the Warrior lives inside of you, NiTawis. We will prepare you to open to it. This is Masato. He will teach you how to channel its power and release its full strength. Do what he tells you, exactly what he tells you, and do not resist."

"This is your destiny," Masato said. "You must join Proteus' Warriors."

Vaughn stared at the floor and stood stubbornly silent. Hannah sensed that the moment had come to compel him to choose sides. Hannah grasped his forearm and spoke with the full Voice of Command. "Look at me, NiTawis." Vaughn reluctantly raised his eyes from the floor and looked down into hers. "I say to you now, NiTawis, that a day will come when The Spirit of the Warrior will be all that stands between your father and certain death. If you heed us, you can save his life. If not, then he will surely die." Hannah watched defiance and fear and belief war across his face until at last a stony look of determination settled there. He looked up into her eyes and grasped her shoulder.

"My name is NiTawis.

CHAPTER TWENTY-FOUR

PÁIHUÁI

GEORGETOWN, DC SATURDAY
JUNE 3

Proteus moved Sheila along with Starkey into the Society enclave after Vaughn's attack. Proteus and Master Yamashima insisted that she did not travel outside until the danger passed. The confinement chaffed.

Sheila thrust her Bo staff violently forward in the final strike and finished her Kata. The "Guard the Mountain Staff" training form was arduous. She bowed deeply and took her final position, facing west. Her posture erect, she trembled slightly. Her black Gi clung to her skin and the red dragons on her sleeves were dark with sweat. Her right hand held her staff upright at her side and her left formed an open blade hand extended forward in challenge. The toes of her black leather shoes were aligned with a red stripe that marked the position of the beginning and the end of the Kata. Master Yamashima sat silent on the edge of the tatami mat opposite her. The blue, cushioned floor stretched away behind her across the dojo to the wood framed walls. He had watched Sheila perform the violent yet fluid attacks and defenses, whirling, spinning, striking, and blocking. She completed all fifty-four movements flawlessly. The surrounding dojo still rang with the sound of Sheila's final Kiai. It reverberated off the high walls and ceiling above them. Sheila's powerful cry no doubt echoed through all the floors above in the Society building.

Sheila watched as Yamashima rose to his feet in one smooth motion. His black and red silk Gi shimmered with his movement, reflecting the early sunlight from the skylights high above the dojo. "Good, Sheila. I found your Kata most acceptable. We will move next to the Katana for your sword forms."

Sheila placed her staff on the long wall rack of weapons that held staffs, swords, and smaller hand weapons. She retrieved her Katana. As she unsheathed the sword she paused briefly to regard the white cranes engraved on the blade. Placing the sheath back on the rack, she walked smoothly back to the floor mat. She strove to make her motion graceful, confident. She inserted the long sword into the black belt of her Gi. She took an open, resting stance. Her breathing slowed. She stood, her every muscle taunt, her body charged with energy from the Kata. She held her body and mind in a balance of outer tension, inner calm. She waited, unmoving, for a long moment, then spoke. "Master, may I ask a question?

"Of course you may, Sheila."

"What is the purpose of the Warriors? And what do we do here as students of Zen?"

Yamashima smiled. "That's two questions. But they have one answer. We are Warriors of humanity, aiming to save all sentient creatures," the Master said.

"Proteus said there were five Warriors," Sheila said, "but I only count three."

"One of those you have not met. Darake has answered the call," the Master said.

"Ok, with this Darake that ought to make four living Warriors, counting Jack, and Masato. But two are still unnamed. I asked Proteus to identify the fourth, but he told me I should speak to you first."

Yamashima smiled at her. "That is as it should be since the fourth Warrior is my student and friend."

Sheila sensed movement behind her. Turning her head she saw a very large man moving across the other side of the dojo floor. The man's gait looked effortless, fluid, but somehow strange. He walked with his heels raised and his weight forward on his toes as if in the midst of a Kata or training form. His arms, held stiffly downward, did not move. His large, powerful looking hands, held close at his sides, turned upward to extend forward. He looked neither left nor right, holding his body rigid as he walked across the shining wooden floor beyond the mat. But he did stop and look her way when he reached a set of double doors at the other end of the dojo. There he turned and gazed at her for a moment. When his eyes found hers, she felt her pulse leap and a slight tremor shook her shoulders. Now she could see his face. Sheila thought he looked Chinese or Tibetan. His long, straight black hair hung to his shoulders and was cut in square bangs where a jagged red scar seared his forehead. She thought he wore his black Gi, trimmed in white, like a second skin. Barefoot, he stepped—toes turned inward—through the doors and disappeared.

Sheila turned back to see Yamashima smiling and nodding. "Yes, it is time you met him. In the midst of all that has happened I thought it best to wait for a quiet moment. You have just seen Páihuái. He is the fourth Warrior."

Sheila broke her stance and stepped forward. Questions poured out of her. "Who is...how do you say his name?"

"It is pronounced Pa, as in papa, then whee. Páihuái. It means wanderer."

"Where did he come from? Why haven't I heard of him, or seen him here?"

Yamashima laughed. "Patience, Sheila, all your questions will be answered in a few moments. Return your Katana to the rack. We will visit him now and you must carry no weapons. Come with me."

Yamashima led Sheila across the dojo and through the double doors. A long wood-framed hall lay beyond with a series of intersecting hallways and doors. At the end of the hall they passed through a set of large glass doors and out into an enclosed sky-lighted garden. Proceeding in silence, they walked along a winding path of limestone pavers and gravel surrounded by bamboo, lush green plants, and the sounds of trickling water. Sheila thought the air smelled of lemon and gardenias. *How can all this be in the Protean Society building? It seems to go on and on.*

"Master, are we still inside the Society building? All this seems to be too much to fit in," Sheila asked.

"Yes, and no," the Master said. "Part of our building, or compound, really, lies on a parallel plane in quite another place. Think of it as a set of doors that open onto another place on earth where we have our Sanctuary, and lots more space."

Sheila pondered that bit of news after they took a sharp turn through the bamboo and reached a small Japanese house built of wooden columns on stone with a large roof and deep eaves. A Shoji-screened door framed with dark wooden posts and beams stood open.

Yamashima rang a tiny, quiet, brass bell that sat on a low copper table by the door. After a moment he went in, motioning Sheila to follow. He spoke softly over his shoulder. "This is the entrance to his home."

Sheila found herself in a large, high ceilinged room with a peaked roof supported by natural wood timbers. The walls were hung with shoji screens over rice paper with several floor-to-ceiling hanging scrolls. Sheila saw white cranes as in the dojo on two of the scrolls. They were painted on backgrounds of grey with the striking colors of pink blossoms and brilliant green leaves. Tatami mats covered the floor and a low mahogany table sat along one wall. It held a simple white ceramic vase with one single stalk of flowering Hibiscus. Páihuái stood in the middle of the tranquil room, and large though the room was, he dwarfed it, making it feel small around her. He stood with his back to Sheila and Yamashima.

Yamashima spoke in a quiet, kind voice. "Páihuái, I have brought someone to meet you."

Slowly Páihuái turned around. He stood silent, arms held tightly at his sides. He gazed into the distance over Yamashima's right shoulder.

Taking the cue, Sheila spoke quietly also. "Hello, Páihuái, I am Sheila Cartwright. I am pleased to meet you." She held out her hand to him.

At the first sound of her voice he stiffened. Then she saw him shiver as if a chill ran through him. He slowly raised both his hands and took hers and held it between his two great palms. Then he inclined his head to look down at her. His dark brown eyes reached hers and the startling depth of his gaze swept her away. She felt a great surge of warm energy wash over her and through her, a wave of compassion and caring. Sheila felt surrounded and bathed in waves of love and acceptance.

After long moments Páihuái withdrew his gaze and released her hand, his arms dropping once more to his sides. Sheila felt faint and stumbled, but Yamashima caught her arm.

Yamashima's voice sounded hushed and reflective. "He has never done that before with anyone. He has recognized something in you. I am very sur-

prised. We will leave him for now. Goodbye, Páihuái, we will come back soon."

Páihuái sat down on the tatami mat, in half-
lotus, his eyes straight ahead, as if to wait. He removed a wooden flute from inside his Gi. He began
to play.

Yamashima led Sheila back through the lush
garden. He stopped amidst the green stalks of bamboo that lined the path and turned to face her. "Are
you all right, Sheila?"

"Yes, but I don't have any idea what just
happened." She turned to look back at Páihuái's open
door. "I've never felt such pure unmitigated love
from any other person. Not even my parents. No,
wait, cancel that—I should have said especially not
my parents."

"Páihuái has the attitude of a warrior, but the
gentle, loving heart of a child."

"But who is he? Where did he come from?"

Yamashima led her further along the path. He
stopped beside a small pool, and stood watching the
Koi gather, hoping for food. "I found him in a remote
mountain village in China near the Tibetan border
where I went to study White Crane Kung Fu with a
reclusive Shaolin monk." Yamashima told her the
monk called him Páihuái, which means wanderer. He
was found wandering between mountain villages.
The village people had fed him and cared for him

since they discovered him. They came to revere him as a kind of silent saint. When Yamashima finished his studies with the monk and started back on the mountain path, Páihuái followed him.

"I led him back when I discovered him. I thought the old man must have need of him. However, the old monk sent him after me, believing it to be Páihuái's destiny." Yamashima told Sheila he saw several similarities to Masato in him, like Páihuái's great size, of course. So he brought him here to Proteus. Later Páihuái's DNA tests revealed the Archarans mutated him, even though there was no previous report of alien mines in China or Tibet. But Páihuái's existence raised the question of alien presence, and the area measured in the hundreds of thousands of square miles, sparsely populated.

Yamashima reached out and touched her arm affectionately. His low voice carried an unusual urgency. "I want you to understand something extraordinary just happened. Until just now, only the old monk and I have received that full, open sharing of love and oneness with Páihuái. He has taken you to be his friend, a rare and infinitely valuable thing. Please visit him again this evening and talk to him as you would to me. He is silent. He has never uttered a sound, but do not think for a moment he is mentally slow. He is not. He will not reply, so simply sit and talk to him—or just sit."

"But what do I talk about?"

"Calm your mind. The right words will come. I think you will find he is with you now, and always."

Sheila stood quite still and mentally pictured Páihuái sitting as she left him. Then she felt a sudden clarity of thought, as if a veil inside of her mind flew aside. She sensed Páihuái's presence there just below the surface of her conscious thought. At the same time she began to hear a low musical tone, like his wooden flute holding a sustained note, and then the tone faded and grew quieter, but did not entirely disappear.

Sheila answered Yamashima. "I have never experienced anything like this, Master. I feel his presence in my mind. I hear him, not thoughts, but a tone, like music. It feels strange, but comforting somehow. What's happened? Am I imagining this? Is this real?

"Yes, Sheila, it is real. Páihuái is capable of a dramatic kind of empathy, a kind of psychic harmony. I don't know why, but he has chosen you, joined with you as he did with his old Master and with me."

CHAPTER TWENTY-FIVE

ALKIRA

GEORGETOWN DC SUNDAY JUNE 4 8AM

Starkey woke early. First light lifted the shadows in the corners as it traveled across the dormer room upstairs in the Society building. He experienced a moment's disorientation that quickly faded. He knew well where he was and why. All the revelations of the day before flooded back. He pushed back the checkerboard quilt and put his bare feet on the smooth oak floor. He moved carefully so as not to disturb Sheila. His clothes sat waiting on the French Empire chair by the bed. The dreams he recalled were benign and he found himself smiling into the antique mirror of the chest of drawers as he dressed. Starkey stretched his shoulders back and reached upward, his hands steepled in the Sky Earth pose. He marveled again at the tremendous vitality he now felt since the metamorphosis. The physical strength of his body seemed matched today by clarity of mind and an almost buoyant mood. A clear, blue sky lay beyond the dormer window, and he could see the Potomac River flowing gently below. Wolf raised his head and watched Starkey dress from where he lay on the braided, oval rug. Sheila rolled over in the bed.

Wolf rose as Starkey reached down to place his hand affectionately on the wolf's head. Starkey marveled at this also. *It's as if we've always been together.*

Starkey placed his hand on Sheila's shoulder. She opened her eyes slowly.

"I'm still waking up," she said. "Can I join you later downstairs?"

Starkey leaned down and kissed her. "See you there."

Starkey smelled coffee as he and Wolf descended the long, curving staircase. He noticed for the first time the richly finished, wooden, wainscoted walls and the large portraits hung along the staircase. Starkey thought he recognized George Mason among them.

The beckoning smell of coffee led him across the red oriental rugs of the entry hall. Starkey knocked on the open door of the drawing room. Wolf stood waiting beside him. Starkey could see Proteus floating before a small console along the back wall beside a large, floor to ceiling window. The early sunlight shone through the white lace curtains that hung beside Proteus. The warm light of a multi-colored Tiffany lamp nearby reflected from Proteus' mirrored surface.

"Come in Jack. There is coffee on the side-board, please help yourself," Proteus said. "There is water in a bowl there on the floor for Wolf also. When you have your coffee, come and take a seat. I have something to show you."

Wolf followed Jack in and, after a drink, lay down by his chair. The air began to shimmer before the large brick fireplace. The ornate, carved, and gilded mantelpiece disappeared. A large view screen formed and Starkey saw the fuzzy image of a tall figure standing amongst hanging, dark grey curtains or stage backdrops, and heard the murmur of voices off screen.

Proteus passed his hands over the console and the image resolved. "You have come at a propitious moment. We are watching this scene in real time. You see before you a woman we will call Jill Brown for the moment. We have caught her on camera in the wings of the Sidney ASPN studios. Please watch."

Starkey studied the image of woman who stood silent and still. Her black, silk crepe Chanel pantsuit fit her closely and took full advantage of her towering, fit body. Her black stiletto high heels pushed her height well above the top of the metal door frame behind her. When the call came, she cut an imposing figure as more cameras picked up her entrance. She walked lithely, confidently, into the studio set, with camera flashes going off and the press milling beneath her like children. She passed in front of the hanging FIBA logo backdrops and crossed behind a table that held a basketball and a heavy cluster of taped microphones and cords. She seated herself in the single chair behind the bundled microphones under the bright spotlights. Her opaque aviator sunglasses reflected the many flashes of the cameras.

A sportscaster's voiceover described the highlights of last night's game as she walked in, the final game of the International Basketball Federation playoffs. An inset screen ran a video of Brown's last aggressive drive of the game and her prodigious leap for a dunk shot that scored the final goal and won the championship for her team, the Aggies.

Brown adjusted the white silk Hermes scarf laid about her broad shoulders, crossed her long legs, and folded her hands on the table before her, scarlet fingernails gleaming. The scarf covered most of the tattoos on her neck, but a few peeked out above it. The half sleeves of her suit top revealed her long, heavily muscled forearms and the multi-colored, Neo-Aboriginal tattoos that decorated them. Tightly braided cornrows pulled her hair back across her scalp and fell in long strands about her shoulders. Her rich, dark chocolate brown skin and high, prominent cheekbones sharply defined her face. She sat completely still, radiating perfect calm, her expression unreadable. Slowly her imposing and regal presence brought silence to the room.

The sportscaster began again in his formal, British accent. The camera switched to the greying, middle-aged man in a navy blazer, white shirt, and striped school tie. "Miss Brown, this is Alfred Wilson here with ASPN. Congratulations on your high-scoring game last night. It capped a championship season for the Aggies."

Brown nodded her head slightly, but did not speak.

Getting no response, Wilson went on. "We also should congratulate you on your selection for the WNBA All-Star team for the fifth consecutive year."

Brown's face remained closed, her body unmoving. After a long moment, she responded with a clipped "Thank you" delivered in a deep and resonant voice.

Wilson's voice betrayed some frustration with her minimal response to his praise. "We're going to look again at a replay now of your final drive to the basket in last night's game." The small inset expanded to cover the entire screen.

Starkey watched as the camera zoomed in on a basketball court and focused on Jill Brown as she slapped the ball out of an opponent's hand at half court and began a furious drive to the basket. Dwarfing the other players around her, she leapt from the foul line, surging high above the height of the basket. As she began the leap, she struck the last opponent guarding her in the chest with her shoulder and sent the woman bouncing into the stands. Still rising higher, she palmed the basketball and jammed it down into the net, nearly ripping the basket off the backdrop as she grabbed it on the way down. The studio audience sat stunned.

After a long moment, the sportscaster continued. "Miss Brown, are you aware that Pam Carter who guarded you on that play is still in the hospital with a broken shoulder and other injuries?"

"Yes." The camera focused again on her expressionless face.

"And that three spectators were briefly hospitalized?"

Brown did not answer and sat unfazed.

The camera switched to Wilson and he leaned forward. "The referees didn't call a foul on the play, but some people are saying you used excessive force during your approach. How do you respond to that?"

For the first time Brown's voice took on a sharp edge and her broad, Australian accent came through. "I don't respond to vague statements like 'some people are saying,' do I, Mr. Wilson? But I'll tell you this. Pam Carter is a good ball player, but last night she got in my way and she knows it. End of story."

In the hushed murmur that ensued, a female voice cut through. "Miss Brown, Lois Chandler here, ABC Melbourne. There have been rumors of your retirement at the end of this season. Would you care to comment?"

Brown's face seemed to soften slightly. "Lois, I'm not thinking about that. After the All Star game next week, I'm going to rack off and drink some beer, and that's all I can tell you." Brown then rose abruptly, turned to show the camera her broad-shouldered back, and walked off camera and out of the studio.

The viewing display shimmered and disappeared. Starkey sat back in his chair, staring at the fireplace once more. Now he knew why Proteus asked him to join him early this morning. *Wow, she's a piece of work.*

Proteus spoke first. "Her true name is Alkira. As you have no doubt guessed, she is an Australian Aboriginal. She took the name Jill Brown when she left us five years ago to "hide in plain sight" in her present life. She is the fifth Warrior. What is your first impression?"

"She damn sure looks the part. She scares me." Starkey stood up and walked to the window beside Proteus. He looked out on the traffic of the forming rush hour that slowed out on K Street for a few moments. He turned back to the room. "Her attitude might be all for show. I don't know. I've never heard a professional athlete say anything quite so cold and callous on camera."

Proteus moved to hover at Starkey's shoulder. "I don't think her attitude is contrived. She left us in anger, and it appears her anger has not abated. Alkira evinced strong frustration with our long, seemingly endless conflict with the Archarans. If she went seeking an ordinary life, women's pro basketball is hardly ordinary and she certainly hasn't kept a low profile. Perhaps she chose poorly. 'Don't listen, don't talk,' doesn't seem to work as well in the world of sports media as it once did, and in the last few years she has been plagued by questions of transgender and sexual orientation."

Starkey turned and cracked a smile looking at the SyLF. "You mean 'Don't ask, don't tell.' She shouldn't be surprised. Looking and acting like that, what would you expect? But it's not her sexual identity or her mental health that concerns me right now. I want to know if she's on our team or not. I certainly don't have a problem with her being angry—I'm angry. Hell, we're all angry, particularly Master Yamashima. He's ready for all-out war today, regardless of the covenants and need for secrecy. He told us that at our first meeting here."

"When she left us she left no impression she might come back. She will not respond to my messages to her. So, since she has always been closest to Darake," Proteus paused, "I have asked him to reach out to her. He arrives tonight, and perhaps we will learn more about her then."

CHAPTER TWENTY-SIX

THE GATHERING STORM

GEORGETOWN, DC SUNDAY
JUNE 4 6PM

Delicious smells escaped the Society dining room. Starkey stood on the threshold with Wolf beside him and surveyed his surroundings. The elegance of the room struck him. For the first time Starkey questioned the reason for all this. Why all the opulence? Starkey could imagine the benevolence of the Proteus' benefactors, the Museons. But what purpose did the Society fulfill that this building resided here in Georgetown. Starkey had never thought to ask. He continued to marvel at the many portraits of Jefferson and the Jeffersonian period décor around him. Ivory walls rose to a twelve foot ceiling adorned with dark-stained crown molding.

Chair railing framed the walls above carved oak wainscoting. His eye came to rest on several large landscape paintings hung above sideboards along the length of the room. Starkey thought one could be a Constable, or perhaps a Turner, eighteenth century anyway, without a doubt. A recording of a solo violin played softly, a Bach sonata he thought. *Jefferson would have felt at home in this room.* Surely that was the intent, but why? Starkey made a note to ask Proteus. Starkey added it to a growing list of questions. Not the least of which was how he and Sheila were to make a living if they couldn't go back to their old lives.

Starkey and Wolf passed two floor-to-ceiling windows, framed with dark blue velvet drapes that opened on the Georgetown waterfront park beyond and under the freeway bridge. The setting sun still lit the Virginia shore on the far side of the Potomac River. Stepping thru the doorway, Starkey saw Masato standing by the stone fireplace at the far end of the room. The man wore a black tuxedo that closely fit his broad shoulders and narrow waist. One elbow rested on a carved marble mantel piece. The Zen priest raised a champagne flute in greeting.

Preserving this section of the society building's former use as a tavern, six circular tables, each with seating for eight, held the center of the room. Shelia stood and waved from where she sat in the far corner. Sheila stood out in the grand room. She was dressed in a simple, black dress. She sat down again under a portrait of Franklin Roosevelt and flashed a smile that invited Starkey to join her.

"Come on Wolf," Starkey said. "Let's go see Sheila." Starkey took in the buffet's offerings as he passed. Lunch was hours ago and his new body burned calories like crazy. He nodded to NiTawis and his father at a nearby table. Sheila didn't wait for him, obviously. A half-empty plate of oysters on the half shell sat in front of her.

Sheila held up a forked oyster as they approached. "Jack, these oysters taste like they just jumped out of the bay at Crisfield."

Starkey sat down, regarding her. Sheila smiled and outshone the silver candelabra. A damask table cloth and silver-trimmed place settings surrounded her. *All this in the face of the danger that threatens outside these walls.* Starkey turned to look at the rest of the dining room. Proteus had told them who would have arrived by this morning. Masato and NiTawis and his father were there, but Starkey did not see Darake and Alkira. He would know Alkira, having seen her on video, and Proteus' description of Darake should be enough to identify him. No doubt Proteus had filled those two in about Starkey and Sheila as well.

Wolf continued on to greet Masato. The Japanese man bent down to place his hand on the wolf's head. Starkey and Sheila watched as the wolf padded over to the table where NiTawis and his father sat. Wolf greeted Pop Vaughn first. The older Piscataway man still wore bandages on his arms and shoulders from the Okee's attack at his trailer, but he sat upright at the table, smiling down at Wolf.

"Wolf has taken a special interest in NiTawis," Starkey said.

"He surely has," Sheila said. "It's almost like he's known them before."

Starkey wondered if Proteus placed wolves with Sooleawa's people in the past. Starkey thought NiTawis looked strong. The man held himself erect, but Starkey could see the man's hands seldom stayed still. His fingers drummed on the table top. Starkey wondered whether NiTawis felt comfortable with this formal setting. The Society and the assembling team of Warriors would all probably feel as strange to NiTawis as it did to Starkey.

Pop Vaughn rose from his chair and knelt down to greet Wolf. He allowed the old man to hold his head between his hands and stroke his fur. Starkey watched the two stare into each other's eyes, and Pop Vaughn slowly nodded his head. Wolf looked over his shoulder at NiTawis who nodded to him also. A small smile appeared on the Indian's face and his shoulders lowered. Wolf had taken the Indian as one of his people and Starkey had wondered why since the night NiTawis broke into Sheila's house. Starkey respected Wolf's acceptance of him and so took the Indian man on faith. Still, remembering NiTawis' capture and metamorphosis by Erebus, Starkey lacked confidence that NiTawis could be trusted not to fail them.

Starkey turned back to Sheila. "You came down to dinner early," he said. "I thought we said seven o'clock."

"We did. I decided I should. I need a full night's sleep tonight. I've got to be in the dojo to practice at o'dark hundred in the morning before The Gathering. Master Yamashima tests me tomorrow afternoon. The "Guard the Mountain Staff" form he's got me doing is a bitch. But don't tell him I said that."

"This is the first time you've ever complained about the Master's training."

"It's not the training, it's the confinement here. I'm not used to being controlled, and I'm restless. What about my students?"

The confinement chaffed. Starkey understood. But what could they do? He changed the subject back to training.

"You've moved so far beyond the normal training the Master provides to his students for self-defense. I see now that he predicted your role in what has happened. And he saw that you would need higher forms of offense as well." Starkey said. He squeezed her hand. He watched as the SyLF that Hannah Cassidy called Mythecus floated by, platters and tureens on hovering trays in tow. Hannah rose from a nearby table and met the chef. She directed the placement of the steaming dishes on the sideboard buffets. Starkey thought the SyLF was a little overdone in his tall white chef's hat, double breasted tunic, and a bogus pencil-thin moustache. Starkey stifled a laugh. The food, however, was not in the least comical. It smelled delicious.

Sheila speared another oyster and dressed it with Tabasco and lemon juice. "You'd better get some of these before they disappear," she said. "By the way, do we call her Hannah Cassidy or Sooleawa today?"

"I think she'll answer to either, but she looks like she's in her tavern keeper persona right now." Hannah's long colonial dress swept the oak flooring as she crossed the room to their table. "Are you reliving your old tavern days, Hannah?" Starkey asked.

"Good evening Jack and Sheila. Yes, I suppose I am, but why not? Souder's Tavern is here all around you. It's at the very core of the society building. For your information, *Jack Starkey*, I have been keeping these rooms in order for over two hundred years."

"No one has told me the story of how the tavern evolved into all this." Starkey said.

"Well," Hannah said, "that's too long a story for now, but that side board with the buffet sat in the old tavern. Under these fancy place settings are several well-worn tables that came from its dining room…"

Sheila interrupted. "But Hannah, what about Thomas Jefferson? Where does he come into it?"

"Well, for one thing Thomas Jefferson sat in that very chair when I gave him a dressing down he sorely deserved. Despite his famous words to the contrary, the man failed to recognize the equality of women and black people. In the end we deemed him to be one of our failures. So much might have been forestalled, you see, the wider spread of slavery and the Civil War. The Protean Society was built on the foundations of failure so we would always remember that "…not even the wise cannot see all ends". And another thing, his views on the education for women…but wait, I am rambling on and on and there's work to be done. We'll have to talk about this later." She started to move away.

Starkey held up his hand to stop her. "Wait please, Hannah, or Sooleawa, may I ask you one more thing? Did you ever have one of Wolf's ancestors with you when you lived with your Piscataway people long ago?

She looked a Starkey for a moment. "Yes, yes, I did. Proteus brought an ancestor of Wolf to live with me and my foster mother after rescuing me from the Archarans. Why do you ask?"

Sheila spoke first. "We have been watching Wolf with NiTawis and his father, Hannah. Wolf seems to already know them, and feel close to them."

"Very good, you two, you have seen the truth. Wolf's breed knows our people in a very deep way, a kind of genetic memory. Ask Proteus about it some-time." Hannah placed her hand on Sheila's shoulder and then moved on to join Mythecus at one of the sideboards, gesturing at a silver soup tureen.

Starkey turned back to Sheila. "I'm starving. I think I'll take your advice and hit the buffet. Don't leave yet, there's more I want to talk to you about."

"Stand back, friends, Big Boy is hungry." Sheila said.

Starkey rose, but stopped when he saw Wolf staring at Michael August. Master Yamashima's assistant stood in a side doorway. Wolf sniffed the air. August retreated—closing the door. Wolf shook himself and came back to stand by Starkey.

"Wolf seems on edge. Is he all right?" Sheila asked.

"Maybe. I don't think he likes August very much. But then, neither do I," Starkey said. Master Yamashima told them that he found Michael August four years ago going through trash cans in the alley beside the dojo. Cold and hungry, the Master took him in and fed him and clothed him. Yamashima took him to a homeless shelter nearby and later gave him a job cleaning up around the dojo. Over time, August told the Master his story of an abusive father and alcoholic mother, and his own alcoholism that brought him to homelessness. He convinced the Master he had studied accounting, and the Master gradually let him do the books for the dojo. Starkey and Sheila privately questioned the wisdom of this, but were reluctant to bring it up. In the last year August displayed strong talent for martial arts and started to teach beginning students. But that didn't explain his presence here at the Society. Now Starkey would bring it up.

"Where is Master Yamashima, by the way?" he said.

Sheila finished her last oyster. "I don't know, but he said he'd be here for the Gathering of the Warriors. I'm going to ask him if he's sure this August is trustworthy. Wolf thinks there's something wrong, I can tell."

"Wolf may simply be missing his mate and their cubs. Proteus said there are seven of them at the

Sanctuary, wherever that is. I didn't have a chance to ask any more about it..." Starkey paused when he saw Darake and Alkira enter the dining room. Starkey wondered how the Sami Warrior wore the fur of the brown bear in the hot DC weather, but the society HVAC handled keeping the temperature comfortable. The giant man moved lightly on the balls of his feet, almost dancing. Darake saw him watching and nodded to Starkey, moving on to the buffet with Alkira trailing. Her many-hued Neo-Aboriginal tattoos rose above the rolled collar of her tunic and ran down her bared arms. Her swagger smacked the spiked heels of her knee high leather boots down against the hardwood floor. Wolf rose and padded across the room to greet Darake and Alkira. Darake placed his hand on the wolf's head and smiled down at him. Alkira fell to her knees to speak to the wolf. He licked her face. She seized the fur on either side of his head and shook it hard from side to side. Wolf growled with pleasure. He seemed pleased to see her here at the society. Alkira made sure her voice carried across the room as she spoke to the wolf.

"If you get tired of that whacker Starkey, you can come and live with me."

Starkey moved into the buffet line behind Darake. He took a plate and surveyed the fare. A huge platter of steaks and chops looked inviting, and a whole, large baked salmon sat next to them. Raw

Oysters and a tureen of what smelled like Cream of Crab Soup steamed just beyond. But only one serving of his favorite, smoked salmon, sat on the nearest platter. Starkey hesitated, but then moved to take it. Alkira appeared beside him, reached across in front of him, stabbed it with her fork, and shoved it onto her plate. She glared at him, daring him to complain.

"Oh please, just help yourself," Starkey said. Alkira turned away, ignoring him. Starkey piled his plate with baked salmon and oysters, filled a bowl of soup, and returned to Sheila's table. Wolf came and sat down beside him. "Did you see that, Sheila? That woman laid the boarding house reach on me and snagged the one remaining slice of smoked salmon right out from under my southern reluctance to take the last one."

"Maybe it's her favorite," Sheila said, laughing. "A girl has to eat."

"No sympathy for the downtrodden here." Starkey said. "I have to admit, even in the midst of all this—I'm worried about losing touch with my old life, losing my job, maybe losing my life altogether."

"What happened to the *new Jack*?"

"He's here with me, yes, but where do I fit in here? Ok, I'm big now. Huge, I suppose, and strong. But except for NiTawis over there, these Warriors have skills way beyond me, and battle experience, real battles, battles to the death, lots of them."

"Remember the Jack Starkey who defeated the Okee by the canal? That was you," Sheila said. She put her hand on his arm.

"Wolf pulled out the Archaran and killed him. I had a lot of help."

"Yes, but *you* saved my life. The old Jack Starkey could not have done it."

"No, I suppose not."

"Patience, Jack, one step at a time. Now I need to go upstairs and get some rest before tomorrow."

Sheila placed her hand on his cheek and held it there for a moment. Then she straightened up and walked out of the dining room.

Starkey watched as Sheila walked away, the tight sheath of her dress revealing the movement of every curve underneath. He saw Alkira turn and manage a smile for Sheila as she passed her on the way out. *So, she can smile. I wonder how Darake convinced her to come back.* Shrugging, Starkey went back to observing the dining room again. Alkira and Darake seated themselves at a table near the windows. They sat alone. Starkey wondered at the Australian woman's rude behavior in the buffet line. Was that a response to him, or did Alkira treat everyone that way? He'd seen her on the sports news the day before and Proteus' briefing prepared him. But what does she know about me? What has she heard?

Most likely she knew he'd only recently experienced the metamorphosis. Would she and the other Warriors accept him? Starkey turned his full attention to the food in front of him. He chewed his last bite as Proteus swept in. The SyLF stopped at Starkey's table.

"Jack, come walk with me. You must meet Darake and Alkira," Proteus said.

Starkey rose and followed the SyLF over to Darake's table. *I suppose now is as good a time as any to find out how they treat the rookies.* Starkey saw Wolf watching.

"Darake, Alkira, meet Jack Starkey, our newest recruit," Proteus said.

Darake rose. The man stood as tall as Starkey, but perhaps a bit wider. "Starkey, welcome, my friend, please join us."

"Thanks, Darake. Hello, Alkira." The woman remained sitting and did not answer. She just stared at him. Starkey took the chair Darake drew out for him. Starkey watched Proteus move on to hover near Masato and engage him in quiet conversation.

Darake picked up a carafe of red wine. "Will you have claret? This is a very acceptable Black Label Bordeaux, my favorite."

Starkey stared at the man.

Darake laughed. "Surprised that a man wearing a bearskin should have taste in wine? Old habits die hard, but I've lived a long time and acquired some sophistication despite my taste in clothes."

Starkey chose a wine glass and held it out. "Yes, thanks."

"Careful. It might be a little strong for someone like you," Alkira said.

"Someone like me? What do you mean?" Starkey asked. But Alkira only smiled broadly, perfect teeth crowding out of her mouth. Starkey thought he'd never seen a colder smile. *Let it lie for now.*

"Darake, can I ask you a question?"

"Of course."

"How long have you been a Warrior with Proteus?"

"I am a Sami, and my people come from Northern Europe. Proteus rescued me from the Archarans on the Kola Peninsula, now a part of Russia. Proteus tells me the year was 1808. I know nothing. I was a mere infant, you see. The Archarans began to infiltrate the area, digging exploratory mines in that remote area and searching for scandium. They kidnapped pregnant women from our villages to create slaves and workers. In the end, the Archarans massacred my village and our entire ethnic group. So the short answer to your question is, over two hundred years."

"That's a long time ago," Starkey said.

"For some, I suppose," Darake said. "But not
in my mind. I still wage that war and I will until my
knife takes the last enemy's head. I have just returned from an Archaran mine and stronghold not far
from there. Or what was a stronghold." Darake's
warm voice deepened and grew harsh. "I slaughtered
them all as they slaughtered my people." Darake's
face darkened and the smile disappeared. Starkey
summoned a great deal of courage and withstood the
fierce look that came into the ancient Warrior's eyes.
"My hatred for the enemy burns in my chest undi-
minished." The change in the man's face froze Starkey into silence. The cheeks drew in and the jaw jutted
forward. Thinning lips drew back from the teeth. A
skull stared back at Starkey. *There is deep darkness
here I didn't even suspect.*

Turning to Alkira, he said. "I saw you on the
BBC in the IBF playoffs. I watched your final drive
to the basket. You're a damn good ball player." He
didn't mention he'd only seen it because Proteus
showed him the game.

Alkira looked slightly mollified. "I'm not
sure I am ready to give up that life. I love basketball.
In that world I have respect, reward, friends, and lov-
ers. But my mentor, Darake, came to get me. He says
I am needed here." Her voice grew deeper still,
sharp, cutting like a scythe. "War comes, perhaps the
battle I have longed for, to fight to win, to destroy

our enemies, to leave their rotting corpses on the ground." She paused. "So I have come. Needed here, *Starkey*, means life or death, not win or lose a basketball game. After you have faced death in battle with these Warriors around you, ball games are tame, no matter how you play. Are you sure you are ready?"

Starkey did not answer. The truth of her words pulled silence down around them once again. Alkira went on, the sad sound of her voice washed over Starkey like waves. "I left the Warriors and the unending years of detente a long time ago because I tired of having no other life. I take little joy from this shadow existence of death and destruction. I wanted love and laughter and none ever found its way here. I still want them." Her fist rose and fell on the table, rattling the plates and silverware.

"Quietly, Alkira," Darake said.

She glared at him, but turned back to speak hoarsely to Starkey. "The fucking humans never suspect the deaths of our Warriors or the sacrifices made to keep their pitiful populations safe. There are no rewards, no thanks, and no hope, nor will there ever be, it seems. Why the fuck should I continue to sacrifice my life for humans who know nothing of what we do?" Alkira hurled the last words like a spear at Starkey, and rose to leave.

Darake caught her arm. "We do it because no one else can or will Alkira," he said. His voice carried finality.

Starkey stared at the two giant Warriors caught in a tableau of fierce emotion. *This ain't the farm team, Jack.* Alkira's words carried a bitter truth. Her questions went to the heart of Starkey's own doubts and fears. He'd never been a hero. He'd never sacrificed anything. Oh, yes, he knew loss. He knew paralyzing pain from his son Ethan's suicide. He knew the sorrow and emptiness of his life after his wife Jane's death. That pain and that emptiness gnawed at his insides still. But could he replace them with the Warrior's life, a Warrior's commitment?

Darake slowly released Alkira's arm. Starkey watched the towering woman stalk out of the room, ducking to pass through the double doors.

"So tell me Darake, is she always like that?"

"No. When she talks to you like that, she's in a good mood. Other times she doesn't say a word for days," Darake said. He rose, putting his hand on Starkey shoulder, a wry smile on his face. "Do yourself a favor, Starkey, when she's not talking stay the hell away from her, you'll live longer."

CHAPTER TWENTY-SEVEN

ABDUCTION

GEORGETOWN, DC MONDAY
JUNE 5 5AM

Sheila Cartwright stood in near darkness before the weapons rack in the Protean Society dojo. A waning half-moon shone faintly through the skylights high above her, illuminating the swords, halberds, and spears that hung there on the wall. The vast underground room stood cool and silent. Perspiration drenched her black Gi during her Kata, and the Gi still clung to her back. Her encounter after the lesson yesterday with Páihuái continued to entrance her. The clarity of consciousness she experienced then persisted and the quiet sound of the wooden flute still played as an undertone in her mind.

She lifted her Katana down from the rack reverently, and paused to regard its beauty in the moonlight. She slid the sword two inches out of the scabbard. Just holding the treasured gift from Master Yamashima boosted her confidence, further dispelling the dark fears that troubled her mind since the attacks at the canal. Michael August brought it to her from the Master's dojo, along with her Gis and bow. The sword was more than one hundred and fifty years old, forged by Master craftsmen in Japan. The blade's spotless steel had emerged from the ancient forge to be welded, folded, and welded again sixteen times. Sheila could not read the Kanji inscription on the blade, but she knew its creator had signed it. The gleaming surface bore an engraving of a dragon, and silver dragons also ornamented the black, polished lacquer of the scabbard. She moved back to the center of the dojo. She continued the practice of her Kata, focusing on the critique Master Yamashima gave her in her lesson earlier this morning.

A low hum and a barely audible pop broke the silence around her. Feeling a sharp pain and pressure on her neck below her, ear she whirled, unsheathing her Katana to face her attacker and confronted a strange SyLF, black and ovoid, hovering a few feet away. Blue lights flashed within the SyLF, illuminating it in the dim light of the dojo. An agonizing pain flared in her neck and shoulder and then swept throughout her body. Nausea and dizziness overcame her. She stumbled and the Katana fell from her hands to the floor as the black SyLF and the dojo around her began to shimmer into whiteness, and then fade to black.

>>>

Wkyak engaged the Archaran warship's camouflage system. Outwardly the ship's black within black surface shimmered briefly and completely disappeared. Had anyone been there to observe, all that could now be detected were the reflected, holographic images of the charged particles of the Van Allen belt surrounding the warship and the solar system and the universe beyond. The Archaran ship sat in orbit above the Earth. Like many others before, the ship approached the Earth undetected by Spaceguard, the combined international efforts to identify approaching Near-Earth Objects. Underfunded and seldom taken seriously by anyone except a few mavericks at NASA and in the US Congress, NASA's Near Earth Object Program launched after the Chelyabinsk meteor impacted Russia in 2013. But the Earth's NEO detection capability, still primitive, proved wholly inadequate to counteract the Archaran's technology. The alien warships flight at near-light speed, coupled with approach vectors whose radiant was subsumed by the sun, shielded them from detection. Once the ships achieved orbit around the planet, the radiation of the Van Allen belt and their camouflage rendered them invisible.

Wkyak's small red form hung in a cramped pod in the deep bowels of the ship. He was suspended from the pod's decks and surrounded by screens and the blinking lights of control surfaces. An umbilical connection emerged from behind his back, linking him to the life support that aerated him, fed him, and recycled his waste. Trioculent like most Archarans, three yellow eyes bulged from Wkyak's small, vaguely humanoid head. He reached up and attempted to smooth the five unruly red hairs that sprouted from his skull, pleased he still grew them. He watched one screen closely that displayed the ship's camouflaged image, satisfied the primitive humans on the planet below would never discover the disguised ship. Reaching forward with one tiny, three-fingered hand, Wkyak depressed the com link and spoke with something like glee in his high-pitched voice to the image that appeared in his screen. "The camouflage is engaged, Prefect Ukruek."

"Satisfactory. Prepare to transport Erebus and the human woman to the MoVR pod," Ukruek said. "Put an Earth-like atmosphere in the pod. And this time, Wkyak, be certain sufficient gravity is engaged to allow Erebus to function. No more errors, Wkyak, or you will be graked and jettisoned—do you understand?"

Wkyak placed one hand between the wrinkled folds of skin at his neck. His voice only squeaked a little. "It will be as you command, Prefect." He turned to the display of the MoVR pod. Erebus materialized on the platform carrying Sheila Cartwright in his arms. The multi-colored light sheath encasing the SyLF and the woman on the MoVR receded down into the platform. Grey, corrugated plastistel panels formed the walls and deck of the utilitarian pod surrounding the MoVR. A single large visual display appeared on the wall opposite.

Wkyak watched as the leering face of Ukruek, Prefect of the Archaran warship, appeared in the display. "Well, Erebus, perhaps you have managed to accomplish your task satisfactorily. Is the monkey woman still alive?"

Erebus paused before answering, blue lights stabbing within, but when he spoke his tone sounded level. "She is merely unconscious." He floated down from the platform and placed the body of Sheila Cartwright on the pod deck. "Why have you insisted we bring her here, Prefect? This was not the plan."

A hatch opened in the side wall of the pod and an utiledroid entered, carrying a small circular device. It hovered beside the body of Sheila Cartwright. One servoarm reached down and attached the device to the woman's forehead. The utiledroid retreated to a corner.

Ukruek struck the com surface before him with one small black-gloved hand. "Wkyak, probe the monkey's mind. I want to know what the old fool of a SyLF, Proteus, is planning and who these *warriors* are."

"At once, Prefect."

The Prefect's leering face now filled the view screen in the pod. "The plan, as you call it, Erebus, is what I say it is. You do not have the capability in your hole in the ground to extract the information I require."

Wkyak gloated when Sheila's body stiffened and began to writhe. Her torso jerked upward, balanced on the back of her head and heels, and fell back to the deck. Her body continued to convulse for long moments. When her body stopped quaking, the utiledroid came forward and removed the device from Sheila's forehead and exited.

"The extraction is complete, Prefect," Wkyak said.

"Scan for references to Proteus and report." Ukruek's image focused on Erebus. "Now you, SyLF, can move to the next stage of what you call the plan. The *plan* is for you to do as you are told. You and the human will be moved back to the planet.

Have your mining drones completed construction of the false landing platform on top of the island and camouflaged its appearance?"

"The work will be completed shortly, Prefect, but the island is often frequented by human rock climbers and our false rockslide, signs, and camouflage will not fool the public and the authorities for long. The force fields and holographic images will be discovered eventually. We must provoke Proteus to attack soon."

"Then, Erebus, simply place MOVR portals at the entrances to the area. We will give any interlopers a little ride to the outer atmosphere and see which ones can fly. Let a few monkeys disappear."

Erebus paused before answering. "Disappearances will only draw the attention of the human authorities, undermining our efforts at secrecy. It will jeopardize the mining operation at this location, Prefect."

"Grake their *authorities.* You mouth the fears of weak-kneed politicians and simpering bureaucrats. I abhor these clandestine operations. If I had my way, I would grake every last human on Earth and scour the planet of their primitive cities. Then we could mine at our convenience." Ukruek paused and seemed to consider this. "Very well, we will prod Proteus and continue this charade. The abduction of this human woman should provoke him. A few hints to the old SyLF and his warriors from our mole should suffice. We will let them monitor a transmission saying we will land on the island in two of the planet's days. Notify us when preparations are complete. We will allow Proteus and his warriors to detect our arrival. When they attempt to rescue her and they are distracted with the Zlayers on the island our mole will lower their shields and the destruction of Proteus' lair can begin. Go, Erebus, and do as you have been told."

Erebus took up Sheila and stepped into the MoVR, disappearing.

Ukruek struck the com link. "Now, the useless SyLF is gone. Tell him nothing more about our strategies. Analyze the data from the extraction. Find out what the human knows about The Protean Society. How many of these reported warriors are there? See if it confirms it is his center of operations on the planet. Have you completed the geological survey of this island, Wkyak?"

"Yes, Prefect, the mesomorphic rock structure, and the fault line are perfect, but will we not compromise the mine and betray our presence?"

"Perhaps it is time the humans learned their true place in the galaxy, regardless of what the Inner Council of the United Planets believes. We require scandium. This site has been a loss from the beginning and Erebus has failed. Grake him and them all. I

intend to destroy Proteus' organization and crush re-
sistance on this planet. Get me the confirmation.
Place the ship on war footing and notify the Zlayrers
to charge up and prepare to deploy. Soon we will see
what these *warriors* are made of."

CHAPTER TWENTY-EIGHT

ASSEMBLY

GEORGETOWN DC MONDAY
JUNE 5 9AM

The tall plate glass windows of the Society's third floor conference room looked down at the Potomac River's edge. The ruins of the Washington Aqueduct Bridge stood below. The moss-covered stone work of the remaining twin arches stepped out into the river. There C&O Canal boats had traversed the river, mule teams pulling the boats loaded with coal and produce along the aqueduct to Alexandria, Virginia. Across the Potomac and beyond stretched Key Bridge and the glass towers of Rosslyn. Rush hour traffic stalled both ways over on the bridge and directly below on the Whitehurst Freeway. The morning commuters, trapped in inbound cars, faced the bright sunlight of a hot summer day to come.

Starkey could hear horns blaring below. He reached down to place his hand on Wolf's head. "The people in those cars struggle and strive, live and die, Wolf, and most don't even suspect they aren't alone in the universe and have never been."

And I was one of them until a few short days ago.

Starkey turned from the river view back to the large, mahogany wainscoted room. A sweeping oval table with ten red leather appointed chairs commanded the center of the space. Busts of men and women sat on pedestals circling the table. Portraits hung on fourteen foot walls behind them, reaching up to the painted ceiling panels. Starkey recognized many of the men and women portrayed, but many he did not. Walking around the table, he read the brass plaques on the unfamiliar ones. A bust of Isaac Newton stood before a portrait of Caroline Herschel, astronomer. A portrait of Abraham Lincoln and his son Todd hung behind a bust of Rudaki, the Persian Classical poet. Next to him stood a bust of Elise Meitner, a mathematician, unfamiliar to Starkey. Euclid, Aristotle, Galileo, Madame Curie, Alexander the Great, Siddhartha Buddha, Shelley, and Shakespeare, all these and many, many more graced the walls and pedestals around the expansive room. *I wonder if Proteus knew them all.*

Starkey heard the double doors behind him open, and turned to see Proteus glide in. Alkira entered next, swaggering in dressed in black motorcycle leathers and tall, studded boots. Ignoring Starkey, she sat down in the chair farthest from him. Darake came behind her, still wearing the fur of the Brown Bear over his shoulders despite the August heat. He nodded to Starkey and sat down beside Alkira. Masato and Master Yamashima entered side by side, the Master dwarfed by his huge brother. The two brothers sat together, speaking privately to each other. Dave Vaughn stopped in the doorway, appearing hesitant. Hannah Cassidy came up behind him and, taking his arm, led him to the table and seated him beside her. Proteus moved to the end of the table before a tall, standing portrait of Jefferson. Proteus indicated a chair beside him for Starkey. Wolf lay down beside Starkey. Michael August came in last and stood beside the open doors.

All eyes rested on Proteus. Starkey leaned forward, resting his forearms on the burl wood table top and watched him survey the assembly in silence. White lights flickered faintly within the semi-opaque surface of the SyLF's form. A Longcase clock struck nine times from its corner. Proteus turned to him, the obvious question in his eyes—*Where was Sheila?* The chair beside him sat empty. He stood and walked out in the hall. She missed breakfast. And that was a first for Sheila. He sat down and turned to the Master.

"Have you seen Sheila today?" he asked.

"No, she skipped our practice, this morning," Master Yamashima said, "and that is completely out of character."

"I don't know what's keeping her, Proteus. I haven't seen her since last night. Should I go and find her?" Starkey said.

"No, we will give her a little more time, but we must begin." Proteus turned to address the assembly. "For the sake of NiTawis, Darake, and Alkira who recently arrived, I will begin by summarizing recent events."

Proteus related the first attack on Starkey at the canal, his rescue of Starkey and Sheila Cartwright from the under-river mine, the battle on the parkway, and Starkey's metamorphosis. Finally he described Dave Vaughn's own metamorphosis and the failed attempt to kill Starkey and Sheila. Proteus told the assembly Vaughn came from a line of Piscataway descent mutated long ago and was coerced to act for the enemy by the Archaran SyLF, Erebus, in order to save his father's life. Vaughn's father was brought to the society enclave after his capture in order to ensure his safety. Proteus placed particular emphasis on Vaughn's recruitment by Hannah Cassidy who named him NiTawis.

Proteus also told the assembly the Archarans, their monstrous Okees, and mutated human soldiers continued to kidnap pregnant women up to the present day on that stretch of the Potomac River along the C&O Canal to obtain the fetuses for DNA manipulation. "Starkey and Sheila discovered the Archaran's presence and the hidden mine, and the ensuing threats of violence caused me to call you all together today."

Darake interrupted. "Proteus, how could the enemy and their operations go undiscovered so long right under your very nose? The disappearances and kidnappings of pregnant women should have told you the enemy worked here long ago. I followed far fewer clues to their mine on the Kola Peninsula across the entire length of the Russian steppes."

"Alas, that blame would fall squarely on my shoulders, Darake, if I had them," Proteus said. "I am at fault, yes, for searching the world and failing to look so close to home. A recent article in the Washington Post indeed raised our suspicions. We now know the enemy has utilized a superior camouflaging system here along the Potomac that defeated our probing. Fortunately Master Yamashima closely monitored Jack, and when the attack on him took place our failure to detect the enemy's presence became clear, unmasking the false canoeing society. Otherwise we might be ignorant of their presence still. My watchfulness looked too far afield, or I slept at the helm. Take your choice."

Master Yamashima spoke then, his quiet voice clear and direct. "Recriminations are not useful, Darake. However it has occurred, we face a dangerous threat and possible invasion. This is not the first time our enemy has employed weapons and tactics outlawed by the United Planets' Covenants. Their very presence on Earth is an egregious violation. Why are we surprised they continue to escalate their weaponry and their transgressions? Our enemy grows bolder and I believe a violent attack is imminent."

Starkey saw white lights began to flicker within Proteus once more as he spoke. "Yes, I am afraid this is true. Our friends on the inner council have sent me disturbing news. What I have feared has come to pass. An Archaran warship has entered the solar system and this time they have sent a prefect with a history of savagery. It is believed he has transported part of a legion of Zlayers, the most formidable of the SyLF soldiers. We can look for little restraint from this one. He seems to have no regard for the covenants or the life of other species."

Starkey's patience ran out. "Are we enough to meet these SyLFs that are coming? Are there no more Warriors anywhere? Why is there is an empty chair there beside Darake? Is that for Páihuái? With me being a rookie and another who has little or no training, I'm worried, and frankly I am not sure about the commitment of some of us." Starkey looked at Alkira first and then at Dave Vaughn.

Alkira rose from her seat, towering over the table, reached across, and pointed a finger at Starkey's face, her voice a snarl. "Who are you to criticize my *commitment, human?*"

Darake's voice beside her asserted calm. "Alkira, sit down, you can kill him later. Right now we have Okees and Archarans to kill."

Alkira jerked her head toward Darake, then fixed her eyes again on Starkey and sat down slowly. She held up her left hand palm open and Darake struck it with his clenched fist. The sound alone shook Starkey deep inside.

Proteus went on as if nothing had occurred. "Páihuái does not join us here, Jack. That seat belongs to The Old One. It stands empty, reserved, but he has not been seen for many hundreds of years. We do not know if he is alive or dead, but he has not answered the call."

"Hundreds of years?" Starkey said. "He's hundreds of years old?"

Alkira laughed out loud. "Hundreds? Again you know nothing, white man. The eldest is *thousands* of years old. He was the first of us. Proteus has not seen fit to tell you? We do not just die, we must be slaughtered. And some of us are not that easy to kill."

Starkey had forgotten Hannah Cassidy told him she had lived for hundreds of years, born in a distant past. He'd just put it inside in the midst of all the revelations of the past week.

Alkira is starting to get on my nerves. When he spoke to her now, sarcasm soured his voice. "Well, it may be impolite to ask a lady her age, but I'll risk it, Little Miss Charming. How old are *you*?"

Alkira rose half way out of her chair but Darake caught her arm and pulled her back down.

Master Yamashima cleared his throat. "Alkira, it would be best if you remembered that Jack Starkey is newly a warrior, but he is also my disciple, and not the easy prey you seem to think."

"She would not be alone," Darake said.

Masato spoke for the first time. "No warrior here shall ever be alone." Masato's words hung in air like the echoes of a distant storm.

Starkey watched Darake and Alkira as the aggression drained from their faces in the long silence that followed. *Shit. Now I know who bats cleanup around here.*

Proteus broke the silence, his voice stern. "Enough. This gets us nowhere. There is much Jack and NiTawis do not know, Alkira, but as it has been done down through the ages, it is our charge to take the new Warriors as our brothers, to teach them, and, yes, lay down our lives to defend them, as you would

Darake. Do you pledge to do so Alkira? Choose now."

Alkira seemed to battle within herself. At last she stood and reached across the table to Starkey and held out her right hand, palm open. Starkey rose and struck her palm with his fist. She walked around the table and stood by NiTawis, offering him her palm. At first NiTawis just stared at her hand, as if unsure what to do.

Hannah leaned over and gripped his shoulder. "Rise, NiTawis, become the Warrior—it is your destiny."

The Indian stood and it seemed to Starkey that NiTawis grew taller still, and wider at the shoulder. Now he stood eye-to-eye with Alkira and looked into her fierce gaze. Lifting his hand from his side, NiTawis slowly rolled his fingers into a tight fist and swung it powerfully, striking her hand with great force. Her hand did not move.

"Now," Proteus said, "we can begin. Michael August took on the task of monitoring for enemy transmissions. Michael?"

August came forward to stand at the head of the table beside Proteus.

August wore the black Gi of Master Yamashima's dojo well. In another setting he would have seemed a tall man, broad of shoulder, and strongly built. But among these Warriors, he seemed almost diminutive. His shaved head framed an unremarkable face, save the eyes that were large and deep blue.

August's voice sounded even and measured. "We have intercepted a transmission that indicates an Archaran ship will land on an island north of us, along the Potomac, within a few days. The ship is already in orbit around the earth. It is waiting for the completion of a camouflaged landing platform being built to become the base of their operations."

A screen appeared before Jefferson's portrait, and a map of the Potomac River north west of Georgetown came into focus. The map centered on the Carderock Recreation area just off the Clara Barton Parkway. "The ship will land on Vaso Island, an island that is chiefly frequented by rock climbers who go there because of its high, steep cliffs. The only access to Vaso is by water. The Potomac branches there, flowing past both sides of the island."

"For what reason would they land there?" Master Yamashima said.

Masato waved a hand to dismiss the idea. "There is none. Why risk discovery? They can materialize their Okees and soldiers anywhere. They have no need of a land base of operations."

Darake slapped the table with his open hand. "It is obvious the arrogant *Kuss* continue to think us ignorant fools. This landing platform is a trap, and this intercepted transmission is a fake, designed to lure us onto the cliffs of that rocky island."

August did not answer. His eyes were fixed beyond the table to the open doors where Páihuái stood.

Master Yamashima, turning, spoke to the giant, silent man. "What is it, my friend?"

Páihuái's great hands held Sheila's Katana.

CHAPTER TWENTY-NINE

ARROGANCE

VASO ISLAND MD MONDAY
JUNE 5 12 NOON

Sheila woke to a massive migraine and over-whelming feelings of nausea. After a time, her blurred vision began to clear. Bright lights shone down from the ceiling, nearly blinding her. She tried to raise her hand to shield her eyes, but sharp pain lanced up her arm and into her shoulder. *Bruised but not broken, but where am I?* She mentally seques-tered the pain and managed to cover her eyes until they became accustomed to the light. She lay on a dark, uneven stone surface patch-worked with wet lichen and moss. Fingers of cold clutched through the silk of her black Gi. She reached out to touch the gray wall beside her. Constructed of small, interlocking clusters of hexagonal cells, the walls and ceiling formed a cube around her that was perhaps eight feet on a side. The wall felt warm, plastic to the touch, but the damp air chilled her. She tried to stand, pushing her back up against the wall, but dizziness overcame her and her legs buckled. She slid back down heavily, her head spinning.

A panel in the wall ahead slid open and the black SyLF who attacked her in the dojo floated in. Fear impelled her and she managed to stand this time, repressing the vertigo. She caught her balance and took a defensive posture. The SyLF hovered in the darkness of the opening, blue lights flashing slowly in his core. Sheila waited, silent, trembling.

"Is Starkey the father of the child?" the SyLF said.

"You're Erebus," Sheila said.

"Oh very good, *human*, full points, but I asked you a question." His voice reminded her of Proteus', but higher pitched and more arrogant, condescending.

"I don't know what you're talking about."

"The fetus you carry, human. You're two m-months pregnant, or didn't you know? Is Starkey the father or not?"

That explains the nausea. "Why do you care who the father is? You're going to kill me anyway."

"Oh, we're quick aren't we? If the father is Starkey, then the fetus m-may be useful. Is he the father?"

"Maybe, maybe not, I have sex with so many men it's hard to keep track," Sheila said. She watched the blue lights flare faster inside the SyLF.

"How m-many Warriors does Proteus have? What are their names? Answer me, human."

The vertigo came back and Sheila began to sway. She fell back against the wall and collapsed. Erebus swept forward extending a handheld device. She recoiled, but he placed it against her neck. Sheila felt a sharp pressure and then the pain lessened. The dizziness and nausea cleared. Erebus took her by one arm and raised her to her feet.

"Come with me," Erebus said, "I have something to show you."

A door in the wall of her cell slid open and he led her out onto a vast, circular platform open to the sky and constructed out of the same grey steel-like plastic as her cell. Sheila realized the platform sat high in the air. Off to her right, she could see the Potomac River far below, the current flowing around small islands and rock formations. It looked like the area above Carderock where she and Starkey jogged along the C&O Canal. An enfolding mist rose from the river to meet the unbroken grey clouds above. The air shimmered, surrounding the platform in all directions, as if it lay inside a cloud roiled by winds. Here and there rock formations thrust upward through the platform, like granite mountains in a dark, plastic sea. *We must be on top of an island in the river.* She twisted to look behind her. Off in the distance through the trees she could see cars moving slowly along the Clara Barton Parkway on the shoreline below. All around her working figures resembling Erebus hovered at the edges of the surface of the platform, attaching panels to the stone of the island. An odor of burning plastic, melting stone, and hot metal filled the air as the workers fused the panels and the stone.

"Where are we? Why have you brought me here?" Sheila said.

"We are on Vaso Island," Erebus said, "but we have m-made some improvements. And you, Sheila Cartwright, are bait to lure Proteus and his Warriors here for a surprise party."

"I don't see any drinks and chips. It doesn't look like much of a party to me," Sheila said.

Erebus extended a gloved hand towards the center of the platform. "Observe."

A slight movement of his hand caused a momentary discontinuity in the air in the midst of the platform. Slowly, row after row of hovering SyLFs, larger than Erebus and grey in color instead of black, appeared. They were more cone-shaped than ovoid like him. Another wave of his hand set the SyLFs in motion, flying upward in tiers of interweaving, concentric circles. Sheila watched as they hurtled faster and faster. Energy beams leapt out of their three revolving limbs, striking at the other SyLFs that passed them and producing a fierce, high-pitched tumult that assaulted Sheila's ears. But the SyLFs were not damaged. A semi-opaque force field spiraled around each and the pulsing beams were deflected and glanced harmlessly away.

"How do you like m-my warriors, human? They are called The Zlayers."

Sheila watched the violent martial display. She said nothing.

"There are hundred and twenty of my Zlayers in this unit. Your R-romans called it a m-maniple, quite a useful tactical unit in confined spaces—they learned that from us. Now, there's one m-more thing you should see."

At a signal from Erebus, one Zlayer, darker in color than the others and larger, moved off towards a large, obelisk-shaped rock formation rising erect out of the platform. The Zlayer discharged a single energy burst at the granite. The rock simply ceased to exist. The shock waves shook Sheila, followed closely by an echoing thunderclap.

"Well, Sheila Cartwright, do my Zlayers and their fusion beams impress you? How will your swords and sticks and arrows stand up against this?"

Sheila wrenched her arm free of his grip and stood apart to face the SyLF. "I suppose your Zlayers might do some damage if our people stood perfectly still and were as dumb as the rocks you've destroyed, but they won't and they're not."

"Arrogant yet? I can m-make you suffer more, human."

"So why haven't you done it? No, you wonder if your torture will harm my child, don't you? You don't know it isn't Starkey's."

"It is only one fetus. We have m-many. We have 'sovans to spare and we can always get more humans. You unsuspecting humans are easy prey."

"But if it is Starkey's child, you want it unharmed because it will be second generation, don't you? That makes it valuable to you, doesn't it?"

Erebus hovered silently, core lights flickering.

Sheila heard a static pop. "Erebus, I did not order drills for my Zlayers." Sheila turned at the sound of the metallic voice, and she saw an Okee appear. The huge pterodactyl-like shape emerged out of a column of shimmering greyness. A black, shiny lizard-like skin covered its wings and body. The monster hopped forward toward them on two clawed feet, beating its wings. Towering over them, the long yellow talons at the end of the wings extended, grasping. It made rasping, guttural sounds. Sheila shrank backwards, but quickly recovered her courage and took her defensive stance.

A panel opened in the monster's carapace revealing Ukruek.

"I am merely testing the anti-gravity field, Prefect," Erebus said, "your Zlayers are functioning perfectly."

"So I see, but you overstep your authority. Do not presume to deploy them again, SyLF."

"As you wish, Prefect," Erebus said, "I did not expect you until the base platform construction concluded."

"Obviously. I came to verify the plastistel platform is permanently fused to the rock of the island. It is critical to the deployment of the energy beam. Wkyak has made you aware of our requirements, I presume?"

"Yes, Prefect, I have chosen this island because the ancient m-metamorphic rock throughout this region contains the necessary faults and sheers. The fault line continues downriver. But he did not tell me why you r-require it to be so."

"That is all you need to know, SyLF. The rest of the plan is not your concern. I will inspect the fusion of the platform and the stone now."

"I guarantee its permanence, Prefect."

"If you are wrong it will be your last failure, Erebus. Our leaders are not pleased with your performance here. Your mining operation has never met its production quotas. This is the richest scandium deposit site on this planet, and yet you have produced the least. Why is that, I wonder?"

"The other mines are located in geographically r- remote areas," Erebus said. "That greatly r- reduces the possibility of human discovery. The proximity of this m-mine to an urban area has created tremendous security issues and slowed our progress."

"Our Masters care little for your excuses, SyLF. They do not put scandium in our holds. You overestimate the intelligence of these primitives," Ukruek said.

Sheila saw another, slightly smaller Okee materialize behind that of Ukruek. This Okee managed to bow stiffly, and a whining voice emerged from the monster's carapace. "They have received our false transmission, Prefect."

"Satisfactory, Wkyak," the Prefect said. "You may keep your precious hairs a little longer." He started to place a small red hand on his own bald pate, but quickly withdrew it.

"So Erebus, while you were playing commander, we have learned Proteus has only six Warriors. Two are newly mutated and probably of little use, and there are a few miscellaneous hangers on. It is laughable. He still holds these pitiful few to the ancient covenants, and allows them only primitive weapons. But, regardless of their effectiveness, we have plans within plans."

"Of course, it is as I told you, Prefect," Erebus said. "Proteus is a social scientist. He loves these humans. He has no m-military m-mind. Violence is abhorrent to him and so he is vulnerable."

"It seems you were right this time, Erebus. It will be a very short confrontation, hardly worth the effort." The Okee's carapace snapped closed and it turned and began to hop away. Sheila heard Ukruek's voice as he and Wkyak dematerialized. "Then we can go back to the Fringe where we enjoy our graking without this dallying with secrets and subterfuge."

Wkyak and Ukruek materialized on the Archaran bridge. "Ukruek, Erebus will likely be destroyed when we strike the island with the disrupter beam," Wkyak said.

"He has outlived his usefulness in any case," Ukruek said.

>>>

Master Yamashima rose from his chair and went to stand by Páihuái in the doorway, reaching up to place his hand on the man's upper arm. "What is it, my friend? You hold Sheila's Katana. Has something happened to her?" Páihuái bent down to one knee to look into the Master's eyes. Starkey saw the Master tremble slightly and then turn back to the room. "Sheila has been abducted. He will show you where they have taken her."

Starkey felt like the walls and ceiling were closing in on him, pushing him down inside himself. *No! Why did I even I tell her about the Anomaly and bring her into this?*

Páihuái walked stiffly to the head of the table where Michael August stood. He stared down at August until the man stepped aside. Páihuái pointed at Vaso Island on the map that displayed the Potomac Valley at Carderock.

"The enemy has taken Sheila there," Yamashima said.

"How does he know where she is, Master?" Starkey said.

"Páihuái and Sheila have bonded. I don't expect you to fully understand, Jack, but I assure you the connection between them is real. Think of it as a kind of empathy, a kind of psychic harmony. Trust him."

Starkey watched as the silent Páihuái came to stand beside him, and looked down at him, great hands flexing as if in angst.

"Of course we know this is a trap," Darake said.

"Yes it's a trap and Sheila is the bait, and it's my fault. Why are we sitting here talking about it instead of doing something? Starkey said. "She may still be alive."

"They have reason to keep her alive, Jack, and we will act soon. But some preparation must be made." Proteus said. "First, Michael you have penetrated their masked communications? What can you tell us about the island and the Archaran's defenses?"

The man's voice held a trace of condescension. "The news isn't good. The landing platform stands nearly a hundred feet in the air, and holographic camouflage and MoVR interfaces surround it. But that's not the worst. This Prefect, Ukruek, commands a full maniple of Zlayers armed with fusion weapons."

"Ok, someone help me out here. What's a maniple?" Starkey said.

"One hundred and twenty SyLFs, Jack." Masato said.

"Our enemy grows careless," Proteus said. "This time their transgressions are so heinous I believe full intervention can be justified. Surely the council cannot fault us this time. I may be stabbed with mine own petard in the end, but intervene we will."

"That's "hoist with", not stabbed, Proteus. Do you mean that at last, Proteus?" Darake said. "Do we finally fight to win?"

"Yes, Darake, this time we fight to win. The time for weapons détente has ended. They think me weak, but Sun Tzu, the Museans, and I began to prepare for this enemy long ago."

Pretend inferiority and encourage his arrogance. "I should have known," Starkey said.

Proteus moved to Darake's side and held out his open palm. Darake rose and turned to face him. He straightened the fur of the great bear draped about his shoulders. He looked around the table, took the eye of each Warrior in turn, and held it before moving on. Then he drew his arm back, slowly at first, but it began to accelerate even as it swung forward, until his body blurred in the motion. The sound of his fist striking Proteus' upraised palm struck a death knell.

"This time, my children," Proteus said. "We go to war."

CHAPTER THIRTY

ATTACK

GEORGETOWN DC/VASO ISLAND
MONDAY JUNE 5 2PM

Masato entered the transparent circular chamber, stepped onto the platform, and turned to face the team. Starkey slipped aside from Alkira and the others, moving himself into the circles of sunlight that cascaded down through a series of skylights in the high ceiling.

Proteus waved his gloved hand and an opaque beam of light sheathed down around Masato. "Our friends on the inner council, the Museans, prepared for this conflict long ago despite their abhorrence of violence. They provided us with the tools and weapons we would need in the dire conflict they foresaw."

Starkey watched as Masato's dark silk suit blurred and disappeared and a cobalt blue uniform replaced it. The uniform clung closely to the shape of Masato's body, revealing the taut, massive muscles throughout his torso his suit had hidden. The tunic and leggings were featureless save one emblem, a circle on the left breast that shone with its own inner light, illuminating the minute stars that radiated outward.

"Nice fit, but blue just isn't my color, Proteus," Alkira said. "Does it come in black?"

"No, Alkira, but the boots are black," Proteus said, as the light sheath withdrew and Masato stepped out. "The uniform carries its own shielding and stealth camouflage, and..."

Darake interrupted. "What will it shield us from, Proteus?"

"Almost everything, Darake. There is no technology currently known in the galaxy that can penetrate this uniform's shielding or betray its stealth camouflage once it is engaged. Inside the shield, a stable environment suitable to your requirements is maintained. The uniform carries enhanced tracking and communication abilities as well, but more on that later."

"So we are invincible," Starkey said.

"It would be better not to think of yourselves as invincible. If you were to step into a MoVR that transported you into distant, empty space, the uniform's power would eventually fail," Proteus said. "Being transported to the center of the sun would do it also, D.O.A. There are galactic energies that can destroy you still."

Starkey watched Masato vanish, reappear, and do it again.

"The uniform's systems are thought-activated." Masato said.

"Yes, Masato. After you are all uniformed, please practice control of these systems. It will be intuitive, but you don't want any surprises," Proteus said. Páihuái appeared beside him, and one by one the Warriors took their turn in the circular chamber and came out in uniform.

Proteus led them down a staircase out of the tower, their footsteps echoing on the marble floor of the long hall. Glow lamps hung near the ceiling, il-luminating racks of weapons extending into the dis-tance on both sides. "Here you will find weapons like those you now use, but with some changes. The Musean technology has been at work here also."

Moving across and a few paces down, Alkira reached up and took down an Aboriginal Fighting Club that caught her eye. "This is a twin of my own, Proteus." She took a few trial swings with the weap-on. "It is well-balanced and it fits my hand as if de-signed for it. But a club is a club, Proteus."

"It was designed for you, Alkira. But that Fighting Club, like the StarMoVR, contains a micro-nomic particle/antiparticle energy system. Once thought-activated by you, anything or anyone you

strike with it will be destroyed. Completely annihi-
lated. Do you understand?"

Alkira stepped apart from the group and held
the club at arm's length, for it began to glow.

"Not here, Alkira," Proteus said. "I'm sorry
there's no dojo time with it, but the Archarans have
left us no choice. There is simply no time."

Master Yamashima moved close to Alkira
and stared at the weapon as Alkira powered it down.
"What is a StarMoVR, Proteus?"

"I jumped ahead of myself or ahead of you in
any case. You will see. Each of your customary
weapons is duplicated here and similarly powered,"
Proteus said. "Your crossbow and darts, Darake and
your long knife are here. Masato and Jack, your Katana and Bo are also here."

Masato and Jack moved along the hall and
took down the weapons that matched their own. Jack
wished for straps and clips to carry his scabbard and
Bo on his back and they appeared on his weapons.
He engaged them. He stepped further down the
weapons hall and practiced withdrawing his sword
and retrieving his Bo. His confidence grew with each
flowing, supple movement.

"I would prefer my own weapons," Master
Yamashima said.

"I thought you might, but the Musean versions of yours are here, also, should you want to try them," Proteus said.

NiTawis spoke for the first time. "I have no weapon."

Sooleawa pushed him aside and came forward, taking down a large club from the wall rack, carrying it in both hands. She held it up before his eyes, her slight form tiny beside the huge man. "Do you recognize this?"

NiTawis took the offered weapon from her and turned it over slowly in his hands. "Yes, Sooleawa, it is a Gunstock Warclub. My father gave me one of these for the coming of age ceremony at my first pow-wow. But that one was just plastic." He stood holding the club, head down, silent and lost in thought, for a long moment. "I had forgotten."

Adjacent to the Warclub hung a long, bone-handled curved knife. Sooleawa gave that to him also. "Look at me, NiTawis. You were born to carry these weapons, as you were born to be a Native American Warrior. When you raise them in battle today, remember what and for whom we fight." NiTawis raised his head and took the knife from her, nodding.

Darake found his Juoksa Bow, a quiver of arrows, and a knife that matched his own and came to stand before Proteus. "Thank you for these, Proteus," he said, hefting each. "What finally pushed you over the edge?"

"The enemy has gone too far, Darake. They threaten the very existence of the human race and the earth upon which you live."

Starkey rode the elevator to the roof surrounded, shoulder to shoulder, by the Warriors and Proteus. He emerged onto the edge of the helipad. The black helicopter perched in the center of the expanse. Turning his head, he watched the shimmering stealth waves flow in the air, circling the Society building in pale oranges and pinks. The nearby buildings of Georgetown and the DC skyline stretched beyond the stealth concealment. White cumulus clouds floated in a brilliant blue sky above them.

The team gathered around Proteus. "The time for the détente is over. Observe," he said. He raised both hands and extended them, palms open. The black helicopter faded and disappeared as a simple cylinder, perhaps thirty meters long and fifteen meters in diameter appeared, with ancillary attached shapes and configurations. Starkey thought it was blunt, designed for function, and not form. A hatch opened vertically in the shining black surface of the cylinder's side. The exact size of the StarMoVR baffled Starkey, for it dwarfed the helipad, seeming to extend beyond the edges of the roof into the stealth waves.

Proteus turned to face the Warriors. "This is a scout starship and an integral MoVR. It is powered by an undetectable particle/antiparticle annihilation system. You may call it a StarMoVR. It will transport us to our enemy's location instantaneously, and therefore unseen. It has on board energy weaponry superior to that of our enemy, which I will use in the last resort. These ships have not been deployed in your solar system until now, and the Archarans have nothing like them. Let me be clear—I prefer not to escalate weaponry and technology too far beyond what our enemy has fielded. Retaliation will come and further escalation will result, without a doubt. Détente implies progression, so much is self-evident. However, this conflict cannot be lost. I believe the future of the human race will be jeopardized if we show weakness before the Archarans and this prefect."

"Proteus," Starkey asked, "what about Sheila? We can't go in with guns blazing. We could kill her ourselves."

"Michael has found her life signs in a small structure at the rear of the circular platform the enemy has built. We will transport you and Master Yamashima to a spot just outside the building. First,

however, Masato and the rest of the team will begin
the assault from the opposite end in a position to attack and destroy the Zlayers. Their attack will cover
your rescue effort. Hannah and Michael will remain
here to coordinate. I suggest Wolf remain here with
Hannah and NiTawis' father. But that decision is
yours, Jack."

Starkey looked down at the wolf by his side.
"Wolf, go to Hannah. Protect her until I return."

Proteus watched Wolf pad away and then
turned back to the Warriors. "You here on this ship
are the only individuals on earth, indeed anywhere
outside the inner council, who know of the tools and
technology you have been given. But after today,
well, the cat will be set amongst the canaries. I am
sorry to say today everything changes in our battle
with the enemy. We may no longer be able to hide
our presence on the earth, and this ancient conflict."

Proteus directed the team to board through
the waiting hatch. Once aboard and seated on the
bridge, Proteus spoke. "StarMoVR—I assume command and activate Control."

"Welcome Proteus. Control activated.
Ready," said the StarMoVR.

Starkey sat at Proteus' right hand, watching
the view screens set in the forward panel of the
StarMoVR, and the rest of the team arrayed themselves in seating that advanced to the rear of the ship.

Proteus swiveled in his chair turning to face the team. "Are we ready, my children?" Heads nodded as he looked at each in turn.

Alkira, seated at the rear, held up the palm of her right hand and Darake leaned across the aisle and struck it with his fist. "But where is Páihuái?" Alkira said. "I didn't see him board."

A hoarse voice behind her broke the silence that followed, uttering just one word, "Sheila."

Everyone turned to see Páihuái standing behind them clothed in the uniform of the Warriors. His head brushed the top of the bulkhead and his shoulders stretched across the compartment.

Starkey turned to look at Master Yamashima beside him. "That is the first word I have ever heard him speak," Yamashima said.

The look on Páihuái's face was grim. Starkey watched his hands making fists, opening, and closing. *I think somebody's in a lot of trouble.*

Alkira reached across the aisle and pushed Darake's shoulder. "He wasn't there before."

"I know. How does he do that? I can't do that."

"Welcome, Páihuái," Proteus said. "Now we are all assembled, let's hit the road, Jack. StarMoVR, acquire the coordinates and position us above Vaso Island."

Starkey experienced a moment of vertigo and the cabin around him blurred for an instant. He looked up at the view screen nearest him and saw what must have been the Archaran's platform and the Zlayers below.

"We are in position, Proteus." said the Star-MoVR.

The sound of a violent slap turned Starkey's head and he saw an emergency light blinking red on the bulkhead. A hatch opened beside Páihuái. Gripping the sides of the hatch Páihuái launched himself out of the opening, into the air, and disappeared.

"Control, track Páihuái on the view screens," Proteus said.

The team watched his image as Páihuái shot downward and landed below them at the perimeter of the Archaran's circular platform. He landed standing upright, knees bent, the platform bending beneath his feet.

"Look at that," Starkey said. "He dropped a hundred and fifty feet."

The Zlayers below detected Páihuái and rose, hovered, and turned. The ranks and files circled and repositioned along the platform to target Páihuái. He began to run towards the SyLF soldiers, accelerating until his motion blurred. Their energy beams bounced harmlessly off him. By the time he reached the first ranks that began firing, he had disappeared completely, but cut a swath through the SyLFs. Their bodies ricocheted upward and away, exploding, disintegrating.

Alkira looked at Darake and gestured at the screen beside them. "I have to get him to teach me that."

Alarms continued to blare and the red emergency lights flashed aboard StarMoVR. "Páihuái has bent the hatch assembly when he struck it. It will not close," Proteus said. "The Zlayers are targeting the ship." Starkey saw beams of energy that coursed upward but deflected and disappeared just off the surface of the hull. "Opening that hatch has betrayed our presence," Proteus said.

Starkey saw Páihuái reappear, breaching the last ranks of the upward exploding SyLF soldiers. He stood before a building at the far side the platform. Páihuái tore away the door and threw it aside. He entered, disappearing inside.

Proteus swiveled to face the team. "Páihuái has jumped the gun. We must move quickly now. Masato, prepare your team to MoVR down to the platform. Destroy the remaining Zlayers and any Okees you may find, but attempt to capture the Archarans they carry. We ought to question them," Proteus said. "If you find a SyLF configured like me, disable it and bring it to me. Control," he said to the ship, "activate the MoVR, and transport the team to the coordinates I have provided."

Sheila withstood the torture Erebus inflicted on her, but only just. Exhausted, she quailed as she saw another Archaran-bearing Okee looming over her. Then there came the sound of Páihuái's flute. It rose and grew louder inside her mind.

A voice screeched from the open carapace of the Okee. The Archaran pointed its small red finger at the SyLF. "Erebus, have you learned if the child is Starkey's?"

"No, Sykyak."

"Your pitiful attempts to extract information have failed. Watch and learn." Turning to Sheila, the Okee flexed its claws. "Human woman, I will show you how the Okee extracts information."

"Do not harm the embryo, Sykyak."

"Grake yourself, Erebus." The monster shoved Erebus aside and stooped and seized Sheila's arms in its claws and began to squeeze, slicing through the plasticast sleeves left over from her previous injuries at the canal and into the flesh, cutting deeper into the wounds in her forearms. Blood pooled, arteries burst, the scarlet stains streaming down her arms and onto the floor. Sheila screamed.

The door of the enclosure ruptured outward and Sheila saw Páihuái stoop and enter. He stood, filling the entrance, his head grazing the roof.

"Sheila." She felt his agony and anger surge and engulf her. Sheila watched as he disappeared only to reappear instantly beside Erebus. Páihuái's great arm swung, blurred, and struck the SyLF, sending it crashing off the walls around the chamber. It caromed into the corner, its head separated from its body. Páihuái seized the Okee by the chest with both hands squeezing, and lifted it into the air before him. The Okee began to scream and claw at Páihuái, huge wings flapping, attempting to pull back. Sheila saw energy waves flow out along Páihuái's arms until smoke began to rise from the black surface of the Okee's hide and flames spouted from its three yellow eyes and its open maw. The monster struggled briefly and then hung limp in his hands, consumed by fire. Still Páihuái continued to hold it aloft until the Okee completely burned to ash, save the carapace containing the Archaran. As the Okee crumbled away to fine black dust, the box holding the Archaran emerged, red hot in Páihuái's hands. Sheila heard shrill screams and the sound of scratching from inside the box.

The box melted slowly in Páihuái's hands, dissolving and dripping into a reddish grey puddle on the floor. Turning to Sheila, he tore away the chain that held her to the wall, carefully severed the collar, and took her up in his arms. He placed her gently over his shoulder and moved out of the building, supporting her with one arm. Sheila twisted to look ahead as Páihuái began to run, striking and impelling upward the Zlayers who advanced, attacking, and the platform blurred and disappeared. Páihuái feared the outcome of the battle and took Sheila as his own, charging himself with her safety. When they reached the end of the platform, Páihuái leapt into the cloud that hovered beyond the island, over the edge and into the air. Sheila recoiled in fear as they plummeted down towards the river channel, but they slowed in the air and a haze formed around them and obscured the rocks and forest and river below. Páihuái landed almost softly in the shallow water. He waded across to the shore beyond. Holding Sheila close, he climbed the river bank and avoided the ranks of police and firemen and soldiers that gathered in the parking lot by the parkway. The explosions emanating from the strange cloud drew the attention of the crowds and emergency crews. When Páihuái reached the road he cradled Sheila to his chest and began to run again back towards Georgetown. Sheila lost consciousness as they gained speed. The road and traffic began to blur and disappear.

CHAPTER THIRTY-ONE

COLLATERAL DAMAGE

VASO ISLAND MD MONDAY
JUNE 5 4PM

The images of the blurred backs of Alkira and Darake began to sharpen for Starkey, and their surroundings came into focus. Ahead of them Masato strode, ignoring the enemy's energy beams bouncing off him harmlessly. The Warriors followed him across a grey, plastic-like platform that stretched away from them, interrupted here and there by protruding stone outcroppings. An indistinct cloud seemed to encircle the platform and the island, but beyond, Starkey could glimpse trees and a highway on the adjacent hills. He thought he caught sight of fire trucks and police cars and green Humvees along the parkway below also, but there was no time to look more closely. *All right, Jackie, keep your eye on the ball.* Starkey stepped hesitantly forward as frequent deep vibrations rose from below the platform, jarring him. The Zlayers he saw from the ship began to lay down a barrage of their fusion beams, arms rotating, targeting the advancing Warriors.

Masato reached the first of them. His Katana sliced outward, arcing, and struck the first of the Zlayers. The enemy exploded as it hurtled upward. Darake began to fire his crossbow and each dart destroyed a Zlayer. Alkira darted forward, bent low at the waist, and swung her fighting club in a blurring motion that struck a Zlayer mid torso and disintegrated it. She paused momentarily to stare at the empty space left behind, hefting her club, then continued to advance, dancing, striking, and destroying the enemies as she reached them. Starkey and NiTawis followed closely behind the three and dealt similarly with Zlayers they encountered, mopping up what the others did not destroy, their weapons exploding and disintegrating their enemies. NiTawis moved clumsily at first, but effectively, his mistakes forgiven by the shields of his uniform. Gradually he achieved a rhythm, moving among and striking his enemies. Starkey found his years of martial arts in the dojo with Master Yamashima had prepared him well for this enemy and this battle. *But of course, the Master knew.*

Ahead of Masato, Starkey saw a larger, dark grey SyLF move out from behind the line of Zlayers. It rose and lowered, and rose again, circling above Masato, more maneuverable than the other Zlayers. Whirling above Masato it fired its three fusion weapons in rotation, targeting him. But the beams bounced harmlessly away and Masato disappeared, reappeared elsewhere, leapt thirty feet into the air, and struck the attacking SyLF across its chest with his Katana. The dismembered SyLF fell back to the platform, began to vibrate violently, and then crumbled, finally exploding into nothingness. Three more of the larger Zlayers appeared but were dispatched by Darake and Alkira.

"These machines pose no threat to us, Darake. Proteus has prepared us well," Alkira said.

"Do not become complacent, Alkira, remain vigilant."

Dispatching the last of the Zlayers, Masato turned to face the team. "Sheila is imprisoned in that enclosure on the other side of the platform. Come..." But his words were cut off as a violent quaking of the island began. Deep rumblings came up through the rock amidst the screech of stone shearing away stone.

Starkey stumbled, but caught his balance as the platform heaved powerfully upward and fell back down. Stress cracks began to form in the surface. Starkey watched as the cracks expanded, hurtled across the length of the platform, and began to widen, waves forming in the surface, racing away, the edges buckling.

Proteus's voice spoke in his mind, communicating with the Warriors. "A strong energy beam has been directed from space at the mesomorphic bed rock structure under the island and strong seismic waves have been released. The shearing forces are threatening to break the island apart. I believe the Archaran ship is creating ruptures in faults beneath the river."

"What about Sheila?" Starkey said.

"Páihuái has rescued Sheila, and they on their way back to the society building. Her vital signs are strong, Jack. She's going to be ok," Proteus said. "Masato, I am going to withdraw the team. Control, recover the team."

Starkey's surroundings again blurred and he found himself back in his seat on the StarMoVR. Starkey felt the knot in his stomach begin to soften. *Sheila is alive and safe.*

"Time to go," Proteus said. "The ship has repaired the hatch and our stealth technology is functioning again."

Starkey saw the stealth waves surround the ship on the view screens. He waited for Proteus to tell the ship to acquire coordinates. But the SyLF paused, seeming to listen. "The energy beam is growing stronger. The seismic waves are growing more violent."

Starkey began to hear a low rumbling that grew slowly louder into a vast roar. He recognized the sound of grinding stone on stone. The rumbling swelled until it broadened across the full range of human hearing, deepening and vibrating inside Starkey's gut. The platform and all of Vaso Island shook and began rocking. Vaso heaved and pitched on its bedrock foundations.

"The island is breaking loose," Proteus said. "The Archaran's energy beam is disrupting the entire geological structure of the island and the anti-gravity force that fielded the Zlayers is shifting it."

"That means landslide," Masato said.

Starkey, riveted to the screen, watched as the island pitched and shook and finally broke loose and began to move off its bedrock foundations. Slowly, inexorably, Vaso Island in its entirety began to move down the river.

Proteus took the StarMoVR up to five hundred feet. From this height Starkey thought Vaso Island resembled nothing so much as a stone railroad spike with the sharp end pointed downstream. Airborne, just clear of the river's surface, Vaso ground its way directly down the Potomac. Small islets, rocks, and trees were crushed and mangled under its pitiless advance.

"Proteus, we've got to do something." Starkey said. "It's headed for DC! A whole lot of people will die if it reaches the city."

"I see it, Jack. I know. It may be that the StarMoVR can move it out in to space, or at least slow it down. Control, acquire the 3-dimensional co-ordinates of Vaso Island."

"The coordinates are acquired, Proteus," said the StarMoVR.

"Now move Vaso Island out beyond the orbit of the moon," Proteus said.

"I am unable to comply. The object is too heavy and too dense."

"Control, can you stop or slow its motion in any way?"

"I am applying the MoVR beam now. The object is slowing. Full power is being utilized, but it is not sufficient to halt its advance."

Starkey sat back down, helpless, as the island continued its slow grind down the river towards the city. He looked still further downstream and there stood the American Legion Bridge, perhaps two hundred yards away. He could see lines of traffic crossing the bridge both north and south. "Proteus...Proteus," Starkey said, reaching out to clutch the screen with both hands. "No, no, no, slowing isn't good enough, if the island keeps on it's going to hit the 495 bridge. It's rush hour. There are hundreds of people in those cars."

Proteus turned to face him. "I know, Jack, but the ship is doing all it can. It doesn't look good."

"Doesn't look good? *Doesn't look good?* Is that some kind of SyLF detachment?" Starkey screamed at Proteus. "*Save those people!*"

Proteus sat silent. "There may be one thing, but I would risk further exposing our presence here on earth."

"Don't you think a whole island crashing down the river has exposed everything already? And is that more important than saving all those lives? Either you are the friend of humanity or you are not. Which is it?"

"All right, United Planets be damned. Control, position the ship between the island and the bridge."

Starkey watched the screens as the ship hurtled down river and acquired a new position. He saw the advancing island rise up in the forward view screen.

"Control, place the MoVRbeam just off the front hull of the ship and against the rock of the island, reverse polarity, ease it into place, and then begin slow, forward thrust," Proteus said.

Starkey felt the MoVRbeam engage the weight of the island and the ship rock backward. The cabin vibrated and jerked as the ship retreated under the strain and the ship's engines began to race and scream in protest. Starkey could hear the sound of the forward hull buckling.

"The MoVRbeam is engaged. The stress on the ship's outer structure is beyond acceptable tolerance. There will be damage," said the StarMoVR.

Starkey heard a gasp and turned to see NiTawis rising out of his chair. "We are being pushed back toward the bridge." Alkira reached across the aisle, grasped NiTawis' sleeve and pulled him back down. Starkey saw an understanding pass between the two.

"Control, increase thrust to maximum," Proteus said.

"Maximum thrust engaged, Proteus."

Starkey watched the rearview screen as the bridge lurched ever closer. Long lines of cars were stopped on the bridge. The ship remained invisible to them, but people were getting out of their cars and pointing up river at the island's approach. Many placed hands over their ears as grinding roar of stone against stone and the crashing of trees drew closer. Vaso Island in all its enormity advanced inexorably downstream towards them, heaving and rocking across the rough river bed.

First the bridge lay fifty yards behind the ship, then twenty-five. The ship moved perceptibly slower, but backward still. Onboard systems were overloading. Warning lights flashed and emergency alarms blared. Proteus sat in silence, head bent forward. The Warriors watched the screens, the island looming above them and the bridge nearing from behind. Ten yards, five. Starkey felt the rear of the ship strike the bridge. The sound of concrete cracking and splitting began, and the powerful groan of bending steel. Now Starkey could hear the screech of brakes, tires sliding on pavement and the sound of cars crashing.

NiTawis' voice rose higher. "The ship is forcing a bend in the bridge."

"The stress on the forward bulkheads is approaching critical. Structural failure is imminent," said the StarMoVR.

Then, all motion ceased.

Proteus lifted his head. "Control, report."

"The forward motion of the island has ceased."

Starkey saw Alkira raise the open palm of her right hand to NiTawis. He struck it with his fist and then grasped her hand and shook it, something more passed between them. Alkira saw Starkey watching and looked away, withdrawing her hand, but slowly. Starkey marveled. Alkira has accepted him. Why? Perhaps Wolf's acceptance of him has opened a way. In an unspoken way Wolf bound them all together.

Masato's voice cut through the sounds from the bridge. "Proteus, Sheila is gone and there's nothing else here. We have been deceived. All this is by design."

"Something tells me we need to be back in Georgetown," Starkey said.

"Control, acquire the coordinates for home base and take us there," Proteus said. "I think we need to circus the wagons."

Starkey almost laughed. "That's circle the wagons, Proteus," he said.

CHAPTER THIRTY-TWO

ELDEST

MUTUO EASTERN HIMALAYAS
MONDAY JUNE 5 4PM

Ku'en?

Sooleawa, can it be you?

You are alive. Yet you did not answer the call.

I am dying, Sooleawa. In a few hours the long story will be over.

No, you may not die. You are needed here. We are overmatched. The Archarans have sent a starship and a reckless Prefect. Everything we have striven for may be lost. We need the MoVRstone and we need you. Come now.

I am tired. I am done, Sooleawa.

One last battle, Ku'en. The voice in his mind paused, and then went on. *Ku'en, Proteus and our Warriors must survive.*

Ach. I have heard this all before.

I need you, beloved.

And aching memories of forgotten joy and sadness and love and longing broke through the sludge of great age and the lost years, opening like lotus blossoms there in his mind. One long groan of acceptance followed.

One last time then, Sooleawa.

He opened his eyes and the roof of the cave came into focus. Soft glow lamps hovered high above him, illuminating the painted and carved ceiling and walls, reflected in the seams of crystal that striated the roughhewn surfaces of the cavern. His old friend, pain, coursed through his limbs and he closed his eyes again. *I don't know if there is one last time left in me. Ach, but it does not matter in the end.* He would die soon in any case, be it here or somewhere else. If the LyFE Stone did not kill him, he could answer the call. Then the enemy would probably kill him. It would be worth the agony of the rejuvenation just to see Sooleawa again. His wives were all dead. They could no longer be jealous of her.

He opened his eyes again and turned his head. B'rtha, his youngest, knelt beside him holding his hand. Ku'en thought her the most beautiful of his offspring. Something sapient shone in her face. She devoted her life to caring for him in the long years of his decline. Her face strongly resembled that of her mother who was his last wife. B'rtha's small brown hand looked tiny in his great leathery palm. He was grateful once again his DNA differed from the Homo sapiens and the metamorphosis did not take away his virility.

"Hello, little one. You at least have not deserted me."

"Many others have been here, Eldest. You have never been alone."

"Still, whenever I open my eyes you are here. Where is your brother, T'an?"

"You sent him to watch the Han and their machines that build the tunnel, Eldest. He sent word the rains caused landslides again and they have abandoned construction for this year."

"Good." *These Han, so determined they are to breach our solitude with their road and civilization. Why must the last untouched Eden be violated by their bulldozers and concrete?* He shifted in the thick brown bearskins that covered him and rose up painfully on one elbow, fighting against the vertigo. "Has your brother shown you the inner alcove and my pouch?

"Yes, he made me promise never to go in or touch them."

"Never mind that now. Bring it to me, B'rtha."

One last time, Sooleawa, I will try. Ku'en watched B'rtha's short, stocky figure rise and walk out of the chamber. Her rolling gait showed a slight limp. He fell back down to the skins, his head spinning. He raised one long shriveled arm and looked at its thinness. The skin hung limp and flaccid from the bones. Would the muscle and sinew reconnect, rebuild, and grow strong again? Proteus warned him when the stone first lay there in his hand in the dim past that there would be a limit. The stone itself warned him the last time he used it. "All things must die, Ku'en," the stone had said.

"Ach, if it is so, then let it be so."

B'rtha returned carrying a brown, scarred leather bag. She knelt beside him again and held it out, offering it to him.

"No, you open the bag, little one, and give me the red stone you will find. Try not to touch the others. The one you want is shaped like a sitting bird."

She pulled a stone from the bag and held it up. "This one?"

"Yes, place in my hand."

"What is it, Eldest?"

"The LyFE Stone."

"Where did it come from?"

"It came from a distant star, a gift from a friend long ago. He called himself Proteus."

"What does it do?"

"Many things. First it gave us language and reason and craft long ago in the ancient past before the coming of the Sapiens. Today it may make an old Warrior young again. It has rejuvenated me many times to live many lifetimes and defend us and the Sapiens against our enemies. Today it may hasten my death. I do not know. For I was not always the shrunken and feeble one you have known in your young life."

B'rtha's voice sounded patient. "I have heard your stories many times, Eldest, the stories of your great battles with the enemy in foreign lands beyond the mountains."

"Yes, that is what I have become. I am the Eldest, he who sits by the light of the glowstones and tells tales of the heroic past to children." *One last time, beloved.* "Help me to sit up, child." B'rtha knelt behind him and put her hands under his shoulders. With her pushing he managed to sit up and cross his legs into a half-lotus. The dizziness came again. He covered his face with his hands until it past. B'rtha drew the bearskins over his gaunt shoulders.

"Go and sit over by the wall and observe, so you may tell my sons what you have seen when they return," he said.

"Eldest, my brother told me to keep you quiet, lying still. He said you must rest."

"That time is past, little one."

"Eldest, father, you are too old to be a warrior."

"That remains to be seen, little one—now do as I have told you. Your brother will have questions when he returns."

Ku'en held the LyFE Stone in his hands, palm under palm, thumbs together. He centered and calmed his mind. In the silence of the cave the stone's awakening began as a low sound in his mind that became a soft tone in his ears and the tiniest vibration in his palms. The red stone slowly grew larger, heavier, and warm to the touch. Ruby red lights sprang upward, spiraled, and orbited above the stone, circled for long moments and flew inward again and illuminated the core. The stone's beauty stirred his pulse. He sat more erect. There came a familiar voice.

"Rejuvenation or death, the odds are even, Ku'en."

"Wasting no words as usual, I see, Stone."

"My design does not support casual conversation—as you know well."

"So you have told me countless times, my old friend. In any case, I welcome death here and now,

Stone, or by my enemies." *One last time, beloved.* "Proceed."

Each time greatly resembled the first time the metamorphosis took him, but the pain of rejuvenation grew worse with every repetition. He felt his heartbeat grow faster still. The familiar, sharp clarity of mind came, when all things seemed to interlace and become one. His eyesight became sharper and shapes and colors grew more vibrant and more distinct. A tremendous sudden surge of strength and vitality flowed through his limbs and he leapt to his feet, watching his frail arms begin to enlarge, muscles expanding, filling with blood and tissue. His enfeebled chest swelled and he grew taller and broader and denser rising to his full height of some nine feet. But now as always before the pain of rebirth began. It erupted at the base of his skull in the old brain and bent him double, forcing him down to his knees. He threw back his head and cried out in agony. The cells in his body expanded, divided, stretched, and doubled, each one a tiny burning coal of memory. His back arched and he thrust his arms up and backward, pilloried in pain. Screams escaped from him again and again with the coursing waves of pain. Then the dreams began.

In the first dream, as always, Ku'en saw Proteus for the first time. Ku'en and his clan, now called

Denisovans by scientists, belonged to an early species related to modern man. He and his people crested a steep hill and found themselves in a grove of ginkgo trees, a bright yellow carpet of their leaves at their feet. He placed his leathery palm on the rough, striated bark of a ginkgo, pausing to rest. A hooded shape appeared and hovered soundlessly before them. Ku'en recoiled in fear and turned to scramble away with his small group back down the hill, but the voice sounded in his mind and froze him in place. His body turned to face the hovering figure.

"I will call you 'Ku'en'." The figure raised his gloved hand holding the LyFE Stone and a blinding light shone out from it and engulfed the group. The light passed through Ku'en's raised arms and hands, into and through his mind, illuminating corners that had been dark and inaccessible. Links were formed and neural networks organized. Neurons fired and chemical messages spread. Logic and knowledge appeared with images of animals and plants and the names for these and of other things. With them came the gift of speech and language.

The hooded figure spoke aloud. "I am Proteus. You are Ku'en, the First, named for my creator."

The first word Ku'en spoke aloud was his name. He stood straighter, squared his shoulders, and turned to survey his clan. He looked back at Proteus and said his name "Ku'en", pointing to his chest.

Proteus lifted his hand and pulled off the hood and the robe revealing his silver, ovoid shape. The surface of the figure reflected the bright sunlight above. Ku'en and his clan shrank back and covered their eyes again, but peeped through their fingers. In time they grew used to Proteus' presence and the changes he brought to their lives. He taught them to sharpen their spears by fire-hardening them and gave them the names for their weapons. He brought the first wolves to their firesides that would become their hunting companions.

Then Ku'en dreamed the dreams of his first metamorphosis, of the battles, blood, ashes, and death. Across the years he strode, leading his small tribe of Warriors, always driving the Archarans and their slaves before him, slaughtering the Okees. Over and over through the ages he battled, grew old, and rejuvenated to fight again, down through the millennia.

The dreams faded and he awoke as the pain subsided. *Strong.* He leapt to his feet, flexing great long arms and giant hands as more power and more power coursed through them and his flesh filled his ancient skin. He straightened and stretched further, towering over B'rtha. Ku'en held up the LyFE Stone before him and gazed at it. *One last time, beloved.* He placed the stone back in the bag.

"Eldest," B'rtha cried, staring upward, she looked awestruck. "Is that you?"

"Yes, little one, it is I. It appears I am a Warrior still. But a Warrior also needs a weapon." He searched among the bearskins where he had lain until he found a huge stone ax. He hefted it twice, savoring the feel of it in his hand again. He ran his forefinger down its handle to his mark and then swung it upward in an arc until he held it high above his head.

He threw back his head and shouted. "I AM KU'EN." His voice rang throughout the cavern, reverberating off the walls and echoing down the passages. Ku'en reached down and took the leather bag gently from her hand. He took a leather thong from the bag and fastened the ax to his waist above his leather kilt. He removed a brown and unremarkable stone from the bag also, and hung the bag over his shoulder and around his neck with the rawhide strap. He held the stone in the palms of both hands. *This life is over.*

"And now, little one, I must go. You will tell your brother that Sooleawa has called me to fight our ancient enemy. He must look to see me no more.

"Eldest—father, wait."

"There is no more time, B'rtha. MoVR Stone. Take me to Sooleawa."

"There is death, Ku'en," the stone said.

"So be it. Proceed. I AM KU'EN.

CHAPTER THIRTY-THREE

ISLAND IN THE STREAM

CARDEROCK MD MONDAY
JUNE 5 5PM

"Jesus, Mary and Joseph, Frank, tell me I am not seeing this," John Petrucelli said.

Frank Novovaski watched as Vaso Island rocked off its bedrock foundations and slowly began to grind south down the river, crushing trees and smaller rock formations in its path. After seventeen years of debunking Iowa crop circles, ancient alien frauds and swamp gas space ships, Novovaski had skeptical down. But whole islands just up and taking a trip downstream? *It's got to be Aliens this time.* But he didn't say that out loud. "Ok, this Oberlin thing is really starting to piss me off. I got one nerve left and it's getting on it."

"What makes you think this is tied up with that?" Petrucelli said.

"I just know it—that's all."

They watched until only the top of the island and the cloud that obscured it could be seen above the trees, and then the island disappeared altogether.

"I would say islands picking up and moving all by themselves like that wasn't normal. But I know how you hate it when I say things like that," Petrucelli said.

"You know, I actually don't mind this time."

Petrucelli sat quiet for a moment. "Shit, Frank, it's headed for the American Legion Bridge and it's rush hour."

"I know. I also won't mind if you drive too fast this time."

Petrucelli drove furiously out of the parking lot and raced down the park road to exit onto the parkway towards Georgetown, but their progress slowed with the heavy traffic. Siren blaring, Petrucelli weaved in and out of the frozen lanes of cars, finally riding on the shoulder. Novovaski rolled down the window of the Black Suburban and waved at the gawkers, shouting at them to make way. He scanned the dense forest on the river side of the road, hoping to catch sight of the island. Once or twice he glimpsed it, but he could always hear it, like the sound of sixty-five bulldozers shoving boulders downriver, relentless and dismaying. His stomach started to get queasy. Then the forest buffer with the shoreline rose and widened out and the undergrowth thickened and obscured his vision. Helicopters roared overhead, and police and emergency vehicles trailed behind the suburban, sirens screaming at the paralyzed traffic. As they crept past the David Taylor Model Basin on the left, Novovaski saw traffic clogged the entrance to 495 ahead. A dull pain started in his stomach, up high, the site of an old ulcer. He put his hand over it.

"There's not enough shoulder to get by up the ramp and onto the bridge, Frank," Petrucelli said.

"Never mind the bridge. There's nothing we can do up on the damn bridge anyway. Just stay to the right on the parkway and pull off down under the damn bridge. I know we can see the river from there."

The American Legion Bridge loomed up and stood overhead. Petrucelli parked on the shoulder beneath the span that crossed over the parkway. The bridge abutments marched across the Potomac here, carrying nearly a quarter mile of concrete and steel highway, vaulting on huge piers, and crossing the rocky water from Maryland to Virginia. Novovaski heard horns blaring from above and voices reverberating, echoing under the bridge, and knew some traffic must be stopped. Novovaski got out of the

Suburban and stood by the SUV watching upstream. The pain in his stomach sharpened. Soon the sounds from the bridge above were drowned out by the thundering sound of the onslaught of the island. Now he could see the top of the island, high above the trees on the shore beside him, as it continued to grind its way downstream, laying waste to everything in its path.

Petrucelli got out and came around to stand beside him. "Do you feel that?"

Novovaski could feel it. The SUV began to vibrate and the ground beneath his feet started to tremble. He looked up and saw the bridge begin to shake. The sound of rocks breaking and trees splintering and falling roared louder as the island neared the bridge. The soaring stone cliffs of Vaso Island ground their way into view. It approached the bridge, the remaining distance shrinking. But now there came another sound. A kind of continuous thundering echoed off the bridge abutments—deafening him, and he heard a heightened screeching and groaning, the sounds of bending steel and concrete shattering. He saw a span of the bridge out in the middle of the river bend inward, even though the island hadn't reached it. Large pieces of the bridge railing began to twist, tear free, and fall, unraveling like string back towards him until it hung in segments, ripped apart and falling near the SUV. He stood frozen as he watched a huge chunk of concrete fall from the bridge down onto the hood of their Suburban, crushing it and shattering the windshield. Flying glass exploded outward, striking Novovaski in the face. He staggered, but recovered, and carefully picked the glass off his face. He turned to see his partner on the ground, Petrucelli's face mostly covered with glass, his eyes closed, and a deep cut across his forehead. The bent windshield frame lay half across Petrucelli's chest. Blood ran down his cheeks onto his starched white shirt and Armani tie. *God, he would hate that.* Novovaski knelt down and started to shift the windshield frame off his partner.

"John. John, are you all right?" he said.

At the fierce sound of steel bending above him, he looked up to see another hunk of the bridge railing falling towards him. It struck the roof of the Suburban, bending it inward, and shattered, hurling concrete debris at the agents. Struck in the chest, Novovaski fell backward to the pavement. Everything went black.

Wkyak sat at his console and watched as the Zlayers on the platform fell one after the other, utterly destroyed by the enemy Warriors. The Zlayers' weapons failed to damage even one of their enemies.

No, things were not going well, and he knew Ukruek would take it out on him, as always. The platform began to vibrate and rock violently. He refocused the monitor from further out, seeing the whole Vaso island scene from a greater height. The island broke loose and moved off its foundations. He hit the com button, pleased he had something good to report. This time he might just escape more abuse.

"Prefect Ukruek, the disrupter beam and the Zlayer's antigravity platform together have broken the island loose and it is moving down the river as planned," he said. "The distraction from our attack on the Society building will be completely effective."

The prefect appeared in the wall screen above. "Lucky for you, but how do you explain what these Warriors of Proteus are doing to our Zlayers? They're completely graked."

"Well, that is, unfortunately, not going as well as expected."

"No kokee, Wkyak, but I asked you *how.*"

Wkyak squeaked. "I don't know how, Prefect, but they burned through our soldiers like RkSak across CleMatika. One of the Warriors defeated both Erebus and Sykyak, destroyed them, and freed the woman."

"Yes, well, those two are of no consequence. Their usefulness was over. Their purpose there was diversion only, but even so we could not afford to lose that many Zlayers."

"The failure belongs to Erebus. His faulty intelligence gathering set up this disaster. Erebus told us the Warriors used primitive weapons only. But they swept us from the platform, disintegrating our Zlayers, and they suffered no casualties, not even one. Our weapons couldn't touch them," Wkyak said.

"Obviously, Wkyak, our enemies on the United Planets' inner council have broken their own covenants in order to aid the humans. Either Proteus, the 'social scientist,' has been replaced by a military leader, or else Erebus misjudged him. It may be this Proteus has himself decided to escalate his weaponry. Either way, you should have anticipated this and prepared. Where are they now?"

"Proteus has moved his ship downstream from the island and attempts to stop its forward motion as you planned."

"Then, Wkyak, *as I planned*, obtain the coordinates and take us into position over the Protean Society building. Forget the Warriors and our losses. You will pay for that later. We must destroy their stronghold now while Proteus is still occupied with the island. Signal our mole to drop the society's shields. It is time to finish this little farce."

"Yes, Prefect."

"And stay alert, Wkyak, Proteus will come eventually. You must be prepared to focus the MoVR on each warrior and transport them into the outer atmosphere as they appear, *safely*. When we have destroyed this Society and this little operation ends, we will bring the Warriors on board the ship and cold-suspend them for later use."

"Is that wise, Prefect?" Wkyak said.

"Our sponsors will want their DNA, and their weaponry, so they must be preserved. Do you understand? If you lose or damage even one you will lose those precious red hairs of yours and the bald head they fail so miserably to cover."

Wkyak placed his hand carefully on the top of his skull. He thought it better to say nothing.

CHAPTER THIRTY-FOUR

TREACHERY

GEORGETOWN DC MONDAY
JUNE 5 5PM

Páihuái rested Sheila on the stretcher in the society's basement infirmary and arranged her injured arms at her sides. She had passed out on his shoulder before they reached the society building, and she didn't wake. He put two great fingers alongside her cheek and held them there for a long moment. He brushed away the hair that covered her eyes. A blanket lay on a nearby table, and he took it up, shook it out, and laid it over her. His hands dropped to his sides and hung there, opening and closing. He stood beside the stretcher watching her, bent forward, up on his toes, silent as the white room that enclosed them.

Panacea appeared in a doorway and glided forward, carrying plasticast sleeves and a coverlet. A table bearing instruments trailed behind her. Her white robe hung loose about her, and she threw her hood back, revealing her face. Páihuái straightened and locked his eyes on hers, unmoving. She paused to observe the tableau for a moment, and then spoke. Her voice sounded warm and yet firm, brooking no disagreement.

"Now, Páihuái, you are in the way. I see what you feel, but stand on the other side if you want to watch. I have to remove the old plasticasts and address her wounds. I am certain the enemy has reopened the old ones and cut even deeper than before."

He side-stepped around to the other side of the stretcher and focused on the SyLF. She scanned Sheila with the hand-held diagnosticator. Páihuái leaned in as Panacea pulled aside the blanket and further scanned Sheila's arms, taking readings. The SyLF nodded without comment, seeming satisfied. She began to laser away the old sleeves from Sheila's arms. As each plasticast peeled away, he saw the old wounds had begun to heal, the flesh rejoining and smoothing, but just below those sutures deep cuts had pulled them apart again. Páihuái saw white bone showing amongst the torn tissue. His body shuddered, but he did not look away. He placed his hand on Sheila's shoulder. Panacea took a clear container of blood from the table beside her. She pulled up Sheila's Gi pants leg and attached the container along Sheila's calf. She cleaned the new and old wounds and disinfected and re-sutured them. The laser suture lines were doubled now, a chevron's V. Finishing, she recovered Sheila's arms with plasticast sleeves. The chevrons remained visible inside the sleeves.

Páihuái felt NiTawis' father enter the lab and come to stand beside him. The old man reached up to place a hand on his arm. Páihuái tore his eyes from Sheila's arms and fixed them on Panacea's face and her two large, spherical eyes. Pop Vaughn spoke as if for Páihuái. "Will she be okay?"

Panacea's voice held reassurance. "Yes, but this time she will need rest to recuperate. The wounds are deeper and she has lost more blood," Panacea said, her hand on Sheila's forehead. She turned to look up at Páihuái, her voice kind, but firm. "Leave her care to me, Páihuái. Your job here is done and the battle has begun."

Páihuái stared long at Panacea, and then, with the slightest nod, turned as if to go.

Pop Vaughn caught at his sleeve. "But he has no weapons, Panacea."

"Páihuái will not touch weapons, Pop, and we don't know why. But, when he chooses to, Páihuái channels an energy, a destructive power unique to him.

"I don't understand," Pop said.

"Not even Proteus or our Musean creators fully comprehend. But the time for talk is over. You, Páihuái, silent Warrior, are needed above. The enemy comes, and now is your hour. Go, there is evil."

Sooleawa put her head down on her desk, cradling it in her arms. The effort to contact Ku'en drained her. Her ability to reach the minds of the Warriors in remote locales around the earth resulted in the defeat of the enemy many times, but the mind links that were so effortless in the past had grown debilitating in the last year. She didn't have the size or all the strength of the other Warriors, but after her own metamorphosis her mental abilities facilitated Proteus' success over the centuries. Did the mind link cause the headache that began at the base of her neck and rose to attack her temples? Perhaps her abilities waned. Had the weight of the years eroded her gift? *After so many centuries, have I begun to grow old?* Be it strain or age or failing ability, explanations changed nothing. But Ku'en held the LyFE stone. If he survived should she rejuvenate as he had done countless times? Today five hundred years seemed long enough for anyone to live.

The pain lessened. She sat up straighter and rubbed her temples with her fingers. She looked about her small office that sat on the second floor above the K St. entrance of the society, but images of the past superimposed themselves in her mind's eye. Reaching out to Ku'en breached the walls of memory, and now like hungry birds they crowded in. First she saw herself in her native village on the banks of the Potomac River, collecting fresh water shells in the shallows as a child. Then there came the dark time of her capture by the enemy. Her earliest memories of Proteus and her rescue next, and then Ku'en rose up in her mind. He frightened her at first. He and all his people were so huge and so different. The first time she saw him he stooped to offer his great finger for her to hold with her small hand. He smiled his gap-toothed smile at her, and spoke her name sound by sound, as if each syllable felt strange in his mouth. Though he seemed kind, still she remained frightened of him until the day the Archarans with their Okees and slaves attacked Proteus' stronghold at Point of Rocks by the Potomac River. The walls exploded inward, killing three of the Warriors. The enemy came surging in, so many of them. But then Ku'en came and rescued her, took her up in his arms and drove through the waves of attackers, his

giant ax arcing, smashing through the ranks of enemies that came, until there were no more. Then he
took her to safety up river. *How could I not love him,
then?*

The memories drifted away like scarlet leaves
on the wind. She extended her hands into the pool of
sunlight that entered through the oculus above her.
The window cast its circle on the shining surface of
her desk. The age spots on the backs of her hands
were expanding, and her fingers had begun to twist
with arthritis. She rubbed her fingers. They felt cold.
Her office and the Society building beyond gathered
a stony silence, as if waiting and she felt uneasy.
Soon it would all begin, she knew. *What should I do?*
It did no good to worry, everything that could be
done had been, but the fears played and replayed in
her mind. Would Proteus and the Warriors survive at
Vaso? Would Ku'en come in time? Would he come
at all? She took up the green deck prism in her hands
that Jefferson gave her and extended it forward into
the sun circle. The sunlight shone through the prism
and cast a green halo onto her desk. *What would you
think of all this, Thomas?* Holding the prism calmed
her, and warmed her fingers. But she felt the unease
return, an anxiety. But what?

Wolf made a small noise at her side. She
looked over at him and reached out to place her hand
on his back and stroked his ashened white fur. The

best of all his forebears carried that color also. Other colors had come and gone down through the centuries but the ash-colored wolves were the smartest, largest in size, and the most devoted. She ran out of names for them, and so this one became just Wolf. The wolves had grown long-lived and more and more human-sensitive in their behavior with each generation over the centuries, until at last they became capable of forming a bond with humans beyond anything, save perhaps that of identical twins. Wolf embodied the best of the best. She believed he often knew what she thought, even at times what she felt. So when the day came she was reluctant to let Proteus take him to protect the child, Starkey, but though sad, she knew no other guardian could have been more constant or steadfast. Starkey represented the future, and the priority of his safety overrode her tremendous feeling of loss. She reveled in the wolf's presence today, even though she knew it would be temporary.

"Yes, Wolf, Ku'en will come. That is, if the LyFE stone's rejuvenation restores him this one last time. He does not know."

Wolf looked up into her face. His silence held intent. His body stood taut, as if poised to spring. He raised his head higher and with his nose he directed her attention to the door of her small office. He padded over and stood by the dark oaken door. He turned to look back at her. He gave low growl. At that moment an alarm bell began to sound.

"That's the shield alarm, the shields are down." Sooleawa leapt up, sped through open the door, and rushed up the wide, curving staircase beyond. Why were the shields down? What was Michael doing? Michael August should be in the control room above, monitoring the society's systems and coordinating the operation at Vaso Island with Proteus. As she took the stairs two at a time, she repeated her old suspicions to herself. She had never been completely comfortable with August, but Master Yamashima championed the man. Proteus' faith in the Master's judgement was paramount, and the SyLF tried to quiet her unease.

When she reached the control room door she found it locked. She pounded on it. "Michael, open the door, it's Sooleawa." When no answer came, she put her shoulder against the door and burst it open. It slammed against the wall.

August turned in his chair at the control center. He smiled, but his face twisted as he did so. "Hello, Hannah. Or do you like Sooleawa today?" August's usual obsequious tone had disappeared. "It's surprise time." His voice sounded a sing-song.

Hannah took two steps into the room and stopped as Wolf approached her side and stood stiffly, growling. "No, Wolf, stay," she said, placing her hand on the wolf's head.

Multiple screens above the console behind August showed scenes of the battle at Vaso Island. She saw Masato and the Warriors advancing, destroying the Zlayers. Red lights on the console flashed and the shield alarm continued to sound. She heard Proteus voice speaking to the Warriors. Then her eyes lowered to a weapon she didn't recognize that appeared in August's hands, some kind of gun. She stared at his blue within blue eyes, her suspicions resolved. No, she felt no surprise. *Traitor.*

Holding herself still she forced her voice to be calm. "Michael, why are the shields down? We will soon be under attack."

"That's the surprise, *Hannah*, the attack starts now, but I am not part of *your* 'we', *my* 'we' comes to destroy you." Michael August raised the gun higher to aim at her head.

"You, Master Yamashima's disciple? What kind of vile creature are you that you could betray the man who took you in, fed you, and clothed you?" The disgust in her voice was mirrored in the darkness and anger on her face.

"That gullible fool? He is not *my Master.* No, *primitive*, my Masters live across the galaxy. Proteus' foolish naiveté and that of Yamashima will reap their reward today."

"You can't win. Your Masters have always failed in the past and they always will."

"No, *primitive*, it is your pitiful secret society and its foolish détente that have failed," August said, rising.

Wolf continued his low growl and crouched, ready to spring.

Hannah slide one foot back into a defensive stance, raising her hands in a Wing Chun position. "You assume too much, traitor. Even if Proteus and the Warriors fall, one comes who will destroy you and your Archarans," Sooleawa said. *If only I am right. Where are you, beloved?*

"Your threats are empty. This time our Masters have sent a prefect who does not fear to scour you humans from the surface of the planet. Too long you have thwarted our efforts. Your Proteus and his Warriors are about to meet their end. Now you will die, primitive."

Sooleawa saw his fist tighten on the gun. Just as he fired, she dove beneath the fusion beam into a forward roll, but the beam burnt down across her back, laying open her spine. Coming up out of the roll, her knife-hand broke August's clavicle. August staggered, but recovered as she fell, her deep wound gushing blood and spinal fluid onto the floor. Paralyzed on her back, she watched as August raised the weapon over his head in both hands to hammer her with the fusion gun. But he had forgotten Wolf. Hanna heard him snarl and saw the wolf arching through the air. August lowered his weapon and fired at the wolf, cutting a blaze along his shoulder. Heedless of the pain he must have felt, Wolf took the traitor at the throat. The great wolf locked his jaws around the man's neck and ripped out the man's jugular vein with one fierce twist of his head as he rode August down to the floor. Wolf, growling on, tore at the man's head and face until blue discs fell from the man's eyes revealing large pupils that leaked yellow fluid on the floor. Wolf did not stop tearing at him until Sooleawa called his name. He returned to stand over her and she raised her head and looked at him. She held one hand out towards him. He came closer and placed his forehead against her face.

"Goodbye, my friend. Go find Jack Starkey, protect him." Her eyes closed.

She started awake when a fusion bolt struck Wolf then, cutting his body in half. His head and shoulders fell beside Sooleawa's. She saw the Zlayer SyLF who shot Wolf hovering in the doorway. The Zlayer aimed his weapon at her.

Ku'en came.

Shoving the Zlayer forward, he stooped to enter the room. Ku'en's axe sang in its arc, blurring in its speed. The axe struck the Zlayer in the back, cleaving, dismembering. The pieces careened and exploded against the wall where they fell. Ku'en stooped, turning the axe's hammer head down, and pounded the remaining fragments into dust, striking over and over again, deep, guttural sounds escaping his lips. He continued pounding until he heard a small sound come from Sooleawa. He shook his head and shoulders violently and turned to see her watching him. He moved back to her side and knelt on the floor beside her. Laying down his stone axe, he took her up in his arms. She lay quite still at first, opened her eyes, and managed a smile. The tears in his eyes overflowed and ran down his face.

She whispered, halting, shoulders quaking now. "Ku'en," she said. "You came."

"Yes, it's me. Ach, but I have come too late, beloved."

"But you have come. And so there is hope."

A spasm of pain struck her body, and her eyes closed, but reopened.

"I will make them pay for hurting you, Sooleawa," he said.

Her body tensed, shook. A strangled whisper forced its way out. "August was a traitor. He dropped the shields. The Archarans are attacking. Save Jack Starkey if you can. Avenge me, if you wish. But stop the Archarans and save the Sapiens, my love."

"I will, beloved."

Her eyes closed. Her back arched and her body twisted. She cried out for the last time.

CHAPTER THIRTY-FIVE

RETRIBUTION

GEORGETOWN DC MONDAY
JUNE 5 6PM

Ku'en clutched Sooleawa closer to his breast
and began to rock back and forth on his knees, strok-
ing her hair. At last he lowered his head and sat still,
ignoring the sounds of battle and carnage filling the
control room around him. Low moans escaped his
lips as he sat cradling her in his arms. The moans
grew louder and more guttural and deeper and more
violent, until they became wails. And the wails became screams. Then they stopped. Echoes bounced
around the walls of the control room.

He lowered Sooleawa back down on the grey
tile floor. Ku'en rose and turned his attention to the
many screens above the control board. On one he

saw and heard the sounds of the destruction at the American Legion Bridge. On another he saw the bridge of Proteus' ship and heard the SyLF's voice ordering the ship back to the Society. Ku'en searched the board until he found the shield controls. He brought them back up. Too late, for he heard the sounds of explosions assaulting his ears and the building quaked around him. He did not heed these things and turned back to Sooleawa and Wolf.

For a while he stood over her, gazing down at her face. He stooped and rested his hand on the wolf's head. Then he picked up his axe and stood. Anger ignited and flamed within him. He felt himself growing larger and larger, until the control room seemed to shrink around him. He thrust back his shoulders and raised his stone axe. The thunder of his voice caused the walls to shudder and the floor to tremble.

"You who have done this —you will die. I am Ku'en."

He set his jaw and let all the rage inside him rise and burn, until his giant body shook. When his quaking shoulders were still he held aloft his axe. An aura formed around the haft and the blade. The stone blade grew heavier and shone from within. The aura from the blade sheathed down around him, until brilliant light shown around his huge form. Then Ku'en, Eldest, first and most ancient Warrior, called to arms by Proteus and the Museans in the distant past, moved out in vengeance. The last warning he gave to the enemy sounded only in his mind.

Now I come.

>>>

Alkira sat silent as Proteus set the StarMoVR down in the underground hangar of the Protean Society. She followed him and the Warriors out of the ship and onto the concrete landing pad.

Proteus gathered them all around before the elevator doors. "We can expect the enemy to attack the society building from above, if they're not already here. The shields were taken down and brought back up, and I don't know why yet. As long as the shields and stealth systems hold, our perimeter should be secure. Masato, take your team and proceed to the roof and prepare to defend."

Starkey moved to stand in front of the SyLF, his face awash with concern. "Proteus, I want to see Sheila before I go anywhere."

"Feeling all clucky are we, Jack?" Alkira said, her sneer undisguised

"Go with Masato, Jack, your skills are best utilized there," Proteus said. "Panacea watches over her. I will check on her. Alkira, come with me. You and I have another errand. You participated in the development of the particle-anti particle weapon that waits for us in storage. I think it's time has come."

"We'll look after your little Sheila," Alkira said, shoving Starkey towards Masato.

Starkey stepped forward and shoved her backwards with both hands. She leapt forward to shove him again, but Starkey caught her arms. They grappled, pushing off against each other. Proteus moved to place his hands on their shoulders and the two Warriors froze in place.

"*Enough*," Proteus said. "You two can play cats-in-a-bag, later." Explosions sounded above. The floor and walls of the hangar shook. "The enemy comes." Proteus released Starkey and Alkira, but beckoned her to him. "Alkira, stand close. We will MoVR together. Masato, deploy your team."

"When this is over, Alkira," Starkey said. Starkey turned and followed Masato and the other Warriors into the elevator, looking back over his shoulder at Alkira. Proteus waved him on.

Alkira stepped under Proteus' outstretched arm and watched as the underground hangar around them began to blur. Proteus transported them to the infirmary where Panacea stood beside Sheila's bed.

Panacea maneuvered to hover between them and Sheila. "Before you start, my patient is still critical, she must not be disturbed."

Alkira slid past the SyLF to stand beside Sheila and look down at her. Sheila opened her eyes. "Hello there, *Sheila*, having a nice little lie down, are we?" Alkira said.

Panacea maneuvered Alkira aside and hovered between them. "Have you not understood? Do you not know what 'critical' means? What are you trying to do, Alkira?"

Alkira moved back and leaned against a door jamb, examining her fingernails. "What does it matter? She's nothing but a *human*, and a weak one at that."

Proteus answered. "Her DNA and yours differ by a fraction of a percent. You are human also, whether you care to admit it or not. She lacks little but your arrogance. That is your weakness, Alkira, and one day it will be your downfall."

"Then let her fight beside me if she is my equal. The particle weapon requires two to hold and fire it."

"No, she is not ready," Panacea said.

"Give her what you gave to me at the battle of Alice Springs, back home. You brought me back from the dead and raised me up to fight again."

Panacea stood silent.

Proteus intervened. "Well, Panacea, will it restore her?"

"Yes, it will. We have used it many times without ill effect."

Alkira saw Sheila try to sit up, but she fell back down. "I can make my own decisions, thank you very much," Sheila said. "I will take it, whatever it is."

"She asks for the Restorative, Panacea," Proteus said. "It is a matter of free will."

"Yes," Panacea said. "But first there is an unanswered question. Sheila, you're pregnant. Did you know?"

"Yes, no, well that SyLF, Erebus, said so when he kidnapped me."

"Well, you are. You must consider your child in this decision," Panacea said.

Sheila lay quiet for a moment. "Will it hurt the baby?"

"No, in fact, our experience has been the children grow strong and healthy, immune to the diseases of human childhood."

Sheila's voice came stronger with a hard edge. "Then if this Restorative works, I will take my chances with the rest of the Warriors. I am not going to lie here and prove Alkira is right, that I'm nothing but a weak *human*. I will fight with the others. If I die, then I die. Give it to me—now."

No one saw Alkira's smile.

Upstairs outside the control room, Ku'en took the main hall, advancing down toward the marble stairs that led up to the fourth floor tower and the roof. Zlayers and Okees appeared from rooms and doorways lining the hall, only to be struck and exploded by Ku'en's axe or disintegrated by the energy beams that leapt from it. Ku'en stormed down the hall, leaping and spinning to strike those who targeted him from behind, to his sides and ahead, as their fusion beams bounced off him without damage. The rage within him cooled and hardened. Cold hatred reigned inside him as he laid waste to all those who appeared to oppose him. Each disintegrated enemy gratified him, and he grunted with satisfaction with each blow struck and each beam that burned through an enemy. At the end of the hall he took the long, arching marble staircase that led up to the roof. Thrusting open the double doors at the top, he saw Páihuái battling Okees, Zlayers and mutant humans across the rooftop and helipad. More and more enemies materialized on the concrete pad, and the surrounding rooftop and tower, though Páihuái destroyed all who engaged him. Ku'en strode forward, nodded to Páihuái, and moved to stand back to back with the silent giant. They conjoined in their destruction of the enemy. Many came to attack them and perished.

A deafening roar that came from above caused Ku'en to look up. The Archaran ship appeared above them. Ku'en saw the society's shielding come on line, colored waves surrounding the roof, but the warship hovered inside the domed perimeter of the shield. A powerful fusion beam fired from a revolving weapons array on the hull of the ship. It tore Páihuái from Ku'en's side, downing him. Moments later Ku'en saw the blue of an Archaran MoVR beam strike Páihuái and he disappeared. Ku'en's axe sent three beams in quick succession that destroyed that weapons array, but another array deployed and fired a beam striking him, forcing him down to his knees, and continued firing at him in rotation. It held him in place, though it did not injure him.

He saw Masato and Starkey materialize on the helipad, followed by Darake and NiTawis. Engaging the battle before them, they leapt high in the air, striking and destroying the weapon that targeted Ku'en, and more of the weapons arrays that bristled along the underside of the hull of the ship.

Rising, Ku'en watched as the ship withdrew two hundred feet or more, and another MoVR beam targeted first Masato and then Darake, and they disappeared. Now all of the remaining weapons arrays began to fire simultaneously. The fusion beams began to destroy the roof and walls of the Society building. As portions of the walls crumbled away, staircases and rooms below became visible. The ship attempted to strike Ku'en with weapons and blue MoVR beams, but he leapt upward and aside, avoiding the beams. Starkey and NiTawis, observing Ku'en dodge the MoVR, evaded it also, and fired energy beams upward, disabling more of the ship's weapons. Then NiTawis, caught by a MoVR beam, disappeared.

Ku'en saw Proteus and Alkira materialize on the roof. A short time after, Sheila and Master Yamashima appeared. Alkira approached Sheila lugging a huge two-handled weapon in one hand. "So you have come, little *human*."

"Screw you, Alkira," Sheila said, grabbing one handle of weapon and lifting it up "So, what is this thing?"

"This, *Sheila*, is a particle-antiparticle cannon, and I promise you, the clackers aren't going to like it at all," Alkira said. "Can you hold up your end?"

"Watch me, *human*."

Ku'en saw Proteus drop a golden force field around the two, and Alkira take aim at the Archaran ship above and engage the weapon. Sheila staggered but caught her balance as a powerful, continuous blue beam began to flow from the weapon, targeting the warship. Alkira stood firm, legs spread in a wide stance. The beam struck the pale orange shielding surrounding the ship's hull, and cracks started to form at the impact point where a small, flaming hole appeared. The Archarans responded by redirecting all their fusion weapons fire at the two women and their cannon, but Proteus' shielding held.

"You," Ku'en called, beckoning to Starkey and drawing him to his side. "Tell Proteus he must search for the missing Warriors out in the earth's solar system. I believe the enemy has moved them there for a purpose. I don't believe they wanted to destroy them, or they would have used other weapons."

"What are you going to do?" Starkey asked.

"When that cannon has burned a hole in the ship's shielding wide enough for me to fit, I am going to take these *gaak* for a little ride." He removed the small, unremarkable brown stone from his pouch and held it up before Starkey's eyes. "This is the MoVRstone, a gift from Proteus and the Museans in the dim past. Remember it, for you may see it again. It is one of a kind, Jack Starkey, bear that in mind."

Turning, Ku'en approached the four. "Proteus, when the breach in the shielding grows wide enough, use your MoVR to send me through." He held up the MoVRstone for the SyLF to see. "If I can reach the Archaran ship, I can end this here."

Proteus nodded. Ku'en watched as Alkira and Sheila's cannon continued to burn through the warship's shielding. The flaming opening grew wider, wider still, then wide enough.

I come, Beloved. "Now, Proteus," he said.

Proteus raised his arm and engaged his MoVR beam. Seconds later, Ku'en found himself grasping the superstructure under the Archaran ship. One hand clutched a strut on the hull overhead and he hung by that arm. He raised the MoVRstone up in the other hand. He shouted above the roar as he began to swing the stone upward.

"Farewell, Proteus. MoVRstone, take me to the center of earth's sun."

There came a familiar voice. *"There will be death, Ape Man."*

"So be it. Proceed. I AM KU'EN." And he slammed the MoVRstone against the hull of the Archaran ship. Ku'en hung on and watched as the small brown stone became a glowing ember, then star bright, and acceleration stretched the light out and away, pulling him and the ship towards the sun.

>>>

In the battle cruiser above, Wkyak watched
the screen as a huge man shape appeared on the underside of the ship. Its voice was amplified and
Wkyak's com computer translated its words, "MoV-
Rstone…take me…center of the sun…"

Wkyak wilted. "Kokee. We are graked, completely grake…"

Starkey stared upward. The Archaran ship
and Ku'en disappeared. Nothing remained but the
stealth waves surrounding the society and the DC
skyline beyond. The MoVRstone fell through the air
and landed at his feet on the helipad. Ku'en's scarred
leather bag fell nearby. The bag fell open and
Ku'en's axe lay exposed. Starkey stooped, picked
them up, and hung the bag over his shoulder. He
gripped the handle of the axe, and stood looking at
the small brown stone in his hand. He looked back up
into the empty sky above. Sheila and Proteus came to
stand beside him and Sheila reached up to place a
hand on his arm. Alkira stood apart beside Master
Yamashima.

"What is this thing, Proteus?" Starkey held
the small stone out towards the SyLF.

"That, Jack, is a MoVRstone, a product of a
technology that, with good cause, is now outlawed in

the galaxy. I should say *the* MoVRstone since to my
knowledge it is the last one that exists. I gave it to
Ku'en in the dim past for a task, and I have regretted
it several times over the years, for the Eldest's
judgement sometimes appeared, well, emotional. But
he would not give it back."

Starkey weighed the stone in his hand.
"Ku'en showed it to me and told me to remember it.
He said I might see it again. I know he wanted me to
have it," Starkey said.

"There are more things in the galaxy and on
earth, Jack, than you have dreamed of heretofore, but
we now must search for our Warriors. Keep the stone
and Ku'en's things for now, we'll discuss it later."

Starkey looked around at the devastation of
the roof top. Stairwells and rooms on the floors below stared back at him, exposed and naked in the
wreckage. "Ku'en said the Warriors would be out
around the earth, orbiting. He thought the Archarans
wanted to preserve them for analysis." He walked
over to the SyLF.

"Yes, we can hope for that. Come Sheila and
Alkira. Hiro, move closer, I will MoVR us all down
to the control room. The stairs and elevator are gone.
We will begin the search for the Warriors. I have
every hope they are still alive. Their uniforms will
have protected them." The roof grew indistinct and
faded.

Starkey expected the control room, constructed of the heaviest shielding, to remain intact. He did not did not expect what they found. Sheila made the first sounds as they materialized. She placed her hand over her mouth and stifled the scream that began. Michael August's body lay on the tile floor, neck torn through, the head almost severed from the body. Yellow fluid leaked from the eyes. Sooleawa lay dead nearby upon her back, her body arranged as if in burial. The remains of a destroyed Zlayer littered the corner nearby. Proteus lowered close to the floor, hovering beside Sooleawa. Wolf's body lay beside her, burned into two halves.

"Michael must have been an Archaran spy." Proteus' words hung in the air of the control room like a black miasma.

Starkey knelt beside Sooleawa, placing his hand upon Wolf's side, his head bowed. Master Yamashima knelt beside him and placed his small hand on the great shoulder.

Alkira spoke from the doorway. "There's a bloody great pile of Zlayers outside and many more down the hall."

"Ku'en has been here," Proteus said.

Starkey rose. Sheila came forward and stood beside him, pressing her shoulder against his.

"This is my failure." Master Yamashima said, standing. He moved to the doorway, shoulders sunken, and turned back to stare at the carnage. "I should have seen through August. I am at fault."

Proteus rose also. "I put Michael August in charge of security here, Hiro. Further, self-reproach is not productive. The enemy deceived us, not for the first time."

"Hey," Alkira said. "We have four Warriors missing, maybe stranded out there somewhere in space. Could we discuss who the donger is after we find them?"

"Yes, Alkira, you are right," Proteus said. "We shall dissemble no more. Control, activate."

"Control Activated, Proteus."

"Initiate full withdrawal, Control. Take us to Sanctuary."

CHAPTER THIRTY-SIX

CONCRETE

ANDREWS AFB TUESDAY JUNE 6

"I would say it's impossible for a whole god-dam island to sail down the Potomac and crash into the American Legion Bridge," John Petrucelli said, "but I know how you hate it when I say things like that." Petrucelli clutched the tube of the IV that ran from the clear plastic bag down into his arm, shifted slightly and rolled over to face his partner.

Frank heard a small groan push out as his partner's turned. "Oh, so we're awake again are we? Yeah, well, I do hate it and you already did fucking say it. Three times," Frank said.

"Well, that's what happened, Frank."

The hospital room at Andrews started to get fuzzy around the edges, and Frank struggled to stay awake. *The drugs must be kicking in...* When he woke up again, their boss Bill Carnegie stood between Frank's hospital bed and Petrucelli's, talking to the other agent. Carnegie must have been speaking before Frank woke. The man's grey flannel suit hung about him in a hundred wrinkles. His tie hung loose, his shirt collar unbuttoned. Frank thought Carnegie looked worn down, frayed at the edges. Stubble of beard darkened his jaw line.

"...the agents you left behind at the scene reported that one minute the damn building was there and the next minute it was gone," Carnegie said.

Frank struggled to sit up. Sharp pain ripped down his leg, the broken one. "Ouch. That makes no sense whatever."

"Oh, hey, Frank. I'm glad you're awake. You need to hear this. No, it doesn't make sense," Carnegie said, "and it gets worse. When they reviewed the drones' recordings of the scene they showed the impossible—the society building simply disappeared, one minute standing there, big as life, the next minute gone. Except for one frame." The man paused.

"Go on, don't keep us hanging. What did that frame show?" Frank asked.

"That one frame showed a different scene altogether. In that shot the society building had sustained heavy damage, like it was bombed out." Carnegie reached back and massaged his neck. "That

shot was superimposed over the other shot of the un-
damaged building like a ghost image. Both appeared
together in the last frame before the building disappeared completely."

"How do you explain that?" Petrucelli asked.

Carnegie shrugged. "I can't. The agents on
surveillance there also reported feeling the ground
shake repeatedly, though they saw and heard nothing.
They described it as earth tremors. But the science
guys say that the instrument readings show no seismic activity took place."

"Did they ever see Starkey? We know he
went in there," Petrucelli asked.

Carnegie eased over to the window and
grabbed a chair. Frank heard planes taking off and
landing during the night from the runway across
from the hospital, the noisy C5 turbofan engines
struggling to lift the heavy Air Force transports. Carnegie pulled the metal chair up between the two beds
and sat down, crossing one leg over the other. He
leaned back and took a cigarette out of his pocket
and held it between two fingers, but he didn't light it.

"Nobody saw him, or anybody else for that
matter, near the scene," Carnegie said. "Starkey has
disappeared without a trace. He hasn't been back to
his apartment, and nobody at his work has seen or
heard from him."

"What about that girlfriend of his, Sheila Cartwright?" Petrucelli asked.

"Same. She's disappeared, too. And we've questioned the Smithsonian guy, Cassavetes, twice. He doesn't know any more than we do. We've tapped his phone and we've got a tail on him," Carnegie said. "But so far nothing. I think he's telling the truth."

"What did he say?" Petrucelli asked.

"Just what you guys recorded in the Hauptman garden that day about the DNA results," Carnegie said. "He knew Starkey and Sheila were going to the Protean Society that night, but he hasn't heard from them since. We followed up on Starkey's story about the canoeing society, the one you recorded in the Haupt Garden in his conversation with Cassavetes. The society building is abandoned and looks like it has been for a long time. The stairs lead down to an empty cellar and go nowhere else. We found no trace of the tunnels he talked about, huge machines, guys with funny eyes or anything else."

Frank ran over it in his mind. Starkey's disappearance and the whole Protean Society building's vanishing made him crazy, sure, but his nightmares under medication here in the hospital these two last nights were about islands—big, stony islands that came crashing down rivers, smashing into bridges.

Petrucelli must have been thinking about the same thing. "Actually, boss, I don't really give a fuck about Starkey and the *Protean Society*. What I want to know is, how did that huge fucking island break loose and come charging down the Potomac like a goddam Amtrak train, crash into the bridge, and drop chunks of concrete on me? I mean, look at me. A concussion, broken ribs, do you want a list? How do the science guys back at headquarters explain that?"

Carnegie shook his head. He looked at the cigarette in his hand. "They don't. They've got some theories. Wilson, as usual, says there's alien science at work here."

"Well?" Frank asked. "For once I agree with him. I mean islands don't just… "

"Enough, Frank. I don't know. But say it is aliens. We still have no proof," Carnegie said. He raised his hand and rubbed his temples with two fingers. We need a ship or a corpse, something physical.

"Corpse? How many people died when that goddamn island smashed into the bridge?" Frank asked.

"One hundred and sixty-seven dead and more injured," Carnegie said.

Petrucelli tried to sit up, but failed. "Jesus, Mary, and Joseph, the count keeps going up. How many corpses do you need? Do you really believe there's no connection between that and the Protean Society?"

Carnegie stuck the cigarette in his mouth and lifted both hands from his lap, holding them out, palms up, shrugging his shoulders and shaking his head. "Look, John, what the hell can I do when the only thing connecting the two events is they're both impossible. Nobody can figure out how any of it happened at all, let alone find any connection between them."

"You heard the recording of Starkey and Cassavetes," Frank said. "You know NIH found alien DNA. Have you talked to them?"

Carnegie laughed. "Oh, yeah. They tried to cover it up, but there's little doubt. We've confiscated all the samples and the research, and cautioned the lab people, but there are rumors flying around anyway. Christ, the UFO fanatics are having a field day."

"Look, boss, the DNA led us to the Society, and Vaso Island sits, correction, used to sit, only a few miles away in Carderock." Frank said. "There were earth tremors in Georgetown for Christ's sake. An entire goddamn building disappears and an island lifts off and crashes into the *American Legion Bridge*. Do you really think that's all a coincidence?"

Carnegie rose, straightened up, picked up the chair, and moved it back to the window. He put the cigarette behind one ear and shoved his hands down in his pockets. "No, John, I don't." He turned back to face the two agents. "But nobody who hasn't been on the front lines of this investigation will buy it, unless we have evidence that proves the connection. They will pass it off somehow as a natural disaster."

"Oh and what might that be?" Frank asked. "If they don't believe the scientists at NIH, what will they believe?"

"You know the answer to that. They'll hush it all up unless you bring me, you should pardon the expression, concrete evidence. Bring me the corpse of an alien, or a living one, or at least find Starkey or Sheila Cartwright so we can question them. Until then, we're stuck sifting dirt in Georgetown where a building used to be but isn't, and analyzing pieces of rock from an island sitting in the middle of the Potomac where it is but ain't supposed to be." Carnegie turned to stare out the window again.

"So," Petrucelli said, "what do we do now? After we get out of these hospital beds."

Carnegie didn't answer at first. "We'll continue to search for Starkey and we'll question Cassavetes again. Our forensic teams are going over the Society site and the island, so maybe we'll get a break there. One thing for sure and certain, my boss is going to give me hell, because there will be a congressional ass kicking and the last ass kicked will be mine."

CHAPTER THIRTY-SEVEN

SANCTUARY

CAPE YORK PENINSULA
QUEENSLAND AUSTRALIA
TUESDAY JUNE 6

The ruins of the Protean Society building, a stark and bitter reminder of the battle with the Archarans just days before, stood below. Starkey and Sheila sat on a balcony of The Sanctuary high above the green of the gardens that surrounded the damaged society building. Masato had warned Proteus that AFOSI agents were investigating prior to the battle. Watching Cassavetes they may have spotted Starkey and trailed them to the society building. Therefore Proteus engaged total withdrawal, removing all traces of the structure from the Georgetown site and MoVRing them here. Beyond the gardens, dense rainforest covered the surrounding hills of Northern Queensland's Great Dividing Range and ran down to river flood plains below.

"It would be a beautiful view," Starkey said, "if it weren't for that." He raised his hand and pointed at the ruins.

Sheila slid closer on the ornate wooden bench and lifted Starkey's arm onto and around her shoulders. "Can we try to look beyond that? Why is Proteus preserving it anyway?"

Starkey pulled her closer still. "I don't know—every glimpse of it rakes up the memory of Wolf and Sooleawa's deaths. It claws through my mind again and again." Starkey's shoulders shook once. He closed his eyes and focused. He could almost feel the touch of Wolf's fur beneath his hand. "But Wolf is still here with me in spirit, and in my heart."

"I see them, too," Sheila said, "lying there side by side in the control room. But at the same time it all seems so unreal now, their deaths—and the battle." Sheila paused and Starkey turned to look at her, a large granite Buddha behind her framing her face. "I know we're lucky to be alive, but I still feel angry," she said. "I mean, here we are in this beautiful place, but our whole lives have changed again. Those two murdered, and Páihuái still lost …"

Starkey cut her off. "Wolf got that son of a bitch, August, though. I just wish I'd been there to see him do it. But what the hell do we do now?"

"Did you really like your job, or your old life?" Sheila asked.

"No, I hated much of it. Apart from knowing you and having a few peaceful pints at the pub, my life bordered on disaster, but I endured it. Oh, and my chief solace, running by the canal and the Potomac has been taken away too."

"You're not the only one affected here, Big Boy."

Starkey turned on her, frowning. "That 'Big Boy' stuff is starting to get on my nerves, Sheila. I know your life's been ripped apart and stitched back together too. But what if you could go back to your dojo and your life? Would you want to? You don't look so different."

"Not on the outside, maybe," Sheila said. "But after being kidnapped by aliens and nearly dying, I think maybe I've changed a little also."

"I'm sorry I, shouldn't have spoken like that," Starkey said, reaching out to take her hand.

Sheila moved closer to him. "It's ok, I might have just a little trouble convincing myself teaching karate to kids is that fascinating after battling Archarans and saving mankind."

Starkey laughed. "It does tend to trivialize things, doesn't it?" But he continued more seriously. "Now it feels like my former life held little real purpose. But this one does."

"There's no going back now. If we tried we'd always be looking over our shoulders anyway, expecting the Archarans and their Okees and Zlayers to come out of every dark corner." Sheila put her arms around him, pulling him close.

"Let them come." Starkey raised one hand and rolled it slowly into a fist. "I don't fear them anymore. No, you're right. There's no going back, and I know where this new road leads. It is the Warrior's road. I have a purpose. Death to the Archarans."

Sheila took his face in her hands and turned it towards her, and Starkey saw lines of worry on her forehead. Her green eyes were wide and her mouth hung open until she spoke. "Jack, your whole life can't be about revenge."

He gently pulled her hands down. "Look, I woke up with the images of Sooleawa and Wolf lying dead in that building over there," he said.

"I know, Jack, it doesn't get any crueler than that, we will never forget, nor forgive," Sheila said. "But we still have lives to live. I understand now, why Alkira went back to the old life."

Starkey understood, also. They must try to find a way to live full lives, even in these circumstances. He used to enjoy shopping for food, even paying for it, and cooking. Now the SyLFs did all that. Things he needed just appeared. They didn't need money. Proteus provided all. And what about his apartment, and his job? And his few friends? How long would they wait before they declared him dead? He wondered if they even missed him. Maybe Masato could tell them how he's adapted.

Sheila put two fingers over his mouth when he started to speak again. "Wait, did you hear that? It sounded kind of like a cicada, but not."

Starkey looked down into the trees below. "I heard it, a bird maybe. The shields around The Sanctuary let in the sounds of the birds, and the smell of the rainforest, but without the humidity. I'd like to know how they do that."

Sheila laughed. "Fascinating, I'm sure. I'm happy we can hear the birdies and smell the green stuff, and all of that, as long as the shields keep the mosquitoes out."

Starkey shrugged. Sheila slapped him on the leg. "You don't care because they didn't even bite you back before you became Big Boy." Starkey took his arm off her shoulders. Sheila pointed down the hillside below. "I wonder what those small shrubs are with the beautiful white blossoms."

"*Eucryphia wilkiei,* in the Latin, Sheila, or Leatherwood, they are a species unique to these hills," Proteus's voice came from behind them.

Starkey leapt to his feet, spinning in the air. He dropped his guard when he realized who spoke. "Proteus, why don't you just yell 'Boo'?" *How long will it take for my nerves to get back to something like normal?*

"Sorry I startled you. I didn't lower the eaves intentionally, Jack." Proteus said. "The bird you hear is the Cicada Bird, but perhaps I can do more than identify the flora and fauna here at the Sanctuary for Sheila. Sit down, Jack, the time has come, as the walrus said, to talk of cabbages and things."

"That's 'cabbages and kings', Proteus," Sheila said.

The SyLF floated forward and descended to their eye level, with the morning sunshine reflecting off his shining surface as he hovered just above the dark wooden floor. Proteus' two large, spherical eyes rested on them. He paused before speaking. "I know I should have introduced you to the Sanctuary when we first arrived, but there has been much to do. So let me do it now."

Starkey heard the sound of a temple bell somewhere off in the distance. He made an effort to center and focused on Proteus. The SyLF told them the southern Sanctuary, the most secure of their installations on Earth, sat in a wilderness area near the top of the York Peninsula. The Upper Peninsula lay hundreds of miles from the nearest road in the far Northwest of Australia. The surrounding rainforest, trackless and almost impenetrable in its long rainy season, hid the compound amidst canyoned sandstone hills and mountains. Musean stealth technology surrounded the grounds and the buildings, and the shields prevented intrusion, rendering them invisible and undetectable on the ground or from the air. The central building had stood for thousands of years, but Proteus modified it many times to better minister to the Warriors that came there. Now it took the form of a Buddhist temple and gardens, and had done so since the introduction of Buddhism to Japan. When other locations came under attack or were destroyed, or their security was breached, The Sanctuary survived to harbor the Warriors. Never large, it adapted in size to meet the Warrior's needs of that time.

Proteus turned away and looked beyond the balcony to the ruins of the society building. The Cicada bird called again.

"But what about the people who live in these forests, Proteus, haven't they bumped into it ever?" Sheila asked.

Proteus turned back to answer. "No one lives here, Sheila. It's an uninhabited, trackless wilderness and always has been. Only a few of Alkira's people, the Aboriginal Australians who live nearer the coast, may have "bumped into it", as you say, down through over the centuries. She thinks she is the last of her people who knows anything is here."

Proteus gave them good news. Delphius, the Guardian of the Sanctuary, had found and transported all of the missing warriors to the Sanctuary. They were scattered throughout the solar system. Páihuái, the last to be found, had been MoVRed farthest away by the enemy, out beyond the orbit of Pluto. Now all the living Warriors were retrieved. Fortunately the Musean uniform's shielding technology made it possible for Delphius to locate the Warriors, track them, and communicate with them. In the past they had had only Sooleawa's mental ability to learn of their whereabouts and reach out to them.

Sheila leaned her head into Starkey's chest. "I knew Páihuái was still alive out there somewhere. I could hear him."

"Yes, Sheila. Master Yamashima told me this also," Proteus said.

Sheila sat up. "Where is the Master, Proteus? I haven't seen him since you brought us here."

"He is in retreat. He spends his time in meditation. Masato visits him. Each of the Warriors chooses their own form of recovery. Páihuái has another house here like the one you saw in Georgetown and he is there, but if anything, his silence has grown deeper."

"When can I see him?" Sheila asked

Proteus reached out to touch her hand. "I think you will know when the right time comes, Sheila. We must all confront the outcomes of the catastrophe in Georgetown. Our Sooleawa, tragically, is no more. The Eldest, Ku'en, greatest of our Warriors, sacrificed himself for our survival. Your companion, Wolf, is gone also. Fortunately he had cubs. And then there is the terrible loss of humanity, for no less than one hundred and sixty humans died on the bridge. We have suffered tremendous losses."

Starkey shivered. It seemed a cold breeze swept over him, though he knew the Sanctuary's climate was controlled. He rubbed his shoulders and then placed his hands first on his knees, squeezing, then on his stomach. He felt a nausea rise.

"Having Wolf alongside me began to heal the open wound I carried everywhere. He didn't replace Ethan and Jane, but his companionship eased the pain. Now his death has torn that wound open again." Sheila reached over and lifted his hand into her lap.

Proteus glided closer to Starkey, hovering by his side. He placed his hand on Starkey's shoulder. "But now, Jack, healing can begin here as it always has done. For ten thousand years Delphius has pro-

vided a retreat here for grieving, wounded, battle-
worn Warriors to recover in mind and body from
their long battles with the Archarans. That is the answer to your question that I overheard, Jack. That is
what you do here and now, Jack and Sheila, and it is
the now you must focus on. We believe that the destruction of the Archaran warship will forestall any
imminent incursions. This has been their pattern.
Their homeworld is far across the galaxy."

"Does that mean it's over for now, Proteus?"
Sheila asked.

"No, Sheila it does not." Proteus said. "You
missed the assembly of the Warriors and the sharing
of intelligence when you were kidnapped. We believe stealth mining transport ships may still orbit
Earth. In the past they have not been a strategic threat
as they attempt to operate in secret. Masato has
searched for sites in the ocean north of the Japanese
mainland. Darake has reported suspicious seismic
activity near the Kuril Islands of Russia. No, it's not
over. We have a respite, but we must remain on our
guard, and we will oppose them until the cows come
back to Capistrano."

"That's *swallows*, Proteus, but never mind
that now. How can we just evacuate?" Sheila said.
"We left that huge island sitting in the middle of the
Potomac and the American Legion Bridge in ruins. Is
there nothing we can do?"

"No, I'm afraid not. I wish we could send Panacea and all her resources to aid the injured, but already we have exceeded my authority here. Open interference is not permitted, as regrettable as it is. It appears harsh to you, and to me, but it could change the entire future of the planet and the human race if we were to openly aid them."

Sheila leaned into Starkey's chest. He placed his arm around her shoulders.

"Regrettable doesn't cover it, Proteus." She said. "All those people died."

"It is a burden I have borne in this war for thousands of years."

CHAPTER THIRTY-EIGHT

RAPPROCHEMENT

BETHESDA MD
NORTH QUEENSLAND AU
WED JUNE 7

Starkey's condo had been ransacked. Drawers stood open, their contents jumbled or strewn on the floor. The rest of his small efficiency looked the same. Books and magazines scattered about, lamps turned over, couch cushions unzipped and removed. The generic pictures that hung on the beige walls were pulled down, their backings torn out and discarded. The Murphy bed was stripped, mattress upended and pillows shredded.

Scanning the room, Starkey laughed. *Look at this place.* His file cabinet stood empty. His camera and photo albums were missing. Starkey flexed his shoulders and lifted his head. *Whoever did this will be watching the building.* He'd been right to use the Eldest's MoVR stone to bring them directly inside the Grosvenor condo. But he'd been wrong to come back at all. Starkey wondered who the searchers were, and how they knew his identity and where he lived. The Archarans could have no need to search his apartment. *The AFOSI agents must have done this. Wait, Cassavetes must have talked.* Well, he'd told the anthropologist to tell the truth. It didn't matter, now. Nobody lived here. Never did, really. He wanted to get in touch with Cassavetes and tell the man he'd been right all along about the bones. *Okees. All true. The monsters couldn't be more alien.* He liked Cassavetes. He thought the man would be worried about him. He'd be curious, certainly, and Starkey owed the keeper of The Anomaly something, after all. *But I can't risk involving him further.* The Air Force agents would be watching him for sure. Maybe the Archarans didn't know about Cassavetes. Starkey could hope. Just the same, he should watch over the man, if Proteus ever let Starkey leave The Sanctuary again after this.

He'd been warned. Proteus made the risks clear. Starkey knew he shouldn't go back to his condo in DC right now and maybe ever. Sheila tried to talk him out of it. But in the end, she'd come along. For Starkey there was really no choice—a dead son, and a dead wife. He couldn't just leave their photographs behind. Two frames lay face down on the top of his mother's scarred old cherry bureau. Starkey turned over the photograph of his son Ethan first and picked it up. The gold colored frame felt small in his hands. He brushed the dust away that obscured the boy's image. Starkey expected the usual blurred vision and tears on his cheeks that often accompanied holding his son's photo after his death. This time they didn't come. He bent down and rested the photo in the brown leather duffle bag on the parquet floor. He picked up the other frame and turned it over. Jane looked back into his eyes. The old pain started to knot up his stomach, but then Starkey tilted his head to one side, and held the photo first at one angle, then another. He side-stepped and held it higher to give it more light. *Wait a minute, where had the reproachful look gone? Was there always a slight smile on her face?* He carefully arranged Jane's photo in his bag beside Ethan's, knowing the prints were made from film and he had no digital copies.

Sheila stood in the hall watching him. "Whoever they were they were very thorough."

Then he heard the sound of footsteps running, approaching in the outer hallway. *Yep.* "Time to go." He wrapped his arm around Sheila and handed her his duffle. He took out the MoVR Stone and held it up. "Home, James." As the room faded and dis-

solved, Starkey glimpsed a faint shimmer in the corner by the bed, as if dust still spiraled upward, reflecting prismatic sunlight.

>>>

Traveling with the MoVR felt like waves
pushing him back and forth, as if he stood at the edge
of the ocean, chest deep. Starkey liked the feeling.
This, their room at the Sanctuary, felt odd at first,
foreign. Well, it was Australia, but he grew to like
most things about it. Not exactly home, but comfortable. He took the duffle bag out of Sheila's hands
and helped her over to the bed. "Sit down here until
the queasiness passes," he said.

"I don't know if I'll ever get used to traveling
like that. And why the rotten eggs smell? Where does
that come from?" Sheila said. She lay back, spreading her arms and smoothing the saffron bedspread
with her hands. She pulled one golden, embroidered
pillow close to her, hugging it tightly to her chest.
"But I can get used to this."

"That pillow's a little much for my taste, but
if you like it." The Sanctuary bedroom, like all of the
rooms in the buildings and alcoves in the gardens
around them, juxtaposed the simplicity of Zen with
vivid color and texture. Unadorned pine and cedar
furniture contrasted with the brilliant reds and golds

of the silk-like fabric that covered the upholstery and formed drapes and curtains. Vertical hanging scrolls and paintings on silk adorned the walls, depicting flowers and traditional Japanese animals. Outside, silent stone Buddhas stood under the shimmering green and blue flying canopies of pavilions. Austere crushed-rock gardens, raked in waves daily around the large, quiet stone islands, butted up against deep borders of yellow and red flowers. Starkey opened the bedroom window, allowing a breeze to ventilate the room. A murmur of distant chanting streamed through the air like music.

Starkey sat down beside Sheila on the bed. He took her small hand between his two. Perhaps Jane's photo prompted it, because her old phrase "relationship discussion" popped into his mind. "What about us, Sheila?" he asked.

She sat up, rearranged some pillows, and leaned back against the carved cedar headboard. "Okay, what about us?" Sheila put her hands around his face, pulled him closer, and kissed him on the mouth.

After they made love she lay on his chest, her face and lips against his skin and her arms draped down over his sides. He reached to retrieve a cover for her, but she woke and slid off, curling up beside him on the bed and pulling the silken spread over both of them.

He reached out with one finger to lift her chin, looking into her eyes. Somehow the green of her eyes had grown darker, but shot through with gold. *Or am I really seeing them for the first time?* He turned onto his side and raised his body up on one elbow. "I have something to tell you. I am free, Sheila, free of the lingering pain of the past. I feel like the ghosts of Ethan and Jane are gone. You used to say they stood in the corner like specters when we were together. Not anymore." He waited, watching a wide smile stretch across her face. Her answering kiss absorbed all his attention. He didn't tell her about the shimmer in the corner by the bed as they MoVRed out of his apartment. He couldn't help but feel there was a presence there in those spirals.

Sheila fretted. She ought to wake him now and tell him. She couldn't imagine a better time. She couldn't keep putting it off. She didn't know whether to believe the enemy SyLF, Erebus, when he told her about her pregnancy, but Panacea confirmed it. She carried Jack's baby. *I don't know for sure how I feel about it.* She loved Jack, and she thought he loved her, but questions remained. What kind of baby would it be? It would have Jack's genes, some alien, or modified, or something? She knew Jack hadn't been through the metamorphosis yet on the night she conceived. What about her? Did she want to have a baby at all? It didn't seem like the ideal time to start a family with ship loads of Archarans trying to kill them. Maybe they were safe now here in The Sanctuary, but they couldn't raise a child here, could they? Panacea said the tiny fetus tested 'normal', whatever that was, but the first trimester was just beginning. And what about the Restorative Panacea gave when she was wounded during the battle? It hadn't seemed to hurt her at all. In fact, she felt stronger, more alive, and better all over ever since. But what did it do to the baby? It was developed for Warriors after the metamorphosis. Panacea told her the Warriors were sterile. Alkira couldn't get pregnant. *I wonder how she feels about that.* And what if the baby wasn't 'normal'? Could she face having an abortion? Killing her child? She'd always believed in the principle of a woman having a choice, particularly if there was some abnormality. But could she really go through with an abortion? Principles don't live and breathe. What if the baby lived to be healthy, but strange, alien? What then?

Jack woke, turned over to face her, and opened his eyes. "Hey, good lookin'."

"I'm pregnant." She might have been more tactful, she supposed. She watched emotions cross his face. Then he smiled, sort of. That smile looked like a bag full of worries. She imagined him going through the same fears of abnormality she was.

His first question could have been a bit more romantic. "How did that happen?"

"The usual way, Starkey, we had sex. You know, the thing we did just now, Big Boy." Sheila pushed his chest with her hand.

A half-pleased, half-cocky look smeared across his face. "I know. I mean, I thought you were taking, weren't you…"

Sheila shrugged. "I was."

Starkey's mouth made a big 'O.'

"Panacea told me your sperm have extra 'oomph' compared with fully human males. Well, used to."

"I didn't know that." Then he sat up in the bed, "Wait—what do you mean *used to*, Sheila?"

"Jesus, you don't know? Masato and Proteus didn't tell you?"

Starkey stood up and walked around the bed. "Move over." He sat down next to her. "Tell me what?"

Sheila closed her eyes. "Damn. I have to be the one to tell you?"

"Sheila, look at me. *Tell me what.*"

"Ok. It's the metamorphosis. It makes you sterile."

Jack stood up and took a step back, looking down at her. Surprise, anger, and confusion chased each other across his face. "I don't know whether this is the silver lining or the cloud."

"Whichever it is, this is it, Jack."

The End

L CHANCE SHIVER

L Chance Shiver is a Science Fiction writer living on a small mountain near Asheville, North Carolina. Native to Washington, DC and surrounding Virginia and Maryland, however, he is still deeply tied to Washington and particularly to Rock Creek Park, the Potomac River, and the C&O Canal National Park.

When not writing, Chance tours the southeast playing early Country and Old Time Music with his wife, Susette, as their duo, The Shivers.